Echos
of the Everlasting

Echos of the Everlasting

KYRA ROMANYSHYN

ECHOS *of the Everlasting*

Published by Kyra Romanyshyn, Edmonton, Canada

ISBN:
Paperback	978-1-77354-643-8
ebook	978-1-77354-644-5

DEDICATION

I DEDICATE THIS BOOK TO YOU, READER. Thank you for taking an interest in my story. My hope is this book reaches those who like a little mix of everything; romance, horror, action, mystery, even poetry. May you enjoy this journey as much as I enjoyed creating it. All my love to you and yours. Keep strong, keep grateful, don't abandon your dreams, and remember it's never too late. We got this.

With love, Kyra

Prologue

God 1 "Destruction"
1922

It was getting hard to crawl at this point, the cold seemed to be finally taking its last strike at me. It was a cruel joke, I should've died days ago. This defied reason and logic. Why was I still here? Every single breath I took felt like my throat was tearing, while my lungs felt brittle; as if my next breath would simply shatter them. I glanced over to the pitiful hole in the deep snow I had dug, cursing as my fingers blackened from the cold. She deserved so much more then a shallow grave in this frozen hell. The twisted body of the plane that trapped us here did little to shield from the harsh weather. I had finished the last of the food I managed to find in the wreckage 2 days ago, but the relentless hunger was nothing compared to how my body felt. I longed for death, begged the quiet frozen air with screams into this cold nothingness. I lost my voice within the first 24 hours. I lost her within the first 24 minutes. We were the only ones that woke up. At first I was grateful, that gratitude weaned and mutated into terror the minute I realized we were trapped here, likely to freeze to death, with no form of communication. We were heading someplace warm and we ended up here, the irony was sickening. How I wished I had noticed she was fatally injured, while I remained intact. I would have spent those last 24 minutes holding her kissing her comforting her. The other passengers died on impact, lucky bastards. It took me a day of freezing before I started to burn the bodies for warmth. Then eventually gorged myself with their flesh. I lost any conscience that these were people too and focused on survival. The smell made me vomit until there was nothing left in my body. Somehow after a few days it didn't bother me anymore. But it kept me alive this long. They say madness takes a while to kick in, I'd say, none of those people were freezing in absolute silence and such bitter cold; surrounded by dead people, with nothing but themselves alive for miles. Madness would be a blessing in comparison. I had no company but the rampant begging of a desperate man. Strangely enough in my mind I wanted to die but a primal instinct to survive had taken over, even that seemed to be dissipating now. I was also running out of bodies to burn. I prayed death would take me every minute that passed. Take me back to her. Take me out of this decaying body, and every sleepless night lit by the fire of someone who once lived too; only to be denied every time. Its been 5 Goddamned days. It felt like an eternity. I didn't have the stomach to commit suicide, the instinct to survive was stronger. Soon, I figured I wouldn't be able to crawl anymore. Then I would be stuck freezing in my own filth. I crawled over to another body. Male, probably 50s, his neck was angled in an unholy manner. I took out the pack of matches I had, remembering the reason I had them with me was for cigarettes, I laughed inwardly. Cigarettes, and here I am burning bodies, consuming them like a fucking animal. As I lay by the fire, I was busy praying yet again for the reaper to claim me when I smelled vanilla. Clear as day, like someone was holding an open bottle of vanilla extract under my nose. Could it be?- but she was- I glanced over to her shallow grave. She always smelled of vanilla.

"Aurelia?" my wife's name came out of my mouth as an unfamiliar rasp barely audible to my own ears.

My tongue thick like molasses, and my mouth drained of everything but a trace of saliva.

I looked back to the fire, I was staring at bare feet, blue and crystallized in the dim light, dancing slightly. A white billowing dress against blue frost kissed ankles. My eyes travelled slowly up over the dancing body of my wife. If I could cry I would have. I was afraid to meet her eyes. Suddenly her lips were on mine, colder then the ice and snow around me. Like a kiss with death itself.

"I love you." She whispered into my mouth parting with each deep kiss.

"God I love you, I loved you so much. I miss you Aurelia."

I knew she was dead but I wanted to hold this hallucination as tight as I could. It was such a blessing compared to this torture of reality. When I did finally pull away to look at her eyes. I fell back slightly, they were not my wife's eyes, they were bright burning red. She laughed. Not my wife's laugh. A demon wearing my wife's body like a Halloween costume from Hell.

"It's time." it sing-songed. A haunting melody of eternal Damnation.

I went, willingly taking her hand as she brought her mouth to mine again.

God 2 "Creation"
1952

"Can we stop at the diner up ahead?" my wife's voice tilled as she propped her feet up on my dash.

I wanted to say no. I was tired of driving, my eyes were burning. I just wanted to get us to the hotel. I glanced at the dash clock it was 1am. What kind of diner was open at 1am? I grit my teeth and pulled up to the diner without a word of complaint. She let out a happy sigh and glided out of the passenger seat; almost forgetting her shoes. I heard a little splash as she exited and she yelped. I couldn't help laughing a bit to myself. Her head popped back into my car, her painted lips pursed in playful distaste.

"No need to laugh, that water was cold! Now hurry up I'm starving."

she slammed my door and I flinched a bit. My car was a red Volvo P1800. I liked classic cars. Emma usually took care to tease me about it every chance she got. I sighed and rubbed my eyes, following her slowly into the diner. The waitress seemed just as displeased that we were there as I was to have stopped in.

"We close in an hour" She said to us blandly.

She was a heavy women, with tired uncaring eyes and greasy brown hair slicked up in a tight bun. Her mouth a fine line.

My wife smiled totally unfazed by the waitresses demeanour.

"I'd like a cheeseburger with a salad please" she smiled politely and the waitress took the menu roughly out of her hand.

I smiled a bit, "At this hour?" I said playfully.

She just smiled slightly, shook her head and looked out the window.

"Coffee, black, I will get a slice of pie too, thanks" figured the sugar mixed with the caffeine would help me drive in a bit.

"Who gets pie at 1am?" My wife teased back.

"A cheeseburger is way weirder." I laughed.

She stuck her tongue out at me.

The waitress didn't even attempt to hide her annoyance. She sighed loudly as she retreated back to the kitchen. After a few minutes my wife looked at me with thoughtful eyes and sipped at her water. God she was beautiful. Her beauty never weaned or faded over the time we had been together. Tonight she was just wrapped in dark jeans and a red blouse, her long dark hair was twisted into a mess of a bun on her head with a red bandana tied around it like a headband. Her lips were painted red to match, her eye makeup light, making the blue in her eyes stand out.

"Thanks for stopping." She half smiled.

I nodded in reply. We ate in comfortable silence, paid and headed back to the car. I grabbed Emma's waist and pinned her against the hood of my car. She erupted in light giggles. I kissed her slowly, drinking her in, biting playfully at her lip. I traced my mouth to the hollow of her throat.

"If you EVER slam my doors again" I said in mock threat as I nipped softly at her neck.

"There will be consequences"

"And is this the consequence of my actions?" She breathed against my ear planting a light kiss to my neck.

"Just wait until we get to the hotel" we laughed and pulled away from eachother as we climbed into the car.

By now it was well after 2am and we still had about 30 minutes yet to go, to get to the small town we were stopping in to visit family. The sugar and caffeine did little to ease my exhaustion. We had been driving for 10 hours straight already. My eyes were begging to close. We started back on the highway. About 5 minutes into the drive Emma spoke up over the soft tune of the radio.

"Hey..babe?"

I looked slightly to her. "What's up?"

Emma folded her hands over and over in her lap, something she did when she was anxious.

"I think you are going to be a father."

My eyes darted to her and I couldn't help but smile, even as panic crept in, but I wanted to be calm and collected for her sake.

"Really?" I asked not taking my eyes off her.

She stopped folding her hands and gave me the biggest smile I'd seen in a while. I leaned over to her and cupped her cheek with my one free hand, kissing her with fervent. She flushed as red as her lipstick and glanced back to the window.

"Babe! Watch out!"

All it took was a split second and I was too late the vehicle was flipping off of the highway. Emma's blood curdling scream was quiet in comparison to the sudden shattering glass and whining metal as my car crunched against the ground over and over. Until we were upside down and I was trapped staring into her bloodied face and wide lifeless terror stricken eyes.

"Emma. Please no, Emma! Emma! "

I screamed. I couldn't move my body. I closed my eyes trying to calm my panicked breaths. Oh God, why was I alive? I need to move, I need to get her out. The baby- A million things raced through my mind. When I dared to open my eyes again, I was staring into bright burning red eyes, in place of my wife's and her broken jaw moved and a voice that was not hers rang out. I tried to scream but it was caught in my throat. A Demon plaguing my wife's body.

"It's time" it spoke using my wife's broken face to do so.

"For what?" I breathed. I only got an inhuman laugh in reply.

Chapter 1: Present day

WOUNDED

"I am necessary for all life, a complex design, and yet I struggle and grasp against the very lives I strive to protect, wounded, my blood divine, will drench those whom need me to survive."

"Not that one." I said quickly. Rayne looked at me and rolled her eyes.

"Not fancy enough?" she laughed putting the basic dark blue dress back on the rack. I shook my head.

"Must be exhausting to be you Serena. Would it really kill you to wear some jeans? It's not your engagement party after all." Rayne teased.

"It just might! And I DO wear jeans sometimes you know. I just prefer dresses is that such a crime?" I laughed heartily.

"It is your engagement party after all Rayne. If you really prefer I wear jeans I will, but only because you're my best friend."

She looked at me incredulously.

"You are a real pain in my ass sometimes you know"

She grabbed a plain knee length black dress. The sleeves were sheer, which I liked.

"I can accept this. I don't want you to have to wear something you don't like." she nodded to me putting the dress in my hands.

"As you command mistress Rayne" I bowed sarcastically and she laughed as we headed to the counter to pay.

Rayne had been my best friend since we were kids. I only had a couple of close friends. I was excited that her high school sweetheart proposed, they were a good couple. You could see the love in their eyes anytime they looked at one another. Rayne was 24 years old I was 28. We weren't in school together. My mom and I actually used to look after Rayne on the late nights her mom worked. When I turned 12 I started to just look after her myself. We developed a wonderful friendship over time. I also felt protective over her, as if she were my little sibling. Everyone seemed to think Rayne and Matt were too young to marry especially in today's day, where one night stands were more fathomable then marriage. But anyone saying that wouldn't have seen their relationship up close, anyone who knew them thought they were simply meant to be. I hoped maybe one day I would feel that depth of love too. Rayne insisted on buying a new dress for me for her party and I had allowed it but I didn't like people buying me stuff. Rayne took her credit card out to pay; flipping her long brown hair over her shoulder as she did and I turned my attention elsewhere. I checked my phone for the time, it was still early afternoon only 1pm, the party was at 4. The day was warm and sunny, usually we got quite a bit of rain here in our short summer months. The warmer days were welcomed and cherished. I took a deep breath, the boutique we were in smelled strongly of floral perfume. Then, I caught a strong smell of coffee over the warm breeze that was wafting through the open store door. There was a really nice cafe across the street, not a Tim Horton's or a Starbucks but a family joint. I didn't recall it ever being there before. On the patio in a vintage white cafe table sat a couple of gentleman. They looked out of place, both dressed up in tuxedo's. Both actually quite gorgeous and staring?- but they couldn't possibly be looking at me, I was across the street. An arm wrapping around my shoulders made me jump. It was just Rayne.

"Ready to go there, Serena?" she laughed and pressed the bag into my hands. "Come on." I still have appointments set up for us!" She grabbed my arm excitedly and pulled me towards the exit.

I looked back at the cafe but the men were gone. I didn't see them on the wide street either. Strange. Maybe they went inside?

"Do we have time for a coffee break Rayne?"

I motioned toward the cafe. Rayne stopped and followed my gaze. Her eyes narrowed.

"Of course I will feed your caffeine addiction she started slowly. But, looks to me like they stopped serving coffee a long time ago. There's a Starbucks next to the salon. We can stop there!" she bounded ahead a bit.

I looked back to the cafe. Sure enough to my surprise it looked like it burned down many years ago. There was plant overgrowth even. I shook my head. Maybe I needed a coffee more then I thought.

I exhaled a breath I didn't realize I had been holding and headed after Rayne.

$$* * *$$

We arrived at the salon, Rayne was getting her hair done identical to her wedding day idea. To test it pre-hand, was her reasoning.

"Rayne? I'm going to grab a coffee now next door, do you want something?"

I tried to feel enthusiastic about the overpriced coffee, but caffeine is caffeine.

She looked at me from the stylist chair

"Shit, I forgot sorry, I'm okay! You go ahead. Don't be long shes doing your hair next!"

I nodded and headed out of the door. I checked my phone I hadn't heard from Henry yet today. Not that it mattered much. He was probably busy, after being together for 7 years it wasn't that odd to not speak when apart from one another. I was waiting in line and thought back to the men I thought I had seen in the abandoned cafe. I couldn't get the image out of my head for some reason. I tried to remember a detail of their faces. Eye colour something. But my mind was coming up blank. I felt uncomfortable in the memory.

"Miss? Hello?" the barista was calling me shaking me out of my memories. There was a frustrated sigh from behind me. Obviously someone in a hurry. Oops.

"Yes sorry, can I grab just a vente vanilla latte?" She nodded.

"Name?" "Serena." I replied and handed her a $10 bill.

I went to wait for my name to be called. From a table nearby I heard a familiar voice. I turned to look and dropped my phone to the ground. The sound was enough for seemingly everyone to glace my direction. It was Henry, with his ex from 10 years ago. Holding hands when he realized it was me he quickly let go and stood up.

"Babe! What are you doing here? I thought you were getting ready with Rayne?" His ex looked at me with a sickening grin. Everyone seemed to be staring, I hadn't even moved to pick up my phone yet.

"Serena?" The barista called out my order and my name.

There was a wash bucket with a cloth on the counter beside me I grabbed it before grabbing my coffee and dumped it on Henry.

"What the Fuck Serena!?" Henry yelled.

I fought bile that rose in my throat and found a courageous voice that felt unfamiliar to my own ears.

"We are through, get your shit out of the apartment, you are gone by the time I get home tonight so help me God."

I said and stole a glace at his ex who's mouth was gaping like a fish. I smoothed my hair, picked up my phone grimacing at the cracked screen. I then grabbed my coffee and started to walk out. There were a couple voices murmuring, but I walked confidently, holding back the tears the threatened at my eyes. I heard Henry cursing me, saying things that he usually said when he was angry.

"You have no right!" was the last I heard from him before the door closed.

I got back to the salon and I was shaking. Rayne's hair had just finished and she was beaming. She looked stunning. A fancy curly up do with glittering gemstones intertwined in the intricate curls. I tried to smile but found my face felt tight. Her smile dropped when she looked at my face. Damn thought I was hiding it so well. She rushed to me.

"Whats wrong Serena? Why are you so pale?" concern creased her pretty tan face. I sighed and explained what happened. I felt tears burning in my eyes again and I pushed them back. Forcing a smile and smoothing the hem of my floral dress.

"I just ran into Henry, with his ex- dumped his ass."

"But forget it, today is your engagement party, don't worry about this right now. Your hair looks amazing, What's next on the list?" I could see a bunch of emotions behind her eyes as she fought back anger.

"Honestly, Serena you deserve better he treated you like shit anyway. Is he still there?? I'm gonna wring his effin neck" she moved toward the door unable to contain her anger and I stopped her.

The hair stylist called back to Rayne saying she was ready to do my hair. Rayne huffed, and motioned me to go sit with the stylist. I looked at the reference picture for the hair Rayne picked out for me. An updo of course. I loved dressing up but I hated my hair up, I only ever wore it down. I didn't protest and just let the stylist twist my long blonde hair into a series of loops and twirls. My phone kept dinging with texts from Henry. I ignored them. When he called I went to his contact and blocked his number. At least my phone was working despite the cracked screen. I said to myself trying to stay on the bright side of things as usual. When my hair was done I had to admit it looked pretty nice. Rayne gave me an encouraging smile from across the room. I paid the stylist.

"Last stop! Nails!" Rayne had a hard time hiding her excitement.

I didn't blame her. I tried to stay as happy as I could as I pushed Henry out of my mind and hoped he would have all his stuff packed and be gone before I came home tonight. Rayne must have noticed my face change.

"Hey look, if you want you can stay with us tonight." she offered softly.

I shook my head.

"It's your engagement party you should spend a romantic night with Matt, I don't want to hinder you" I smiled.

She opened her mouth to argue but decided against it.

"Well alright, just call if you change your mind." she smiled at me.

We arrived shortly at the nail salon and I flipped through a magazine while she got her nails done. She bounced over to show me her french tips.

"Beautiful! You are going to make Matt fall in love with you all over again tonight, especially with the dress you picked!" I gave her my best smile.

"Not that you need any of that to do so." I laughed gently.

She rolled her eyes.

"I hate dresses, but you are right, and that's my goal!" she paused and grabbed my hands.

"Would you like your nails done too?" after examining my hand she shook her head.

"Ugh never-mind your nails always look perfect length and colour" I laughed a bit. Honestly relieved I didn't have to get them done. She checked her phone.

"Crap! Forget it, we gotta go we are going to be late to my own party!" Rayne pulled me too my feet and immediately hailed a cab.

* * *

Not long after that we got to her house. No one had arrived yet, looked like Matt's ford truck wasn't in the driveway either. I checked my phone it was only 3pm. I laughed to myself. Well Rayne always needed everything perfect.

"We have a whole hour to get dressed and set out food Rayne, don't worry. I will help make sure everything goes exactly how you want." I said.

She hugged me tightly.

"I will go set out all the prepared food while you get dressed okay, then you just have to worry about yourself." I smiled, making a shooing motion with my hands. With that being said, she eagerly bounded up the stairs. When I saw specks of her like this it reminded me of when we were kids. It also showed me how happy she was with Matt. I wandered past the stairs and into the kitchen. The decorations she had laid out looked very elegant just black and white, balloons and streamers. She had a champagne glass tower, and a large chocolate fountain. Matt was a big CEO and Rayne had taken over her moms bakery after high school. Matt's parents died when he was 18 and left him their company and assets so he was pretty well set up before Rayne even moved in. Their ceremony spared no expense. I looked around and opened the two fridges and started taking out all the prepped trays. There was ample fruit and vegetables, meats and exotic cheeses, mini sandwiches, and all sorts of wonderful dessert that Rayne no doubt made herself. The main course one of the 5 star fancy restaurants uptown were preparing and Matt I'm guessing had left to go pick that stuff up. I laid out all the snacks and apps and drinks, taking care to ensure it all was stacked and spread out in the most eye pleasing manner I could. God if this was just the engagement party, I couldn't imagine what the wedding would look like. The idea made my head swim. I grabbed a glass from the cupboard and filled it with icy tap water. After finishing I went upstairs to check on Rayne and change myself. I closed myself into one of the 4 bathrooms and re-applied my makeup. The dark makeup I liked around my eyes made the blue in my eyes stand out. My head was already hurting and I wished I could take my hair down. Despite the fact it did look quite elegant. Images of Henry and our life together flashed in my head now that I was alone and staring into the mirror. He was the only man I had ever been real serious with. I again forced the memories away and reminded myself that it was likely he was unfaithful the whole relationship. Somehow that didn't make it easier. Instead I found myself almost sympathiz-ing and wondering what I did wrong. I dampened a cloth with cold water and dabbed my cheeks and neck avoiding my painted eyes. I slipped out of my floral dress and slipped into the simple black one Rayne picked out earlier at the store. I looked at the floor and saw a pair of strapped black heels laid out. Rayne obviously had picked them for me, we had the same size of feet. Ugh I hated heels, I was already 5'8 I didn't like towering over people. Also I preferred boots to any other shoes, even with majority of my outfits being dresses. I was confused because this was a house party, no one wore their shoes in the house. There was a knock at the door then interrupting my torrent of thoughts.

"Hey, Serena come out and zip this dress please?" I unlocked the door and told her to come in. Before I zipped her dress I held the shoes up to her.

"Why?"

Rayne laughed:

"Remember Serena, Matt is from the US they wear shoes inside, he thinks it's weird and gross that we don't here"

I shook my head and laughed forgetting, then tried to imagine a fancy party where everyone had bare feet or socks and thought it was funny as well.

"I guess I forgot!" I shrugged and zipped her dress. Then sucked in a breath as she did a little twirl.

"So?" she asked me eagerly with her eyes sparkling.

"Well you look absolutely stunning Rayne. As always!" I gave her a hug.

"I'm so happy you found such a good guy. I am proud to be your maid of honour too."

She let out a squeal and motioned me to come downstairs. I slipped the heels on, trying to ignore how sore my feet would be in a couple of hours. I followed her downstairs just as Matt and his best man Allan walked in with arms full of food bags.

"Hey Serena."

Matt greeted me with his familiar warm smile, and looked around at the food. "Nice job it looks very classy in here!"

I grabbed the food bags out of his hands. Allan gave me a nod in hello. Allan I had known as long as Rayne and Matt but we never said more then a couple words to each other really. It's not that he was a bad guy, he was always making people laugh, and I never saw him lose his temper, just something didn't sit well with me about him.

"Thank you, I'm glad. I'll go lay these out, go find Rayne!"

He thanked me and headed to the living room where Rayne was adjusting decorations. He wrapped her in a big hug and kissed her so passionately you could swear it was their first kiss, then he poured over her with compliments on her hair, dress even her nails. I smiled and turned away. Trying to ignore the pang of sadness it brought when I realized I was alone again. Not that Henry was anything like that anyway. I think he just settled with me. I shook my head again trying not to think about it. Allan was standing in the kitchen and offered to help me, so together we set up the rest of the food in comfortable silence.

* * *

Not even 20 minutes later the party was in full swing. They must've had at least 80 people here, no one was dressed crazy elegant, Rayne had insisted on simplicity for the guests. Mainly for me because she knew I would've overdressed. Most people had no problem being super casual, according to Rayne I struggled with it. Although that never bothered me I was more comfortable when I was dressed up. Rayne was occupied with Matt and all their guests so I just kinda hung around snacking on all the food they had. Normally Henry would be here and we would be off playing cards together or something. I sighed to myself. I had to let it go. I glanced to my phone and debated playing a game but decided against it. No way was I going to stand here at my best friends engagement party playing on my phone. Especially since that was my pet peeve, and that would make me a hypocrite. So I instead looked around the room. Most people I didn't recognize. Aside from Rayne's parents whom were in a conversation with Matt's parents. I kept looking and my eyes fell on..Henry? I damn near dropped my glass of champagne. The nerve of him to show up here. He was watching me intently. When I made no move toward him he came up to me and put his arm around me, he reeked of booze.

"Heyyyy baby. You look hot" He slurred.

I aggressively grabbed his arm and tossed it off of me. I tried to keep my voice low and steady as my heart hammered in my chest and I felt like my skin was on fire. I didn't want to make a big scene.

"Get the Hell out of here Henry, I told you we are through. You should be packing your shit."

His eyes turned angry and I felt small all of a sudden. He grabbed my arm again this time hard enough to hurt. He pushed me into the wall. Pinning me with both of his hands. He was always aggressive when he was angry, or didn't get his way. I never measured up no matter what I did.

"You don't get to decide that, Serena." he leaned close to my ear seething.

"The apartment is mine" he growled.

I tried to meet his intensity but I felt like I was seconds from crumbling.

"I signed those papers Henry, not you." he pulled paper out of his jacket.

"Not according to this lease agreement."

He held it in front of my face with his other hand pressed hard into my chest holding me harshly to the wall. I looked to it, sure enough only his name was there.

"You think I'm an idiot?.. You didn't sign shit. Nothing real anyway."

He laughed again coming close to my mouth shoving the papers back in his pocket, he moved his hand aggressively up my leg. His other arm pinning me still. The stench of his booze was making me dizzy.

"Apologize bitch, or you will be the one packing your shit"

His hand curved up to the globe of my ass now.

"I didn't appreciate that little stunt you pulled this afternoon."

I was trying hard not to draw too much attention, as realization dawned how screwed I really was. I pushed him roughly and he only laughed.

"Oh you feisty now bitch?" he kept his hand tight on my arm, and pushed me back to the wall.

"You were always such a weak little thing. Pathetic."

I grit my teeth to keep from whimpering. Then Henry was pulled off of me. I looked up and it was Matt pulling him with Rayne at his side. Rayne spoke first.

"Henry get the fuck out of our house, you are not welcome here. The fact that you even showed up here shows how much of pig you really are. Now get the Hell out of our house and stay the fuck away from Serena." she spat.

I wasn't sure if she had the chance to fill Matt in on what happened earlier or not yet, but regardless he followed suit of Rayne. He was still holding Henry's collar. The other guests were watching now and all I wanted to do was bury my face somewhere and hide.

"You heard my Fiancé Henry, get out if you know whats good for you." Matt followed authority ringing in his voice.

He shoved Henry toward the door. A few other men in the room muttered in agreement. Henry laughed and left. Then everyone was looking back at me. I exhaled slowly. Rayne was watching me with concern.

"Are you okay?!" She looked me up and down.

Meanwhile, Matt locked the door behind Henry and watched to make sure he left.

"I'm fine Rayne, I'm so sorry he showed up." the words tumbled out of my mouth. She shook her head.

"Guys please get back to the party, the situation is dealt with."

Matt addressed the guests and everyone resumed conversations and mingling. Matt came back over to us.

"You okay Serena?" he asked.

I nodded.

"Thanks both of you. I am just going to take a moment upstairs to calm myself okay? I'm really sorry he caused a scene at your engagement party."

I gave an apologetic smile and Rayne nodded.

"Of course, take the time you need, call me if you need me okay?"

I nodded again and started up the stairs. I loved Rayne she knew when to give me space and when not to press. My arm was throbbing where Henry had grabbed me. I rubbed it gently. When I got to the bathroom I exhaled slowly trying to figure out what I was going to do. I looked in the mirror there was a bruise forming in the shape of Henry's hand on the back of my arm. Damn. Why didn't I stand up to him? I wasn't one to be a damsel in distress. I fought my own battles. It was weird for Rayne to be the one protecting me today. Maybe I was losing my edge, maybe I was just tired. Or maybe, I've always been a bit weary of Henry, always watched what I said and did. I knew he had a bad temper. Temper. I shook my head. Why had I felt so afraid? I felt a bit disgusted by myself for not standing up to him. 7 years of my life and I bowed to him, ignored my needs and my wants and became who I thought he wanted and even still that wasn't ever enough. He was just a person. I wasn't some helpless victim. I thought back to the lease papers, I really am out a house. I ran over my finances in my head immediately trying to formulate a plan. How would I get my things without running into Henry? God, I always had my own finances and made sure I could take care of myself, made sure my name was on the lease so I couldn't lose my home but somehow I messed it up. How did he get the upper hand? I took the cloth I had earlier and again dabbed at my sweaty face and neck. It's fine. I had all my bank cards and everything, I would simply get a motel for tonight and sort it out in the morning. Yes. I wouldn't ruin this party for Rayne and Matt by telling them I was out a house. They deserved to celebrate tonight. I would fill them in tomorrow. I'm sure Matt and Allan would accompany me to get my things if I asked, or I could get the police involved if needed. I had options. I calmed my racing heart. Planning relaxed me. I came out of the bathroom then ready to rejoin the group and be there for Rayne and Matt. I bumped straight into a muscular chest and fell flat on my ass. Damn it, like I needed any more embarrassment tonight.

"Are you alright? I didn't expect someone to rush out of the door."

The mans voice was deep and a bit rough. There was a hand extended towards me. He had an interesting ring on his hand Gold with a snake eating itself? What a strange- His hand grasped mine and pulled me to my feet. My hand tingled pleasantly where he touched it. He dropped my hand the second I was on my feet. Words stumbled out of my mouth

"S-sorry I came out really quick, I guess. Thank you for helping me up"

I still didn't look to his face I was far too embarrassed to meet the strangers eyes. "Don't worry about it." he said.

When I refused to look at his face, he moved toward the bathroom door, I could feel his eyes lingering on me, but I didn't move until the door closed softly. I could feel the heat rushing in my cheeks. I went slowly downstairs. My feet were in agony. Rayne was waiting at the bottom of the stairs. She hugged me.

"The party is coming to a close!" she said happily.

She clasped her hands together in delight.

"Aside the little hiccup with he-who-shall-not-be-named-" she joked.

"I think it went really well thank you so much Serena."

She studied my eyes for a while.

"A few guests already left and more will follow shortly, if you wanna go I totally understand. But will you be okay going to the apartment? What if Henry is there?"

"I can handle him, he's just annoying when hes drunk. Maybe he did clear his shit out."

I said as lightheartedly as I could, hating the full blown lie I was telling so easily and reminding myself that I wanted to wait to tell her all the details of what actually went on earlier. She nodded and Matt came behind her and folded her into his arms kissing her head. She giggled.

"Call us tomorrow if he didn't take his shit we will lend a hand"

Matt motioned to Allan whom nodded stiffly. Rayne smiled in agreement.

I hated lying to them, it wasn't me. I didn't like to lie. But otherwise their night would be ruined and I didn't want to be the one responsible for that. I gave Rayne another hug.

"Thanks guys, I hope you have the best closing to such a beautiful evening!"

I winked to them as I turned to leave. As I closed the front door and walked to my car relief flooded me. I needed to be alone for a bit, I needed to gather my thoughts. One thing at a time. I thought to check my tires and around my car. Everything seemed to be in place, thankfully Henry hadn't touched it. Wait, why did I think he would? God, that whole thing rattled me way more then I thought I guess. I typed the nearest motel into my phones Gps and siri started guiding me. Elder Oak Inn? Weird, I never even remembered seeing that motel. Hmm maybe I should just look up the nearest travel lodge. I went to change the address in my phone and it stopped responding to my touch.

"Great." I muttered out loud to myself.

I sighed. I guess that fall did mess my phone up. I would get a replacement in the morning.

"Well, Elder Oak Inn here I come." I buckled myself and started my car.

I was thankful it was a warm evening. I rolled the windows down for fresh nighttime air. It smelled slightly of rain and I silently hoped it would rain. About 20 minutes later I pulled up to the inn. Sure enough the sign did say "Elder Oak" it looked a bit out of place among the larger chain motels. Also it seemed to be nestled in the middle of a large parking lot, that was mostly empty of cars.

"Where did you take me siri?" I thought out loud.

There was also a lot of vegetation around the building, relatively uncommon here as we spent most of the year in snow. I grabbed my emergency overnight bag that I kept in my car and took my keys out of the ignition. Overthinking everything came in handy today I guess. Not that buying stuff would be impossible, just annoying. I closed my car door taking care to triple lock my car as I walked towards the entrance. The air smelled stronger of rain and the sky above started to darken. Looks like I would get my wish. As I got closer to the hotel it looked more standard, aside from all the plants. There was a cafe attached that advertised breakfast. Cool. After breakfast I would run to the mall to get my phone changed out then go back to Rayne and Matt's to explain what happened and ask for some backup to pick up my stuff from the apartment. Then I would start looking at listings. I nodded to myself happy with my plan. I opened the door to the hotel and I couldn't believe my eyes. Inside was immaculate. I sucked in a breath. There was a huge fountain in the centre of the lobby that had cherubs galore surrounded by lush real flowers, above it was a gigantic skylight and the floor looked like polished gold. There was heavy red velvet curtains over all the windows in the lobby and everyone here was dressed to the nines. I looked sheepishly down at my dress. I was under dressed for the first time in my entire adult life. If I didn't know any better I'd say I had walked into a hotel in Vegas. I was about to turn around and walk out, there's no way I was getting a room for under a grand. Looking again, I wondered what else the hotel had to offer. So I walked up to the front desk. The lady had her grey hair in a tight bun, she was short and heavier built, and turned her nose up at me.

"Can I help you?" she said as she eyed my outfit with distaste.

"I'd like a room for a few nights, if there are any please."

The words fell from my mouth before I thought much on it.

She cleared her throat loudly.

"I don't think this hotel is in your price range." She said with a dismissive wave.

I was going to turn around and leave, I'd been through enough for one night. With another look around the hotel, I found my voice.

"Pretty presumptuous of you to think I can't afford a place like this. I asked for a room if there was one available please." I placed my credit card on the desk.

The lady looked at me for a minute glanced to my card, and looked a bit confused.

"My apologies." She gave me a small bow.

"We only have the presidential available. Its $20 a night."

I laughed out loud before I could stop.

"$20? I'll take it for 7 days. That was cheaper then the cheapest most run down motels.

What the hell. For presidential? Can't afford it, what did I look like? I complained to myself. The lady sucked in a loud breath and the two other ladies at the desk their eyes widened. It was like they thought I was dropping thousands or something.

"You got it Miss! There is complimentary dinner of your choosing to those who stay in our presidential and you have unlimited access to the hotels services."

She handed me a sheet of paper listing said extras. I didn't look at it yet.

"You did say $20 a night, yeah?" I asked just to make sure.

"Yes of course. But we include many things with that. It will be well worth your money I can assure you." She nodded her head to me.

She handed my card back.

"Sorry we still only take cash or cheque right now." She spoke hesitantly.

I dug in my wallet I was pretty sure a had a few hundred dollars stuffed in there. I handed her a $100 dollar bill and two twenty dollar bills. Her hands took the hundred dollar bill unsteadily and her eyes widened yet again. What was the big deal? I pay $100 for a few groceries. She handed me my room key, which was an actual key, not a key card.

"Again, I do apologize for my rude interactions. Please let me know if there's anything I can do to make your stay here better." She smoothed her bun nervously. It was like they thought I was royalty or something. I just smiled and made my way toward the gold carved elevators. I looked at the tag on my key, 13th floor. Huh. Most places didn't have a 13th floor for the stigma attached to the number. Mind you most places weren't like this. I opened my phone to google this inn, see if I could figure out why it was so cheap, or what it was for. I couldn't fathom a place like this costing only $20 but my phone wouldn't work. Figures. Well I will figure that out tomorrow. Least I had a bed tonight. I put my cell back into my bag and pushed the button to the elevator it hummed and chimed as the doors opened. No way. There was a bench in the elevator and an assistant that pressed the buttons for you and held your bags. He nodded a greeting to me dressed as a bellhop you would see in an old movie. What a strange place.

"Floor miss?" he smiled waiting to push the button for me.

"Oh, sorry yeah the 13th floor." his eyes widened as he pressed the button for 13.

"You need not apologize to me miss." he said kindly.

I just smiled.

When the elevator opened again he tipped his hat to me and handed me my bag. "Enjoy your stay, miss" The doors closed on his smiling face. Am I dreaming? There's no way a place like this exists not in 2024. Certainly not for $20 a night, There was a small hall lit by elegant chandeliers and there were three presidential suites up here. The walls had huge framed oil paintings. I shook my head in disbelief. I looked down at the key I had room #2 exhaling I used the key to unlock the door. It was also weird to have a real key instead of a card to scan. I opened the doors and the lights automatically flickered to life. I had to steady myself on the door frame to keep from falling over. The room was bigger then my entire apartment. Full kitchen, full dining area, two living rooms and what looked like a library with books and a fireplace. The furniture was all stuff you would have found in a vintage furniture store. Marble floor. I was stunned. There were several windows lined with the same curtains as the lobby. I dropped my bag to the floor and slipped my shoes off, locking the door behind me. I walked to see the entire room. My feet were aching from the heels. I wanted to call Rayne and tell her about this place but my phone still neglected to work. I sighed and placed it on the counter. I made my way around looking for the bathroom. When I opened the bathroom door there was a huge clawfoot tub in the centre of the room. An elegant sink and all the walls were lined with mirrors. There was a shelf with a bunch of different soaps, and bath accessories. On a rack hung several lush towels. Huh no shower head though? Strange. I started to run the bath. I went to the sink and started to wash my makeup off. I unpinned my hair and relief tingled my aching scalp. I looked though the different bath scents, all in pinup style tins. I settled for lavender. I slipped my dress off and couldn't help but let out a satisfied whimper as I stepped into the hot lavender scented water. Just what I needed. To melt the days stresses away. I stayed in there for what felt like hours. My long hair draped over the side of the tub. Felt so good to be free of hairspray and pins and the dreaded heels. I got out and I slipped into the hotel robe, it was silk and felt great against my bare skin. As I went to drain the tub there was a knock on the door and I froze. "Yes?" I called out

"Miss, your dinner is served."

Oh I had forgotten! I wondered what the food would be like.

"Coming!" I called out.

I opened the door and the mans face flushed bright red.

"Oh miss! I'm so sorry to have caught you when you are indecent!"

He looked away quickly and just gently pushed the table of food into my room. I stared dumbfounded for a minute. It's just a robe?

"It's not a big deal. Thank you for the food." I smiled but the man hadn't looked back at me.

"Just ring the bell by your door when you want the dishes taken away."

He excused himself, half falling over on his way to the elevators. I shook my head. The food was delivered on a genuine silver platter. I went to close the door and hesitated when I heard a faint voice.

"We don't have much longer you know. We need to figure this out and fast."

I lingered for a second. Then another mans voice piped up. Deep, rough and familiar?

"I'm aware of the time frame. We still have 6 months, that's a lot longer then you might think. I know we have a huge list here but-"

His voice dipped lower and out of my earshot. The second man sounded like, the man I bumped into at the engagement party? With the strange ring on his hand. What was the likelihood of that? I closed and locked the door. Maybe I would run into him at some point. At least that proved this place was real. I removed the lid of the dinner. Expecting maybe a burger or something. It was lobster tail, lamb cutlets, vegetables and a creamy soup. There was a secondary tray with an array of tarts and mousse. Also a bottle of champagne, and a large pitcher of ice water.

"Holy shit" I couldn't imagine even eating all of that to myself.

I pulled the wheeled table to the large dining space and started to eat. Everything was absolutely amazing and cooked to perfection. I put the remaining dessert in the fridge for later as well as the unopened bottle of champagne. I polished the main course off. I rang the bell for someone to come this time I just left it outside, being that I was still in my robe I didn't want to make anyone uncomfortable. I heard the table get rolled away. I wasn't sure what time it was being that my phone didn't work, there didn't seem to be any clocks in here either. There wasn't even a tv. I looked thoughtfully around the room. I may as well check for books. I haven't read a book in a while. My fingers ran along the leather bound books. Perusing titles. I had loved to read in the past but with phones and computers and tv I spent my time doing other things. Maybe that was the point of this place. Take you back to your roots. I started reading the titles as my fingers traced each one. 'Mythology, Greek Myth, Gods and Goddesses, The Theory of Time Travel, Paganism, Spells and enchantments. There were a number of occult books. Hmm. I tried the next shelf. Romances, Shakespeare, Poetry. There was one book that looked out of place it was bound in something thicker then leather and it had no title on the spine and no author name either. I almost grabbed it then changed my mind. I was quite tired. I wonder what kind of people rented this suite out for them to hold these books. I decided to go lay in the massive king sized poster bed. I lay in the dark and quiet for some time. My mind was rampant. I allowed myself to think of Henry. I allowed myself to be sad now that I was alone. I cried silently, overwhelmed by everything suddenly. Realizing that Henry wasn't who I thought he was. Yet I knew didn't I? Why else did I walk on eggshells around him all these years. Why else did I make myself smaller, confine my personality, all those years moulding myself to be exactly the girl I thought Henry would want only to not recognize the person I was anymore. Only to be replaced. I supposed it was freedom, but it was daunting here alone in my thoughts. After I calmed down I felt acceptance and just hoped it would be smooth to grab my stuff. I fell into a fitful feverish sleep.

Chapter 2

LOST WHISPERS

"I am the sound you hear when you are alone, when you are scared, a whisper in the dark, a flutter in the tree, a sudden chill, I wear many faces, but I am lost to your sight, ever lingering, especially at night."

"There I could feel the plane drop much too fast. Oxygen masks fell from the compartments above. Screams of so many people. Ears popping, and then the impact. So cold, everything was so cold. I just wanted warmth. Dead everyone was dead... I'm so cold. My head is in agony, the air is too harsh in my lungs..

Then I am in a car, Soft tunes, then the sudden whip of the vehicle, crunching metal, shattering windows, so loud in my ears, Blood, metallic and bitter it's all I can taste in my mouth my body crushed..I can't move, my face doesn't feel right, oh God help me. Please help me. "

* * *

I awoke drenched in sweat and in the midst of a scream. I put my palm to my clammy forehead and caught my breath. What a vivid dream. I rubbed my arms and pushed my hair back off of my face. It clung wetly to my neck. The sun was just starting to poke in. That would mean it was around 6am. I was still in the presidential suite, that part hadn't been a dream I suppose. I dragged the covers off and stretched. I pulled the curtains aside and admired how the sun spilled into the room from the huge windows. Looking out the window was a small courtyard, not one you could see from the front of the building or the parking lot. It had what looked like a pond, lush flowers and arches of vines. Like something out of "The Secret Garden" meanwhile it was spring here in Edmonton, still traces of snow and no vegetation. I wondered how to get to the gardens. I shook my head. This place made no sense. I walked over to the washroom, washed my face with ice water, re-applied my mascara, brushed my hair and teeth. I tried to see if my phone would work, when it didn't I wasn't surprised. I pulled a long red dress out of my bag. Might fit in a little better here with this dress.

"Well at least my regular style would look normal here" I laughed out loud to myself.

I pulled the dress up onto me and dug in my bag praying I had something other then Rayne's heels to wear. I found some black ballet flats at the bottom of the bag and let out a sigh of relief. Again, sometimes overthinking everything came in handy. I slipped them on grabbed my wallet, phone and keys. Time to check out that cafe downstairs I thought to myself. I locked my door behind me and stood in the Hallway a moment. I started to walk towards the elevators but I stopped when I heard the men's voices again.

"The book isn't here. Nothing that we need is here it seems! It's the same tail we've been chasing all these years to no avail!"

There was a slam that maybe was the bathroom door or something. Then the mans voice I recognized responded.

"It has to be. I've done the research and this is the right time period, the right place. We have to keep looking we don't have a choice! We can't afford not too." his deep voice was calm but there was an urgency in his words.

Did I just hear him say time period? Okay, so they are wackjobs, that's comforting.

"Then recheck your research! We must have missed something. I just want-"

His voice was droned out by a fight that was happening in the first presidential suite. A man and a women. I pressed the button for the elevator. It was hard not to hear the fight they were yelling quite loud.

"You told me you were leaving her!" The women's voice shouted.

"I am! I have, I'm with you aren't I?" The man yelled back.

"Then why she calling the hotel asking bout you, hm?" The women challenged.

I rolled my eyes sheesh. Just another unfaithful couple how original. The elevator dinged and the same boy from yesterday was there he greeted me and pushed the button for the lobby. I heard a room door lock as the elevator started to close. Was it those guys? Or the pissed couple, I wondered to myself. The doors closed before I got my answer. When I exited into the lobby, I immediately felt much more comfortable then I had last night. I wasn't under dressed and no one was giving me a second look. I walked past the desk where the ladies greeted me warmly. I turned into the cafe, I was excited to try the breakfast. The cafe was stunning. Retro but elegant to match the rest of the hotel. I went to the counter and a girl greeted me happily.

"I will get a coffee please, and the breakfast special today whatever that is." She nodded.

"Sure thing miss, that will be $3 please."

"$3? is- did I hear that correctly?" the shock was evident in my voice. She gave me a puzzled look.

"There are cheaper options if you just want eggs or pancakes if that's too expensive. The special comes with quite a bit of food though."

She gave me another genuine smile. I handed her a $5 bill and told her to keep the two dollars. She squealed loudly and hugged me over the counter.

"Thank you so much, I can't even tell you how much that means to me!" her excitement over $2 made me feel uncomfortable. I shook it off.

"No worries!" I smiled back at her and took a seat in the window booth. Maybe this place was like a theme park showing you what life used to be like. That didn't make much sense either because then the price to stay would be much higher. I longed for my phone to work so I could call Rayne and tell her all about this place. If I wasn't just crazy, that is. I sighed remembering I also needed to inform her and Matt I was out of a house as well. The girl brought my food over. I gasped a bit. She wasn't exaggerating I had eggs, fruit, bacon, sausage, toast, a pitcher of juice and a small stack of pancakes too. She also brought a fresh steaming cup of coffee with a side of steamed milk. There was no way I could finish all this.

"Enjoy!" she said and half skipped back to the counter.

There were only a couple others in the cafe. Still I couldn't see a clock anywhere. I chewed thoughtfully on the fruit for a minute. Then two men walked in. And I damn near choked on a mouthful of berries. They were in tuxes and they looked identical to the men I thought I saw in the burned down coffee shop when I had been out with Ranye. How the hell was that possible? That was my imagination, right? They both turned and stared at me, probably because I was staring at them. They both had short brown hair and both had a shadow of facial hair. The man on the left was noticeably muscular under the tux probably 5'11 and had these bright blue eyes you could lose yourself in. The one on the right noticeably toned and a bit taller maybe 6'1 could see some tattoos sneaking out of the tux sleeves and collar. His eyes more bluish green. Brothers maybe? I realized I was still staring as they walked toward where I was sitting. I flushed and accidentally knocked the sugar caddie to the ground, little packets of sugar sprawled out all over the floor. Oh god. I stumbled out of the booth to start picking them up and saw another hand helping. The ring. I recognized it. The same guy I bumped into at Raynes? How? I looked up to meet his eyes, sure that my face was a bright ugly red. I met his greenish blue eyes. A flair of recognition flashed in his eyes. Crap he remembered. The other man just stood watching.

"You really seem to be a clutz hey?" He offered warmly in his rough voice.

"Uhh-huh honestly not usually." I laughed a bit.

"Thanks for the extra hand though" I had to turn from his eyes.

I put the refilled caddie back onto the table. I could feel his gaze linger on me. I could also feel his friend or brother or whoever staring harshly at me.

"My names Damon by the way. Seems only fitting considering we have run into each other twice. My brother there his name is Darren."

He motioned to the other gentleman. I nodded in reply and glanced to Darren. He gave me a nod.

"What about you? Whats your name?" Darren said it came out more of a demand then a question, his gaze steadfast.

"Heh forgive my brother, he can take a bit to warm up to."

Damon laughed and clamped Darren on the shoulder.

"Serena" I gave them both a small smile.

"Well Serena, nice to meet you." Damon said and Darren motioned him to go sit down.

"Enjoy your breakfast Serena." Darren spoke with a hard edge to his voice.

Damon looked at me for another second, then he turned and walked toward Darren. They sat a few tables away from me. I ate in silence. The brothers were talking but it was far too quietly for me to pick up what they were saying. Although I really wanted too. I noticed they occasionally looked back at me, almost like they were talking about me. I tried to shake it off. There's no way they were the same guys from before right? That never happened. It couldn't have, the cafe building didn't exist anymore. I sipped my coffee and looked out to the parking lot. My car was sitting there, beside it there was a black Volvo P1800. Wow, you don't see many classics nowadays. I finished what I could of breakfast. The brothers were lost in hushed heated conversation. I started towards the door, when I exited I realized it was raining slightly. I breathed deep. Enjoying the cold mist falling on me for a moment. I didn't glance back at the hotel. Then I headed to my car, time to go get my phone fixed. I went to start my car and stopped when my phone rang. Confused, I looked down and saw my phone suddenly had 48 unread texts mostly from Rayne a few from Matt. And 26 missed calls from Rayne. I picked up on the third ring.

"Rayne, hi I'm sorry my phones been-" She quickly cut me off

"Thank God you are alright! I've been trying to get a hold of you! I've been so worried." she practically screamed.

I had to pull the phone from my ear because her voice was so loud.

"Serena did you not go to your apartment last night? Where were you? Where are you now?" she was speaking so panicked and quick that a knot started to form in my stomach.

"No I stayed at a motel. I can send you the address I want you to see it!"

I responded trying to keep things light.

"Thank God you didn't go home Serena! I thought you were dead!"

The blood drained from my face and my skin erupted in goosebumps.

"Rayne what are you talking about?" there was a breadth of a pause on her end.

"Serena, I'm so sorry there was a fire-" She spoke her voice cracking.

"I thought maybe you got killed, oh God I'm just so happy you are okay."

"Rayne wait- what fire? My apartment?-"

"Your entire apartment building went up in flame last night Serena! Henry was in the list of deceased in the news this morning. I couldn't get a hold of you and your name wasn't there so I-" she broke off in sobs.

"I'm so sorry Serena. I was just so worried"

I was having trouble finding my voice. It wasn't really my apartment, Henry wasn't the best person, but didn't mean he deserved death, not nearly. I swallowed the lump in my throat. I couldn't grasp or believe Henry was dead, my eyes teared and my chest felt tight. That also meant, I've lost all my stuff. If there was insurance it wouldn't go to me, because my name was never really on the lease no evidence of it being mine. I ran my free hand through my hair roughly over and over and paced outside of my car.

"Do they know what caused it?" My voice was much calmer then I felt.

"A gas leak they think, but there are suspicions of arson, I don't know it's ongoing investigation it only happened a few hours ago!"

She stopped crying.

"Where are you? I will come to you, you shouldn't be alone right now. We can go by there later to see if we can find any of your belongings."

I took a few minutes to respond.

"I-yeah-I'm at Elder Oak Inn" I started slowly.

There was a few minutes before she talked, I could hear her typing in the name of the motel into her phone.

"I can't find that on google maps, are you sure that's what it's called? Ugh nevermind, just drop a pin to me okay?"

I did as she asked.

"I will be there in 20 minutes okay?"

"Sure no worries." I said.

Rayne paused told me she loved me and hung up.

I leaned back against my car trying to steady my breathing. I looked back toward the hotel, I could see Darren and Damon getting up to leave. I watched them leave the cafe and head to the main hotel door. I averted my gaze. Immediately piling together in my head my finances and what I would need to do, what I would need to buy. I needed a place to live regardless. I was so overwhelmed I didn't see or hear the brothers come up to me.

"Hey again, sorry we just saw you pacing when we left the hotel. Everything okay?" I looked up to meet Damon's sincere eyes.

I glanced over to Darren who stood coldly eyeing me carefully. Why did I want to answer him? Why did I feel a sudden rush of need to dive into everything that just happened? It was strange to feel so pulled.

"I- I'm fine just waiting for my friend." As I said it the words felt like I was swimming against a rushing river. They felt forced.

Darren's eyes widened, Damon's face changed for merely a second shock evident in his eyes, which he quickly smoothed over. Darren was the one who spoke.

"Alright, well have a good day Serena." He said without a hint of warmth in his voice and gently touched Damon's shoulder urging him long. Damon gave me a brief smile confusion was still clouding his beautiful eyes. They walked toward the old classic volvo together without so much as a glance back at me. I ran my hands through my hair. I hoped Rayne would show up soon, I felt compelled to leave and head to my apartment to see for myself. Instead I steadied my breathing and waited patiently. Rayne pulled up maybe 10 minutes later. She seemed to barely put it in park and turn the engine off before she was tumbling out of her drivers seat and rushing toward me. Her arms wrapped tight around me and we both almost fell over for how hard she hugged me.

"I'm so glad you are alright. You scared me to death you know." she said quickly studying my eyes,

"Me too, thank you for calling me, I'm sorry for missing your calls. My phone stopped working last night, I was going to head for a new one this morning but it seems fine now somehow."

I held it up for her to see. "Maybe the hotel just had bad reception."

I shrugged and motioned to Elder Oak Inn where I stayed. Rayne followed my motion.

"Oh Serena.. please tell me you don't mean to say you stayed there?" She grimaced.

Confused I looked again to the hotel. To my stricken horror it was in ruins. It looked condemned and abandoned for quite some time. So long that plants had begun to overtake it. What the Hell-but those guys-? Everything was real? Was it not? I pressed my palm to my head, it was the exact same as before with the cafe.

"Serena, you weren't squatting were you? That place looks like it would kill you just for entering it's premises. Wait please tell me you weren't drinking?

I should have known you wouldn't want to face Henry after last night. I should have made you to stay with me and Matt."

I looked at Rayne her face was a mix of concern and disgust. I looked again at the ruin. I started to scramble for an answer in my head. There was another motel in the next parking lot over. It looked like somewhere you rented by the hour but that was better then what Rayne was thinking. I took a deep breath.

"No, of course not!" I forced a light laugh.

"I just pointed in the wrong direction I meant there."

I pointed to the other motel. "Obviously."

Rayne's face relaxed.

"Why a shitty motel instead of somewhere nicer? There's so many hotels around."

"I was just tired Rayne, I punched in directions to the nearest place to stay and I ended up here."

"Alright then, phew at least you stayed somewhere with a bed, shelter, food and rodent free I would hope"

She laughed at her own joke, I tried to smile but my face felt tight. Was it a dream? Did I just stay at that other motel and think I ate the food I did and saw the people I did? It was really just like that old coffee place from yesterday. Rayne's voice cut through my thoughts.

"Didn't you say you wanted to show me the hotel? Because it was 'amazing?'"

She looked at the deadbeat motel again in disbelief.

I again forced a bit of a laugh.

"Nah, I was being sarcastic. It was shitty I just wasn't ready to face Henry. Also Rayne, when he came up to me last night, he showed me the lease papers-" I trailed off.

"And?-" Rayne said raising her eyebrow, not letting me drop the conversation.

"My name wasn't on them. I have no proof of ever living there. I wanted to wait to tell you because I didn't want to ruin Matt and your beautiful evening. It was Henry who would kick me out, I would have been out a house, regardless of the fire."

The word "Fire" felt strange leaving my lips, I guess I still didn't really believe it.

"I was going to tell you guys today and get a hand with grabbing my stuff. Then start hunting for another apartment, after I fixed my phone."

The words fell quickly from my lips. Rayne was used to my rambling though thankfully.

"That spineless dick!!" she spat.

"He so got what was coming to him!" I flinched a bit at her words.

"It didn't warrant a death sentence Rayne." I said sharper then I intended.

She just shook her head.

"Well lets at least see what we can salvage from your apartment yeah? I'll drive. Also you should stay with Matt and I. Not this greasy motel."

I almost said yes but then again something was pulling at me, maybe the motel was what I thought it was last night? I needed to figure out where the hell I actually was last night. I didn't think I could shake not knowing. I had to piece together my reality, and differentiate it from fantasy.

"We can go to my apartment and I appreciate the offer to stay, but I will stay here for a while." I gestured to the motel.

Rayne looked at it distastefully. She opened her mouth to protest I was guessing but I cut her off before she started.

"I paid for the week in advance, so I may as well just stay here get my head straight. No offence but I will need some space after.. everything you know?"

I gave her a soft smile. Her face relaxed in understanding.

"Sure, whatever you need okay?" she half hugged me and we started toward her car. She unlocked it with the fob and I looked around again. But there was no evidence of last nights splendour here anymore. I got into her Jaguar. Matt bought it for her a couple years ago. She kept it very clean, I sat down worried I was going to track dirt or something. I never felt overly comfortable in such fancy cars. I also preferred to drive myself, but I took the mental break panning over everything I did last night, all the people I met, or thought I met. There was no way that was imagined? Maybe the old looking motel was the one I went into and since I was quite stressed I thought it was elsewhere. I hoped that was it. I hoped I could piece this together. Then there was the deal of my burnt apartment. I sunk back in the passenger seat. Feeling mentally exhausted. It wasn't even 8am yet. Rayne glanced at me when we stopped at a red light.

"Are you okay?" the light went green before I replied and the jag revved up.

"I'm as okay as I can be. I guess I'm hoping some of my stuff survived the fire." I said honestly.

"I hope so too."

We drove in silence until she pulled up to my apartment on 95th. The building was charred black not completely destroyed the upper left half of the building was still standing, aside broken windows and charred walls. The same could not be said for the right side. My apartment was on floor 9 of 15 . I counted the lines of windows floor 9s windows were mostly destroyed it looked like unlike floors 11-15 which were mostly ruined. The base of the apartment complex was still in okay shape considering. I sucked in a breath. I glanced at Rayne her lips were moving in silent count, probably checking my floor too. She pulled the jag into a stall and shut the engine off.

"You ready?" She looked over to me and I nodded unbuckling myself.

We walked toward the base of the apartment building. The building still had some emergency crews around the base and some police officers were standing by the entrance. One guy and one girl. The guy made eye contact with me.

"Excuse me, Officer? Is there any way I can get up there to see if anything in my apartment is salvageable?" He glanced me up and down.

"Floor?" he brought out a notepad.

"Floor 9 apartment 9"

He seemed to be going down a large list on the notepad.

"Can you show me some ID? "

"Of course" I pulled my drivers license out for him to look.

"You didn't come home last night? I'm sorry to tell you this but the man that was in that room perished due to smoke inhalation earlier this morning."

He said it in such a "business as usual" tone it bothered me quite a bit.

"I heard, thanks" I looked away from him. Swallowing tears that threatened.

The female officer glanced at me and gave me a sad smile.

"I'm sorry for your loss" She said her voice lacking much warmth but I still appreciated the sentiment.

I couldn't imagine part of my job to be telling people their loved ones were dead. I was much too empathetic. I remembered once when Rayne and I were kids, Rayne was maybe only 5. Her mom gifted her a kitten. She adored him and named him "Poof". I remembered one night I was looking after her while her mom worked late and she said she wanted to take Poof out to play. I said okay and we took the kitten outside to play. Well low and behold while we were outside in the garden I was reading a book and Rayne started crying. I rushed to her and she pointed to the sky and said

"Birdie took poof"

I remember tearing up and crying right alongside her while trying to explain best I could that Poof wouldn't come back. The officers voice broke my reminiscing.

"That floor has been cleared to return to, you'll need an officer to go with you as we are taking precautions to ensure your safety. I'll call someone over. Are you both going? I will send two guards with you." He didn't wait for our reply.

He spoke into the radio: "Send me Smith and Wesson."

I glanced at Rayne to see if she picked up on what I picked up on. She just gave me a half smile, obviously not hearing what I just heard, or she simply didn't know. Smith and Wesson was a gun company prior to the early 2000s. Before they changed their name. Weird co-incidence. When the men approached my jaw must have dropped. They looked equally as shocked to see me. Darren and Damon? I immediately averted eye contact. I looked over to Rayne waiting for her signature nudge or smile when someone was attractive. But she seemed unfazed.

"Ah officers Wesson and Smith please escort these young ladies to Floor 9 room 9." I swallowed glancing back at them.

They were both eyeing me, confusion and something else- caution? In their eyes. I looked away again.

Darren spoke. "Follow us please."

Rayne started walking and I had a hard time making myself move. Rayne noticed and put her arm around my shoulder.

"Hey it's going to be okay, I know it must be hard to see your apartment like this, but it looks like some stuff is probably going to be salvageable. More then we thought even." She said encouraging me.

Little did she know my unease had nothing to do with my apartment. She dropped her voice to a whisper.

"Trust me it's safe if they are sending these old officers with us. They would send strong hot young officers if there was any worry of danger."

I stopped in my tracks. What the hell did she just say?

"Old?" I glanced to the guys they definitely heard us.

"I don't know Rayne they look pretty young to me. 30?" I said a bit louder so they could hear me.

The brothers both looked at me now and both of them had a look of unease when I said this.

Rayne stifled a laugh. "30? You need to get your eyes checked those guys have one foot in the grave."

I glanced back to them slightly, we were heading to the elevator. They were very clearly the young hot men I kept running into. There was no way. The elevator roared loudly to life making a clanking sound when Darren pressed the call button. My heart fell to the pit of my stomach. Rayne tensed. The guys shifted on their feet.

"I think we should get out and take the stairs." Rayne said before I could.

"Yes Miss." Damon replied.

We stepped out of it before the doors closed. When the doors did close there was a horrifying crash as the elevator let go. Damon spoke into the radio. "Attention please let all other officers and civilians know the elevator is out of commission."

A voice crackled back "Copy that"

"Out of commission?! You almost got us killed going in there! You should really consider retirement." Rayne roared directed at Damon who just nodded to her. Darren looked like he was trying to hold back a smile. Which he was successful with.

"Rayne relax, we are fine." I spoke gently. She glared at me.

"Someones a softie for the oldies" I tensed at her comment.

"They had no way of knowing it was going to crash." I said calmly. Rayne shrugged. "I guess."

We walked up the cement stairs, they were covered in soot from the fire. We climbed to the 9th floor door. The hall to my apartment didn't feel welcoming anymore. Not knowing about Henry not knowing it wasn't ever mine to begin with. When the 4 of us entered the hallway, there was ash strewn all over the copper rug. We stopped before the entrance of my apartment. Damon took a master key and unlocked it for us. We stepped into the kitchen as we entered. The apartment was trashed. It was like someone had broken in. My hand came to my mouth in shock. I was expecting my apartment to be burnt, destroyed, but not rummaged through. I didn't really know how to process it. Rayne put her hand on my shoulder encouraging me.

"Don't worry, it looks like you'll have more of your stuff then you thought."

I swallowed a bit and could feel the guys eyes on me.

"Is this how you left it?" Damon asked.

A small wave of sadness washed over me. I liked a clean place, Henry was messy but I cleaned up after him. I would have never left my apartment in this much chaos. Furniture toppled over, clothes strewn everywhere, broken glass from all the windows was from the fire. There was ash over everything. The photos that lined the walls were smashed everywhere. I ignored Damon's question and felt immediately guilty for doing so.

"Rayne I'm going to go to the bedroom to see what I can salvage-" I started slowly. "Could you please gather the pictures from the broken frames in here for me?"

I didn't wait for her reply and walked to the bedroom. I needed a moment alone. Mostly because I felt like I was losing my mind, what Rayne said was in my head, I didn't get how she could think they were old. Also they had very fake sounding names. But what purpose would they have to be impersonating officers? I approached the bedroom slowly the door was slightly jarred. I pushed it lightly. The first thing I saw was the bedroom floor was an outline in chalk where they I assumed found Henry's body. I gripped the door frame afraid I would fall over and fought tears. The wall had something written, in-blood? Now I did feel faint. Darkness crept my vision as I let out a loud breath. Arms caught me. Strong and unwavering before I made it to the floor.

"Hey, hey hang on..I got you." I couldn't open my eyes yet but it was Darren's voice, not Damon's.

Strange Darren usually wasn't the one talking to me. I felt him lift me from the ground. It was effortless and smooth, and I felt cool and calm, as if I was in a cold lake on a hot day. A freezing cloth was pressed to my forehead and I felt Darren move me so my head was on his lap. Then he gently grasped my long hair and pushed it off of my forehead and to one side leaving my neck exposed, where he moved the cloth too. I shuddered slightly at the movement.

"Hey, Serena are you with me?" He said quietly.

I wasn't crazy, he used my name it was them. Why did this feel okay? I opened my eyes then. I felt lost in his eyes for a moment, but his face was not friendly, it remained collected and professional.

"Y-yeah I am alright. Thank you. Where did you get a cloth?" I sat up and he pulled me to my feet immediately.

"Counter, thought you might faint, wanted to be prepared." he said emotionless.

"Oh, well thank you again."

He just nodded.

I glanced to his hand. He and his brother had matching rings it seemed. I looked to the bathroom mirror it was spider-ed, but in the mirror Darren did look old. He didn't even look like Darren older, he had different eyes, face shape. It was like a totally different person. I was so startled I almost fell again, his hand was quickly and firmly at the small of my back. I looked to the mirror again and there seemed to be a haze of coloured smoke surrounding his reflection. Darren met my eyes in the mirror.

I looked away and instead met them in person. I scrambled for something to say.

"I-I thought I saw blood, I thought I saw blood on the wall- but I was told Henry died of smoke inhalation. There wouldn't be blood?- Right?"

I looked away from him and grasped the sink. Darren's eyes widened a bit and he left the bathroom. He flicked the bedroom light on and talked into his radio.

"Attention all units, please revisit all apartments for signs of break-in and injury after the fact. Apartment number 9 has blood and is in turmoil, clearly a break in after the body was removed."

A loud voice crackled back "Copy that agent. Finish quickly and bring the civilians down. Execute caution offender could still be in area."

"Yes sir." Darren clicked the off.

I turned the water on and splashed some on my face taking a deep breath. I looked around the bathroom for my belongings. I found my makeup bag untouched and grabbed it. I walked to the closet in the bathroom, grabbing an old tarnished leather bag. I tossed the makeup pouch into it. The closet had a metal tin can in it. I looked down and saw scraps of my clothing. Had Henry been burning my clothes? I tried to turn the closet light on but it wouldn't go. The window wasn't bright enough to see into it. I switched the flashlight on my phone. My side of the closet to my surprise was mostly empty. It was usually overflowing. My dresser in the closet was also empty. More then half my clothes were gone. There was a handful of dresses a couple tops and a couple bottoms I scooped it all into the bag. I gathered a few silk nightgowns, and all the under garments and bras I could see. It didn't amount to much. I had one pair of shoes left only. Doc martens. I was surprised to see my most expensive pair of shoes being the only one there. No other boots heels or flats were here. I reached to the top of my closet where I had a lock box. It was still closed, but the dial was very loose, like someone had tried smashing it open. I pushed the code it opened and thankfully everything was there still. I had a few grand in cash, my social security, my passport, my birth certificate my health care card and my heart necklace. I slipped it around my neck. Having missed the familiar weight of it. My bank cards and everything else had been with me. Now I knew I had everything that was vital. I had a vintage set of a hand mirror and brush. I threw those in the bag too. My jewellery box was emptied nothing left. I sighed. Nothing else seemed important enough to look for. I started into the bedroom. Darren was staring at the wall with the writing on it.

"What does it say? Does it say something?" Darren's head whipped around to me. "Don't worry about it, is there anything else you need in this room?"

His eyes went to my throat.

"Where did you get that necklace?"

It was the first time I heard a hint of anything other then professionalism and ice in his tone. It was soft- sad?

"I..I have had this for as long as I can remember."

I fingered the heart pendant gently. Darren shook his head slightly.

"Come on, we gotta go if there's nothing else Miss."

We got back to the kitchen and living room. Damon glanced at us. His eyes also falling to my neck. Except he didn't mention it.

"She fainted." Darren started.

Damon opened the fridge and tossed a can of coke to me.

"Here drink this, it'll help." Damon flashed me a smile.

"Unfortunately that's about all there is in this kitchen most of your appliances are gone and most of your dishes have been broken. I'm sorry."

I caught the can midair while he said this. I tried to return his smile but I couldn't.

"Thank you. I got the most important things at least."

Rayne came bounding toward me, she handed me a bundle of photos and my laptop. The screen was cracked bad.

"I got the computer to turn on it's still working right now and we can get it repaired I'm sure!"

I returned her smile. "Thank you." I held the photos to my chest.

"If there is nothing else, we should escort you back down, there needs to be another investigation, the break-in happened after the initial clear out."

Darren stated with no empathy in his voice. Damon shot him a look.

"That is if you are ready to go of course. I can't imagine how hard this is, I'm glad you got the most important stuff." Damon offered me a sympathetic smile and Rayne hugged me.

"W-who's blood is on my bedroom wall-what was the writing?" I started my voice sounded distant to my own ears.

"Blood?! What the fuck! Henry died of inhalation didn't he?! Who's blood?" Rayne rebounded.

Damon looked to Darren and some silent look passed between them that I couldn't pin point.

"We will take care of it, we don't know right now. It is best if we take you both back downstairs." Damon said.

Darren looked away from us, he was difficult to read. Honestly I didn't want to see the blood or the chalk outline again.

"Yeah let's go."I said quickly.

Rayne shot me a baffled look.

"Don't you want to know?"

"Not really. Honestly I need some food."

It was a white lie, I felt sick to my stomach, mind you food might help. I did want to know what the writing was, but I would find out secondhand, I didn't want to see it. A look of distaste crossed her features then she laughed a bit.

"Always thinking with your stomach hm?" She nudged me.

"Yeah." I tried to sound humorous but it came out very plain.

"How did you fit your whole wardrobe in that bag?" she motioned with her head slightly.

I looked at the bag.

"I didn't it's all that's left."

"You mean the sicko that broke in robbed your clothes?!"

"No, they nabbed most of my jewellery, my shoes were gone aside one pair oddly. Thankfully they didn't get into my safe. No, Henry was burning them, there was a tin pail in the closet. He probably tossed my other garments, I don't know"

I shrugged.

I glanced to the guys they were both listening intently to what I was saying.

"That's totally screwed up. I'm sorry Serena." She hugged me again.

Over her shoulder Damon looked concerned but Darren was fuming. It didn't make sense. It's not like this was their apartment or their things.

"We will get to the bottom of this." Darren stated, heat edged in his voice.

"Let's go back down ladies. Like my partner said, the officers will take care of this. We will contact if there are any updates."

Damon said as he opened the door for us.

It killed me how professional they sounded. How well they were selling the lie.

"Okay, come on Rayne, I wanna get out of here."

She followed close behind me and Darren followed behind her with Damon leading. We reached the lobby doors. Damon and Darren broke off to talk to other officers. While they were still in earshot Rayne piped up.

"You know for old guys they climbed all those stairs no problem hey? Guess as an officer you gotta stay in top shape but like my grandpa struggles with one flight never-mind 9 at once."

I could see Damon smirk over her shoulder. Darren was talking with another officer and I wasn't sure if he heard what Rayne said or not.

"Rayne your grandpa is pushing 90, what age did you say you think they were?"

"Like at least 75. Why how old do you think they are?" she paused for a breath then continued

"Oh right you're insane and think they are 30 or some crazy thing." she laughed. "Well regardless, lets go get you some new clothes!" She flashed her black credit card. "On me of course!"

"Rayne- I love you but I'm not a charity case. I have money." I looked down to the ground. My mind was everywhere.

"Yeah I know, but I also know you would do the same for me. You just lost all your stuff. I am the one that introduced you to that douche bag, the least I can do is buy you some clothes! You'll need your money for a new place among other things you lost. Just let me help you? For once? Please?"

She gave me a fake pout that worked back when I used to babysit her. I sighed and she smiled clasping her hands together in delight, knowing full well she won me over.

"Let's hit up the downtown boutiques!" she unlocked her car.

"Rayne no, if you are buying me stuff can we go thrifting?" She twisted her face.

"Ugh. I can afford the nice dresses you like! Probably even nicer then what you had before!"

"I know, but I buy all my clothes secondhand I can't justify spending so much on clothes." I shrugged, I had always been more frugal so to speak, Rayne had not.

Rayne rolled her eyes.

"Fine. But let's go to a couple boutiques too." She nudged me playfully.

"If you insist, and only if we get food first." She smiled in triumph and started the car. I buckled in.

"You got it! The melting pot is downtown!"

Rayne was difficult to argue with and she was just trying to be a good friend. I shouldn't fight her so hard.

I shot her a look. "How about Boston pizza?"

"Olive garden?" She countered.

"Sure." I felt my stomach rumble. Pasta was always a nice comfort food to me.

Shopping, all I really wanted was to go back to the motel and prove to myself that I wasn't crazy. However it was only noon.

We pulled up in about 10 minutes to Olive garden. I thought back to the food I thought I had last night and wondered again if that really happened or not. There was a black honda SUV behind us, the windows were tinted so dark you couldn't see a driver. I watched as they mimicked every turn we took since leaving my old apartment. Maybe I was being paranoid. When Rayne pulled in to park in the restaurants lot the SUV continued straight but pulled into the next parking lot. I'm just losing my mind. I concluded to myself. We got into the restaurant it was pretty dead.

"Remember when we used to come here as teenagers after we got our first part time jobs?" I laughed a bit.

Rayne smiled.

"Yeah you mean when you got your first job. We used to fill up on the endless salad and bread then only order an app or something the waiters hated us!"

I sometimes forgot she was so much younger then me. We laughed together at the memory, and for a minute life seemed less dark and confusing. A young man approached us.

"Afternoon ladies can I get you both drinks to start?" He placed a bowl of salad and warm bread on the table.

"A glass of your finest red please." Rayne ordered without looking at him. He looked to me.

"Honestly, just water thanks."

Rayne raised an eyebrow at me. "What, no coffee?"

Of course I wanted coffee, weird how I didn't order it. The waiter looked back to me.

"If you have lattes I will have one, if not just a regular coffee please."

He nodded and left.

"You are really off today hey? Who can blame you though." Rayne said nonchalantly while piling salad onto her plate and mine.

The waiter was back with our drinks. She sipped thoughtfully on her wine.

"Ready to order?" He asked pen poised over his notepad.

"I will get the house special." Rayne stated and handed him the menu.

"I will get fettuccine Alfredo with shrimp please."

I gave the waiter a smile which he returned.

"Great I will check in with you ladies soon"

He left and Rayne took another sip of her wine. I didn't ever really drink, only occasionally. Rayne on the other hand did daily.

"Serena this might be a stupid question but are you okay? I looked up a repair shop its not far we can get them to fix your laptop."

"Thanks Rayne. Yeah lets get it fixed." She nodded in reply.

"Well honestly I don't know, maybe I'm in shock but I'm okay. I guess just hoping for more answers about everything sooner rather then later."

I shrugged a bit.

"I get that. Do you want to look for a new place right away? I can help you, we can drive around too, we have all day."

She sipped her wine again, this time downing the glass she waved the waiter over.

He came quickly, "Yes?"

"Another glass." The waiter nodded and left. I folded my hands together a couple times.

"You could say please you know, he's just working."

Rayne looked up at me breaking a piece of steaming bread off.

"Didn't I say please?" The waiter returned with her glass.

"Thank you." Rayne said.

The waiter nodded and left again.

"Happy?" She laughed a bit.

"Overjoyed. Such a big girl you are using your manners" I said sarcastically.

We both burst out laughing.

"Does that mean I get dessert?" She teased back.

We both laughed again. The waiter returned with our food.

"Thank you!" We both said at once then laughed again.

The waiter looked confused then said "No problem, enjoy."

It felt really good to laugh with Rayne like this. We ate the rest of the meal quickly and silently. Rayne picked up the tab and we headed out the door. I felt much better then I had before we got to the restaurant. We stopped in a boutique around the corner similar to the many Rayne took me too yesterday. There were 3 dresses that stood out, one red one black and one pink. Rayne followed my gaze and searched for my size in each. She ushered me into the change room excitedly. I undressed and pulled the pink one on, it was billowing with fairy style sleeves. Next I pulled the red one on it was knee length strapless with a heart neckline, also billowing. The black one was more sleek but down to my ankles, the sleeves were lace and so was the top of the dress. I redressed.

"How's it going in there?" Rayne called.

"I simply love them! I'm just trying to decided which one to take!"

"Take all three Serena it's okay! We got a lot more shopping to do as well!"

I went to look at the price the dresses were around $120 each.

"Rayne-" I started and she cut me off.

"I swear if you tell me they are too much money. I'll have your ass. I told you it was my treat!"

God I would not spend $120 on a dress ever. I opened the change room door to her eager face. She yanked the dresses outta my hands and booked it too the counter.

"Rayne!" I yelled frustrated.

A couple people looked my way and I sighed and came up to the counter behind her.

She handed me the bag.

"There you go!"

Tears of gratitude pricked my eyes and I hugged her tightly.

"Hey, relax its the least I can do. Next boutique!"

She started towards the door, I grabbed her arm gently.

"How about we drop my laptop off, then go thrifting please? It's not just about money but I find it relaxing to sift through stuff."

I gave her a half smile.

"Of course!"

We crossed the street to drop my laptop off. It was a small shop and the technician greeted us with just a nod. We were the only ones in here. I approached the counter. The guy didn't raise his head, he was reading his cell.

"Hello, How are you today?" I started

"Fine. Repairs are billed per hour. Screen fix is $50 flat."

"Screen fix please."

He looked at me bored and took the laptop from my outstretched hand.

"Name? Cell number?"

"Serena" I wrote my cell down for him.

"It will be ready in three hours."

I thanked him and we left. We walked to the car and Rayne punched in her maps thrift stores nearby. The first one we stopped in was mostly furniture and housewares. I made a mental note to return here once I found a new home. The second had a huge selection of clothing and accessories. We spent the afternoon here and I managed to grab ample clothing for a fraction of what Rayne spent on me. Rayne even found some stuff she bought. My bill for three huge bags of clothes was around $100 she spent only about $40 in her one bag of clothes. I couldn't help but laugh.

"See? Isn't this better then a boutique? More variety and less money!"

Rayne laughed. She was about to say something when her cell rang.

"Hello babe." She said, she smiled at whatever he said back to her.

"I miss you too handsome.. Dinner?" She glanced at me.

"Go have dinner with your soon-to-be Husband it's okay, you spent the day with me we can grab my laptop and if you don't mind just dropping me back to my car at the motel. I will make do!"

"Are you sure?" She asked looking at me.

"Very."

The thought of being alone for a while despite how much fun I had with Rayne was compelling.

"Id love to grab dinner, where should I meet you?" She laughed.

I couldn't hear what Matt was saying but Rayne's cheeks flushed.

"I love you so much" Rayne said and hung up.

She was still beaming when she hung up.

"Let's go get your laptop!"

She pulled my arm and broke into a run, I laughed and ran with her.

"Where is he taking you, that's got you so hyped?"

I raised an eyebrow as we approached her car.

"The rotating restaurant! We haven't actually gone before."

"Oh wow! Me either, let me know how it is!"

We pulled up shortly to the repair shop where I grabbed my laptop, Rayne waited in the car. We spent the car ride singing songs from our teen years. Not long later we pulled up to the motel. I was relieved to see my car. I glanced to Elder Oak in hopes it was magically functioning. It was still in shambles. I sighed slightly.

"What's wrong? Change your mind about this shitty ass motel?"

"Oh no, honestly I really am looking forward to sleeping it's been an emotional day. Thanks for making the afternoon so great Rayne. You really are amazing."

She smiled and handed the bags to me, from the boutique and from the thrift store.

"Okay give me a call tomorrow! Oh and check for bedbugs." She laughed.

I rolled my eyes.

"Well you make sure you wear a dress tonight! Matt deserves to see you dress like a girl here and there!"

I laughed playfully. She stuck her tongue out at me.

"Oh that's ladylike Rayne" I used a mock disapproving tone.

Rayne scoffed.

"As if. He's marrying me he knows what he's getting into."

We both laughed as she waved and pulled away. Leaving me alone in the cool quiet nighttime air with arms full of bags. I decided to put them in my car for now. As I locked my vehicle, I noticed the black tinted SUV parked across the street. I was fairly certain it was the same one I thought was tailing me and Rayne earlier. I swallowed and dismissed it as paranoia. Locking my car again I started to the motel.

"Let's see where I really slept last night, shall we?"

I said out loud to the mostly empty parking lot. Speaking out loud usually calmed me, but not this time.

Chapter 3

SCARLET OFFERING

"A reflection cannot exist within boiling water, at your most vulnerable you feel your most powerful, a scarlet offering to, absolve, absorb, retain, still the waters and now return home to yourself."

I came up to the "pay by the hour" motel. I was looking all over for anything that that held even the faintest resemblance to my memories from last night. The cracked uneven cement that lead up to the motel was not kept well. The plants outside were mostly dead or dying. I walked in the lobby and the door chimed. It was just your average motel lobby. It was crammed though with desks that were too big for the space and worn leather couches. The lady at the front desk looked at me with not much emotion in her face or eyes. She seemed very bored or tired, possibly stoned. Dull black hair, maybe 56 years old.

"Can I help you?" she asked, her voice cracked a bit like she had a cold.

"Uh maybe, see I think I stayed here last night?"

"You think you did? Were you drunk or something?" she asked casually.

It probably wasn't uncommon here for her to see many drunk people. I forced a laugh.

"Yeah a little." She just shook her head. "Name?"

"Serena Moonshale" The lady clicked on her keyboard.

"Nothing under that name, would you have used your stage name?" She asked me. I tried not to get too insulted as I knew what kind of motel this was.

"I'm not a dancer or anything like that."

I looked down embarrassed for having to say that out loud. I had nothing against people in that lifestyle it just wasn't for me.

"Oh my bad. Well did you come alone or did a man take you here, could it be under his name?"

"I came alone, I remember that much. Oh wait, here."

I passed her the antique key I still had from last night.

"My dear is this some sort of joke? No hotel or motel that I know of uses keys like this. Not today's day and age. All chip cards hun. I'm pretty sure you didn't stay here, sorry. I can get you a room though.

There are some men looking for an escort as well, I can point you that direction."

"I'm not an escort either." I said a little exasperated. I would be lying if I said it didn't irritate me a little.

"Ah, gotcha well then get out of here, good luck in your search. I would give you a room anyway but it's Saturday night so."

She dismissed me with a wave of her hand.

"Thanks anyhow." I said politely.

I let out a breath and headed out the door. I looked first to the SUV that was still parked across the road. I couldn't tell if anyone was in there or if it was just parked. Part of me wanted to approach it, to ease my mind. But then that felt idiotic because what if it was someone following me? Like here I am on a silver platter, let me make your job easier! I'll just wonder right up to your door. I laughed a bit to myself. Dark humour at my own expense. I was probably wrong anyway, why would anyone follow me? I looked back to my car it was still one of the only ones in the lot. Except, the volvo? The guys were here again. I wondered if I could speak to them, double check that it was indeed them at my apartment earlier. Well maybe I could ask them being that we stayed at the same spot, unless I imagined that too? I walked up to their car but to my dismay it was empty. I checked my phone it was only 7. I looked up to Elder Oak Inn yet again. When I came last night I remembered it didn't look condemned until I had left. When I first got there last night it looked completely normal. Now, there was a chain metal fence around it that had a "No Trespassing" sign nailed to it and under that a yellow sign stating the building was condemned. I looked back again I could still see my car.

"Should I just-?" I thought out loud. "Open it?"

I rattled the gate a bit and it opened with a loud metallic groan. I looked around again afraid someone heard it but no one was here to hear it.

"I guess I got this far."

With another quick look around I slipped past the gate. I turned around to close the gate behind me. When I looked back I fell to my ass in shock. The path was lit with flowers. I could see the cafe sign I saw last night, The big ornate doors and lights on inside. I stood up, the gate I closed was now just a simple gold painted picket fence. I tried to check the time but my phone wouldn't light up.

"No way" I couldn't believe my eyes.

"How do I test this? I must be losing my mind."

I grabbed the gate again and walked through it. To my utter shock I was back in the parking lot the gate I was holding was the chain link. The building was yet again in shambles. My car was where I left it. I did this several times and the same thing happened each time. So somehow this was real. I walked to my car the SUV was still parked but this time the window was down. All I could see in the moonlight was an elderly man with very pale eyes. The window wasn't down the last time I looked. He was not looking my direction however his eyes were fixated on something up ahead on the road that I couldn't see. Hmm maybe it was nothing. I got to my car and grabbed my bags and my laptop. A final test to see if the items came with me still. I closed and locked my car. When I looked back the SUV was gone.

"Well okay then. Here goes nothing"

I grabbed my bags and my laptop, locked my car and headed to the gate. When I came on the other side I still had everything I had grabbed from my car in my hands.

"No friggin' way."

Despite how surprised I was it was hard to contain how happy I was to be back in this place. I opened the doors, all of the splendour from last nights memories was here, and the same lady from last night greeted me.

"Ms Moonshale! How delightful, we weren't sure you would make it back for dinner! Would you like the same as last evening or would you like something different today? Oh! Timothy come get

Ms Moonshale's bags for her please, take them up to her suite for her."

Timothy came over dressed similar to the gentleman in the elevator from yesterday. I let him take my bags and I came to the front desk.

"I would love the same thing as yesterday actually." I smiled politely to the receptionist.

"Of course, go get comfortable it will be up to your room shortly! Just, maybe perhaps wait to be in a night gown until after the meal comes tonight?" She winked at me.

I thought back to how uncomfortable the guy that delivered my dinner last night was when I answered in a robe.

"That was unintentional, I won't do it again." I said and gave her a smile which she warmly returned.

I rang for the elevator and the same guy from last night greeted me. Timothy also followed behind me with my bags.

"You must have gone a long way to reach that boutique." He nodded to the bag.

"Oh well I have a car so it wasn't that far." He looked at me shocked.

"One day I would like a car myself, I'm glad you had a nice day. I hope it continues. Have a good evening"

He dismissed me as Timothy and I walked to my suite.

"I can take it from here, Timothy. Thank you"

He handed my bags to me and tipped his hat, heading down the service stairs. I turned the key to my room. I opened the door and it was just the same and I let out a happy yelp, louder then needed, but I couldn't contain it.

"I guess I'm not crazy after all, what a relief."

I closed the door to my room and leaned against the door dropping my shopping bags at my feet.

"Wow, this really is stunning. I will have to take Rayne here tomorrow!"

I started to unpack my bags. I unpacked the thrift bags first happy with how many different outfits I had grabbed. The weather here was usually cold so I had warmth to add to my regular outfits. I put everything in the closet. I unloaded the bag from the boutique next. To my surprise there were about 5 extra dresses in there, a gorgeous jacket, a blouse and a really nice pair of jeans.

"What!" I exclaimed out loud.

The three dresses I picked were in there too. There was a sticky note.

"Don't be mad I thought these would look amazing too, (Even the jeans haha) I grabbed them while you were in the washroom! Love you! Signed Rayne."

I shook my head but also brought my hand to my mouth in shock, tears threatened but I didn't shed them.

"Oh Rayne this must have cost a grand. I owe you big time."

I said out loud and checked if I could call her, but my phone wasn't working still. "I guess maybe they just don't have reception here, this place wasn't exactly ordinary."

I put the rest of the clothes away. At the bottom of the bag there was another bag. "Oh, Rayne"

I opened it and it had a bunch of pairs of gorgeous nightwear and lingerie.

"God, I don't even know how to thank her for all this."

I put those away too and glanced around the room. I pulled the curtains closed. Then I heard faint voices. The guys! I jumped up and pressed my ear to the wall. Realizing in that moment that I should really mind my own business. However, I wanted to talk to them to see if they could tell me why this place was hidden. They must know too they were outside of it like I was. Damon was talking.

"Well what did you say the sigil was on her wall, I didn't recognize it myself."

"It's.. Demonic Damon. Dark and very old. I'm telling you we need to figure out why it was there, sooner rather then later." Darren was talking hurriedly.

"She could be-"Damon started but Darren cut him off:

"No she doesn't seem the type you should have seen her faint, her face I'm excellent at seeing falsities and that wasn't fake. She was terrified and confused."

"I believe you, and I feel the same, but it must be something, we saw her this morning at the hotel cafe, then we saw her out there." Damon said, there was worry in his tone.

"Well I don't know. What if she's misleading us still somehow" Darren stated.

I couldn't believe what I was hearing these guys say. Demonic? What like in the movies? God well I wonder if they are even officers or not. Cultists? I pulled away from the wall until I couldn't hear them enough to make out what they were saying. That's what I get for eavesdropping I guess. There was a knock at my door then and I opened it to a giant tray of food. My stomach growled loudly. The gentleman delivering it was the same as last night.

"Here you are miss. I apologize for my outburst yesterday I just-" He trailed off.

"It's quite alright I should have been more careful as to what I was wearing when I opened the door. I hope you have a good evening and thanks for the food."

I smiled he tipped his hat and left. I paused in the hall half tempted to knock on their door.

"I will just eat this first I think" I whispered out loud to myself.

I pulled the trolley in to my room and locked the door behind me. The food was incredible yet again.

"God maybe I should just live here, it would be cheaper then any mortgage or rent by a long shot. Although I'm still unsure if this is reality. I would feel better if I talked to the guys."

I swallowed the last bit of food. I went to the bathroom mirror to smooth my hair, I spun a bit in the mirror. Sweet I managed not to get anything on my white dress. With a deep breath I decided I would go see them.

"Why am I so nervous? I guess probably cause they are over here talking about demonic things. What if they are cultists? I don't know, they seem like good people. I am usually pretty good at reading characters." I spoke to myself out loud. That was something I usually did.

I swallowed my food and went to the door. The hallway to my relief was empty. I moved to the first presidential suite and hesitated to knock. Damon was talking.

"Did you happen to see if she was back in the hotel tonight?"

I let a small breath out and almost changed my mind about knocking but I stood firm, listening. They were talking about me, this proved it. My only question was why.

"I did a sweep but she could just be in a room or not back yet. If she even returns." Darren said with the usual cold edge in his voice.

"Any lead on the book?" Darren continued.

"Not yet, but it has to be here somewhere." Damon replied.

I decided to knock then. Their voices fell silent and there was some shuffling. I fiddled with the hem of my dress, suddenly wondering if I had made the right choice. I literally heard them talking, I was pretty sure they were psychopaths and here I was offering myself to them. Where was my conscience? Something stronger then fear pulled me to stay. The door cracked open. Damon and Darren were both standing there, when I met their eyes Damon's looked surprised and cautious. However in Darren's eyes there was a rage boiling. After a moment I found my confidence.

"I'm sorry I couldn't help but overhear you were looking for a book."

I hadn't thought about saying that it just came out of my mouth, without so much of a thought, like it wasn't even me talking.

An image of the black book hidden in my bookcase came to mind. As I thought it the book literally materialized into my hands. I dropped it startled and yelped. Damon and Darren shared a look of horror. Damon reached down and grabbed the book. I stepped back and Darren lunged forward grabbing my arm and half dragged me into their room, his other hand clasped tightly over my mouth, muffling my scream. Damon had the book in his hand as he quickly latched the door. Darren pushed and held me roughly to the wall.

"I'm going to die." Was the only thought in my head.

"Oh my god please! Stop Darren. Please! You are hurting me!" I screamed struggling against his strength.

Damon tossed Darren a knife which he caught with his left hand, his right arm held me pinned against the wall. He brought the blade to my throat.

"Darren! Damon please, please stop! What did I do? Please don't hurt me!" I struggled against him as hard as I could. My eyes were burning and blinding with tears.

"What are you? Speak." Darren held the blade closer to my throat so close if I swallowed too hard it would cut my skin.

"What are you talking about!! Please!! I don't know anything!"

"What. Are. You." Darren seethed. "Don't make me ask again."

"Darren maybe we should-" Damon started. "She looks genuinely petrified"

"Shut up! Demons lie, they pretend Damon!" He pushed me harder against the wall.

"I'm not a demon! Please you guys are sick- I can get you help. Demons don't exist- please"

"Then how the hell did you get this book!" Darren's eyes bore into mine and now I had so many tears streaming down my face it was hard to see.

"Oh god I don't know! Please I don't know. You can have it, just let me go!" Begging seemed pointless but it's all I could do. I had never been so scared in my life. Suddenly a strange sensation covered me and I felt one hundred percent unafraid. I immediately stopped crying and thrashing and pleading. I became clear and focused.

"Get off of me! Let me go!" I pushed against Darren as hard as I could. The blade fell from his hands and he *Flew* backwards hitting the far wall just missing Damon by a hair. I stared in utter shock. Damon suddenly looked nervous and he came barrelling towards me.

I pulled my arms up covering my face and head.

"No! Please I don't know how I did that! Oh God I don't know how I-"

I looked down in horror at my hands and crippled against the wall, falling to the floor and resuming crying. All my fear flooded back.

"Oh god is he okay-" I heard a groan from Darren as he got up.

"Whats happening to me!" I screamed and cried violently. Cradling myself in my arms, I just looked at the floor and cried.

"I'm so sorry.. I've never-you gotta believe I've never-" I felt Damon's arms come around me.

"Kill me..just kill me..just get it over with please.. please" I begged in a voice barely above a whisper. I accepted that I would not make it out of here alive, and I suddenly didn't want too. This was all too much.

"Shh" Damon was trying to soothe me. Darren got up.

"Damon what the hell are you doing?! Put that bitch down!"

Damon unwrapped one hand from me and held it up to Darren.

"Stop. She's not a demon, and if she is, shes possessed and has no idea what's happening to her. Look at her Darren. I mean really look at her. She is beyond terrified."

Darren looked to me and I met his eyes, my eyes were still blurring and burning from the stream of tears. His expression softened and turned into something that looked remorseful.

"We have to make sure." Darren said his eyes not leaving mine.

"We will." Damon said as he put me in a chair from the table.

"Grab that rope." Damon commanded.

Darren started to wrap my hands with rope from the curtains. Damon moved to wrap my legs. I let them because I was too afraid to do anything else. When the rope was secure Damon moved to grab the knife and the book. I blinked out all the tears left in my eyes and took a shuddering breath. The rope dug tightly into my skin and it stung.

"What do you want with me?" I looked to Darren who stared at me distrust obvious in his expression.

I suppose I wouldn't trust someone that just threw me across a room either. I eyed the knife Damon held in his hands. It didn't look like a regular kitchen knife. It was gold with various engravings. The blade was the length of a dagger. He came closer and I realized it was in fact a ceremonial dagger. Like something straight out of a TV show. It had similar markings to their rings. Damon finally spoke.

"Where did you find this book?" He held the bound book in his hands.

Darren rolled his eyes as if he thought this was useless. I would answer everything they asked and prove myself to Darren.

"I found it on my bookshelf in my suite next door, last night after I checked in."

"Have you ever seen it before last night?"

"No. Never even touched it, I- I don't know how it ended up in my hands at your door. I don't know how to explain it. It sounds insane."

Damon took a minute before asking another question. Darren let out a frustrated sigh and ran his hand through his hair.

"What if this is pointless Damon?" Darren yelled.

Damon shook his head.

"Give me a minute, we can at least talk to her. Like you said we gotta know for sure."

Darren sighed and moved to the kitchen.

"What are you doing Darren?"

"I'm going to get her some water."

Damon nodded and turned back to me. I didn't like how he said water.

"I will answer anything you ask, but don't talk about me like I'm not in the room."

I said way more confidently than I felt.

"Alright." Damon stated.

"Why don't you tell me how the book came into your hands, no matter how crazy it sounds." Damon urged softly.

"I heard you guys talking about a book and when I got to the door and brought it up the image of the book on my shelf popped into my head and- It just sort of appeared. I gotta be losing my mind."

Damon nodded. Darren brought the water to my lips to drink.

"Poisoned?" I whispered, his face was inches from mine.

"Won't hurt you none, unless you are a Demon of course."

Darren said with challenge in his tone.

"Fine. If only to prove you are crazy."

I took a couple sips, it was just water. Darren stared slack jawed at me and Damon gave a very slight smile.

"She's not a demon Darren."

"Well she's not human either!" Darren roared.

"We don't know that!" Damon rose his voice.

"I am human, guys so are you. There's no such thing as monsters and demons. Movies aren't reality. You guys need help-"

"We need help? A human can't throw someone across the room like that."

Darren's words stung. I clenched my jaw, that's true. Okay let's use it to my advantage then I thought quickly to myself. My body was screaming fight not flight.

"Okay." I breathed. "Since I'm a bit tied up at the moment I would appreciate some answers too. And being that I apparently have inhuman strength I am sure if I tried, I could get out of these bindings no problem."

I ignored the loud scoff from Damon. Darren to my surprise looked almost amused.

"You make a fair argument I suppose." Darren said as he ran his hand roughly through his hair again turning away from me.

"You guys are not cops are you?" I asked breathlessly.

Damon laughed a bit "No, not really."

"Then why were you at my house posing as cops?"

Darren interrupted:

"Damon we can't trust her! We don't know what she is! How is she even in this hotel Damon have you forgotten?"

"Then do more of your absurd tests like getting me to drink water." I challenged. Darren and Damon both looked at me. A slight smirk played at Darren's mouth. "Ladies choice. Not all the tests will be quite so..refreshing. I promise you that." His eyes held a strong challenge and for once I felt, I wasn't going to back down. Damon spoke before I got the chance too.

"Darren, take it down a notch. If she isn't human then shes being complacent regardless." Damon said lightly.

Darren shot him an irritated glance. I grimaced at being called complacent but I was a people pleaser at heart.

"It wasn't just water, it was holy water." Damon explained.

"Holy water? Like blessed water? Are you guys religious or something?"

"Or something." Darren answered instead of Damon.

"We are working on stopping the apocalypse-" Damon started Darren interrupted him.

"That's smart Damon tell her everything before we even know if we can trust her! Are you forgetting she threw me across the friggin' room no less then ten minutes ago?"

He swiped with his hand over his bleeding nose. His shoulder looked out of place and he was cradling his left arm.

"The end of the world? You guys are seriously insane. Darren come here, please." I coaxed.

He turned his head to me.

"Yeah right." He approached me with a silver knife.

"Woah hey!" I yelped.

"Don't worry okay? We are just trying to see if you can hold it." Damon explained softly.

"Jesus fine I'll hold the knife." I snapped. Damon handed it to me gently,

while watching me cautiously. It did nothing. I shrugged and Darren clenched his jaw, grabbing the knife back. He nicked my arm with it.

"Ouch! Hey!" The blood trickled down my arm. Damon let out a sigh and went to grab a bandage, he wrapped my arm carefully.

"It's not that big of a scratch, you don't need to bother wrapping it." Darren stated.

Damon continued anyway.

"There Darren, satisfied? That covers most of the list."

Darren gave a heavy sigh.

"Yeah okay. But we still don't know where that strength came from. Or much else." He narrowed his eyes at me.

"Can you please untie me now? Now that I've passed all your so called "tests". The least you can do is give me some answers." I said bitterly.

Darren looked back "You are strong enough to rip them yourself I'm sure." He matched my tone.

"Darren enough." Damon moved to untie me.

"Wait let me try to get out." I thought maybe too confidently.

Damon's eyebrows shot up. "If you insist."

"Show us the monster you are." Darren challenged.

I struggled pathetically against the bindings for about 5 minutes before Damon just untied me.

"See? I'm no monster, I honestly don't know where that strength came from and I can't summon it on a whim. I don't know how I got the book. I don't understand it, it's never happened before today okay?"

"We believe you Serena." Damon answered.

"Darren do you also believe me?" I tried to meet his eyes.

Darren sighed. "For now."

I started to walk up to Darren he didn't shrink back.

"Can I see your arm please?"

He stopped cradling it. "Why?"

He didn't move closer to me. I looked behind me to Damon.

"Damon can you go get some ice and a bucket of warm water with soap?" Damon looked to Darren who nodded.

"Sure I'll be right down the hall." Damon exited the room. I looked back to Darren's eyes. Confusion clouded them. "What are you doing?"

"Look I'm a nurse aid, your shoulder is dislocated I'd like to fix it, if you'll let me. I never intended to hurt you." He studied my eyes for a second.

"I'm fine. I've been in worse shape."

"You aren't, no thanks to me, look I really just want to help you okay?" After a moment of consideration he spoke.

"I guess." His voice softened and he moved closer to me.

"Good. Because after this I really need to know what's going on." Darren looked away from my eyes for a sec and nodded.

"Okay on three, one-" I popped his shoulder back and he groaned loudly.

"You friggin' said 3." he grunted and shook his arm a bit.

"Better?" I offered a small smile.

"Yeah, thanks." He stroked where he cut me gently.

"I'm sorry for that"

"It's barely a cut I'll live. I trust you had your reasons"

"We just- we have to make sure that's all." He cleared his throat.

"I get it and I'm sure I'll get it a lot clearer once you guys explain things to me."

I adjusted my tone to playful.

"If not then I suppose I will just kick your ass again, since somehow I can."

Damon entered then "I don't doubt that" Damon said while laughing.

"We will see about that. I think you are at a disadvantage, since you can't control it yet." Darren said without matching my playfulness.

Damon handed me the water, cloth and ice.

"Here have at it. He could use the TLC." Damon joked.

Darren glowered at him.

I started to dab with the warm cloth on the cut under his right eye. He pulled away from me.

"Damn it Darren just let me clean you up. Please. It's the least I can do."

"I'm not a friggin' child, I can clean up myself." He snapped.

"I didn't say you couldn't. Please stop pulling away." I said softly.

"Jeez Darren just let her help. I'll get some drinks for us."

Damon moved to the kitchen to fix drinks. Darren moved back toward me.

"Fine. I just don't get why you are being nice." He said.

I gave a small smile and began dabbing under his eye again.

"What's there to get?" I shrugged slightly. "It's just how I am."

Darren studied my eyes again. I admired his like I did the first time I met him.

"Serena, whats your poison?" Damon asked.

I don't really drink, coffee would be nice." I said without breaking Darren's eye contact.

I moved the cloth to his blue swollen nose. I dabbed the dried blood there.

"I think I broke your nose. I'm so sorry Darren really. I didn't know."

"Yeah, feels like it. You apologize too much. Do you know that?"

"I'm aware." I reached and cracked his nose back in place.

"Ow! Damn it. A little warning next time!" He jolted back a bit.

"I would apologize but someone told me I apologize too much."

I gave him a small smirk. Damon broke into a laugh in the kitchen.

"Man she's got you there."

Darren just rolled his eyes. I continued to clean the cuts and blood on his face then handed him ice to bring the swelling down under his eye where there was a nasty cut and a bruise. I moved towards the kitchen and Damon handed me a hot cup of coffee with steamed milk.

"mm thank you." I brought it to my lips the scent alone calmed my nerves.

"Of course." Damon gave me a brilliant smile.

"Thanks for patching grumpy up over there." He nodded to where Darren was sitting holding ice to his cheek.

Darren glared at him. "Shut up Damon."

Damon laughed

"Don't take it personal, he's like that with everyone."

"Trust me, I don't." I didn't look to see Darren's face.

"Look I have been really patient but can you both tell me whats going on now please?"

"Gladly." Damon said and motioned to the couch.

"Well I'm sure that will be more comfortable then being tied to a chair."

"I'd bet as much. But if not we can always tie you back up milady." Damon laughed again.

Darren moved to the couch as well. When we are all seated Damon spoke.

"Ask what you want to know. We will tell you what we can."

All the questions in my mind raced and I found it hard to decide what to ask.

"You guys said you were trying to stop the apocalypse?"

"Damon shouldn't have told you that." Darren piped up.

"Okay, but what does any of this have to do with me?"

"Honestly we don't know. We didn't originally think it had anything to do with anyone else." Damon started

"The fact that you have that book and that it came to you makes me question it myself." Darren added. Damon nodded in agreement.

"Okay, what's this book?"

"It's ancient. We have been tracking it for a while now." Damon said.

"Tracking it?"

"It's hard to explain." Damon continued.

"It's black Magick. Probably the most dangerous and sought after book in history." Damon continued.

"Why would that be in a hotel room randomly.?"

"That's what we want to know and why it responded to you" Darren said.

"I don't get what it has to do with me." I sipped my coffee.

"It's hidden with blood magicks so that means you are a relative of a previous owner of the book." Damon said.

"Or an extremely powerful being, where this type of magick feels it is drawn too you." Darren added eyeing me cautiously.

Damon shot him an irritated glance.

"What? Your the one who insisted on telling her this stuff." Darren rebuffed.

"Well keep the book, by all means I don't want anything to do with it. I trust you guys know what you are doing right?"

"We plan to destroy it. However we might need it to stop the apocalypse." Damon stated.

"With how dangerous you are saying it is, I think that's a good bet."

"We just don't know how to destroy it yet, and we can't until we know we don't need it." Darren added.

Damon took a sip of his coffee.

"Well you could burn it?" I suggested.

"You think something this powerful can be destroyed so easily?" Darren said with frustration in his tone.

"Darren, she's just trying to help."

Darren downed his drink, the ice clinked around in the glass noisily. He stood to fix another.

"We don't need to involve her, Damon. It's our fight not hers."

I grit my teeth a bit and took a long sip of my coffee, contemplating my next question.

"She's already involved Darren. It's better if we give her more information."

"No it's better to send her on her way. Knowing less." Darren said darkly.

"If I may, I would like to hear more about everything. Honestly everything is strange right now."

Darren shook his head in irritation but didn't protest further.

"Why were you guys dressed as cops and at my apartment?" I asked after a moment of heated silence.

"We were investigating the fire." Damon stated

"Okay but why, why have you been following me? And why did my friend say she thought you guys were old?"

"We had no idea it was your apartment, we were shocked to see you as well." Darren answered.

"Oh." I felt my cheeks flush.

Damon chuckled. "We use minor spell work for what we call a "glamour", we need to get into a lot of different places at multiple levels of security to track down everything we need to."

"In order to stop the apocalypse?"

"Yes." Damon replied.

"We didn't think it had anything to do with you until I saw the blood in your apartment. That was the first inclination it might have something to do with you, our second, was the book." Darren began.

"Oh- right." My mind flashed back to the unpleasant memory. "But you can't think I did that? The blood-" I trailed off disturbed by the memory.

"No, I don't but the sigil was demonic and we had our suspicions, we were going to track you down if you hadn't shown up at our room." Darren took a sip of his new drink.

"Am I in some sort of danger?" Darren looked away when I said this. Damon's face looked at me with genuine sympathy.

"We don't know yet, but it's possible." Damon stroked my hand gently.

I didn't move from his touch. It felt warm and lovely like it had back at Rayne's.

"Why were you at my friends engagement party Damon? I-I recognize your touch." I paused for a bit and cleared my throat. "Er- I meant ring."

I grimaced feeling embarrassed by how I worded that. Damon looked at me with furrowed brows.

"We thought there was something at that house, we were checking in on the richer families in the area. It wasn't there so don't worry."

I was suddenly overcome with the need to sleep.

"Okay..look guys I have more questions but I'm exhausted. I'd like to go now."

"Of course." Damon stood up and went to open the door for me. Darren watched me walk.

"One more thing." Darren started. Damon looked at him with confusion in his expression.

"Yes, Darren?" I said simply.

"How do you get into this hotel if you know nothing of Magicks?"

I stopped in my tracks.

"What do you mean?"

A scream from the hall echoed before I got the chance to hear an answer. Darren and Damon sprung to their feet and barrelled into the hallway. Damon grabbed my hand and dragged me with them.

"Get her back to her room." Darren ordered.

Damon guided me to my door.

"Lock it, don't come out until we tell you too got it?" Damon said hurriedly.

I didn't reply and Damon closed the door to my hotel room. I latched it behind him.

I flipped the lights on. My mind was swirling. I again wished my phone would work. I thought I should maybe call the police? I guess and tell them what? What if they see the hotel like Rayne did? A knock at my door pulled me from my thoughts. I opened it. Damon gave me a half smile and walked in Darren followed behind him.

"What happened?"

"Nothing just the couple fighting in the first suite. Fight got out of hand. They are checking out. A window got broken and she screamed." Damon said.

"You guys are okay then?" I asked.

They nodded.

"Well we won't keep you. I'm sure we will see you for breakfast." Damon smiled.

"Goodnight." Darren closed the door behind them.

God this was a lot to process. They tied me down and yet why do I want to see them again? They talked about the end of the world and demons and magic, like insane people. So why did it not scare me? Is it because somewhere under my logical thinking I believed them wholeheartedly? I sighed out loud and walked to the bathroom to run a bath. Rose scented this time. The hot water felt amazing on my skin. My skin was raw where they had the ropes, otherwise I felt fine.

"I think I'm going to offer to help them." I thought out loud to myself.

As crazy as that sounds especially out loud. I think I'm going to offer to help them stop the apocalypse they so believed in. Partly because I was afraid they were right and I couldn't imagine, knowing about something like that and not helping. Also maybe it would help me find out more about why that book sought me out. I actually wanted to believe in magic. Who wouldn't? Like all the fantasy novels I loved so much. What if a lot of that was in a sense real? It couldn't be all evil and dark, could it? I stayed in that tub inhaling the floral scent until I was too tired to think anymore. I pulled myself out of the tub and dressed in one of the nightgowns from my apartment. I checked my phone again and still nothing. I climbed into the soft bed, happy with my choice and drifted into another fitful sleep.

Chapter 4

TRANSPARENT

"Transparency exists, within the sky, high above your dreams to fly, clarity, peace, below the waves of crystal blue waters, wonders unexplored, we seek clarity, but can we handle true transparency?"

"*There I could feel the plane drop much too fast. Oxygen masks fell from the compartments above. Screams of so many people. Ears popping, and then the impact. So cold, everything was so cold. I just wanted warmth. Dead everyone was dead... I'm so cold. My head is in agony, the air is too harsh in my lungs..I held the dream longer. Arms wrapped around me. My legs are broken it's impossible to move. His arms are so strong so comforting. He's telling me he's gonna save us, he pulls us out of the wreckage, but I know I will die. The voice sounds achingly familiar. I long to see his face. I long for warmth.*

Then I am in a car, Soft tunes, then the sudden whip of the vehicle, crunching metal, shattering windows, so loud in my ears, Blood , metallic and bitter it's all I can taste in my mouth my body crushed..I can't move, my face doesn't feel right, oh God help me. Please help me. I held longer to the dream. I hear his voice pleading begging for me to be alive, but I cannot move my mouth to reply. I want to stroke his hair, I want to tell him I'm here but I can't move. His voice too is familiar, safe. I wanted to see his face, I wanted to speak.. what about the baby?...What will happen to our baby?..

I awoke drenched in sweat and panting. The same dream, but I was able to gather more information this time. Something about this place, sleeping here this dream seemed to reoccur. I wondered if it still would tonight and every following night. If I could somehow unravel the mystery of it. It felt so raw and real.

I rubbed the sleep from my eyes and stretched my arms. The sunlight was poking through my curtains and I drew them back happy to see another sunny day.

"I wonder if it's just always warm and sunny here, guess I will see when I leave later." I said out loud to myself.

I went to the washroom, bathed quickly and dressed in a red dress today brushed my unruly hair and painted my eyes. I stopped to grab my bag, keys and cell. I figured no point in not going back to the cafe for breakfast. With how cheap everything was. I turned to lock the door to my suite, Damon and Darren were just heading out as well. Damon was wearing a black dress shirt and dark blue slacks Darren was wearing a light blue dress shirt and black slacks. Both looked gorgeous as per usual. I sighed slightly. Everyone dressed so nice here. Damon smiled when he saw me and Darren gave me a nod in hello. Darren had a black leather jacket draped over his arm and Damon has a brown leather jacket draped over his. I smiled.

"Good morning."

"Agreed." Damon said eyeing me shamelessly.

I felt heat rise to my cheeks.

"I was just going to grab breakfast downstairs. Would you guys care to join me?" Darren's face held a subtle surprise and Damon outright smiled.

"You sure you want to after everything?" Damon asked

"Very sure. You guys still owe me some answers." I looked away from them and walked to the elevator.

"That's fair." I heard Damon say behind me.

"Look we have a lot of ground to cover today, after last night maybe we should just leave her alone." Darren was speaking in a hushed voice probably only meant for Damon to hear.

I debated acknowledging out loud that I had heard him and decided not too. I pushed the call button for the elevator.

"Yeah I get it but she may still be a part of this." Damon replied.

Now I really wanted to interject. I still didn't.

The boy that usually ran the elevator was not there it was a young girl this time.

"Going down miss?"

"Yes, all of us are I motioned to the guys." Her eyes dragged over them lustfully.

"Of course" She replied and waved us all in.

I felt a strange protection over the guys, as I watched her eyes never leave them. I shook it off. They were gorgeous who could blame her?

Gorgeous and possibly psychotic. I silently reminded myself.

We entered the lobby. The Lady that usually greeted me at the front desk piped up.

"Good day to you miss! And gentleman." She added afterwards with a huge smile on her face. Damon and Darren both said hello and I smiled.

We entered the cafe. It was strange because no more then 12 hours ago I was afraid these guys were going to kill me, and here I was this morning getting breakfast with them. Maybe I was the insane one, I felt a certain level of safety with them for some reason too.

We settled into a booth. They sat together and I sat opposite.

"So Serena, what do you want to know?" Damon started.

The waitress came before I could reply and the girl at the till I tipped yesterday waved excitedly at me. I smiled back and gave her a small wave. The waitress was a slender blonde with sultry eyes.

"What can I get you all?"

"I'll have the special and a coffee please." The waitress nodded.

"Same here actually." Darren piped up.

"Same, thanks." Damon replied, handing her our menus.

"You got it." She smiled at us and walked away. Returning shortly with 3 cups of steaming coffee.

I took a sip before speaking.

"I want to help."

Darren almost spat his coffee in shock.

"You can't." He wiped his mouth with a napkin and the bit of coffee that spilled. He pulled a flask from his jacket pocket and added some to his coffee.

"What do you want to help with exactly?" Damon asked.

"Damon she can't help us."

"Darren maybe I can help. The book was drawn to me and I-"

Darren cut me off.

"No. Absolutely not."

Darren was shaking his head and downed his coffee.

"Darren hold on. She might have a point."

"We aren't here to babysit. The world is ending. We don't have time to entertain you." Darren said giving me a sharp look.

His words bit into me a bit.

"I am not a child as to quote you last night. I'm not trying to burden you, I think I could be useful." I pressed.

Darren scoffed. "You think you could, being the main point."

The man had a sharp tongue, every word cut deep.

"Why do you even want to be involved?" Damon asked kindly.

"You can't seriously be considering this Damon can you?"

Damon ignored his brother and kept his eyes on me. I took a breath.

"Look, I don't know anything about spells, or demons or apocalypses I admit. On the other hand though I am good at finding things. You guys said you had a list of items you needed. Maybe I can help."

Darren put his cup down roughly, the sound made the waitress look over.

"Can you fight? Do you know anything about what we are up against, what sacrifices this will entail, the danger?" He challenged.

"No." I paused considering how open to be. Darren shook his head in irritation and looked away from me.

"I clearly have strength, hidden somewhere within me. The book you said was impossible for it to come to me, but it did. What about what you said last night about needing magic to enter this hotel. I think I am already involved whether I want to be or not. I'm obviously not normal. But if I'm not normal then I don't know what I am. Maybe you can figure it out."

I stared at Darren for a couple minutes then glanced to Damon whom was looking at me with creased brows.

"I need your help too. Is what I'm trying to say. I for some reason believe you both can help me." I looked down into my cup. Feeling odd being so open.

"No, it's not happening." Darren stood up roughly from the table and told the waitress he would take his food upstairs. He exited without another word. I looked to Damon.

"Pay no mind to Darren. He has the temper of a toddler."

His confession did little to comfort me. I just looked down again feeling guilty for aggravating Darren so much.

"Look, I hear you Serena. But have you taken into consideration what you would be giving up?" Damon said.

I focused on his eyes again, blueish green, so strangely inviting. I found my voice.

"Giving up?" I paused to laugh humorlessly.

"I have no home to go back too. My boyfriend is dead. My mother is ill and I have not spoken to her in several years. I already lost my dad and I have no siblings. I just have Rayne." I broke eye contact again.

"I'm sorry about Darren and I'm sorry your life has derailed, you do understand, we don't owe you anything. But you are right. I think you are already involved. If you are the best place is with us. You also have to understand, if you are involved it's safest for your friend if you are not around her much."

He ran his hand gently over his jaw.

"Take today to consider if you are really interested in this. If you are, we will give you a run down tonight of everything, if not. I understand."

The waitress dropped our food off and had someone run Darren's up to him.

"What about Darren?-"

"Darren may seem cold, cruel. Really he's just very protective, and damaged. You have to get to know him to see the better side of him. I will talk to him."

"Alright, I will take the day then. I will see you guys later?"

Damon smiled. "You can bet on it." He threw a couple bills down.

"That should cover everything, yours too." I opened my mouth to protest.

"After last night it's the least I can do." He spoke before I could.

I nodded.

"Thank you so much."

He smiled and left.

I stayed a couple minutes sipping my coffee. Darren seemed dead set against anything to do with me, I mean I did beat him up, but even before that. Damon was opposite. I really do want to help them, I mean I don't want the world to end. I wondered if I should check out the rest of the hotel. Looking outside I would guess it was around 9am Rayne would be up. I can look around later. I should meet her see if she can get in here maybe. It would be so much less overwhelming to share all these things with her.

I waved to the waitress and smiled she did the same and I left the front of the hotel. Sure enough when I looked back again it was back to its condemned shambles. It also wasn't sunny like it looked out of the window. It was cloudy and smelled of rain. I approached my car and stopped briefly when I saw the black SUV back sitting in the parking lot this time.

"They must live nearby or something." I said out loud to myself.

I checked my phone and I had no missed messages. I dialed Rayne she picked up on the first ring.

"Hey Serena! How was your night?"

"Hey, it was pretty good." The lie sounded smoother then I felt.

"Great!"

"How was your night, did you have a nice romantic evening with Matt?"

She laughed. "It was amazing as always. But I got up early this morning, I didn't want to wake you but I found some really nice apartments! I thought I would save you the trouble."

"Oh, Rayne thank you."

"Want me to meet you at the hotel?"

"Sure!"

"I will see you in 20 minutes"

"Sounds good!" I hung up.

I leaned against my car. Out of the rent by the hour motel stumbled a girl.

She was a gorgeous red head. She didn't have much on it was pretty clear she was a dancer. She seemed drunk or high perhaps both. She had a big burly man on her arm. He was overdressed for the weather with a black trench coat. I watched them for a second. The man looked to me and I recognized his pale eyes from last night. They stumbled to the SUV. Ah okay just a creep on the prowl` for a cheap thrill. I looked away. Something about the guy made me feel uneasy. Rayne pulled in then, she jumped out and hugged me tightly. How had 20 minutes passed so quickly? I thought to myself.

"Ready to find a new home?" She put her arm around me and I laughed.

"God, you make me sound like a stray puppy!" She paused considering a reply.

"I mean you kinda are! How was your night at the inn? You a hooker yet?" she teased.

"Never in a million years." I laughed. She started to half drag me to her car.

"We will see about that. Any attractive guys there?"

My breath caught thinking back to Damon and Darren. She studied my face. Crap I always had a bad poker face.

"Oh my god no way!!! Tell me!" She practically squealed.

I grasped quickly for an answer.

"Of course there are! But any guy hanging out in a dive like that probably isn't looking to play house. Or they are already playing house and they wanna escape their reality."

"Oh please, I'm not saying to marry a guy. Just you know feel around a bit. You never got too you were with Henry so long."

His name cut a bit.

"Oops sorry. Maybe we should just call him Voldemort." I laughed at that.

"Yes, from now on he who shall not be named."

"Deal" Rayne laughed.

"Rayne you also haven't been with very many people!"

"Yeah but Matt is perfect. I don't want anyone else."

I smiled to her. "I know."

"I just want you to find Mr. Right after all those years shackled to that douche is all."

I nodded. "Anyway, so you found some apartments hey?"

"Yes! Let's go!" Rayne said excitedly.

I glanced to the hotel.

"Rayne wait, I want to show you something." She paused at her door.

"Sure, what?"

"Just trust me for a second."

"I always have Serena. What is it?"

"Just follow me for a minute please."

She obliged and I walked her up to the gate of the hotel. She looked at the gate glancing over the "condemned" "No trespassing" and "Danger" Signs. She gave me a strange look.

"Yeah the condemned hotel, burnt down in early 1900's they just left this here. What about it?"

"Come on, let's go in for a second." I asked motioning her to follow me.

She hesitated.

"You gotta be joking! Why do you want to go in there? Don't you see all the signs? Ugh we are going to get some sort of disease just from touching this gate."

She looked at me again disgust in her expression.

"It's still operating." I said, realizing how insane that sounded.

"Serena no! It's not. There was an explosion here it killed everyone inside, hundreds of people died in there."

She motioned to the building

"It's in shambles. Are you feeling okay? Look do you need to just rest today?"

"I know what it looks like Rayne and I know you think I'm being crazy, but this is where I've been staying the last two nights."

She looked at me in horrified disbelief.

"Serena tell me you are not *squatting* in an abandoned condemned building? Also it's probably haunted! Do you not know your history? Never mind strewn with a hundred years of built up filth. Rats even probably. Maybe some crackheads?"

"I didn't know about the history. But I know- Rayne, just come in the gate it'll make more sense."

"Fine. Let's walk into this nightmare. Only to prove you need some therapy."

I nodded, feeling guilty about making her worry. I opened the gate and walked through, she followed me. The hotel was how it always was every night I'd been here. A crash of relief flooded me. If she can get in here too then that meant I could include her in everything. I turned to her beaming, But she crossed her arms.

"So where's the "Operating" part of the hotel?"

She looked more concerned then angry.

The relief turned to total dread in my stomach.

"It's just a shell of what it used to be. Are you sure you are feeling alright? Look you didn't really stay here did you? Cause if you did, we should make a stop to the medi clinic and get you a tetanus shot.

It's clear you can't be by yourself right now and I will make you stay with Matt and I. I will set you up in the guest room."

It was obvious she didn't see what I was seeing. I scrambled pathetically for a reply.

"April fools!" I tried to force a laugh. Rayne's eyes widened and she looked quickly at her phone. Apparently it was working. I checked my own but it wasn't working.

"Oh my god Serena what the hell!! It is April 1st." She started to laugh.

"Fine! You got me but can we get going? I got a great day lined up for you."

"No more stupid pranks okay? I fell dirty just having stepped in that gate." She looked to me. I didn't reply.

I looked back to the hotel. It looked totally normal and fine. Maybe the guys were right. Which means there was something unnatural about me. Oh God okay, I gotta think. Rayne was on her phone and mine still wasn't working we started to walk back to the car. The moment I stepped through the gate my phone picked up a signal and started working again.

"What-?" I said under my breath but Rayne picked it up.

"I know, ew, who just hooks up with someone in their car like that, in broad daylight too?"

I looked to where she pointed. The knot in my stomach only grew tighter. She was talking about the black SUV that girl and that guy got into. There was fog on the windows and the car was shaking.

"Uh, yeah wow. That's really obvious hey?" But something felt off too me. I clicked "lock" on my key fob.

"Too obvious" She agreed.

We walked past the vehicle and got into her jag. A piercing scream followed by a softer scream came from the SUV. I felt panicked all of a sudden.

"Oh wow and she's a screamer. Sheesh they need to get room. The motel is literally right there." Rayne teased.

"Yeah- well let's go. I can't wait to see what you found." I felt a need to run.

"I can't wait to show you! Also no pranks on my end. I'm too old for that stuff."

I looked at her.

"I'm older then you!"

"Well maybe you need to grow up a bit."

She nudged me playfully and laughed.

I would normally joke back but I felt really strange. I tried to shake it off.

She started the car and drove to the first of 3 apartments she picked out for me.

We pulled up to 97th street. It was close to downtown, so I wasn't too keen on it already.

"I know what you are thinking but this apartment is gorgeous." Rayne said reassuringly.

"I believe you."

We pulled up to a nice gated area.

"I didn't know they had gated communities this close to city centre."

"I know right? It's new but I guess it's too keep all the crack heads and homeless out. For people who want the convenience of downtown without all the negatives. Only locals and visitors are aloud in. Visitors are only permitted until 9pm to avoid issues. Anyone staying longer then that needs written permission to show the gatekeeper. It's safe."

She put the jag in park. The apartment building was really nice with a really well kept front area.

"How much was this monthly Rayne?"

"Don't worry it's in your range. Trust me I did my research on these places."

"Oh I know you are amazing at planning and research. Thank you. I'm excited to see inside."

It was true, I was mostly excited.

We entered the building. It reminded me of an office building everything was very pristine done in grey/white colours.

"It's on the second floor, There's 7 but I know you prefer to be lower down. There's some available on the higher floors if you do change your mind though!"

"Stairs or elevator?" Rayne asked

"Stairs."

"I figured especially after yesterday. I also know you hate elevators."

That's funny, she was right I did hate elevators. However, that fear never even crossed my mind when we at the hotel. I must have looked confused because she followed with:

"Remember when we were at your old apartment with those ancient officers and we damn near fell down the shaft?"

My mind flicked to yesterday. I couldn't believe it was only yesterday. So much had happened since then it felt like.

"Right, yeah that's why" I gave a small laugh and we started up the stairs.

They were well lit with windows not dark like most apartment stairs. We approached the door to the said apartment 123. A real estate agent met us and punched the code into the door. She was medium build and had her dark hair in a high ponytail and had a very high pitched voice. She was dressed in a pink blazer and black dress pants.

"Hey ladies! Welcome!" She waved us in.

"Hello!" Rayne said. I smiled.

We stepped in, it was very nice, the side facing outward was a wall of bay windows. The kitchen was to the left. It was open concept. There was a small electric fireplace in the area meant to be the living room.

We turned right to the bedroom, it had a spacious walk through closet. The bathroom was on the other end of the closet. This apartment felt cold and unwelcoming. It reminded me too much of a hospital.

"So one bedroom" The real estate agent said.

I waited expecting to see more but after walking through the bathroom we were back at the front door.

"So what do you think?" Rayne asked.

"It's nice-I started. How much monthly?"

The real estate agent answered.

"It's $1900 monthly. A steal really with those windows and brand new stainless steel appliances."

Rayne was right I could afford it. All I kept thinking was how cheap that hotel was. The apartment however, it was smaller and pricier then the apartment I had previously.

"Thank so much, I will have to think on it, we have more showings today." I started.

"Totally understandable, let me know!" The real estate agent replied while waving to us as we left.

"You didn't like it?" Rayne said when we started back down the stairs.

"It's not that, I guess I want to kinda stay within or under the price my old one was." I gave her a small smile.

"Makes sense! This was the most expensive and the one I figured you would like the least. Just wait until you see the others!"

I gave her an encouraging smile. "I trust they will be lovely!"

"Oh they will. We can grab lunch after we view these."

"Sounds great."

"The next one isn't super far." We climbed into her jag.

She was humming to some pop song on the radio and I was lost in thought. Apocalypses, demons, fantasy land stuff right under our noses all this time. How blissfully ignorant all us humans seemed to be. I wondered if other people other then the guys knew about this battle or not. It seemed like an awfully large burden to bare. I didn't like to use the word impossible but improbable that two guys could save the world on their own. But what did I know anyways? We pulled up to an older looking apartment building 120th street

I liked that this one had some distance from downtown. I was opposite of Rayne in the sense that I preferred to be further from the hustle and bustle. Her and Matt's place was in the richest neighbourhood closest to downtown. Also gated but all the houses were minimum 1 million. I couldn't justify spending that much on a place ever, but maybe if I could afford it, I would think differently.

"Don't let the outside fool you" She said as we got out of her car.

I glanced around the area was not well kept and the building was an ugly brown. It looked almost like a prison. It only had 3 floors. The same agent met us outside this time.

"I won't." I replied.

"Hi girls! Welcome!"

"Hi, how are you?" I started

"Great and come on in!" She punched the code and the door buzzed open. This apartment building felt cozier. It was done in warmer colours.

She took us to the 3rd floor.

"Room 321" I thought back to the first apartment. "123" Weird coincidence.

We took the elevator this time.

"If you ever decide to walk up the stairs, for whatever reason they are well lit by windows. It's a standard now!"

The real estate agent piped up as the elevator dinged.

We approached the door and she lead me in. This one also had bay windows. The kitchen was done in granite and marble. There were two bedrooms in this one. It was bigger then the first by a landslide but still smaller then my old apartment.

I liked it better. It didn't remind me of a hospital like the other one. It was nicer then the outside showed as well, which would detour break in's.

"So?" Ranye was smiling.

"I like this one a lot better then the first one. How much?"

"It's $1400! Including utilities and such." I nodded. Not a bad price.

"Take me to the last one before I decide please"

"You got it!" Rayne let the agent know we would consider. We went back downstairs. This apartment felt cozy but stuffy to me.

When we were in the parking lot Rayne spoke.

"Okay so this last one, I think will be your favourite. It's almost out of town though not overly far from the motel you are staying at."

"Okay beautiful, lets go."

We drove for a while. We passed the motel. I looked for the guys volvo but it wasn't in the parking lot anymore. The SUV however still was. I looked out the front instead. About 15 minutes later, we pulled into a line of what looked like cottages. My heart soar a bit. There were huge oak trees lining the street.

"Rayne these are houses?" I started.

"Oh I know!" She was fighting a happy squeal.

I loved the area. It looked very Victorian.

We pulled up to a cottage number 6. The yard was a bit overgrown. There was a huge garden, that just needed some TLC. We pulled into the drive. I couldn't hide my excitement. The real estate agent was leaning against her car. She smiled when we pulled in and gave a small wave.

"Oh my God Rayne! Are you telling me you found a house I can afford?"

"Yes!" She practically screamed in delight.

"It is old and needs a lot of work but I thought you might like it. You are very into DIY so it's also a project for you essentially! It's just a bit far from the city."

"Rayne the outside even I can picture making this so beautiful."

There was ivy crawling up the house. Like something out of a fairytale.

"I know this isn't what you like Rayne." I laughed.

"Oh I wouldn't ever, but we like different things and that's okay." She smiled and half hugged me.

We walked up the cement steps and the agent opened the door. Inside, I felt a rush of happiness and I felt very warm and welcome.

The entryway was small and lit by a chandelier. The stairs were straight ahead. The doorways were all arched. The paint on the walls was yellow and peeling. To the right was a kitchen, with ample cupboards and a small dining area lit by a big window. To the right was the livingroom it had a fireplace. A real one, there was a cove attached that was small but would be so nice to curl up with a book.

We went upstairs to three bedrooms two of the three were loft bedrooms. The master had a bathroom attached and a spacious closet. The other bathroom was right by the front entrance with a pocket door. All the rooms had big windows.

"Is there a basement? I asked.

"Yep." The Realtor took us toward the back door under the front staircase there was one descending.

We went down it was a small open room. Furnace was separate and there was a new washer and dryer against the left wall. We walked back upstairs to the back door. The back yard had another overgrown garden and an old hand dug pond and many mature trees. It was bigger then an average backyard. There was an old shed too.

I grabbed Rayne's arm excitedly. "How much?"

"With how old it is, they are only asking 170 thousand. We got an inspection done as well there's nothing overly concerning. It just needs some TLC.

"You would need 10k down." The Realtor added. My face must have fell because Rayne spoke.

"Matt and I will cosign the agreement. We know you need to re-buy furniture and everything. We don't want you to drain all your savings."

"Rayne you don't have to do that!" She immediately dialed and face timed Matt. She turned the phone to me.

"Guys, no."

"Serena, do you love this place?" Matt said over the phone.

"Yes, but I don't-"

He held the paperwork up against the screen.

"Rayne figured this place would win your heart everything's set up if you decide you want it!"

Rayne smiled satisfied with everything. I knew they had me beat on this.

"You know me too well Rayne, you knew I wouldn't let you so you did it anyways. Thank you. Sincerely. Thank you both. I need some time to think it through."

Matt nodded and Rayne and him said goodbye and that they loved each other.

"Rayne this is amazing, are you sure?"

"Of course! If roles were switched you would do the same for me you know you would." She smiled.

I hugged her tightly.

"I would. For sure. Well lets get some lunch? I'll consider it overnight and let you guys know tomorrow."

"Sounds perfect to me!" she chirped and said goodbye to the Realtor.

"Thank you very much. We will be in touch." I said to the Realtor and shook her hand.

"Great. Thanks ladies." she replied as Rayne and I started back to her car.

"There's a local dining area not far from here, want to check it out? We can scope the area of your new home!"

"Sounds like an excellent plan, thank you!"

We drove around the block. There was a sign for a lake.

"There's a lake nearby?"

"Yes! I totally forgot, I know you always wanted to live close to a lake."

"Ah Rayne I'm so excited. Thank you!"

"Does that mean you are going to let us cosign for you?" She glanced to me.

I thought to Darren and Damon. Remembering the more pressing issue.

"I just, I guess I need a bit of time to think it through."

I wanted to tell her about Damon and Darren. Also I mean, a selfish part of me wanted to continue to live in ignorance. I suppose that opportunity flew out the window already. I couldn't possibly ignore the end of the world now that I knew about it. I just couldn't. I wondered if I could have both. Live in my dream home and ward off the apocalypse.

"Suite yourself. Here we are."

It was a cute diner. Retro looking, lots of rock music memoir. My stomach grumbled and I checked the time. It was already after 3. No wonder I was so hungry.

"I bet they have amazing cheese burgers." I said excitedly to Rayne.

We walked in and Rayne looked at the music memoirs with distaste. I couldn't help laughing.

"What are you a music critic?"

"No, I mean well who likes rock?"

"I do!"

She rolled her eyes.

"Oh I know, but you like all kinds of music Serena"

I shook my head. "Not all. I'm not a huge fan of screamo or rap"

"Rap is the best." she argued

"I think all music has it's own charm I suppose, I just prefer some genres over others. I like music that tells a story" I looked to her.

"Songs that are just about partying, money, drugs and sex aren't as appealing to me I guess." I shrugged.

She shook her head at me.

"Ugh, you always with the moral high ground. So kind and loving to everyone and everything around you."

"Is that such a bad thing?"

"No, it just makes the rest of us look bad." she laughed.

"It might screw you over too. It has before." She looked at me with a semi serious face.

"I do have a back bone in my defence."

She put her hands up in mock surrender. "I'm just saying"

The host greeted us. He looked like he was a hardcore metal head himself. Most of the staff did. I loved it.

"For 2?"

I smiled. "Yes"

"Follow me"

We settled into a table in the back.

"Worlds best cheeseburger" I read out loud. "Well, I guess I know what I'm having!"

Rayne rolled her eyes. "Gross"

I just chuckled. "To you, to me I love all food."

"Yeah well SOME of us don't have an amazing metabolism like you." Rayne countered.

I just rolled my eyes. "You have no reason to be insecure Rayne."

She really didn't she was beautiful and she was slightly muscular. Whereas I was more average looking.

"Yeah I know! But I have to watch what I eat and I work out a lot."

"I would rather not have to work so hard for it, you know?" She explained.

"I get it." I gave her a sympathetic smile.

The server came by his face was loaded with piercings, he was wearing a band tee, all the staff seemed to be doing the same.

"What can I get you fine ladies tonight?"

"Water please. I will order the worlds best cheeseburger" I said. He smiled.

"What side?"

"Caesar salad please." He didn't look to Rayne yet and she started ordering.

"Bloody Mary, I will have a tossed salad too please."

She handed him the menus.

"Wait, just a salad?" he confirmed.

"Yes."

"Rock on." He laughed as he left the table. I laughed too.

"This place is awesome." I said excitedly. Rayne raised her eyebrows.

"I know you like high class restaurants and I appreciate you taking me here instead."

"You owe me." She laughed.

"Indeed, for far more then just this Rayne. Thank you I'm blessed to have such an amazing best friend."

"Hey don't sell yourself short, you are too."

"Oh I wasn't." We both laughed the food came quick. I took a bite of my burger. It was juicy and loaded with flavour. Rayne watched me for a second.

"Is it deserving of the name?"

"Beyond." I said after swallowing.

"How's your salad?"

Rayne laughed a bit. "It's good, for a salad."

"You'll live?" I joked.

"Hopefully. If not I'm going to haunt your ass." She shoved a forkful of salad into her mouth.

I smiled and finished eating.

"Let me pay this time Rayne."

"If you insist."

"I do, please you've done way too much for me. I just want to give a little back."

"Fine." She waved the server over, I paid and we headed back to her car it was almost 6 now.

I felt a strong urge to return to the hotel all of a sudden.

"Well, where too now?" Rayne asked unlocking the car.

"Honestly can you please drop me back at the hotel actually?"

My tone came out more serious then I meant it to. Rayne looked suspiciously at me.

"Are you sure you wanna go back to the dingy hotel?"

"Yes, really I am."

She sighed. "Well alright, but get me an answer soon. The sooner we get you outta that dodgy place the better!"

I offered a small smile.

"I will get back to you."

"Are you sure there's no guy?"

"Rayne seriously! No." I laughed. "I would tell you."

"I would hope so."

There was a hollowness in my stomach. I wanted to tell her I just didn't know how. I decided to watch out the window the rest of the ride back as I thought about what to tell the guys.

Chapter 5

LIFELINE

*"Breathe in, breathe out, I am the blood running through
your veins, connecting you to yourself, breathe in, the chaos of
uncertainty, to unearth what lies beneath, breathe out, find your
pulse, such beauty can be found within yourself."*

W̲e pulled up to the parking lot 25 minute later. There were flashing police lights everywhere. Rayne gasped.

"Something happened!"

Panic settled into my core, and I immediately worried about the guys.

"Pull up, Rayne."

She did and put the jag in park. I looked to my car it was untouched, but there was police tape beside my car.

I unbuckled and jumped out.

"Serena, wait! Where are you going?"

She unbuckled and followed me out.

I approached the tape, just in time for them to zip up a black body bag.

"Miss, stay back please."

One of the officers rose their hand and shouted at me as I approached the tape. Rayne was close behind me. The officer he had slicked back black hair dark eyes with a heavier build.

"Holy shit, someone died?" Rayne said loudly.

I ignored her and looked rapidly around for the brothers volvo.

After a couple seconds. I spotted it parked in the usual spot up front they were both leaning against the car talking. Both were dressed as officers and I assumed didn't look like themselves to other people. Relief flooded me.

"Serena! You can't stay here. You have to come with me." Rayne said interrupting my thoughts.

"Rayne, it's okay. I will be safe."

Astonishment graced her features.

"Are you kidding me?! Serena that is a dead body!"

"Yes, I know."

"Why aren't you freaking out!"

Rayne was yelling so loud a couple officers glanced towards us. Truthfully she had a good point. I should be scared. I was worried sure, but I was able to stay calm and I didn't feel afraid.

"A dead body!" She said louder and more flustered, emphasizing the word *dead*.

"Look miss, We are going to have to ask you to calm down. Did you know the deceased?"

"I don't think so! I sure as Hell hope not!" She was still yelling.

"Okay then, I'm going to have to ask you to leave the scene for now."

"But-" She protested.

"You too" He motioned to me.

"My cars right there." I pointed.

"If that's true, we have to search that vehicle it was too close too the scene and we will have to ask you some questions."

Rayne's face held more shock.

"She wasn't even here today, she was with me!" Rayne interjected.

"That's fine miss, your friend isn't in trouble" The same officer said calmly. Rayne's face calmed slightly.

"Rayne it's okay, thank you for today, go rest and get out of here. Drive safe and I will call you later."

"Are you serious?"

"Yes, I promise I will be fine."

"Okay..just make sure you call me!"

"I will."

"You better!"

I watched Rayne head back to her car. I felt guilty for pushing her to leave but she was clearly panicked. It was better and safer for her to be home with Matt. I wanted to talk to Damon and Darren. I started toward them and the officer stopped me.

"Can you answer some questions please?"

I looked toward the guys.

"Yeah, anything you need."

"Miss, when did you leave this morning?" The officer asked me.

"I left around 9am." He was writing on a notepad.

"Okay and did you happen to see a girl with red hair come out of the motel over there?"

My stomach twisted.

"Yes, I saw a girl leave there."

"Did you see where she went?"

"She went into a black SUV with a man, I didn't get a good look at him. Or the vehicle"

The officer was writing everything quickly.

"She's the one we just zipped into the bag."

"Oh God."

"Anything you can remember would be helpful about the guy she was with."

"His eyes were pale, I'm sorry I didn't look long and I left right after for the day."

"I understand. Thank you miss. Call us if you remember anything else. "

"Do you still need to check my car?"

"No, you are free to go."

"Thank you, I hope you find who did it."

"That's our job. Have a good night now."

Damon and Darren were watching me, I started toward them as the cops cleaned up the scene.

Damon gave me a smile Darren kinda just nodded.

"Do you guys know who?-"

"Who did it, no but we have a pretty good idea." Darren spoke matter of factly.

"What did you tell the cops?"

"I just told them I saw a red headed girl come out of the motel earlier this morning with a guy and they got into a black SUV."

"Is that all you-" Damon started.

"All I saw?-" I finished. Damon nodded.

"Well I thought I saw that same SUV yesterday, but I can't be sure. So I didn't mention that"

Darren and Damon exchanged worried looks.

"Anything else?" Darren pressed.

"All I remember is he had eerie pale eyes" I shook my head cringing at the memory. Darren's eyes widened.

"Can you describe them better?" Damon pressed.

"Uh- well they didn't look like any eyes I've ever seen before. Like a pale almost white."

"That sounds like-" Darren started.

"Yeah, we will have to keep our eyes out, it does fit the MO"

"The prey though?" Damon continued

"It's where I would, if I were it." Darren added.

They needed to stop talking like I wasn't here. I waited patiently listening to both of them, instead of making any remark.

"I suppose, most of the girls there would have few family and friends that would look for them." Damon continued.

"It does make sense, but usually they don't hunt like that. They like more of a cat and mouse thing." Darren adjusted his tie as he said this.

"Less they were desperate or had ulterior motive?" Damon answered.

This was getting too strange. I decided to speak up now.

"What do you mean Prey? Are you guys saying this was not some deranged human?"

They looked to me like they forgot I was even here.

"We are talking about a demon." Darren said eyeing me carefully.

"Are you serious? Demons are real? How do you know for sure?"

Darren gave a humourless laugh. It was the first sign of anything less then robotic from him.

"Everything of your nightmares, of your horror movie entertainments, of your books. Everything is real documentation"

I felt the blood drain from my face.

"Yeah don't sugarcoat it for her Darren." He gave Darren a look of irritation. Darren just shrugged.

"Whatever, she's considering joining us in this fight there's no time to ease her into it. You know that Damon."

"You okay?" Damon looked over to me.

Darren scoffed loudly, eyeing me coolly.

"We can't tiptoe with you, so if you decide you want to help us. Which I still don't get why you would, nor do I think you should. You've got a lot to learn, and very little time to adjust. Otherwise you will only slow us down. I'll be in the diner." Darren stalked off behind the gate.

Damon exhaled loudly.

"Look I'm sorry for Darren. I guess now would be an appropriate time to check if you had come to a decision? Do you really want in on all this?"

I took a second to calm my racing thoughts. How could I say no? There's no way I could go about my life knowing it was all going to end sooner rather then later, and that I could maybe help stop it. There was no way I could pretend I was just a regular person after what happened the night before. I stared into Damon's eyes. They were so sincere and warm to me. My last thought was the house Rayne found today, but that seemed selfish to want now. I took a deep breath.

"Yes, I want in. For more reasons then one." I smiled lightly and Damon returned my smile.

"Okay then. Let's go inside and we will tell you what you need to know." He offered his arm for me to grab.

"Shall we, Serena?"

"Okay, I'm as ready as I will ever be."

I wanted to grab his arm, but I refrained. He didn't seem bothered by it.

"Wait-Damon." He stopped walking.

"What's wrong?"

"Nothing, just does this building look like a broken down building to you, with "condemned" and "Caution" and "No trespassing" signs?"

Damon looked at it.

"You are seeing it's reality yes. Outside the veil."

"What does that mean?"

"Well traditionally these types of thresholds can only be crossed by someone who isn't full mortal. That's why we seemed confused to see you outside of the hotel."

"Wait- so are you telling me I'm not a human?"

"No- I'm not saying you aren't but that is something we will have to look into. You are seeing it how humans do but you can cross through without anything. Mortals can enter if they know the ancient magics which is what Darren and I thought originally. Clearly you do not use magic to get through though."

He motioned to the gate we walked through.

"So what does this place look like to you?" I asked. "Do you see it's reality?"

"It looks like the hotel 100 percent of the time. There is a lot of warding on this building so it's protected from most things."

I nodded taking that in as we entered the door. I guess most things was referring to all the nightmares Darren mentioned were real.

"So when I tried to bring Rayne here and it was just a condemned place inside and out to her?"

"Well that means your friend is full mortal."

"But I'm not? And that would mean you and Darren aren't either? Or do you know the magics to get in?"

"Let me explain with Darren okay?"

"Okay, no worries."

Damon looked and smiled at me.

"I know you will have a lot of questions and it will be overwhelming to learn everything we need to teach you. But I do believe you'll do well with it. We will answer all your questions."

I returned his smile.

"Darren doesn't think I will though, right?"

Damon paused for a second.

"No, he doesn't but Darren is difficult. He takes warming up to, and doesn't trust easily. Try not to take it too personal. I know I told you that already, but really. He's cold with me too and I'm his brother."

"Why though?"

Damon laughed a bit. "Well that you would have to ask him yourself, and when you find out, let me know too, would you?" He paused to chuckle.

"Look we will go through what we can, if you decide you don't want in after all I would understand."

Darren caught the last thing Damon said as we entered the diner and walked up to the table.

"I agree with Damon, for all of our sake, I hope you don't want in." Darren downed a beer and motioned for another one. The waitress nodded. She was the same as last night.

"So everyone in here, the workers, customers, other people staying at the hotel none of them are full mortals?"

Darren fixed Damon with a look of annoyance.

"She should know about this place." Damon answered.

"The workers here are the workers that died on the day of the fire many years ago that actually took this hotel with it." Damon stated.

"Is that why everything so cheap?"

Damon laughed. "It's basically stuck operating in the year it was destroyed."

"Wait-so you are telling me all these people are dead?"

"Dead and unaware they are dead, endlessly looping in what their day to day life looked like the year this hotel got blown up." Darren answered.

"The guests too?"

Darren shook his head. "Many guests here are ones that died, but all the guests back then only the richest of the rich would stay here so everyone was once of great import, that's why the staff treat us that way."

"Well are there other non-mortals here though? Like us?"

"Places like this are warded against the things we kill, so essentially yes. It's a safe haven for those who can access it." Damon answered this time.

Darren looked to Damon.

"You told her she isn't mortal?" Darren's tone was ice.

"No, I said she may not be full mortal, she sees the shambles of the hotel like the mortals do but when she enters it is like this." He motioned his hands.

"She didn't use magic to get in, I walked in with her. She can just walk in."

Darren looked to me and narrowed his eyes slightly.

"You thought you were mortal?"

I shifted uncomfortably under his glare.

"I guess I thought I was possibly crazy or dreaming. I tried to rationalize, but today when Rayne couldn't enter the hotel and everything with you guys- I mean I grew up with my parents, in the city. I went to school, I work and am looking for a new place to live. It all seems pretty normal to me, until the other night with you guys, that's when I started to question everything. I want to know what I am probably just as much, if not more then you do. I simply can't sit idly by when I know there's a fight to keep the world from ending, it's just not in my nature to do so. So please guys let me know what's happening and how I can help."

Darren looked down and Damon nodded. I started to speak again, feeling like I half won Darren over with my confirmation of helping.

"Okay...now that it's settled. Are you guys not human?"

"We are human." Darren answered.

"We think we are, we just happen to know a lot about this stuff. Our parents were killed when we were young."

Pain flashed in both their eyes as Damon said this. Darren chugged his drink and motioned for another.

"She doesn't need the family history Damon. It's not vital right now."

"You're right." He replied.

I really wanted to know more about their past, but I was being my overly trusting self.

"So Darren you said everything of my worst nightmares was real?"

Darren nodded and Damon scoffed slightly.

"Not all, surely" Damon rebuffed.

"Enough though." Darren countered.

I thought back to horror movies.

"Okay, I'm going to run through a list in my head then."

Damon nodded encouraging me. Darren took a long swing of his drink.

"Possessions?"

"Very." Darren answered

"Are they similar to movies?"

"Not the vomiting sick, climbing walls stuff. But they lie, they hide, and they usually murder the host. Speaking in tongues that kind of thing. They know how to blend into regular day to day life." Darren met my eyes.

"So scarier for sure." I said.

"Werewolf's? Dracula?" Damon laughed a bit

"Yeah not like twilight. But werewolf's and Vampires are very real" Darren answered cooly.

"I was thinking more "Underworld" or "Queen of the Damned" for those actually."

The corner of Darren's mouth threatened a smile, but he didn't follow through.

"That's more accurate. However, in reality they are pure malicious." Darren said.

"Ghosts are real then?" I gestured to the staff. "Are they dangerous?"

"They can be. Poltergeist's, people that died violently or a death where they felt they weren't ready to go." Darren continued.

"Is anybody really ready to go though?"

Darren's eyes looked distant for minute.

Damon spoke up after glancing to Darren.

"Ghosts can be complex. Some are harmful, some are playful, some are helpful. Pretty much anything you can ask about exists. In some form or another."

"Wow, so we really do have a reason to fear the dark. But are there not some beautiful things? Like mythological?"

"What you hoping for unicorns or something? Leprechauns that shit rainbows? The tooth fairy? Santa Claus?" Darren said sarcastically.

I was taken off guard.

"No-I meant like dragons, sirens, Cerberus kind of thing."

"Not everything exists on this plane of existence. Some things cross that should not as well. Most things are evil in one sense or another." Damon answered instead.

"Okay, well let's circle back to this. What's our main threat right now? Outside of the apocalypse of course."

"Demons." Darren answered plainly. "Friggin Demons are everywhere. Part of the apocalypse."

"So how can you tell if someone is a demon?"

"Usually by their eyes, but they are intelligent enough to put contacts onto their hosts eyes."

A chill ran through me.

"So you said the man that killed that girl, that was a demon?"

Damon pulled out a notebook type thing, it looked like something a hot topic would carry. Witch wannabee and bound in leather.

"We have been tracking them. There are several types of demons from each circle of Hell. Right now we have mostly run into black eyed. They hold power over the void and are excellent at possessing people, but they are the lowest ring of demons. They possess for fun and for murder. They are careless but not stupid. Until tonight when you said you said pale eyes. We haven't run into a pale eyed demon yet." Damon continued.

Darren looked hesitant to say much.

"If that demon is more powerful and more intelligent, why would it show it's eyes?"

Darren raised his eyebrows, as if he was impressed with my question.

"That's what we have been trying to figure out, we will have to read through some more old books upstairs. It's possible it underestimates us, but that's best case scenario." Damon said.

"How do the demons understand that you are a threat though? If you haven't shown any sort of aggression?"

"That's a good point, but Darren and I are well known in the Demon ring. They know to watch out for us."

"It is possible that this Demon doesn't associate with the lower class Demons." Darren started.

I thought for a minute.

"Or it wants you to know it's here for some reason." I said slowly.

Damon and Darren looked at me like they hadn't considered that as an option.

"She has a good point Damon."

I was shocked to hear Darren agree with me.

Damon rubbed his chin. "Why bait us though?"

"Maybe it doesn't think you guys are a threat."

Darren scoffed and Damon nodded. "You might be right Serena."

"So you guys, what kill these things?"

"I wish, no the best we can do is send them back to Hell." Damon said.

"Like priests do?"

"Yeah but we are no saints." Darren looked back to wave the waitress over again.

She sauntered over.

"Darren" she started. "I'm gunna have to cut you off after this one."

She batted her eyelashes slightly and adjusted her body so her cleavage was more prominent.

Darren seemed completely unfazed by her obvious attempt to be flirtatious.

"No, I'd like to order some food this time."

She seemed slightly hurt by his cold tone and instead pulled her notepad out.

"I'll get a cheeseburger, thanks."

"Sure thing." she said.

She wrote that down and turned her attention to Damon and again resumed her obvious flirtation.

"How bout you handsome?"

Damon gave her a smile and gave a glance at her cleavage that she was trying so hard to show off.

"I will take the rice bowl, unless of course, you have a better suggestion?" He smiled and winked at her, she twirled her hair in her fingers.

"My pleasure."

"It will be." Damon said seductively.

He paused for longer on her chest then necessary, obviously pretending to read her name tag. "Jane"

Why did this bother me slightly? I was annoyed with myself for feeling like that and looked down at the menu.

She let out a giggle, and wrote his order down. She then glanced at me.

"How about you? Aren't you lucky to be dining with Elder Oaks finest."

I laughed it came out smoother and more real then it felt.

"Oh I'm very lucky. I would love a cheeseburger and Caesar salad please."

Darren looked up at me for a second. A strange emotion in his eyes that I couldn't pinpoint. His tone was ever so slightly softer then usual. Damon also looked at me softly.

"Cheeseburger? Thought you would order something like Damon did" Darren said simply.

I laughed for real.

"I love a good burger, you don't know me that well Darren, I might continue to surprise you."

The emotion in his eyes was gone as quickly as it arrived.

"Not much surprises me."

"Maybe because you never look for anything outside of what you know. You seem too assume a lot. It doesn't leave space for anything to surprise you when you are in denial of the possibility of things being different then you think they will be." I said this lightly.

It made Darren look in my eyes again.

"She's kinda right dude." Damon laughed. "I'll also get pie. Of course.. Cherry if you have"

The waitress replied then.

"Great, I will ring that up." She left running her hand over Damon's shoulder as she did.

"You should lighten up Darren" Damon said after giving the waitress another flirty smile.

"Oh shut up Damon, we are literally in the midst of a friggin' apocalypse and your focused on getting laid"

"You need to get laid Darren, it's the end of the world, may as well enjoy what we can."

"Unless we stop it. If your done drooling, how about we finish, what we came here to finish." Darren gestured to me.

Curiosity piqued me. I took that as an invitation to resume my questioning.

"Damon, you said most people here are ghosts, how are you planning to get with Jane?" I asked.

Damon smiled. "Kinda a strange kink there Serena thinking about sleeping with ghosts."

I felt my face redden.

"No- I-"

Damon just smiled and continued.

"Totally valid question, she's not a ghost. She's the daughter of an old buddy we knew. She's in the business."

"You mean, people that are trying to stop the apocalypse?"

"No, other people that kill monsters for lack of a better word. Her old man was great at catching vampires."

"No one else knows about the apocalypse. Just Damon and I and now you are working on it." Darren answered.

"Why would you not want more people on it?"

"Cause Darren is a piece of work." Damon joked rolling his eyes.

Darren glared at him.

"It would be counter productive to alert so many people. It would cause panic and the families that take care of the other monster populations would drop what they are doing for this, sending what's normally pretty under control into utter chaos." Darren explained. There was so much harshness in his voice. I considered what to say for a minute.

"If the world does end, wouldn't that be worse then more creatures prowling about then usual?"

"Exactly my point." Damon interjected and motioned to me.

Darren looked at us both for a second.

"No, cause we are going to stop this, and when we do, it would be better for the creatures to be under control. Then we won't be fighting creatures pointlessly and trying to stop this shit simultaneously. It's a waste of time, energy and resources."

"That's a big if Darren." Damon sounded slightly heated.

"We will stop the apocalypse Damon. I'm your older brother. Trust me on this. We will stop it. We have no other option. We have to, and we will succeed."

Damon nodded. "Yeah, okay man."

I felt it would be pointless to argue. They both made valid points, I wasn't sure which option was better. So I held my tongue and changed the subject.

"Alright, so how do we stop the apocalypse?" I paused briefly.

"That's probably the strangest thing I've ever said out loud you know."

Damon laughed. "I can imagine. Welcome to crazy town. You are adjusting well though, if that helps."

I slowly exhaled. "Thanks."

Darren grabbed the notebook from where Damon had it.

"So to stop the apocalypse, We have to hunt down legendary artifacts essentially."

Damon raised his eyebrows.

"Give that back." He grabbed the notebook from Darren.

"You fight, I research. Therefore I can explain my own notes, thank you."

"No need to have a hissy fit." Darren tossed the pen back at Damon.

"Here's your pen too, you whiny girl"

Damon scoffed. "I'm not whining."

"Sure friggin' sound's like it." Then he said in a mock whining girl voice "My noteboooooook"

It was the first time I ever saw Darren joke around.

I stifled a small laugh.

"What?" Both Damon and Darren said at the same time then they glared at each other.

"It's like dining with an old married couple."

"Well get used to it, Darren is a pain in the ass."

"So legendary artifacts-" Darren started.

Damon held his hand up.

"Knock it off!"

Darren sat back and almost smiled. Then motioned for Damon to continue.

I couldn't help but laugh again.

"As Darren was reading in MY notes."

He fixed Darren with a glare. Darren just shook his head and rolled his eyes.

"We are hunting supposed legendary artifacts. They have been stowed away all over the world since the beginning of time."

"How many artifacts are there?"

Darren answered instead. "666"

"What like the Devil's number?"

Darren nodded.

"Well how many have you guys gathered?"

"We have 600. We have been tracking and trying to pinpoint where each artifact is hidden, so far we have located 56."

Damon slid the notebook over for me to read it.

"So you have no idea what the last 9 are?"

"Not just that," Darren continued. "We aren't even sure what they are."

Damon looked down a little defeated.

"We will though. Especially with your help Serena." Damon smiled.

"I don't know how much help I will be, but I'm willing and able."

Darren gave a small nod. "Hopefully you will be more help then hindrance."

"Darren don't be such an ass." Damon said then looked to me.

"Serena you already have helped. You located item #648. That black magic book."

"I think that was just a fluke." I said sheepishly.

"You better hope it wasn't." Darren said.

"Darren honestly. You know how that book works. It was attracted to Serena. It doesn't just lay around in the open."

"Fine. But we don't know why it was attracted to her."

"Darren, I don't know why the book came to me either. If that makes you feel better. But I hope we can figure it out and I can be of more help to you guys."

"Okay, well. Good." Darren looked at me a second.

The waitress came with the food then.

"This looks incredible Jane. Thanks." Damon smiled to her.

"You able to locate the shapeshifter?" Jane lowered her head closer to Damon.

"Yeah. He's over there in the corner booth. I got it under control though. I'm going to send my dad after it. As for you though-" She paused and leaned toward Damon's mouth. "My "Shift" Ends in 35 minutes."

Darren Scoffed. "Get a room for God's sake"

Damon ignored him.

"Some of us are hungry." Darren said annoyed. Damon continued to ignore him.

"Damon started "Yours or mine?"

"Why not both?" The waitress again stroked Damon's arm as she walked away.

I laughed. "You two hook up before?"

Darren groaned. "Yeah anytime they cross paths. Like friggin' rabbits."

"I think you are just jealous Darren." Damon started and took a spoonful of his veggies.

"Yeah yeah. Shut up and munch your greens. Rabbit." He took a bite of his burger. I smiled a bit and ate mine too.

"How's your burger?" Darren asked.

I thought back to the joint I went with Rayne earlier in the day. Then thought about the house she had found me. I knew I had to stay with the guys. I needed to figure out how to turn Rayne's gracious offer down.

"I've had better. But good. You?"

"This is the best damn burger I've ever had. Where have you had better?' Darren asked.

"Hm a little joint about 20 minutes from here. Rock themed. We will have to check it out sometime. I'm sure their other food is good too Damon, if you don't like cheeseburgers."

"Well that sounds great." Damon replied.

Darren nodded. "Can't turn a good cheeseburger down."

I smiled.

"So what's the first item we need to get?"

"It's suppose to be here in this hotel. With the book. We will start looking tomorrow." Damon answered while eyeing Jane across the diner.

"We will just meet up in the morning then?"

"Well I know what I'm doing." Damon said his eyes not leaving Jane.

Darren rolled his eyes. "I'll be at the bar"

"I think I might look around the hotel a bit then turn in myself. Should I be worried about what Jane said, the what was it? Shapeshifter?

Damon moved his eyes to me.

"No, Jane's family is in charge of shapeshifters. It will be taken care of."

"Got it. What an organized underground community."

"Can't imagine it, if it wasn't." Damon replied.

"We all help each other out too." Darren added.

I nodded. Jane came and cleared the plates. Damon paid the bill, and Jane pulled her apron off and gripped his arm.

"Night guys." He said as he walked out with Jane giggling beside him.

Darren chugged his beer.

We sat in silence for a minute.

"Are shapeshifters dangerous?"

Darren looked a bit confused by my question.

"They can be, but normally won't bother you if you aren't bothering them. You for sure don't want to get on their bad side. They would change into you and they can make you the most wanted person in the country, or they just kill you. Kind of a staple for most monsters."

"I see, so do you kill them if they aren't hurting anyone still?"

"Each family lead group is different in their styles and preferences."

"Oh okay."

"Do you have more questions?"

I thought for a moment. I had a great deal of questions still. But it was getting late and I figured Darren wouldn't like to be kept. I took a second to admire his blue eyes. Him and Damon had such gorgeous eyes.

"Yeah, but nothing pressing."

"Alright, well if you excuse me, I am going to head to the bar."

I couldn't help but feel slightly disappointed. Damon was very open, Darren was so closed off. It gave me a strong desire to unearth his personality. He's got to have a heart under all that ice. He was funny, maybe I just needed more time around him. I pulled from my thoughts, embarrassed when I realized Darren was waiting for a reply.

"Oh- yes of course. I'm sorry for keeping you. Are there stores and such in this hotel? I haven't really explored yet."

"Yeah there are quite a few, in it's time this hotel was immaculate. Nothing compared to it. I'm sure you can find something you enjoy."

"Okay, Thank you. You are just going to grab more drinks?"

Darren ran his hand through his hair.

"Well my rooms occupied so."

"Ah yes. Of course. How could I forget. Well do you want to stay with me for a bit?"

He looked into my eyes. Considering. I continued.

"I was just going to look at some shops, so if that sounds boring to you, I understand."

"I'm going that way anyhow. I will walk with you."

There was still no warmth in his voice. It sounded more of a command then an offer. Maybe that's just how Darren talked.

"Sure, I'd like that. Thank you."

Darren nodded and stood up, offering his arm to me. How gentleman-like. Guys were just not like this. Damon had offered the same earlier and I had declined. Perhaps that was rude of me? Part of me wanted to say yes to Darren though.

"May I?"

I didn't hesitate long.

"You may." I laughed. "What are you something out of a romance novel?"

His face twisted in disgust.

"No, it's just polite. Romance novel? Hardly. Are you one of those dewy eyed fans of romance?" He scoffed, and went to take his arm away.

"Wait-" I grabbed his arm gently.

"I didn't say no. I was only teasing. And no actually. I read psychological thrillers."

He looked at me for a second and shook his head slightly.

"Okay Silence of the Lambs. This way." He led us out of the diner.

I knew he was making a joke but his face displayed no hint of a smile. His tone was slightly lighter then usual though. I wondered if I could crack him.

"Darren, whats your favourite genre then?"

He glanced slightly to me. I felt his arm tense.

"No, no I'm not doing this small talk Bullshit with you. We have a job to do and you have a lot to learn."

His tone was back to his usual huff. I swallowed and considered what to say. I could have backed down, I realized I struck a nerve. I decided to keep it light instead. I thought to say the total opposite of what I actually thought.

"Oh, then I suppose you leave me no choice but to guess." I made an exaggerated "hmm" sound.

He raised his eyebrows at me.

"It's teen romance isn't it? And you hunt Monsters so definitely: "Buffy the Vampire Slayer", makes sense you based your character off of Angel. Or maybe you are more of a Spike?"

I wasn't sure what Darren would say. I smiled and looked at him expectantly. He took a minute to reply, but I felt his arm relax.

"So let me get this straight. Based on what little you know of my personality you think is either a tortured soul that can't fuck the women he loves because he turns to a monster? Or a whipped broken man on a power trip with stalker tendencies?"

"Well damn, someone sure knows a lot about a show that he claims to not be interested in. Also Spike is just a misunderstood romantic, he loves Buffy, he didn't start off as a villain, and he ends up a hero."

"Anyone ever tell you, you are absolutely terrible at assessing people?"

I made a mock tone:

"Well I never!"

Darren's expression softened. "Sorry for disgracing your fantasy boyfriend." He nudged me playfully. I giggled a bit.

"Well I'll tell you one thing, that is: you are definitely 100 percent wrong." Darren continued.

I smiled slightly.

"So set me straight. What's your favourite genre?"

Darren rolled his eyes.

"I think I will just let you keep guessing." He paused. "Here is the bar. Shops are straight ahead."

I tried to hide my disappointment.

"Ah well thanks for the company.- I will see you tomorrow?"

He let go of my arm.

"We have a ton of ground to cover. Meet us first thing. Take care of yourself."

He walked off without looking at me.

"Bye Spike!" I called after him.

I heard a laugh but I wasn't sure if it was Darren or not. He didn't come back out. I sighed.

It would be nice to get to know the brothers better if we will be working together but I guess that will come in time. It makes sense they were probably stressed out. I couldn't imagine the weight they had on their shoulders. There was so many items to locate. Plus they likely will have to take time to train me in combat as well. I had taken 8 years of martial arts, but I had never handled any weapons. Mind you I seemed to also be a well of untapped strength somehow. I wondered how we would figure that out.

It seemed to me that Damon used Sex to release stress and Darren drank himself to oblivion to deal with stress. I sighed out loud. Neither were ideal coping mechanisms.

"Okay, where too first?" I spoke out loud quietly.

As I was looking at the shops it looked almost like a Christmas village. The shops were lined up, there were fake trees and snow. It was April though so Christmas theme seemed really out of place. Unless that's when this place burnt down. There were white stringed lights all over the walkway and the shops. It reminded me a bit of

Disney village the way the shops looked on the outside, sort of like dollhouse-vintage.

"Are you lost miss?" a mans voice it sounded like it was right beside my ear. I spun to look but there was no one there.

"You look lost..."

I spun the opposite direction but no one was close enough to be speaking like this to me.

"Where are you?"

"Follow my voice"

I listened harder. I walked forward and to the right.

"Warmer.." The voice hurt my ears now it was so loud. I didn't understand why no one else could hear it.

"I'm lost too.. "

I looked at the store signs. There was an antique dealer to the right. I decided to go in there.

"Getting warmer.." I had to cover my ears now. It was so loud.

I walked in and there was a little bell announcing my arrival. An elderly women glanced up and gave me a genuine smile.

"Welcome dear. Have a look around, let me know if I can help you find anything."

I tried to nod but it felt like my head was on fire.

I rushed to the back of the store.

"You are hot! Hot!"

I looked at the back shelf. There was a number of odd items. There was an old lamp. It reminded me of the one from Aladdin. I reached for it.

"Yes, take me!" The voice was so loud that tears pricked my eyes.

I picked up the lamp and the voice fell silent. There was a price tag. $0.05 cents.

"I guess I will have to take you.." I whispered quietly.

I brought the lamp to the counter. The lady gave me a soft smile. Her hair was pulled into a tight bun, with more grey then blonde. She looked maybe in her 70s.

"Ah a Genie lamp. Interesting choice."

She glanced at me.

"You don't mean to tell me there's a real live genie in that lamp?" I sounded as panicked as I felt.

The lady laughed.

"Well aren't you a bit daft. Of course not. That's just a silly fable. $0.05 please."

"Oh-of course. I'm a bit drained tonight sorry"

God had I really just said that out loud? I had to be more mindful. I handed her a nickel. She smiled. I took the bag she handed me and left.

It wasn't overly heavy but I had a lingering headache and decided to check out the rest of the shops another day.

I headed to the elevator. When the doors opened the same boy greeted me as usual.

"Great to see you again miss."

I smiled. "You too."

"Have a pleasant evening. Do you want food brought up tonight?"

"No thank you so much though, I ate already. Oh, do you perhaps have the time?" I was curious what it was and there still were no clocks here.

"Half past 8 miss."

"Thank you."

He tipped his hat and closed the doors after I stepped out.

I walked to my door and paused long enough to hear a couple moans from Damon and Darren's room.

"I guess that means I will have to wait to tell them about the weird lamp." I spoke out loud to myself.

I unlocked my room door and flipped the lights on.

I put the lamp down and as soon as I did. My headache was gone. I walked to the bathroom brushed my hair, and washed my hands.

I decided to go back down considering it was only 830 and the moans next door were making me ache.

"Maybe I can tell Darren about the lamp. He might be less pissy if he knows I want to talk business."

I took the stairs instead. Feeling quite lonely.

Normally I would call Rayne, she was also expecting a call that I couldn't make.

"Unless I got outside of the hotel, for a couple minutes. Why didn't I think of that yesterday?"

When I entered the lobby I decided to try and leave. The lady at the front desk piped up.

"Miss! Isn't it a bit late to go outside alone? Specifically without a chaperone!"

I was confused for a minute then remembered what time period I was in.

"Oh, thank you for the concern, I will only be a minute. Want some fresh air."

"For sure miss! Just be quick now, you hear?"

"I will!"

I stepped out into the night air. It was warm until I got out of the gate. Then I saw it was actually pouring in real time. I walked to my car. My cellphone chimed with missed calls from Rayne. I phoned her, she picked up before the first ring even finished.

"About damn time!" she practically screamed.

"I'm sorry yes. The cops had questions and then I was with Damon and Darren."

I clamped a hand over my mouth, realizing I just said that out loud to Rayne.

"Wait-who? You met two guys?! Tell me everything now!" She exclaimed. All worry was out of her voice.

"It's not that big of a deal I met these brothers, they are both really nice."

"Wait- but at that sleazy motel? What kind of guys are they?"

I laughed.

"I always love that you care so much Rayne."

"It goes both ways! Now stop deflecting!"

"Look they are.. cops." I wasn't sure what else to tell her.

"Cops! Oh wow that's exciting. They are good looking then?"

I thought about Damon's tall toned body with tats sneaking out under his sleeves. His blue- green eyes and soft longer brown hair. Then I thought about Darren with his demeanour that commanded respect. Natural leadership, muscular arms and short brown hair with bright blue eyes.

"Yeah they are both gorgeous, I won't lie."

Rayne squealed.

I thought for a minute.

"They asked me to help them with this case.." I started.

"Really? That's kinda cool. Did you say yes? Please tell me you said yes!"

I laughed. "Yes! So I need a little extension on the house idea"

Rayne laughed. "Of course! I'm happy you are getting out there."

"Why are you still talking to me. Go catch one of the brothers!"

"Okay Rayne!" I laughed. "Honestly don't think they are interested in me."

"Don't doubt yourself. You are stunning and have personality to match."

"I didn't say I was interested even!" I countered.

"Well get interested." Rayne laughed. "Anyway Matt and I are going to watch a show now. Thanks for calling and I'm glad all is good."

"I'll keep you posted! Goodnight!"

"Goodnight Serena!"

She hung up first.

I slunk back against my car only just realizing I was getting completely soaked by the rain.

I unlocked my car and grabbed a dress that I hadn't brought in yet and put it under my sweater. That's when I noticed the SUV from earlier parked in a nearby stall. Panic enveloped me. I started to walk back to the hotel glancing once behind me to the SUV. I didn't see anyone. I picked up the pace and got back to the hotel lobby. Breathing loudly running my hand through my drenched hair.

"Glad to see you got in alright!" The lady at the front desk said.

"But my heavens, you are soaking wet! It's not raining, did you fall into the fountain out back?"

It took me a second to understand why she was confused. Right this place was trapped in some eternal warm day/night.

"Oh I- yeah I'm a clutz." I forced a laugh. "I'm okay just going to go warm up."

"If you say so! You should be more careful."

"I will. Thank you"

I rushed to the elevator, aware of many people staring at me in confusion. I supposed if I were them I would too.

"Oh are you okay miss?" The boy in the elevator asked.

"Oh-yes thank you."

I rushed out of the elevator when we stopped on my floor without looking back at the attendant, and opened the door to my room.

It was quiet in Damon and Darren's room. I glanced to the weird lamp I found and walked to the bathroom. I started to run a hot bath. I guess I would wait to talk to the guys. I wondered around the bathroom in my robe lighting the numerous wax candles in the bathroom. When I finished that I went to the shelves to choose bath salts.

I choose Vanilla scented this time. The rain and SUV encounter had chilled me to the bone, the water felt heavenly.

Vanilla was my favourite scent and I inhaled deeply, letting all the thoughts of the day melt away. I wondered how late it was now.

I heard Darren I was guessing coming back to the room. Jane must be gone by now.

I was looking forward to seeing the guys in the morning.

I settled my head back into the water and started to wash my hair.

I held my breath and closed my eyes, diving completely under water. The whooshing of the water in my ears drowning my thoughts. When I came up for air and opened my eyes. There was a figure standing at the foot of the tub, pale eyes glinting in the dim candle lit bathroom. For a second, I could only stare. My chest constricted in a desperate attempt for oxygen, but I was too scared to inhale.

The figure after a moment reached their hand touching the surface of the water.

Within seconds, my candles all blew out as if there was a sudden wind, and I screamed trying to scramble out of the tub. I screamed again and all I felt was bitter, painful cold. Like shards of ice stabbing into my skin.

"Help! Please!"

It was getting harder to speak and breathe.

I thrashed helplessly unable to move enough to get out of the tub.

To my horror, the water I was splashing in turned to slush, then snow. It began to harden like ice. I was hyperventilating as darkness crept my vision.

"Help me, help me, help me, help me." I said but all that came out was barely a whisper.

Chapter 6

MYSTIC ABYSS

"They say if you stare into the abyss it stares back, some days in your darkness it can feel as though it envelops and consumes you, the funny thing is in darkness the mind will play tricks, the abyss of night brings galaxies of stars to life, all we need seek is one ray of colour to bring us back our promise of light."

There I could feel the plane drop much too fast. Oxygen masks fell from the compartments above. Screams of so many people. Ears popping, and then the impact. So cold, everything was so cold. I just wanted warmth. Dead everyone was dead... I'm so cold. My head is in agony, the air is too harsh in my lungs.. Arms wrapped around me. My legs are broken it's impossible to move. His arms are so strong so comforting. He's telling me he's gonna save us, he pulls us out of the wreckage, but I know I will die. The voice sounds achingly familiar. I long to see his face. I long for warmth. I held on longer, why did this feel like the tub, wait am I dead? An image my husband? Two children, young 2 and 4 maybe, getting ready to board a plane.

Then I am in a car, Soft tunes, then the sudden whip of the vehicle, crunching metal, shattering windows, so loud in my ears, Blood, metallic and bitter it's all I can taste in my mouth my body crushed..I can't move, my face doesn't feel right, oh God help me. Please help me. I hear his voice pleading begging for me to be alive, but I cannot move my mouth to reply. I want to stroke his hair, I want to tell him I'm here but I can't move. His voice too is familiar, safe. I wanted to see his face, I wanted to speak.. what about the baby?...What will happen to our baby?..I held longer to the dream. Younger then we are in the car. Blood in a bathroom, I'm crying arms wrapped around me, there so much blood. "We will keep trying trying for a baby. We will keep trying."

I felt arms wrap around my upper body. Strong and secure. "Serena!" I couldn't open my eyes it was Darren's voice. "Serena! Damn it! Damon I need a hand, grab her too!"

A second pair of warm arms wrapped my lower body. I felt myself pulled from the slushy bathtub.

"Where the hell did it go!" Darren was yelling.

"It's gone Darren I don't know. Friggin just dissipated. Serena! Hey, come on" Damon's voice.

They both sounded so worried. I never heard so much emotion in Darren's voice. But I couldn't move, It was hard enough to breathe.

"Is she breathing?" Damon's voice.

"Check her pulse. Her neck. Keep your arms around her though." Damon again.

"I-I don't." I felt lips on my neck, I couldn't tell who.

Both their arms held me firmly, warmth emanating.

It felt like their lips had graced my skin a hundred times before- but that was impossible.

I must be delirious. I tried to speak, but it came as a raspy breath.

"We aren't warming her fast enough Darren."

"Well- what do you suppose we do!" Darren cried out.

"Take her to the bed. I will find more blankets." Damon said quickly.

I felt Damon's arms leave my lower body and I was cradled against Darren.

"Hang on, just hang in there." Darren's voice sounded so pained.

I felt the bed against my skin. Darren's arms didn't leave me body.

"Damon! The blankets."

"I'm grabbing them!" He yelled over his shoulder.

A minute or so later I felt a heavy weight over my body. Damon must be stacking blankets.

Then I felt Damon's arms around me too. I felt so secure and protected in both their arms.

"Darren if she doesn't come to we need to get her to a hospital."

"I know but it could be anywhere. Serena?" Darren said softly.

I tried to open my eyes. My eyelids felt glued shut. When I did open them my eyelashes were white from what I could see. I was suddenly very aware I was naked under the blankets. My head was turned to Damon. He smiled.

"Hey, look who's back to the world of the living."

I turned slowly to Darren his eyes held a raw pain I had never seen before he smelled strongly of whisky. He looked genuinely relieved.

"You gave us quite a scare." Darren said after studying my eyes for a minute.

"I-I" I tried to speak.

"Hey, it's okay give it a minute you damn near froze to death." Darren kept searching my eyes.

My mind flooded back to the bathtub. That really happened?

"I'm going to get you something warm to drink, I think Darren might be too drunk too." Damon laughed lightly.

Damon unwrapped his arms and moved another blanket onto me. Darren kept holding me and didn't respond to Damon.

I leaned in closer to Darren. He was so warm. He responded by pulling me closer to him.

Damon returned shortly putting a steaming cup of tea on the bedside table. He climbed back into the blankets and re wrapped himself around me.

"Guys-Wh-what happened?" My teeth were chattering, it was difficult not to stutter. My throat felt raw and my saliva felt non existent.

"Want to try and sit?" Damon asked.

I nodded.

They both helped move me to a sitting position taking care in going slow and making sure I was okay.

Darren re positioned the blankets around me. It was getting easier to breathe, each breath I took still felt like cement, but at least it didn't hurt.

Damon brought the tea to my lips and I drank best I could.

"Serena do you remember what you saw?" Darren asked relatively urgently.

"Darren let her warm up at least before bombarding her with questions."

"This is important Damon."

"No-" I started slowly. "You are right, it's important." I took a deep breath. "I saw a man with Pale eyes."

Damon's eyes widened. "The Demon that killed that girl tonight?"

I nodded.

"Are you certain?" Darren asked.

I nodded again.

"Damn it." Darren let go of me and climbed out of bed.

"Well now we know what kind of powers this breed of demon holds."

Damon said as he also let go of me and got up.

"I saw his eyes..my candles all burnt out and then all I felt was ice, like someone threw me into a glacier lake, first it was shocking, then blindingly painful."

Darren's eyes held pain in them as he listened. He grimaced slightly. Damon was looking at me with genuine concern.

"I couldn't get out of the tub, I don't know how- The water felt like I was pushing through slush- then felt like I was trying to swim in powdered snow- then it felt like my body was being encased in ice and that's when I blacked out."

Looking at their concerned faces was hard for me to do, so I decided to lighten the mood.

"I'm just relieved you guys found me, dying the first day on the job would be- well you know. Unauthentic."

Damon snickered. Darren remained like stone.

"No one is dying anytime soon. We will make sure of that." Darren said.

"It's become evident we need to train you faster then I'd hoped." Damon started gently.

I tried to get up.

Damon grabbed my arm to help. I held the blanket around me.

"Well I'm ready to learn."

I glanced down at myself, briefly forgetting I was still naked.

"First though, would you guys uh- get me some clothes?"

I shifted my feet, awkwardly wrapping the large blanket tighter around myself.

"Oh yes- of course of course." Damon rushed to the closet.

He came back out with jeans and a top. The jeans Rayne bought me a couple days ago.

"This work?" He held the clothes up for me.

I nodded and attempted a smile. "Thanks."

"I apologize Serena, we didn't have a choice-we pulled you out of the bathtub." Darren started rubbing his hand along is jaw anxiously.

They both turned away from me so I could get dressed without me having to ask them to, which I was grateful for.

"You don't owe me an apology. You saved my life."

I pulled the jeans up and the top over my head.

"I'm dressed, thank you."

The guys turned back toward me.

"Yeah, but we don't know why you were targeted." Damon started.

"Did the demon look at you this morning?" Darren started. "Did he make eye contact with you?"

I tried to think back. "He glanced at me he didn't seem overly interested."

I gasped slightly out loud.

"What is it?" Damon looked over to me.

"Well- the SUV the demon was in, I saw it in the parking lot tonight."

Darren whipped around to look at me.

"Why the hell didn't you tell us that? Why did you go out alone at night?!"

I was taken off guard by his sudden outburst, then I remembered he was likely plastered.

"You guys were preoccupied, I was going to report in the morning. Darren, with all due respect, I am capable of being alone in the nighttime. I can hold my own."

I said it softly.

I wasn't angry, I figured he was just worried, and alcohol never helps anything.

"Yeah, you so clearly demonstrated that tonight. There are so many things out there we aren't just talking about a random creep." Darren explained sharply.

Damon glared at Darren. "Calm down Darren. We will teach her."

"It's okay Serena." Damon gave me a soft smile. "At least we heard you."

"You are so damn lucky we heard you! If we hadn't-" Darren trailed off.

"Well you wouldn't be breathing, so you wanna help then don't put yourself at deaths door, this is serious, dangerous business. Is there anything else we should know?" Darren's words again cut as they normally did.

"Darren honestly, how was she suppose to know? We didn't even know what this demon was capable of until this happened."

Darren held up his hand. "She is not bait. Don't say it."

"That's not what I'm saying. She got attacked, we saved her and now we know what to watch for."

"She could've been killed." Darren leaned over the counter with his hands in his hair.

"Darren-" I started softly.

I had a strange moment of deja vu looking at him like that and I wanted to stroke his hair softly turn his head toward me and cup his face in my hands.- I shook it off.

"Look I'm alive, and I am not going anywhere so you are just going to have to understand that. But arguing over my being here is pointless, because I can't walk away from this. I will learn. I will. I am obviously already involved. I will help."

He lifted his head and looked at me for a long moment and I spoke up again.

"Yes, since you asked, there is something else you should know."

I motioned to the bag with the Genie lamp.

"I went to check out the shops and this thing- called out to me."

My arm's erupted in goose flesh, as I remembered the loud voice.

Damon went to open the bag. He pulled the lamp out and examined it.

"What do you mean it called out to you?" Darren fixed me with a hard stare.

"I mean..it spoke to me. It sounded human, but off? It called my name. At first I thought it was someone I knew somehow, it was so loud like they were right beside me."

"Were they speaking English?" Damon asked studying the lamp. "Can you hear it speak now?

"I only understand English, so I would have to assume yes? No, I can't hear it right now. When I touched it last time there was loud ringing in my ears."

Darren and Damon exchanged a look I couldn't read.

"You thinking, a djinn?"

Damon nodded. "Pretty sure."

Damon flicked his eyes to me. "When you grabbed the lamp nothing- came out of it?"

I laughed. "What you mean like Aladdin? I get 3 wishes if I rub the lamp just right?"

Damon chuckled. "No Disney here."

"We aren't talking the Robin Williams Genie here Serena. Djinn are nasty sons of bitches. You wouldn't want any wishes from it." Darren spoke up.

"Vampires, shapeshifters, werewolves and now Evil Genies?"

"Djinn not genie." Darren corrected.

"Looks like someone trapped this one ironically." Darren added.

"Awesome. That clears it up. So these things grant wishes that what have a bad twist?"

Damon scoffed. "Not exactly. They poison you. Inject you with a venom that puts you into a coma, where you essentially trip balls for the duration of them feeding on you."

I shuddered.

Darren added. "Kinda, except they place you in your dream life so that it's damn near impossible to wake up from. Then you die when they are done draining your life."

"So they dose you with hardcore LSD?"

Darren offered a half smile. "Pretty much."

"Wow look who almost smiled. Careful might break your cold stone exterior with that." Damon teased.

"Shut up Damon, I was not." Darren rolled his eyes.

I couldn't help but laugh. My heart fluttered to see Darren almost smile.

"Okay so it's trapped in that thing?"

Damon nodded. "Thankfully for us. I will need some time to decipher the writing on here."

"What's the likelihood Serena just located another piece of the 666?" Darren asked.

Damon smiled at me. "High."

"So then why are these items calling out to me?"

"We don't know yet, but it will prove useful." Damon said as he took the lamp to the table.

Damon walked over to my bookshelf.

"This is where you saw the book before it came to you right?"

"Yes."

Damon nodded. "You have a few interesting books here. There are a couple we don't have. We should gather them."

"If this is a piece of the 666, why is there a creature trapped in it?"

"Often these objects are guarded by some supernatural being or force." Damon continued.

"So, what was the book guarded by?" I asked hesitantly.

"We aren't sure of that but that's probably why you had a hulk moment." Darren added.

"Wait,-you think whatever it is- is INSIDE of me?" My heartbeat quickened.

"No-well it's not impossible. We will figure it out okay?" Damon looked at me sincerely.

"Okay. I believe you. But ugh, that gives me shivers. So what do we do about the Djinn?"

"Well we don't let it out, for starters." Darren started.

Damon was comparing a book of ancient languages to the inscriptions on the lamp.

"You mentioned earlier that different families took care of different creatures, who's in charge of Djinn?"

"No one, they were thought to be next to extinct. We could be wrong, they might all be trapped like this one. Waiting for some poor fool to open the bottle." Darren continued:

"Don't tell me we have to open that friggin' thing Damon."

"It's true, this inscription is a ruthless binding spell. It keeps it trapped but this lamp is one of the 666."

"Son of a bitch." Darren turned away.

"You mean..we have to free that creature? Do you guys know how to kill it?"

Damon sighed. "Yeah it's not easy. Darren do you think the knife would work on these?"

"I wouldn't risk it. Once that thing is here. I guarantee it's seriously pissed off about being trapped, we have a very small window before it infects all of us."

Damon ran his hand along his jaw. "We will grab the weapon tomorrow then."

"For now don't touch the lamp Serena, with a binding spell this strong it shouldn't have been able to contact you." Damon wrapped it back in the bag.

"I won't."

"Serena it would be best if you came and stayed with us in our room." Damon started. Darren shot him a death glare.

"You know it's safer, that Demon could still return tonight."

"I couldn't deny that would make me feel safer, but I don't want to impose either."

"Impose, like nearly getting killed, you mean?" Darren started.

"Darren stop. She's coming with us." Damon said firmer then I ever heard him speak before.

Where did the concern Darren had not an hour earlier disappear to? It wasn't bad I was used to dealing with anger. I used to take it as a personal attack, eventually that was so draining that I detached myself from anger.

"Let me just get a change of clothes." I said plainly.

I walked toward the dresser, avoiding Darren's heated expression.

I stopped hesitantly at the bathtub, the ice in it was melting, it looked more like slush now then solid ice.

I shuddered.

"God I can't believe that just happened." I whispered to myself.

"Staying with them is my best chance. I will learn. I can do this."

I paused to grab a nightgown and a dress for tomorrow. Heat rose to my cheeks realizing I was about to room with both of them.

"Get a hold of yourself Serena" I said to the mirror.

I splashed some water on my face then I picked up on the brothers talking.

"She is only going to hinder us Damon this is proof. This. Here. Tonight." Darren was speaking in a hushed tone.

"Darren, she located another piece of the 666, just simply by walking near it. We need her help. We will train her. She will be stronger."

"You better hope you are right Damon. You realize how high the stakes are. The risk we are putting on her?"

"She can handle it."

Damon was so sure of what he was saying it made me believe it too.

"Whatever." Darren said exasperated.

Sometimes I felt like I should let them know their private conversations weren't always private around me, but thought no good would come of it. I would prove Damon right.

I came around the corner with my clothes and robe in hand.

"Alright, I'm ready to go."

Damon smiled at me. He put the lamp on the counter still in the bag and took the book he had been studying.

Darren opened the door and I walked out with Damon following me, Damon locked the door for me.

Darren unlocked the door to their room. I shuddered slightly entering as I remembered what happened the last time I was here. When they were going to kill me, now here I was willingly bunking with them, for protection of all things. The irony was through the roof.

"So you won't be tying me to a chair this time, yeah?" I joked.

Damon laughed. "Unless that's what you are into, no."

I felt my face flush.

"And Darren, I can expect you not to attempt to cut my throat tonight?"

"I'll be on my best behaviour." He said it matter of fact, coolly. Darren didn't play into my joking.

"Well than I guess I'm safe."

I glanced around the room. It was similar to mine, aside from maybe ten times the amount of books. They had two large beds instead of one.

I walked to the couch and put my clothes down.

"I'll take the couch."

"No. Take mine. I don't sleep much anyway." Darren motioned.

Damon's bed was tousled. I'm guessing from him and Jane earlier. I swallowed a bit.

Damon followed my glance. "Yeah better than mine."

"I don't know if I will sleep much."

Damon laughed gently. "Yeah near death experiences tend to do that to you."

Darren was rustling in the fridge.

"Well I'm wiped. Don't worry. Anything or anyone comes, you are with us. You are safe. Alright?" Damon reassured, giving me a smile.

I nodded. "Goodnight then."

"Night Darren, Serena."

Damon went to his bed and maybe a few minutes later was snoring lightly.

Darren shook his head. He was starting to make a sandwich.

I walked up beside him.

"Here, let me."

I grabbed the butter knife from his hands and started to spread mayo.

"What, don't trust me to use a butter knife?" he stepped sideways to give me space.

I paused, looking at the knife. "Don't think you could do much with this." I shrugged.

Darren snickered. "You'd be surprised."

He watched me for a second. "I can make my own sandwich you know."

He stepped closer to me and held his hand out for the butter knife.

"I'm not doubting your mad sandwich making skills Gordon Ramsey. Go sit, I will bring it to you."

Darren smiled. Fully and looked like he might laugh.

I admired it for a second. It sure was beautiful.

"Holy mother of God. You smiled." I teased. "Better call the papers."

Darren rolled his eyes. "Yeah, whatever."

He moved to sit at the table and started palming through one of their ancient texts.

I fixed him a sandwich and fixed one for myself too, considering I wouldn't get much sleep. Not when all I could think about was the Demon.

"So-" I started as I set the sandwiches down. I pulled the chair opposite of him.

"What, going to try and guess my favourite colour now?"

I smiled. "No, we aren't here for small talk. To quote you." Darren shifted in his chair.

"What then?" He took a bite of the sandwich. "Holy shit, this is incredible."

"Did you think it wouldn't be?" I teased.

He shrugged. "I'm particular."

I laughed "That's a staple of your personality."

He took another bite, then motioned his arm for me to continue talking.

"Well, look I trained in martial arts for 8 years I am pretty good at hand to hand fighting, maybe rusty now though."

"That will come in handy. What about weapons?"

I shook my head. "No experience."

He took another bite. I took the break to take a bite too.

"We will have to teach you. A surprising amount of monsters die from things like silver bullets. Just like a human would."

"I'm surprised, I would have guessed most needed like a bone dipped in lambs blood or something."

"Heh, no a fair amount need special weapons but the vast majority doesn't." He glanced around the table for a minute then grabbed the table salt.

"For example, table salt. Lesson 1"

"Are you going to insult that sandwich by adding salt to it?"

"Now who sounds like Gordon?"

I chuckled. "Okay but seriously salt, for what?"

"Sea salt is better, but essentially it's ghost repellent. Similar to sage. We keep white sage and sea salt nearby at all costs it can help cleanse an area infested with spirits."

"What about crystals?"

"Obsidian Crystals for ghosts yes." He pulled a chain out from his white t-shirt, it had a black Crystal dangling from it.

"So if one is actively getting hurt by a ghost then what?"

Darren stood up and rustled in a duffle bag beside the table. I took a couple more bites of my sandwich.

He pulled what looked like nun-chucks out.

"Oh you ninja fight them? Obviously, silly me." I teased.

He made a mock ninja stance, and half smiled. Then held it outstretched for me to see. It was much longer than nun-chucks.

"No, this chain is infused with iron and black crystal. It's been soaked in boiled water containing sea salt and white sage. Swinging it at the attacking spirit, will give you a couple of minutes to breathe."

He imitated swinging it.

"Okay, cool it, Jackie Chan. Before you hurt yourself. Anything else? This all sounds like temporary fixes. How do you put an angry spirit to rest?"

Darren scoffed. "I'm an expert."

"Sure, but you are also drunk."

He rolled his eyes.

"Usually you have to dive into their unfinished business so that they can move on. The spirits that are too far gone, there's a spell to banish them. Or they are holding on to an old belonging of theirs or piece of DNA."

Darren put the chain back.

"DNA?"

"Yeah some people keep locks of hair, baby teeth."

"That sounds very occultist."

"Sometimes yeah."

"Okay and what burn the item or..DNA?"

"Exactly. Fire is purifying."

I finished my sandwich. "Interesting."

Darren sat back down and continued eating. I sat in silence with him for a few minutes while he finished eating, sipping at some tea.

"Want another sandwich?" Darren looked up at me gratitude shone in his eyes for a moment.

I smiled. "Soak up all that alcohol for you."

I moved to the fridge.

Darren scoffed loudly. "I can hold my own. To quote you."

"Sure, but I don't want you hugging the toilet all morning. Speaking of which, here." I put a cup of cold water down for him.

"Drink this too, like at least 3 cups."

Darren stared coldly at me for a moment. Then brought the glass to his mouth.

"What are you trying to sober me up for? I'm a lot nicer this way."

"We have work to do if you do not want me to drag you guys down."

Darren watched me for a minute. "Cheers then"

I brought my tea cup into the air from the kitchen. "Cheers."

In a few minutes I finished making it.

I put the sandwich down for Darren.

"You should get some rest. It's well past 2am."

I looked around for a clock.

"How do you know the time? My phone doesn't work in here and I have never seen a clock."

"Biological clock I suppose, Damon and I live here so."

"Wait-you live here?"

Darren shrugged. "We have for about a year and until we find all the objects here and in the surrounding area, then we move to another place like this. It's mostly protected and cost effective."

I nodded. I couldn't argue that.

"Except for the Demon." I sighed.

"The warding for this breed of demon we need to find, it wouldn't be the same as it's fellow black eyed demons. We will find it."

"Okay. Well what about Demons, can you repel them like ghosts?"

Darren shook his head.

"Different ball game for each race of creature. Damon will give you a run down of demons tomorrow. Anyways, get some sleep you are no use to us if you aren't rested." Darren more or less ordered.

I was very tired, It was also a lot of information to digest.

"I can try." I got up from the table and headed to change in the bathroom.

When I came out Darren glanced at me, and pointed to his bed.

"Sleep. Nothing will get you." Darren said softly.

It was so nice to hear him speak softly, it was such a rare occurrence.

"I know, you need to sleep too Darren."

"Yeah, yeah I know. I will."

I climbed into the bed, and I heard Darren settle on the couch. My eyes felt heavy.

"And Serena?"

"mm?"

"Thank you- for the sandwiches."

I smiled and wrapped myself under the covers. It wasn't long before I drifted into sleep.

Chapter 7

ATONEMENT

"The calm before the storm, a grey area, wondering what the point is, vision blurred by darkness, the light seems non-existent, so easy to drown here, I beg for atonement, with new eyes open, I realize the colours are there, they were always, colours muddled in grey, life is purely beautiful, when you learn to block the grey."

I woke hyperventilating. It took me a second to remember where I was. The guys were in the kitchen. Darren was at the table drinking a coffee. Damon was standing behind the counter. Damon smiled when I sat up.

"Hey good morning. How did you sleep?" He asked.

I rubbed my eyes. Thankfully they didn't seem to notice I was panicked.

I took a moment to calm my breathing.

"Good morning."

Darren glanced to me.

"Hope you are hungry, Damon ordered the whole damn menu."

Damon shot Darren a look sharper then a knife.

"Yeah, wasn't sure what you would like." He ran a hand nervously through his hair.

Darren just rolled his eyes and walked over to hand me a cup of steaming coffee.

"Thanks Damon, that was really nice of you."

I took the cup from Darren. "Thanks for the coffee."

He nodded and walked back to sit at the table.

I sipped thoughtfully for a second.

I would be lying to myself if I said I didn't like not being alone and being cared for. It always felt like I was so busy caring for everyone else, that I put myself and my needs last. It was sweet and different to care and be cared for in return.

I stood up and Damon glanced over to me.

"You feeling better today?"

"Much. I'm just going to get dressed and such."

Damon nodded and I headed to the bathroom.

It looked identical to mine.

I combed through my blonde hair with my hands and used the mouthwash they had in there.

I gasped slightly when I actually looked in the mirror. I had forgotten I hadn't taken my makeup off last night after the bathtub incident. I looked like a raccoon.

"Oh my-" I said out loud.

I grabbed a wash cloth and soaked it with soap and warm water and scrubbed my eyes clean. I hadn't thought to bring makeup over last night.

"Well bare faced it is." I whispered to myself. I wasn't used to seeing myself without makeup. I dressed in a pink flowing dress today.

When I rounded the corner the guys were piling food onto their plates. My stomach growled and I was grateful Damon ordered so much.

I sat at the table both Darren and Damon looked at me.

"So- Darren said he went over ghosts last night?"

"Ah straight to business hey?" I laughed and grabbed a forkful of eggs.

"We have too much ground to cover not too." Darren stated.

"Okay I understand. Yes ghosts. I was trying to ask about Demons"

I moved to stack a plate with food.

Damon smiled "Re-iterate it to me."

"White sage and sea salt in boiling water. You need to help them solve their unfinished business, they will usually leave clues. Some are violent and some aren't. Find what they are bound to and burn it. Object or DNA. Darren showed me the chain for when you are under attack, and black crystal for protection."

"Perfect. Here-"

Damon handed me a black crystal on a chain same as Darren had and same he had wrapped around his own neck.

"Thank you." I gently grabbed the necklace and draped it over my neck.

It clanged softly against my heart necklace that I grabbed from my apartment that I always wore.

"Okay demons are difficult. The black eyed Demons we can ward off with some spell work, to protect an area. Combat wise, we need to bind them to keep them trapped long enough to preform an exorcism." Said Damon.

"Holy water will burn the hell out of them. A good test to see if someone is possessed is with it. We use it in combat too." Damon said.

"Does salt work with demons?" I asked.

Damon shook his head slightly. "Not really. Too powerful."

"Pisses them off a bit, maybe stings the sons of bitches a little." Darren added.

"Okay so are demons always inside of people, or do you see pure form demons ever?"

"You cannot see a demons true form on earth. They need a host to walk around. Other monster's often appear sort of human to the untrained eye. Others are grotesque in appearance. They stick to shadows and come out at night." Damon explained.

"So the person it's possessing do they know what they are doing?"

"Yes. Basically they are locked in their mind but can see and feel everything but they aren't in control of their body" Damon continued.

I took a long sip of coffee.

"That sounds like a nightmare. Do you guys ever follow up with people after you exorcise the demon in them?"

Darren gave me a strange look. "Not really our area. We explain what happened and some safety measures to take."

"I feel like they would need so much therapy but they couldn't say anything much otherwise they would be thrown in the psychiatric hospital."

I took a breath a little afraid to ask the next question.

"Do they ever try to kill the host?"

Damon and Darren exchanged a forlorn expression.

"Usually if they can they will. While harbouring a demonic entity in you, your body starts to shut down the longer you are possessed."

Damon said taking a sip of orange juice.

"Also most demons will eventually tire of the host trying to regain control, screaming and pounding from the inside. Especially if they intend to keep a host long term. So then they kill them." Darren added sadness evident in his tone.

I nodded. "I couldn't imagine that. So the Demon last night- same thing?"

"That-" Damon started. "We don't know right now, they seem to be more vicious then the black eyed ones and harbour power like we have never seen."

"So we don't know how to get it uninterested in me?"

Darren looked down, and Damon's eye's fell from mine.

"Not yet. We will figure it out. I promise." Damon rested his hand on my shoulder for a minute.

"We won't let anything happen to you Serena." Darren looked at me.

His words felt comforting to me, just as Damon's touch did.

I swallowed a few bites of food.

"I believe you."

I thought back to the house Rayne found for me.

"So this life, do you guys ever set down roots?"

Damon and Darren exchanged a look.

"What do you mean?" Damon asked.

"Well have you guys ever had a place of your own?"

Darren shook his head. "We haven't" There was a faraway look in his eyes.

Damon looked lost in thought too.

"Why do you ask?" Damon met my eyes.

"I was just curious that's all."

"We have to move around all the time, we have our whole lives." Damon added. "Bigger things to worry about."

"Of course." I decided to drop the topic for now.

I thought it was sad they never knew anything other then monsters. I was not one to say. My life had been pretty mundane, but I didn't hate it. It just seemed better then being on the road forever, knowing you had somewhere to call home. That you always had something or someone to come back too.

"So what other creatures do we need to worry about. Like that Djinn? You mentioned we needed a weapon, do you know where to get one?"

Damon swallowed a bite of food and looked at Darren.

"We need to use one of us as bait. You need a ceremonial knife dipped in the blood of a person infected with the poison of the Djinn, to kill the Djinn."

"They are the original: "Give you a taste of your own medicine. Karma is a quick bitch on these suckers." Darren snickered.

Damon laughed and I smiled.

"The ceremonial knife, like the one you tried to kill me with Darren?"

I laughed seeing the look on his face.

"Oh I'm only teasing. All is forgiven. You thought I was some sort of monster, we all make mistakes."

Darren's face softened. "You shouldn't be so quick to forgive people."

I shrugged. "There's no reason not to."

Damon spoke up.

"To answer your question, no. They live in ruins usually. Ceremonial meaning historical this time. We need a knife carved of stone dipped in blood of the person infected."

"Basically think caveman." Darren added.

I sucked in a breath. "Wow. Where do you find that though?"

"Usually you can in pawn shops. There's one in this hotel and there's another one few miles from here." Damon said pointing at an old phone book.

"That phone book is the same age as this hotel, lot's has changed since then. How do we know it's still in operation?" I asked, thumbing through names.

"We don't until we go." Damon smiled. "We will go this afternoon."

"Do you think we need to let that thing out Damon? You said the binding was intense. Are you sure we need to unleash it? Shouldn't it stay trapped?" Darren asked.

"Well the fact that it was able to call out to Serena, shows that the barrier is weakening. Also the lamp is one of the 666 it's 100 percent safe to assume this Djinn is a guardian."

"Fantastic. So we have a possible hybrid, seriously pissed off Genie on our hands."

Darren sighed and poured some whisky into his coffee.

"Really, at 7am?" Damon looked over to Darren in distaste.

"Don't worry little bro, it's not your liver."

Damon snickered. "It's not mine that concerns me."

"Whatever." Darren said as he took a sip.

Between the three of us we actually got through almost all of the food.

Damon put the trolley outside.

"I'm going to get washed up." Darren said without looking at us. He closed the bathroom door.

I poured another cup of coffee and helped Damon gather all the dishes.

"Damon, how many items are in and around Edmonton here?"

Damon opened the notepad.

"We are hoping the final 7 are in and around this area, but we don't know. The lamp and book made the list from 9 to 7 missing items."

"How long until the world ends?" I asked hesitantly.

"Judging by all the precursors to the apocalypse. We believe we have 6 months. I know it seems like a long time, but those 7 items, they are hidden possibly all around the world. Most are guarded. We also need to complete 66 rituals, and I have only been able to locate a few rituals this far." Damon ran his hand on his jaw.

"Add travel, sleep to that and you are looking at a lot less time then a full 6 months."

"So, if my math is correct. Each ritual needs 10 items? That would bring it to 660, so one ritual only needs 6 items then? "

Damon nodded. "The final one requires 6 items, all the most powerful items."

"So the apocalypse, how did it say we were going to go?"

"Time is folding in on itself. We aren't certain yet. We are learning as we go. All we know is there's no way anyone will survive it. It has something to do with Hell. Hence the demon problem."

"Unless we stop it."

Damon smiled. "Yeah exactly."

"Then I guess we better get to it." I smiled.

Darren walked out in a bath towel then. "A-freaking-men." he grabbed his coffee cup.

"God Darren put some friggin' clothes on. We have a lady present."

Damon said shielding his eyes.

"Yeah you are one to talk about honouring the ladies." Darren scoffed.

"Oh I honour them." Damon retorted.

My eyes lingered on his exposed chest a half a beat too long. He had tattoos like Damon but more of them, his whole arms coated and he was so muscular. I breathed in as quietly as I could and turned away as he went to walk back to the bathroom.

I downed the rest of my coffee.

"Where's our first stop?"

Damon looked over and smiled at me. "Glad you are eager."

"I guess I'm in favour of the world not ending."

Damon chuckled. "Good. I figured we would go down to the stores, see if anything else calls out to you in this hotel. Then we have to go to Wabamun lake."

My mind flashed to the little cottage Rayne had found for me. A hint of sadness fell over me.

Damon picked up on it immediately. "Something wrong?"

I studied his eyes for a minute. I didn't understand how both brothers always made me feel I could trust them 100 percent.

"Honestly, I was just wondering what to tell Rayne."

"Your friend? About what?"

"Well her and her to be husband made me this very generous offer on a house of my own. That's all."

Damon continued to keep eye contact.

"If you want to say yes, then say yes. Then you have a place to call your own once we fix everything. We can use it as partly a home base too if we ever didn't want to be at the hotel."

I was surprised by his answer.

"Really?"

"Yeah of course. You won't get much use out of it yet but you'll have it when we are through."

I smiled. "Thanks Damon. I will give her a call when we leave the hotel later."

"Good."

Darren walked out fully dressed in a light dress shirt and jeans. Damon stood to get dressed too.

Darren took a seat beside me. I smiled in hello, he nodded.

"Light colours look good on you Darren, they bring out your bright blue eyes."

He scoffed slightly. "Yeah okay."

Damon came out in a darker dress shirt and jeans. I could see the blueish green in his eyes stand out.

I sucked in a breath seeing Damon's Tattoos sneaking from his shirt. I need to get a hold of myself.

"Well you both look great. Shall we?"

I got up first and they followed me to the door.

"Serena here-" Damon handed me the ceremonial knife they were going to use against me.

"Why?-"

"Just to be on the safe side like I said many of these items are guarded. It kills most everything. Darren and I will take the guns since you have no experience with firearms."

I tucked the blade into my boot.

"Thanks, I haven't really used knives much either honestly."

Darren scoffed. "The pointy end goes into the attackers body. You hold the non pointy end, so you don't cut yourself."

"Darren-" Damon started.

"It's fine Damon. It was a stupid remark. I got the message." I chuckled lightly.

Darren locked the door behind us. We started toward the elevators. When the doors opened the same girl from yesterday smiled at us in greeting. Damon and Darren gave her a nod and I gave her a smile.

When we stepped out of the elevator we made a left to the stores.

"Damon do you have any lead where these these might be?"

Damon looked at me cautiously. "I only know there are a couple items in here. I guess I'm hoping that you are the key"

"Yeah, so let us know when your spidey sense's or whatever kicks in." Darren added.

"I'd call it more of a 6th sense."

"Oh, you see dead people?" Darren raised his brows.

"No, but apparently you both do." I laughed.

"You will too." Damon was laughing too.

"Fair point. The crown is rightfully yours."

We paused at the stores.

"Which store did you find that lamp in?" Damon asked.

I looked around for the antique store. Scanning the lines of stores up and down. I looked to the right where there was just a wall littered in photographs.

"It was right over there. I could've sworn." I pointed to the wall.

"Well, think harder." Darren started.

"Hold on- what if-" Damon started.

Damon walked up to the wall of pictures.

"This place burned down in 1920s right?" He started looking at the photos.

"Yeah..and?" Darren said impatiently.

"So all these pictures would be earlier then 1920s or during." I walked up beside Damon.

"What are you looking for?"

Damon looked at me. "Just a hunch. Are you sure this is where the store was?"

"Yeah, it was the first thing I saw, and the experience rattled me a bit, so I didn't actually shop."

"Look at these pictures, do you recognize anything?"

I scanned the pictures and was about to say no when the bottom left image stood out to me. It was an elderly man and women standing in front of what looked like an old frontier building that read "Antiques" I read the description.

"1940?" I looked at Damon. "That's out of place if this burnt down in the 20s. The women, I-I know it's impossible but it sure looks like the women that ran the antique store I went into yesterday."

Darren came then glancing at the picture. "So- it was placed here by someone that can come in and out like us?"

Damon shook his head. "I don't think so..maybe.."

He grabbed the photo off of the wall and handed it to me.

"Hold this a second Serena."

I grasped it gingerly in my hands. There was an immediate searing pain in my hands and I dropped the photograph, shattering the frame in the process.

"Oh-"

When I looked up I was about to apologize but I was too shocked to speak.

We were all at the antique shop. The same one I was in last night.

"No freaking way..." Darren spoke.

"Holy shit." Damon added.

"What just happened?"

"Is this the store Serena?" Damon asked.

"I-Yes but weren't we just looking at a picture?"

I looked to Darren and Damon but they looked just as shocked as I felt.

"Did this happen last time?" Darren asked.

"No! The store was just there. Like any other store, no photo's. I would've mentioned if I got sucked through a picture."

My heart was racing and I ran my hand through my hair.

"Does this mean she's-?" Darren started but Damon cut him off.

"It mean's this has something to do with Cronos." Damon interjected.

"You don't mean-"

Damon nodded.

"The friggin' God of TIME?" Darren ran his hand over his hair.

"It's the only being that has the power to do something like this."

"A God??" I started. They both looked to me.

"There are a lot of God's from a lot of different religions." Damon started.

"They exist though?"

"Yes."

"So we can somehow travel through photographs?"

Damon shook his head. "Not we. Nothing happened until you touched the photo Serena."

"But-I. Look I have no idea why this stuff is happening to me."

Damon gave me a sympathetic smile. "We don't either and we will figure it out together okay?"

"For now let's head back in, obviously there's something that was missed." Darren started.

We walked forward into the store. The same lady greeted me.

"Oh, hello again dear. Come for another look?"

"Hi, yeah I did. I loved it so much last time." The lie came out smooth as silk.

"You brought friends with you. Hello Gentlemen."

Darren and Damon nodded.

"Lovely. Well take all the time you need."

"Thank you."

Darren and Damon started sifting through the shelves. I ran my hand along a few things. I didn't hear any voices or anything. I felt pulled to a glass cabinet by the front. There was a thick book on one of the shelves in a language I didn't understand. Then I heard whispers. I couldn't make out what they were saying. The bottom shelf held a breathtaking Tiara. As I leaned in. The whispers grew louder.

"Serena...Serena..Serena.."

There was a hot pain behind my eyes. I inhaled sharply.

I knelt to the ground slightly.

"Serena!"The whispers yelled and I yelped slightly.

I felt Damon's arms around me

"Serena.. hey? You alright? Did you find something?"

I pointed to the tome. Damon's arms fell from me as he stood up to look at the tome.

Darren came now and helped me to stand the whispers were quite loud. I placed a shaking palm to my ear.

"Darren grab..Grab the Tiara..please."

Darren looked over the cabinet, as soon as he picked it up the whispers silenced.

I let out a shaky breath. Steadying myself on the front desk. The lady looked at me with raised eyebrows.

"You good dear?"

"I-yeah, Thanks."

We will take the tome and this tiara." Damon started.

"How much?"

"Hmm don't you guys have an eye for truly unique items." She started.

"Truly unique?" Darren questioned.

"Yes, this tome is said to be the tome of the dead. Well so the traveller that dropped it off said." She shrugged. "Nutty old bat."

"The tiara is rumoured to be the crown for the first princess." She sighed. "Same nut dropped it off."

"Wow-well those sound valuable." Damon started. "Why not put them in a museum?"

She shrugged again. "If you even believe in that sort of nonsense then I would suppose so. Museums don't make me money though."

"Do you remember anything about the traveller that passed through to drop these off? Did they drop anything else off?" Darren started.

"Actually yes. Two other things. The lamp that this young lady bought off of me yesterday. And this."

She bent down and picked up a tiny black music box.

There was a loud whipping wind sound in my ears as I laid eyes on the box. I had to strain to hear anything outside of the noise.

"Rumoured to have a deadly lullaby." She sputtered, unaffected by whatever was affecting me.

Clearly fully believing it to be the ramblings of the insane.

"The traveller had unusual eyes is all I really remember. He passed through here some months ago."

"Unusual how?" Darren asked.

"They seemed to glow red." She shrugged. "I was a little-" She rose her hand up, indicating she was under the influence of something.

"Yeah- Right well we will take all 3 items." Darren answered.

"Great choices. $20. Since they are a rarity and all"

The sound in my ears was still loud. $20 was quite a bit of money in this time zone.

Another lady came from seemingly no where in the back.

"These items you aren't permitted to sell."

"Oh-mother. I will sell them. It's my damn store."

I looked to the boys we were all in shared shock.

"Mother?- Well you..sure don't look your age." Darren started.

"Well she's a raving old bitch is what she is." The daughter spat.

"I eat well dear."

The "Mother" Was a slender lady with long braided medium brown hair and very light eyes.

Damon looked like he was trying to decipher something.

The lady that appeared looked no more then 30 whereas the daughter looked around 75.

"Oh flattery-from the cockroaches that crawl this planet. How sweet." The lady seethed.

With a flick of her hand, she sent Darren and Damon flying crashing into the far wall of glass hardware. She laughed.

"Guys! No!" I scrambled to my feet. Grabbing at the blade in my boot.

"I've heard of you, Elderwood brothers. I must say, it's quite disappointing you don't live up to your name. I haven't had a good fight in ages."

I glanced to their bodies, they were both too still. Unconscious I prayed.

She continued talking.

"Unless the rumours are true, and you don't remember what you are. How intriguing. Shouldn't be that easy to take down unless you were mortal."

I stood still. She seemed to look through me. The wind whipping in my ears was silenced.

"You will not lay a hand on them."

The women turned her head to me, as uninterested in me as a fly.

"Oh you pathetic little girl." She flicked her hand and I expected to be thrown back but nothing happened.

Fear flashed in her features briefly even the daughter turned her attention to me.

"But how-"

In the corner of my eyes I saw Darren struggle to get up. I needed to buy him time.

"Your tricks won't work on me."

A voice whispered in my head similar to the whispers from the items. "Rhea"

I took a chance and guessed that was her name.

I noticed Damon get up now, when I spoke the name and I made sure to speak up, hoping they knew what this meant because I had no idea. Recognition sparked his features and he mouthed something to Darren. Darren nodded and inched closer.

"I don't need tricks. I will wring your little mortal neck with my bare hands."

I forced a laugh. "Oh really, Rhea? That's cute."

She stopped in her tracks.

"No- you have no right to speak my name off your filthy tongue."

Darren was up behind her now.

"You insult me! Attacking from behind? Cowardly. You believe me to be idiotic. You are all nothing but filthy little vermin." She swung around and gripped Darren by the throat. Damon ducked back down.

"Darren!" I yelped. I lounged toward her with the blade.

"Serena don't!" Damon yelled.

"Insolent child!" She shrieked as the blade sunk into her ribcage.

Her grip loosened on Darren enough for him to start to gain the upper hand.

Damon was right behind me now.

Darren wrestled out of her grip and held her arms back. Standing behind Rhea.

"Don't underestimate us cockroaches sweetheart." Darren seethed beside her ear.

Damon plunged a piece of the broken wood post into her chest and started reciting something in Greek.

I pulled the blade from her arm, it healed almost instantly. "What the-"

I stepped back letting Damon and Darren handle the mother.

I looked to the daughter and she put her hands up.

"I'm not here to fight. I do not participate in this nonesense my mother is caught up in."

"Give me the items." I walked up to the daughter.

She handed them to me. "All yours."

The mother let out a shriek.

"We will remain! You can't stop all of us."

"Yeah well, you won't live to see us succeed." Darren almost laughed.

Damon stopped reciting, and she crumbled to dust in Darren's hands.

The daughter laughed cruelly and clasped her hands together in delight.

"Thank you for releasing me from her" Darren spun round and held the same wood to the daughters throat with one hand his other arm pressed her into the desk. God he was strong.

"Don't be so quick to thank us Hestia." Damon started.

"What big plans does Daddy have for the Apocalypse?" Darren seethed.

She gave an unfriendly smile. "So you've figured out our little family tree huh?"

"Answer the question." Damon demanded.

"Those items will help you. I'm aware of your mission Elderwood's. I'm not on Daddy's batting team, if you remember he wasn't exactly the fathering type."

I wracked my brain for the brief increment of Greek mythology that I had learned.

God of time, this was his daughter and that was his wife. He devoured his children, Rhea wanted them to live. It would make sense for her to pine against her father.

"I still think we should kill you." Darren spoke low and deep, holding her tighter against the desk.

She chuckled. "You don't remember what you are Darren, Damon, do you? What a shame.

Kill me and you will be trapped here. I'm your ticket back to your own time handsome."

She flicked her eyes to me.

"You however, I don't know what you are. I just know you are a key, the items will call to you. How you were unaffected by my mothers powers is beyond me however."

"We are going to stop the apocalypse that's who we are." Damon said anger hinting in his voice.

"Such big talk. If you really are mere mortals now." she narrowed her eyes.

"Get that damn wood away from my throat boy, unless you fancy another nice toss across the room."

Damon nodded to Darren and Darren lowered the wood.

"Good child." She smoothed her blouse.

Darren mouthed to Damon "Child?" and looked like he was about to make a snide remark but Damon shook his head.

I found my voice. "Can you give us some answer's please Goddess Hestia?"

"Oh look at least one of you still have manners. It's revolting how you humans talk about us God's. Talk about a superiority complex."

Darren spoke.

"Seems to me your the one with the complex, we don't worship the old God's anymore. Therefore you've lost power thanks to us."

"Mind your tone with me boy!"

Damon spoke. "Hestia ignore my brother, he didn't mean to offend."

Darren glowered at him and remained silent.

"Well you are a vile little worm aren't you Darren? Damon- not much better. You are both pig headed."

"Goddess Hestia, ignore them both. We just want to keep the world in one piece. Can you please help us?"

"Children" She motioned to the guys. "Take notes, this is how you respect your elders."

"My father has part in the apocalypse. The items will help you. I also have this."

She pulled a map out from under the desk.

"I've marked where some of the items to stop my father are that I know of. I made a deal with the looney red eyed rat that dropped the few items I handed to you."

Damon spoke up. "You made a deal with a red eyed Demon? Are you aware-"

Hestia cut him off.

"Very aware. Demons are not much of a threat to me, just to you wee mortals."

"I understand why you hid from us Hestia." I started:

"You didn't know we were on your side, and you feel inclined to help because we share an enemy and we freed you of your mother?"

She pursed her lips "Precisely."

"I have a few rituals as well." She handed them to me with the map.

"Others you will find in that tome."

"That's all I can really help with. I hope your memories do return Elderwood brothers."

She turned her eyes to me. I kept mine slightly downcast out of respect.

"You.. I don't know what you are but you are important. It's good you are under the protection of the Elderwood brothers. You'll need it."

Before any of us could speak there was a loud noise all three of us cupped our ears and knelt down.

When I opened my eyes we were back in the hotel. Staring at the photo with it's broken frame. The photo was now blanched white. The items and such were in a bag still slung over my arm.

"Are you guys okay?" I looked at their bleeding faces and grimaced.

Confused how no one around us seemed to notice we just dissipated and then reappeared out of no where.

"We are fine Serena, we have had much worse." Damon tried to smile but his lip was swollen.

"Let's just get that stuff upstairs and see what we are working with." Darren stated and started toward the elevators.

Damon gave a half shrug and I followed them.

The girl in the elevator did not even acknowledge how beat up the guys looked. Her eyes merely widened slightly when she smiled in greeting. Perhaps she was being polite. Or maybe everyone here minded their own business.

The familiar "Ding" to the 13th floor rang out. Darren went ahead to unlock the door.

Once we were all inside Darren spoke up.

"What did she mean, who we are? Damon do you have any idea?"

Damon rubbed the back of his neck.

"I have some odd memories, some whacked out but realistic dreams. It's possible we don't remember everything from our past. I mean can you even recall what we were doing before we started trying to save the world? Cause I can't."

Darren groaned.

"No I can't. What- so your saying we have some sort of friggin' amnesia? Isn't that just perfect."

I thought to the dreams I had been having since I got here.

"I've been having some weird realistic dreams as well, just since being here. What about you Darren?"

"Yeah I have."

"Wait you too Serena?" Damon looked to me.

"Yeah, but I don't think it's my life I'm dreaming about. I think it's someone else's."

"Do you guys remember anything from childhood or how you learned so much about what goes bump in the night?"

"Honestly Serena no. But it seems you are caught up in the same sort of thing." Damon answered and Darren nodded in agreement.

"Well if a Greek God was aware and afraid of you I wonder what she knew that you don't?" Myself I mean I remember my childhood, school everything. She said I was something too, which I guess we kinda knew considering."

"I'm going to take a look at the tome." Damon moved toward the bag.

"Hey-" I placed my hand delicately onto his shoulder he relaxed into my touch.

"Let me fix your face a bit.. please." Damon turned to me.

"Sure, but it's not necessary."

"It is, I didn't get injured. It's the least I can do."

"You were smart to say the name aloud you know. It helped us formulate an attack, we would have been going in blind otherwise." Damon said kindly.

"Good. I was hoping it would help."

Damon sat at the table and I grabbed soapy warm water, a cloth and a couple other medical supplies.

I started to dab at his cuts and his lip. He winced slightly.

Darren was watching me.

"You're next." I gave him a small smile over my shoulder.

He scoffed. "I'm perfectly capable of wiping my own wounds. We survived this long without your help."

Man he was stubborn. I kept my voice level and calm.

"I have to stitch your head. Whether you want me to or not."

"It's fine." He said coldly.

"It's not." I offered sweetly.

"Oh Darren don't be such a hard ass. Let her help. She has before." Damon laughed.

"Your lip could use a stitch." I grazed my finger ever so gently over it.

"Whatever you say Doc." Damon smiled. I laughed a bit.

"Stitch his whole mouth shut while you're at it." Darren muttered.

Damon burst out laughing.

I put a couple of stitches in Damon's lip. Then got up and moved to the kitchen.

"Good as new." I tossed some ice from the freezer in a baggy to him.

"For your black eye"

He caught it effortlessly mid air. "Thanks"

"Your up Darren."

"I'm not into Doc/patient roleplay."

Damon snickered. "Sucks to be you I guess."

I laughed a bit. "I'm not a doctor. So you are safe."

"What Darren, would you rather I stitch you up? She's got a gentler touch, I can assure you."

Darren rolled his eyes but moved to sit nearby us. "Whatever."

"Much obliged, grouchy" I stated.

Damon snickered. There was a play of a smile on Darren's lips.

"You will both be the death of me, I swear." Darren said in a softer tone. "Just get the stitches over with."

"The only killjoy in here is you Darren" Damon teased.

I dabbed at the rest of the cuts on his face, wringing the cloth of blood before reaching the worst cut on his forehead, the skin was peeling back slightly. I disinfected it and started on the stitches. Darren sat still as stone, not even wincing. After a few minutes it was done.

"There you go. It wasn't so hard hm?"

I handed him a second bag of ice, and went to put the medical supplies back in the kitchen.

"Yeah.. thanks I guess." He said quietly.

"Don't worry about it. I'm happy to help however I can."

"We appreciate that." Damon said lightly.

I nodded.

"So I heard whispers this time, similar to when I grabbed the Aladdin lamp."

Damon nodded. "I figured as much."

"They silenced when Darren picked the Tiara up. The strange thing is they whispered Rhea's name to me. That's how I knew who it was, but I still am not sure why."

"It's possible there are some guardians that don't want the world to end, or don't agree with Cronos's ideal world."

"We have no way of knowing their true motives though." Darren added.

"So we proceed with caution." Damon finished.

I nodded.

"With a grain of salt then"

Damon was palming through the tome. He pulled a piece of paper out.

Darren's eyes widened. "The ritual?"

"Yeah-it's a few of the rituals actually, and a map of where she believes some items are hidden. She wasn't lying." Damon said then continued.

"Should we send her a thank you basket or something?"

Damon looked to me.

"I think we did enough for her." I said.

"I'm sure us stopping her father will be enough of a thank you."
Darren added.

"Alright. Do we have any lore on the tiara?" Damon started.

"I will look into it then, you got the tome?" Darren agreed.

"Sure do." Damon replied.

"Okay that leaves the little music box. I will take that one."

Damon and Darren looked at me.

"What? We are a team no?"

"Of course. Thanks Serena." Damon smiled.

"Just- be careful. We don't know what it is. Let alone what it can
do." Darren added.

"I will be, don't worry."

I walked over to their mini library and started reading through
the titles.

Many of them were in languages unfamiliar to me.

There was a faded copy of Grimm's fairytales.

I started to wonder why it was there, then imagined it was entirely
possible the fables were in fact a true document if everything else
was real, maybe this was too.

I began to flip through it.

I paused at the story of Ariel. Remembering the Disney
adaptation.

I laughed a bit. I looked at the music box. Hestia's warning that
the box contained a deadly lullaby was fresh in my mind.

I inspected to box. It was black with intricate designs of ships
and sea.

"Guys, do siren's exist?"

Damon and Darren both looked up.

"Yeah, but they aren't like they are in the stories" Damon
motioned to the book I was holding.

"They are ugly, evil, crafty creatures. They do lure people to
the water and drown them. They aren't a bunch of Ariel's" Darren
snickered.

"I would assume not. Have you guys ever run into one?"

"Not really, they aren't extinct but they aren't common either." Damon said instead.

"Do we have any lore on them?" I asked.

Damon stood up and walked to the shelf I was at. He grabbed a book about sea monsters and handed it to me. I looked at it dumbfounded.

"Sea monsters? Are you serious?"

Damon laughed. "Most everything is real. Even the grimm fairytales. Those are usually based on cursed objects."

"Like the objects we are collecting?"

Damon nodded. "Yeah some are cursed and some have guardians like the items today."

"Well colour me surprised."

"Yeah, let us know what you find in there." Darren said without looking our direction.

I nodded and Damon went back to flipping through the Tome.

I opened the book, scanning the index for siren lore.

Flipping to the page, I began to read.

It was pretty standard, they pose as a beautiful women or a dream of some sort to lure victims into the water and then they show their true form and drown them.

I read along. Davy Jones?

"Did you guys know these sirens are soldiers of Davy Jones?"

"Most creatures in the water are. Well the evil ones. There's also King Trident." Damon said.

I kept reading for a moment. Then a photo stood out to me. It was of the music box I was holding.

"I found it." I read out loud to them.

"The original siren song. Trapped in a warded box and used by Davy Jone's to control his soldiers of the sea. If used incorrectly the melody will be fatal to the beholder."

"Holy shit. Well I guess we don't open the friggin' thing." Darren said.

"Unless we need to." Damon added.

"Why would we need this do you think?" Darren asked directing his attention to Damon.

"Well. There will be one item we need from the water, I know that much. We will hang on to it. Keep it here where it's safe and warded and can't fall into the wrong hands."

"Sounds like it could come in handy, we should figure out what that box controls aside sirens." Damon finished.

I nodded and placed the box on the shelf with the book.

"You guys have any luck with your items?"

"It will take me a while to decode this Tome. So far nothing helpful." Damon said exasperated.

Darren spoke up. "Yeah this Tiara did belong to the first women in royalty. It was passed for generations, rumoured to bring protection and luck."

"Protection from what?"

"Witchcraft and some other forms of dark magic.

I exhaled. "Does it say anything else?"

"Yeah actually, that it was stolen back in 1969 by a women who wanted it destroyed. Never turned up again until now. Also the Tiara doesn't work alone it's paired with a necklace." Darren turned the book with the pictures to us.

I gasped when I saw the picture.

"That-it looks identical to my necklace, the one I've had for as long as I can remember."

I pulled the pendant out of the top of my dress to show.

"I thought it looked vaguely familiar." Darren nodded.

Damon came over to look closer at the picture and the necklace.

"You don't know when you got that?" Damon asked.

I shook my head. "Honestly I think it was given to me as an infant I started wearing it when I started school."

"From your mom?" Damon asked.

"No, Great grandmother."

"Well now we know why Rhea couldn't harm you. The necklace protected you, she uses dark magic for most of her powers. Since most people now do not worship the old Gods they often resort to dark powerful spells." Damon continued.

"So this belongs to you Serena." Darren held out the tiara.

"Aren't these items warded?" I took half a step back.

"You do have the necklace."

I rubbed the necklace gently between my fingers.

"Thank you." I said as I took it from Darren's outstretched hands.

When I grabbed the tiara, I waited to see if the voices returned. Much to my relief, they didn't.

"Wow so I guess we are in the presence of royalty huh?" Damon gave a half ass bow.

Darren cleared his throat uncomfortably.

"Guys we don't know that."

I flushed at the idea of being something so extravagant.

"It belongs to you either way." Damon smiled. "May I?"

He was asking to put the tiara on my head.

"Uh-I"

"Damon don't put it on her just incase. We should research it a bit more." Darren said hurriedly.

Damon's smile fell slightly. "Fair point"

He put the tiara on the shelf next to the music box. I exhaled.

"Could have some bad mojo, the other objects all seem to have a bad side." Darren shrugged.

"Most helpful items do have a negative side effect. I should've thought of that."

"Where's the other item you wanted to hunt today Damon?"

Damon studied the map. "There's a museum nearby, they might have the red shoes."

Darren groaned. "Cursed object. That's just awesome."

"It's not far from here."

"Let's go then. I need to call Rayne too."

Damon nodded and Darren moved to the door.

We got to the car and Darren took the keys.

"Shotgun!" Damon laughed.

I rolled my eyes. "I'd rather the backseat, can stretch out that way."

"No one likes riding back." Damon retorted.

"I do!"

It wasn't a lie.

Damon shook his head at me "Well good least then I don't have to fight you for shotgun"

I shrugged. "Guess not."

Darren revved the Volvo to start. I picked up my phone. I had a missed call from my mom and several from Rayne.

I called my voicemail. It was my mothers voice. We hadn't talked in a few years, my body was on edge, afraid of what the voicemail might say. I clicked off of it and went to dial Rayne instead.

She answered on the first ring as always.

"Serena! I've been dying to hear from you!"

"Hey Rayne sorry, I've been busy with-"

"Omg tell me the boys! You are with them right now aren't you! So sexy working a case together, you gotta get a little prisoner/cop roleplay going?"

My face went white hot.

I looked up at Darren and Damon, it was obvious they could hear Rayne on the other end, her voice was so loud. They were both trying not to smile.

"Yes Rayne I'm with them. Working a case that's all."

Rayne laughed loudly. "Sure you go with that! I can't wait to hear all the dirty details- "

I cut her off.

"Rayne focus a minute please" I laughed embarrassed that the guys heard her.

"Okay but you gotta tell me later okay?"

I laughed in spite myself.

"I will report that nothing happened."

I dared a glance at the guys Damon was smirking, Darren was focused on driving.

She blew raspberry in the phone. "Don't be so frigid. No man likes that. But also don't be a slut- I mean that's not what I was saying."

I shook my head at her ramblings and opted for a topic change.

"I will take the house. And I am eternally grateful for you and Matt helping with this"

Rayne squealed in delight so loud, that I had to pull the phone from my ear.

"Yay! Oh my God I'm so happy to hear that! You had me worried you were going to flop on it."

"I'll call the Realtor right away, Matt and I will handle the paperwork. We will have you sign this afternoon for possession. Sound good? Say round 3?"

"Yeah that'll work Rayne. Thank you so much. Really."

"Don't even mention it!" She yelled to Matt over the phone. "Matt babe she said yes!"

Matt let out a loud "Woooo" in the background.

I laughed.

"Thanks guys, talk later?"

"You got it! Byeeee. Oh also..Details! Come on girl get that sweet sweet-"

I interrupted her quickly.

"Rayne oh my god, talk to you later."

I hung the phone up before she could say anything worse. I covered my face with my hands so embarrassed I couldn't even speak.

Damon was looking at me over his shoulder. "You okay?" He was trying not to laugh.

"Oh my god.. don't even say anything, did you guys hear everything?"

Damon couldn't hold back his laugh. I wanted to curl up in a ball.

Darren looked at me in the rearview mirror.

"Oh we didn't hear much except you going after the sweet-" Damon teased.

"Oh my God, Shut up Damon! Jesus." I couldn't help giggling nervously.

Darren was smiling too.

"Your friend is quite the character." Darren said.

"She's spirited. I'm not- it's not"

I fought for words to try to explain I wasn't trying to sleep with them. I fell back against the seat.

"You guys weren't even- it wasn't meant to be heard. I never said to her that I was-"

I kept stumbling pathetically over my words.

"It's okay. You don't gotta defend yourself its all in good fun" Damon smiled at me over his shoulder.

"We are here" Darren pulled into the lot and put the Volvo in park.

We all climbed out. I looked around.

"I've been to this museum multiple times in the past, I had no idea there were dangerous items until now."

"Ignorance is bliss" Darren stated.

Damon held the door open for me.

"Ladies first"

"You are really polite for a playboy." I teased.

Damon put his hand to his chest in mock offence.

"Such cruel words from the beautiful women"

Darren laughed deeply. "She isn't wrong, slut."

"Yeah yeah shut up, virgin. If you didn't act like you had a stick shoved up your petty ass all the time maybe you would get laid more often too."

Darren laughed. "Whatever helps you sleep at night."

I tried to cover my laugh.

We started up the stairs to the second floor.

"It should be up here." Damon said studying the map he grabbed.

I started to hear the ballet to swan lake. It was quiet.

"I-do you guys hear swan lake playing?"

They both stopped to listen.

"No." Darren said "Where do you hear it from?"

I pointed to a room on the right.

"I don't hear it either." Damon agreed and we moved toward the room. As we neared the ballet got louder and louder. I put my hands to my ears.

"We must be close, it's so loud, it's so so loud guys." I bent down to my knees.

"Stay with her no need for her to get so close I will go ahead and see what we are dealing with." Darren commanded and walked forward Damon sat beside me.

He put his hands over my hands to help cover my ears.

"Hang in there Serena."

He said out loud I assumed but I read his lips. The ballet was so loud it drowned out Damon's voice.

Darren came back in what seemed like 10 minutes when it was probably only a couple. He ushered us down the stairs the ballet was still blaring.

Damon guided me still keeping his hands over my ears. I leaned into him.

Only when we left the museum did the ballet silence.

Damon removed his hands and I did too.

"There Serena, you okay?" Darren asked.

I nodded and tried to catch my breath.

"Did you find them?" Damon asked as I gathered myself.

Darren nodded. "Yeah, heavy security."

"Figures." I said.

"We will return tonight. We will need a cover. Cop won't cut it this time I don't think." Darren said.

"Serena you should stay back at the hotel. With how much of an effect they had on you I'm not sure you would be able to help all that much." Darren said to me.

His words stung slightly, but he was right, with how loud it was it rendered me unusable.

Damon shot him a look.

"I agree Darren, it's fine I will hang back but you guys have to promise to be careful."

Damon looked surprised at my response and Darren just nodded.

"Think we have been successful for today. Let's head back. You can meet up with Rayne and sign for your house. Also congrats on it." Damon smiled.

"We will continue researching and see you after we grab the red shoes from the museum." Damon continued.

I nodded.

"Good plan" Darren said as he drove the Volvo back to the hotel.

I drifted to sleep with the hum of the engine.

Chapter 8

TWIN FLAME

"Stare unto me my gaze of flame, let your blood run thick,
molasses in your vein, fiery passion, anger in my glare, I am you
and you are me, to burn within this twin flame."

There I could feel the plane drop much too fast. Oxygen masks fell from the compartments above. Screams of so many people. Ears popping, and then the impact. So cold, everything was so cold. I just wanted warmth. Dead everyone was dead... I'm so cold. My head is in agony, the air is too harsh in my lungs.. Arms wrapped around me. My legs are broken it's impossible to move. His arms are so strong so comforting. He's telling me he's gonna save us, he pulls us out of the wreckage, but I know I will die. The voice sounds achingly familiar. I long to see his face. I long for warmth. An image my husband? Two children, young 2 and 4 maybe, getting read to board a plane. Their grandparents maybe? "We will take the kids for the first week and then meet you there. "Enjoy your honeymoon!" I hug the two children tears spilling from my eyes. A bad feeling. Something's not right. "Maybe we should all go together?..." I held longer..

"You two haven't gone on Vacation together since before the kids were born, enjoy some one on one time!" My husband nods his head. I lean down, I kiss their heads and tell them they are the best thing that ever happened to me and that I love them with all my heart. Their little hands it was like they were gracing my skin now. I wanted to cry harder then I already was. I miss them. I miss them so much.

Then I am in a car, Soft tunes, then the sudden whip of the vehicle, crunching metal, shattering windows, so loud in my ears, Blood, metallic and bitter it's all I can taste in my mouth my body crushed..I can't move, my face doesn't feel right, oh God help me. Please help me. I hear his voice pleading begging for me to be alive, but I cannot move my mouth to reply. I want to stroke his hair, I want to tell him I'm here but I can't move. His voice too is familiar, safe. I wanted to see his face, I wanted to speak.. what about the baby?...What will happen to our baby?..Then an image of us Younger then we are in the car. Blood in a bathroom,

I'm crying arms wrapped around me, there so much blood. "We will keep trying trying for a baby. We will keep trying. We are at a hospital, long needles are being poked into my skin. They hurt. A nurse speaks " As far as fertility treatments go we have given every one under the sun. You may want to look at adoption if this doesn't take, especially after so many miscarries." I held longer to the dream. My husband, the voice so light and loving, so familiar. "Don't worry. I have a good feeling about this one, don't lose hope my darling. We will do this. We can get through this. We will be parents I promise you. "I feel like my body is failing me. It's not doing what it's built to do. I don't understand. " I cry helplessly against his chest. "It's not your fault. Shh now"

When I woke up, I was laying on the couch in the guys room.

"Hey rise and shine" Damon teased.

"Well if it ain't sleeping beauty." Darren added.

I rubbed my eyes. My heart hammering in my chest from my dream.

"Oh God, I don't even remember falling asleep, how did I get here?"

"Carried you. You were out like a light." Damon said.

"The object hunting seems to be affecting you a bit." He continued.

"Here." Darren handed me a glass of ice water.

"Thank you. I don't know I just felt drained. How long was I asleep?"

"Only an hour." Damon smiled. "You still have plenty of time before you meet with Rayne to sign for your house."

"Well thank you, sorry I fell asleep like that."

"You don't need to apologize for sleeping Serena" Darren said without looking at me.

"Have you guys figured what cover would work best to undergo security? What about just a security guard?"

"One of us will pose as a guard the other as a janitor."

"I'm not being the janitor this time" Darren said. "I will be the guard."

Damon shrugged. "Let's flip a coin."

Darren rolled his eyes but pulled an odd looking coin out of his sweater pocket.

"Call it" He tossed the coin in the air.

"Tails"

"Damn"

"What tails?"

"What do you think genius?" He tossed the coin to Damon.

Damon chuckled.

I smiled. "I'm sure you guys will do well. Be careful."

"Always are." Damon said lightly.

"You too, watch out for yourself." Darren barely glanced to me.

They left me in the room.

I took a moment to collect myself. I kept thinking about how excited I was to meet Rayne to sign for that little cottage. I felt selfish for being excited about something so mundane when I was trying to save the planet but something about it felt right.

I put some coffee to brew and sat down. I couldn't get why my mom left a voicemail after not speaking to me for 3 years. I hated myself for being afraid to open it.

We didn't have a falling out exactly. But she ran back to the guy that abused us growing up, after being separated for a long time. I guess I just found it hard to accept. She also never approved of Henry, I met Henry so young and had never been with another person. He was older then me scooped me up young. She didn't trust him. I see now she was just trying to protect me, but I was so defensive. Henry wasn't always bad either, still now after everything I don't believe he was a bad person. Maybe I loved him too hard for too long and it blinded me. I still missed him. Now even still, I felt she was hypocritical running back to the man that hurt us so after so much time. Losing my dad was horrible, I missed him dearly he was an amazing man. Losing him was so hard on my mom, and she stayed single for a long time struggling to keep me and her fed. Then Nick came. He was incredible for a while. He was one of my dads close friends he was really there for us when he died. He was well off in comparison as well. Really helped my mom get us back onto our feet, when she was doing everything in her power to provide for us, working multiple jobs. I had a lot of pleasant memories of Nick growing up. Once I was a teenager though he lost his own father and got into drinking. He was a brutal drunk. Mom always made excuses like it wasn't him hurting us, it was the booze. That's why I never drank. I hated what it turned people into. Mom swore he was not drinking anymore when they got back together, but I could just tell it was a lie. I pulled myself from my reminiscing. I would listen to her voicemail. She was my mom after all, I missed her too she also lived in BC so it was a fair bit of a drive to see her from Alberta. We used to talk on the phone often though.

My thoughts flicked to Darren and Damon. I felt very protective of them, and very safe around them. I also really just wanted to understand what I was. The idea that the demon that tried to kill me was still out there unnerved me. I had so many questions, I wanted to learn more about what they killed and what other people killed. It's like a world of shadows that just always lingered and never saw the light of day. The public so blissfully unaware. Like an underground society of heroes.

I hoped their trek into the museum would go seamlessly. I also wondered what was guarding the item there, and if they could handle it. I mean they have been at this a long time so I shouldn't worry but it was hard not to. I poured a cup of coffee. I carried it to the bookshelf and ran my hand along the titles.

"Demonic races"

I pulled it out. Maybe this would help us identify the demon that attacked me.

I flipped through it my heart racing as I read, realizing these were all real things.

"Black eye demons" I skimmed the article. "Lowest level of demons, no powers aside possession, well trained killers. Easily disguise as humans"

Method to dispose: Exorcism. Weakened deeply and burned by holy water

"Red eyed demons" "The peddlers, deal makers, soul collectors." I kept skimming. "Commonly referred to as reapers. Second tier demons" You will not see them unless you are actively seeking to make a deal, or nearing the veil.

Method to dispose: If you are not the one nearing the veil or in the deal you will not affect them. Only way to send back is for the victim to use a knife blessed by a priest the moment before the deal is up, or the victim is on their last breath.

Exorcism from someone unaffected by the demon will send the demon away temporarily.

"Purple eyed demons" "Abilities concerning heat/electricity and can make a humans blood boil with a single touch." I kept skimming. "Bounty hunters" Third tier Demon "Can possess and kill host from the inside out" Deadly when encountered. Will kill without purpose.

Method to dispose: Must be trapped by a pentagram drawn with the victims own blood. If there is no time to prep this, can be killed with a knife blessed by a priest and coated in the victims blood. Exorcism ineffective. Holy water will only piss it off.

I kept reading.

"White eyed demons"

I dropped my coffee cup and it shattered loudly on the floor.

My hand shook as I guided myself through the article.

"Highest and strongest tier of demon." "None documented" "Handpicked by Lucifer." "Rumoured to have Lethal psychic abilities as well as abilities portraying to cold." No one that has ever seen one and lived to tell about it has been documented" "Most of these knights remain in Hell and do the torturing to condemned souls/ keep order of other demons."

"Rumoured there are only 9 in creation."

Method to dispose: Unknown.

I shut the book quickly, sweat was dripping down my forehead. I swiped my shaking hand over it.

"Oh god. Why is that thing after me?" I whispered out loud to myself.

I spoke out loud when I was afraid and alone usually. It seemed to help settle my nerves.

I looked to the shattered ceramic on the ground and started to pick it up with my hands. I didn't notice it cutting me until I looked at my hands after I threw away the broken pieces.

"oh-ouch." I washed my hands in the sink and grabbed a dish rag to clean the floor. After I cleaned the coffee I decided to reopen the book to the page I was reading for Darren and Damon to see when they came back.

A pang of worry hit me.

"Should I just go check on them?" I wondered what time it was.

I decided to head down to the lobby and I would make my way outside. I could call Rayne and maybe the guys too to check up on them.

I locked the door and headed to the elevators. I greeted the tenant with a smile which he returned. I walked out to the lobby and out the front door. The front desk was busy and did not comment on my leave.

When I got outside I scanned the parking lot. No black SUV. I sighed outwardly.

The boys volvo was not in sight either.

I went to my car unlocking the doors. I checked my phone it was 230. I had no missed calls or texts. The house was about 20 minutes from here, I could make my way there now. I was suppose to sign at 3, Rayne mentioned. I glanced slightly at the notification above my voicemail. I hovered my finger over it. Then I put my phone away and decided to drive to the house. I started my car and exited the parking lot.

* * *

My mind was lost in thought and I could scarcely remember the drive. When I pulled up I saw Rayne's Jag parked in the driveway her and Matt were standing speaking with the Realtor at the front door.

I pulled my car up behind Rayne's she glanced my direction and waved enthusiastically to me. Matt turned and gave a slight wave and a smile. I waved and smiled back.

Suddenly quite excited, looking at this beautiful little cottage that was about to be mine.

I closed and locked my car and hurried to Rayne whom embraced me tightly.

"You made it just in time! We just glossed over all the details!"

"Thank you so much." I hugged her tightly looking over her shoulder to Matt.

"Really, thank you both so much."

"Don't even mention it." Matt smiled and clamped me on the shoulder.

"Sign here please Serena." The Realtor handed a clipboard with papers and pen over to me.

I couldn't help but be a bit nervous. This was cheaper then rent, not cheaper then the hotel, but it would be home.

I hoped that I could help Damon and Darren and keep this house. I signed the paper.

Thank you and congrats, here's the deed to the house it's all yours. The Realtor left the property dropping the keys into my hands. Rayne ran and hugged me again.

"Oh my god, Serena I'm so happy for you! Lets go inside!!"

I smiled back. "I couldn't have this without you and Matt, honestly I owe you guys everything."

"Nonesense!" Rayne laughed.

"If roles were switched I know you would do the same for me."

She wasn't wrong.

"Of course, okay let go inside!"

I started to walk up with Rayne when my phone rang. I didn't recognize the number. Afraid it was one of the guys in trouble I answered.

"Hello?"

There was silence on the other end.

"Hello?" I asked again.

I was about to hang up when a voice came through.

"Serena?"

My heart dropped.

"Mom?"

Rayne spun around and looked at me wide eyed. She knew all about us not speaking.

The line clicked off.

I hit redial and it directed me to a psychiatric hospital in Vancouver.

I felt my phone slip from my hands. Rayne wrapped an arm around me and Matt ran over.

"What's wrong?" he asked.

"Her mom just called." Rayne answered for me.

Matt picked my phone up and put it back to my hand, I glanced at the screen. Just one small crack.

"What did she say Serena?" Rayne asked creasing her brow.

I took a steadying breath. "She just said my name and it dropped the call, I called back and it's from a psychiatric hospital. In Vancouver."

"Oh God. I'm sorry Serena." Rayne hugged me and I made no move to return the embrace.

"We can book a flight and go see whats happening Serena we will go with you." Matt said encouragingly. Rayne nodded in agreement.

"I just checked, the earliest flight we can get is Wednesday, two weeks from now." Matt turned his phone to me.

"Two weeks, it would be faster to drive. Maybe I should just call and see what she's there for. "

"I will book it anyways okay? We can always cancel." Matt said.

I nodded. "Thank you so much, you guys really don't need to do that for me though."

"Nonsense." Rayne said. "Do you still wanna go into your house?"

"Maybe we should hold off hun, she might just want some time to herself." Matt put an arm around Rayne.

"I- yes I'm sorry thank you so much for everything guys but I'm going to try to reach my mom and maybe grab a coffee okay? Just need to gather my thoughts."

"Of course" she gave me a huge smile.

Rayne knew I preferred to be alone when things got stressful. I loved her for it.

"Call us when you want help to settle in or if you need anything okay?"

Rayne said as her and Matt started to walk back to her jag.

I grasped the keys tightly in my hand. Looking to the house that was now mine.

Matt pulled the jag out of the drive and they both waved to me. I managed to wave back.

I went to make sure the door was locked without going inside. I was afraid I would ruin the excitement. It was locked. I put the house key with my car key and walked to my car.

When I sat down I dialed my voicemail as my hands shook.

"You have one unread message, play your message now?"

I clicked 1.

After a moment my moms voice came through. I held my breath.

"Serena, it's mom. Don't be alarmed by where I'm calling from. I just wanted to phone and check in with you and ask if we could see each other soon. I-" There was noise in the background someone telling her to get off of the phone.

"I love you sweetie." Click.

I exhaled. Aside from the background sounded like she was okay, but it didn't answer why she was there.

I saved the message.

It was 430 I decided to head back to the hotel.

I drove mindlessly and before long I found myself back at the hotel. The guys volvo was parked. I was relieved to see their car. I parked beside them this time and got out, locking my door and heading to the lobby making sure no one was watching me, as to regular people it did look like I was sneaking into a condemned building.

"Welcome back miss!" The lady at the desk greeted me.

I waved and smiled and headed to the elevators.

When the door opened Damon and Darren were there. To my delight they both looked like they had no fresh wounds.

"Serena!" We were just about to come give you a call. Damon smiled

"Hey guys." I smiled back.

Darren turned to the bellhop in the elevator.

"Can you just take us all back up?"

He nodded closed the doors, pressing number 13 for us.

We rode up in silence. The bellhop tipped his hat.

"Thanks so much" I said to him as the doors closed again.

"So did you get your house?" Damon asked.

"Yes, I didn't go in yet though." I looked down a bit.

"How come?"

"It's not important" I shrugged it off, I wasn't sure I wanted to talk about it just yet.

Damon looked like he was going to ask again. So I decided to ask another question.

"What about you guys, did you secure the item? Damon held a fabric bag up that had some symbols on it.

"We did." Damon said and smiled.

"No one danced to death?"

"Nah." Darren said. "Swan lake isn't exactly *dance worthy.*"

"Not the ballet shoes type huh Darren?" I joked.

He scoffed. "Talk to twinkle toes over there" He nodded to Damon.

"You?" I couldn't help but chuckle. "Honestly that's pretty interesting."

Darren's eyebrows shot up.

"Yeah so what, Darren you couldn't dance to save your life."

"If that day ever comes I got you to dance for me prancer."

Damon laughed heartily.

"Just Ballet?" I asked.

Darren chortled. "Nah he's the dancing queen."

"Dance kept me in excellent shape" He chuckled patting his stomach.

"So does training combat. Maybe if you spent more time training and less time twirling you would be a better fighter." Darren joked.

"Yeah, maybe if you spent less hours training and more hours dancing you would actually find a women willing to tolerate you for more then one evening."

Darren scoffed. "There's no way."

Damon laughed.

"Oh yeah, a man that can dance, girls melt over it, why do you think I stuck with it so long? Serena back me up here."

Damon nodded to me.

I laughed a bit. "He's not wrong, girls do love when a guy can dance well."

"Well I'll be friggin' damned"

Darren unlocked the door to our room. He tossed the bag onto the counter by the genie lamp.

"How was the rest of your day Serena?" Damon asked as he locked the door behind us.

I glanced to the demon book I was reading. Remembering I needed to show it to them.

"Well aside from signing for my house, I read up on Demons. I found something of interest."

Damon walked over and Darren followed.

They both skimmed over the page I read.

"Damn it." Darren put his hands through his hair and walked to the fridge to grab a beer.

Damon sat down and re-read it several times before speaking.

We haven't run into any of these, just the blacked eyed and well-"

Darren cut him off. "Just the most powerful white eyed un-kill-able one. That what, never has been reported before. No one even seeing it? Oh and to top it all off it's hand picked by the devil himself."

"Yeah, in a nutshell." Damon agreed.

"Well that's just friggin' awesome." The sarcasm was evident in Darren's tone.

Fear crept through me. I thought they would know what to do.

"We will figure it out." Damon said confidently as he flipped more through the book.

"Good find on the book Serena. It's strange I skimmed this shelf countless times and I don't remember seeing this one. Did it call out to you at all?"

"No, it didn't"

"Maybe I just missed it then." Damon continued

"You should stay with us until we figure this out Serena. If that's alright with you?"

My heart fluttered slightly. Of course it was alright. I felt way safer with them then alone.

"Yeah, of course." I smiled. "Not really in the mood to become a human ice sculpture today."

"No kidding." Damon closed the book.

"Let's put up all the warding we know of to start." Darren grabbed a can of spray paint from his duffle bag.

"Spray paint, won't the hotel be upset?" I was genuinely curious.

"You can only see the symbols in black light. They won't scan the room with black light."

"Makes sense."

"We have been doing this a long time Serena" Damon laughed. "We know a few tricks."

Darren started on the spray paint he was copying from the book that I found when I first met them.

Damon grabbed another can and moved to help.

I walked up to look at the symbols they were copying.

"I'm glad that book was useful for you guys."

"Us too, because of the way it came to you, we weren't sure what was in it. But since reading it we have learned a few new things that we didn't before. Like some of this warding." Damon gestured to the book.

"What's tonight's plan?" I asked.

"We were thinking we could all grab supper then kinda do our own thing. Celebrate the few wins we have had in the last two days."

I smiled. "That's a great idea, got to celebrate big and small wins often in a long fight like this, so you don't lose yourself in it."

Damon smiled, "Yeah try telling that to Darren."

I glanced to Darren.

He rolled his eyes.

"There is so much responsibility on our shoulders, I don't see a point in wasting what precious time we have." He took a swing of his beer.

"We don't have the luxury." His voice was sour and he continued:

"You guys go do whatever. I will stay and continue reading where Serena left off."

Darren plopped himself at the table and began thumbing through the book.

I took a minute to try and think about what to say.

"Told you" Damon motioned to Darren.

"Stubborn as shit. I'll be in the diner, care to join me Serena?" He lifted his arm for me to grab.

When I hesitated he put it down non nonchalantly. I took a breath.

"Darren, I understand where you are coming from. But we are no good to anyone if we neglect ourselves. We have to keep our head straight, focus on the bigger picture, yes, but we are no good to anyone burnt out."

Darren shifted in the chair, but didn't reply.

Damon sighed loudly. "She's right man. So Serena will you join me? Talking to him is like talking to a wall sometimes."

I tried again. "Darren." I lightened my tone. "With great power comes great responsibility." I put my hand to my hip and smiled.

Damon burst out laughing.

Darren met my eyes. "Did you just quote friggin' Spider-Man to me?"

I held my laugh back and continued in the same playful tone. "And with great responsibility we hold the responsibility to take care of ourselves too. Yes? That's the only way we can ensure we do our best for everyone else."

I walked past Darren toward Damon and grabbed my coat.

"You coming Spidey?" I said playfully over my shoulder.

Darren slammed the book shut and got up. "Only if you never call me that again."

I laughed. "I won't make any promises."

Damon laughed again.

"Don't." Darren said firmly as he pushed past Damon.

Damon hummed the Spider-Man theme song under his breath. As we made our way to the elevator I laughed.

Darren smiled. "Yeah, yeah okay guys shut up already."

"So dinner first?" I asked excitedly.

Damon smiled at me. "Whatever you want."

We walked out of the elevator and headed to the diner. I glanced around. Damon motioned to an empty booth.

They sat on either side, leaving me a choice who to sit beside.

Darren was glancing at a menu. Damon smiled to me.

After a brief hesitation, I moved to sit with Damon.

I immediately regretted it as Jane bounded up to us.

Darren let out an annoyed low sigh and continued to look at the menu.

Damon flashed her a brilliant smile.

I looked to her and smiled too. "Hi, nice to see you again."

She barely nodded to me her eyes were locked to Damon's face. Damon was looking at the menu now. Not at Jane.

"I'll get chicken pecan salad please" Damon said and looked up to hand Jane the menu. Her smile faltered slightly.

"Sure, love"

"Cheeseburger fries. Thanks." She took Darren's menu. Without really looking at him.

"Fish for me."

You got it, coffees all around?"

"Beer for me, not coffee." Darren said.

Jane rolled her eyes.

"Coffees lovely." I said and Damon nodded.

She walked away glancing back at Damon over her shoulder.

"Um, should I?" I went to move and Damon rested his hand on mine briefly.

"No, Serena it's quite alright." he moved his hand back quickly.

"Okay Jane just seemed bothered that's all."

"That's how he wants her" Darren chimed in.

I laughed slightly. "You are a player aren't you?"

Darren snickered. "Slut you mean."

Damon shrugged and smiled.

Jane dropped the drinks off. Again Damon acted cooler toward her and she was very obviously upset about it, but she didn't say anything. She didn't look back this time.

"I think you are being cruel Damon, she clearly adores you." I said quietly to him.

"Mmm I will make it up to her after dinner."

Darren groaned. "We need separate rooms I swear."

"Hey if you ever manage to get laid, I wouldn't complain about giving the room up."

Plus I figure you would just go self sabotage in the bar after this anyway. I don't judge how you decompress. Although sex is wildly healthier then drinking, I would argue."

Darren rolled his eyes. "Now who's judging?"

"What about you Serena?" Damon looked at me. "How do you decompress?"

I shifted slightly. I was only ever with Henry, never was one to get around. I had a lot of hobbies and interests but none really to decompress. Singing perhaps, but I wouldn't dare say that as it was reserved for the shower. Art, but I was a terrible artist. Reading, but I couldn't pin point a favourite book. Perhaps dancing, I danced everyday regardless of what I was doing.

Our food came as a welcome distraction from the question.

"I like spending time with Rayne." I said after a while. "I like to help people, that calms me."

Damon nodded. "Explains the nursing aid. Think you would've pursued that further?"

"You mean if I didn't have random abilities, a high power demon after me and wasn't trying to save the world?"

I laughed before continuing. "Yeah, maybe"

Damon smiled. "Fair point."

Darren stayed silent as we finished our meals.

Damon paid. I stood up and he waved Jane over. I decided to go to the washroom.

"Thanks for dinner guys, I will get it tomorrow."

"Of course" Damon smiled at me.

Jane brushed past me purposefully, and went straight into Damon's arms.

I laughed slightly. Marking her territory, little did she know she probably wasn't the only one Damon was sleeping with. I hoped my assumption was wrong. I felt bad for her, she clearly liked him quite a bit. I headed to the bathroom not expecting the guys to wait for me to return. The bathroom was empty when I got in. I walked to the mirror, I always left my hair down. It had a natural wave to it. The white dress I was wearing fit my figure beautifully. I wasn't sure what to do with my night. There was a noise in the far stall. Guess someone else was in here after all. I turned the faucet on and wet my hands. I yelped when the water went suddenly frigid. The door to the stall slammed open, but no one came out. I could see my breath now and the mirror began to house tendrils of frost.

"Oh God.. no, not here. The demon." I barely whispered.

I started to move toward the door when I saw a figure in the mirror. A women.

She looked startlingly similar to me, like my own reflection, but her face shape was different, she had dark hair and different eyes.

"Ser....re...na..."

I fell to the floor her voice was like knives in my ears. My hands cupped my ears with all my strength.

The pain and noise was similar to earlier at the museum.

"H..e...lp.."

"Pl..ease."

The words were broken and sounded like they were coming through static.

The frost coated the mirror suddenly shattering it. I screamed and ducked down. Glass slid into my skin. It burned like fire. The voice stopped, the reflection gone. The room was warm again I realized as darkness crept over my vision.

Chapter 9

DREAMSCAPE

"To wander everlasting, through cotton candy clouds, lavender fields, enveloped by warmth, Serenity, I will slumber here forevermore, I ask thee, never wake me."

There I could feel the plane drop much too fast. Oxygen masks fell from the compartments above. Screams of so many people. Ears popping, and then the impact. So cold, everything was so cold. I just wanted warmth. Dead everyone was dead... I'm so cold. My head is in agony, the air is too harsh in my lungs.. Arms wrapped around me. My legs are broken it's impossible to move. His arms are so strong so comforting. He's telling me he's gonna save us, he pulls us out of the wreckage, but I know I will die. The voice sounds achingly familiar. I long to see his face. I long for warmth. An image my husband? Two children, young 2 and 4 maybe, getting read to board a plane. Their grandparents maybe? "We will take the kids for the first week and then meet you there. "Enjoy your honeymoon!" I hug the two children tears spilling from my eyes. A bad feeling. Something's not right. "Maybe we should all go together?..."

"You two haven't gone on Vacation together since before the kids were born, enjoy some one on one time!" My husband nods his head. I lean down, I kiss their heads and tell them they are the best thing that ever happened to me and that I love them with all my heart. Their little hands it was like they were gracing my skin now. I wanted to cry harder then I already was. I miss them. I miss them so much. I held longer. I look to my children, and remember when I first gave birth, when I saw them for the first time. True love. The only form of true love I imagine. My first baby as he was laid on my chest. The feeling of overwhelm. The pain. I remembered not understanding why there was still so much pain when they put him on me. I cried as much as the baby did, I was so terrified I wouldn't do good enough and the need I had to give him the world was inexplicably intense. "Your an amazing mother. Never forget that." My husband kisses my forehead and wraps me in his arms.

Then I am in a car, Soft tunes, then the sudden whip of the vehicle, crunching metal, shattering windows, so loud in my ears, Blood , metallic and bitter it's all I can taste in my mouth my body crushed..I can't move, my face doesn't feel right, oh God help me. Please help me. I hear his voice pleading begging for me to be alive, but I cannot move my mouth to reply. I want to stroke his hair, I want to tell him I'm here but I can't move. His voice too is familiar, safe. I wanted to see his face, I wanted to speak.. what about the baby?...What will happen to our baby?..Then an image of us Younger then we are in the car. Blood in a bathroom, I'm crying arms wrapped around me, there so much blood. "We will keep trying trying for a baby. We will keep trying. We are at a hospital, long needles are being poked into my skin. They hurt. A nurse speaks " As far as fertility treatments go we have given every one under the sun. You may want to look at adoption if this doesn't take, especially after so many miscarries." My husband, the voice so light and loving, so familiar. "Don't worry. I have a good feeling about this one, don't lose hope my darling. We will do this. We can get through this. We will be parents I promise you. "I feel like my body is failing me. It's not doing what it's built to do. I don't understand. " I cry helplessly against his chest. "It's not your fault. Shh now" I held longer, It' later and im holding a positive test in my hands. My body aching from treatment. My heart swelling, nothing but pure joy. I can't believe it. "You are one in a million." I whisper as I caress my belly. "I can't wait to tell your Daddy."

When I came too a waitress was standing over me. She looked almost like a child.

"Oh my God. Are you okay?"

"I.." I looked at my glass punctured hands, blood slowly trickled from them.

"Oh god, I will get a bandage for your arm!"

I glanced over my entire right arm was glittering with glass and blood.

"I-wait."

The waitress turned to me.

"How long have I been in here?"

"I came as soon as I heard the glass shatter! It only took me asking you once for you to come too. What happened?"

I shook my head, unsure how to explain.

"Oh nevermind it, I will be right back!"

She rushed out of the bathroom. I guess that meant I wasn't hardly unconscious for more then a few minutes. How did I dream so much in such a short period of time? And who or what was that women? I thought back to the notes, seemed like a ghost. It didn't hurt me. It asked for help. I'd have to run it by the guys tomorrow, not ruin their night tonight. She didn't hurt me. I hoped no one else was in danger.

The dreams were so real, every time I had them, it felt like I was really there.

The bathroom door opened again and she came bustling in with a first aid kit.

"Here lets clean this up, shall we?"

"Thank you, really so much, how careless of me, breaking the mirror." I forced a small laugh.

She raised her eyebrows at me. "Give me your arm."

I did. She started shuffling in the box. She removed what looked like tweezers but larger.

"This will have to do for digging the glass out."

"How old are you?" I asked after she dug a couple pieces out of my arm.

"Hey don't you know it's rude to go around asking a lady her age, don't you have any manners?"

"Sorry-I you just look pretty young."

"I am young, not that it's any of your business. I'm fixing your arm so you should just thank me then shut your pie hole" she snapped.

I laughed a bit. "Thank you, I'm sorry for asking. I wasn't trying to undermine your obvious first aid skills."

She kept grabbing the glass from my arm in silence for a few moments.

"I'm 12. Well almost 13 so I'm almost a lady okay? And I know what I'm doing." She pulled a bigger piece of glass out and I winced slightly. Least I don't go round smashing mirrors all willy nilly. Are you sure you aren't young yourself?"

"You're right." I smiled to her. "I apologize."

She gave me a small smile.

"How did you learn to do this?"

"Oh what because I'm a women?"

I felt confused for a minute, then I remembered what year this hotel existed in. What a strange thing to hear.

I nodded.

"Well my mom taught me, she taught my sister too but she had more important things, like boys to worry about."

I laughed a bit. "Sister?"

She sighed. "Yeah you met her, you were with Damon and Darren weren't you? Jane is my sister."

"Ah, yes I have met her. Seems sweet."

She twisted her face in distaste. "She's a total harlot. It's embarrassing really."

"Everyone knows you are worth nothing to man when you've given yourself to so many others. How she will find a husband, I have no idea."

I laughed. "That right?"

She nodded eagerly as she continued to pull the last of the glass bits from my arm.

"Damon's just one of many suitors. Almost done. Just need to wrap it."

The last bit of glass she pulled out chimed on the tile. She dumped some vodka on my arm. It stung slightly. Then she proceeded to gingerly wrap it.

"Anyway so if you are interested in Damon I'm sure you have a shot despite my sister. She's got a lot of options and I don't think Damon is her favourite one."

I sucked in a breath, if I had a drink, I would've choked on it.

"I'm not interested in the brothers, we are just friends. We work together."

She raised her eyebrows at me.

"And share a hotel room together, but none of my business." She paused briefly. "Really, they are handsome, just old, you know like you. Jane's younger anyway it wouldn't last."

"Oh? And how old do you think I am?" I was intrigued that she called me old.

"Probably like 30."

I laughed. "28."

"Yeah, old."

"Okay, if you say so."

I probably was considered old in this time. So strange to think at 28 people are still figuring out their lives. But a short time ago, you already had your shit together.

She fastened the bandage. "All set."

"Thank you. What was your name?"

"Jenny"

"Well, thank you Jenny."

"My pleasure, I will sweep the glass. Go chase your coworkers or whatever."

I laughed. "Okay, be safe."

She rolled her eyes. "Safe? What are you my mother?"

"Sorry" I laughed slightly.

"Oh if you see Jane, tell her next time to set me up with someone, I will be 13 in a few days. Time to start looking for a husband."

I shuddered slightly. I couldn't imagine any 13-year-old in our time being remotely ready to date let alone marry.

I left the bathroom. The booth where we ate wasn't cleaned yet but the guys were also gone. I'd guessed Damon was with Jane upstairs, and that Darren wandered to the bar.

I stood for a moment unsure where to go. I could go back to the room start researching where to locate the next of the 666.

"Oh wait" I spoke in a whisper to myself. "Damon and Jane have the room. Guess I'm stranded out here too."

It would be too late to bother Rayne to hangout. I could go back to my own room. The very thought flooded me with dread. I shook it off. I could just walk around the shops, I found an item last time and time travelled of all things. That reality still hadn't really dawned on me just yet. I supposed it wouldn't be a horrible bet. I thought to myself. I started to walk that way. I walked by several shops. I felt no pulls this time. I could hear music coming from the bar. I guessed that was the bar Darren frequented.

I hesitated outside the entrance to the bar, I could hear what sounded like karaoke. A female was singing "Valencia" By: Paul Whiteman horribly off-key and slurred. I could hear a couple people shouting for her to get off the stage. I imagined going up there and singing but I wasn't familiar with any music from the 1920s.

There was scattered applause as she I assumed got off the stage. I was about to keep walking when the applause got louder. The beginning of "Heartbreak hotel" By Elvis started up. I paused slightly. Ah Elvis. But 1920? No, 1950s more so. I wondered if it was maybe someone that could come and go from the hotel, and not one of the ghosts this time. What a thing to do, play music from someone popular in the future but in the past. Maybe I would go in. As I got to the entrance, I heard the next person start singing. His voice was magnetic. He slowed the song a little bit, was singing acoustically. It was strange to hear it without the regular melody. I rounded the corner where I saw blue lights shining to the stage.

"Drink?"

I jumped slightly and turned my head to the bartender.

"Sorry didn't mean to startle you."

I looked to the lanky body of the bartender. He was sporting a dark blonde mullet with dull eyes. He smiled slightly.

"No, thank you very much though. Unless you serve coffee?" I gave him half a smile.

He shook his head and shrugged "No, not here, I'm sorry."

"No problem at all."

"You just want some water?"

"Please."

Suite yourself, milady."

He poured a cup of ice water for me, I thanked him as he walked over to take an order on the other side of the bar.

I took a long sip of water.

My eyes wandered to the stage. Curious to put a face to the voice that drew me in here.

To my shock, there was Darren, singing slowly into the mic and strumming a dark wood acoustic guitar. Oh God Darren's voice was the one I heard. He finished the song in a hauntingly beautiful melody, that was fully his own. There was a heavy applause. He deserved it.

I watched him start up another song, as per request. He started the upbeat "Jailhouse rock" He got right into it, was even dancing as he sang and strummed the guitar. He looked.. happy. Everyone started clapping along to the beat, I joined them. It overjoyed me to see him like this, not his usual gloom and doom self. He got off the stage as he finished the song and moved to sit at the bar. He hadn't noticed me yet. All look of happiness wiped from his face, like a canvas bleached white.

"Darren! You gotta play some more songs for us." The bartender said eagerly as Darren sat down.

"Ah, think I'm done for the night Steve."

"Another whisky then?"

"Yeah, thanks."

Darren was fixated at something on the wall. I toyed with the idea of walking up to him, but then I wondered if I even should. There was a strong possibility Darren wanted to be alone. I turned my gaze around the room once. My eyes settled on someone in the back of the room, that caught my attention. It looked like- Henry? Henry was dead. There was no way- but there he was leaning against the back wall. Beautifully posed. Playing with what looked like a rosary. My mind flashed back to everything that happened. Henry's dead body flashed back in my brain. All the blood in the apartment. I suddenly felt queasy and dizzy. I gripped the bar stool. There was no way he was here, this was impossible. I have to be hallucinating. There was no way. I couldn't slow my breath, it was loud in here and no one seemed to notice my distress. Blackness crept in my vision. I gripped the seat harder but it wasn't enough. My vision blurred and I felt myself fall. There was a commotion of voices as I struck the freezing tile. There was a siring pain in my head as my skull crashed hard against the ground. I struggled to open my eyes. I felt hands grip my body. They were strong and familiar.

"Serena?" The voice was like an echo through deep bush.

"Serena!" More urgent now. Louder.

I couldn't bring myself to open my eyes. I tried to make a sound but it only came out a whimper.

"Should we call an ambulance?" I could hear a girls voice booming.

"Yes! What kinda damn question is that?" Darren sounded absolutely pissed.

I could smell the whisky on his breath. Spiced and warm against my face. I tried to open my eyes again and failed.

"Darren.." I managed.

I could feel wetness from the back of my head. God was I bleeding?

"It's okay, I got you. Don't talk" his tone was sincere.

I obliged as I felt myself slip into sleep this time succumbing to the peace of it.

For the first time in a while I didn't dream.

The only thing I could hear was a constant beeping at first. Then soft murmurs of voices in the distance. I could feel the familiar scratch of a hospital gown on my skin, but I couldn't open my eyes yet. I realized the beeping was the machine beside me measuring my heartbeat.

"Okay, a hospital, great. I must be worst off then I had imagined." I thought to myself.

After that I began to hear the hushed but heated conversation between the guys.

"Well you were there with her! Didn't you see her fall?" I recognized Damon's voice, but the worried tone was new.

"Yes, but not WITH her Damon! I didn't even know she was sitting at the bar until she fell."

Damon exhaled loudly. "Her head is busted open man."

"You think I don't know that, I sat there holding her head with my hand coated in her blood. I got her here, didn't I?"

"Oh yeah you got her here all right, but you didn't see Henry?! Are you absolutely positive? Because you are plastered and you could have missed it."

This made my heart race and the monitor's beeping sped up. Both the guys stopped talking and I assumed looked over at the monitor. I tried to calm myself and slow my heart.

Darren dropped his voice an octave. I had to strain to hear. His voice was steel.

"Don't play me Damon. We both know Henry is dead. I went back and looked after she was loaded into the ambulance. No trace."

"Well incase you've forgotten, in our line of work, dead doesn't always mean gone." Damon said almost matching Darren's steel tone.

"Again! I am well aware-" Darren began, before Damon interrupted.

"Why would she be panicking whilst in shock saying Henry was going to get her over and over again?" How do you explain that Darren! She's not one for a psychotic break."

"I don't know! We will just have to keep an eye out."

"Yes, add that to the millions of things we are already worried about." Damon said frustrated.

"Damon, I'm supposed to be the negative one. You are always Mr. Positive. Don't make us switch roles. Get your head straight. We cannot fail on any account."

The door to the room opened then. I tried again to open my eyes, but my face wouldn't respond. It felt numb.

"Has she stirred?" A male voice sounded. He sounded maybe 65 and quite bored.

"Not yet." Damon answered.

"Hm. Well the anaesthesia will ware off within the hour, she should stir by then."

"What if she doesn't?" Damon asked.

The doctor sighed. "Well we would assume there may be some internal damage to her brain. When she wakes, she will likely be rather confused and may have slight memory lapses from the concussion. The cut was deep and the fall was hard, but I don't think she will have anything outside a concussion and a scar."

He left the room then.

"You're right Darren. Look I'm just worried about her."

I heard his chair scrape loud against the floor as he sat.

'You think I'm not?" Darren sounded hurt.

Damon scoffed at Darren.

"Sometimes brother, I don't believe you capable of anything outside of anger."

Darren didn't reply for a few minutes.

"Let's save the introspection into me for a later date. We have a job to do."

Damon sighed. "We are doing our job."

They stopped talking then and I was lost in thought.

I had been calling out saying Henry was coming for me? God that is embarrassing. However, my mind flashed back to his cold eyes, cruel smile. He had been real, he had to of been? It felt real. But not possible- unless what Damon just said held some truth. He wasn't wrong, there were demons and spirits, it's not entirely unfathomable. This realization made my stomach twist. I wanted to move. I tried again with little luck. I felt hurt for Darren. Surely he could feel more then just, anger? I had witnessed him more unguarded tonight, wrapped in music. Happy. I would call it. Maybe I was wrong.

I tried then to open my eyes again, this time my face reacted to my wishes.

"Thank God" I breathed to myself.

My eyes were blinded by the blazing white florescent lights above my head. I couldn't quite focus on anything. I only saw shapes among the white light.

"Ahh- it's so bright." I groaned quietly.

Damon and Darren both rushed to my side Darren on my right and Damon on my left.

Damon was smiling. "Ah rise and shine sunshine." He laughed.

Darren ran his thumb gently over my cheek, barely contacting my skin.

"Too Bright?"

I closed my eyes again. "Yeah. My head hurts a bit." I tried to move but my body felt too heavy.

"Good to see you up Serena!" Damon said still smiling widely.

"I will get a nurse." Darren said as he abruptly stood up. He was heading toward the call button when the door to the room flung open wildly.

"Serena!?"

Rayne. I recognized her shrill voice immediately.

There was a clamour of voices.

"Miss you can't go in there!" a man said

"Stop! You can't go in there right now" A women tilled.

"The hell I can't!" She spat back and pushed into the room.

I laughed slightly. Rayne took Darren's spot on my left. She didn't even acknowledge the guys. Her eyes were searching mine and frantically looking me up and down.

"OH my God you would not believe how hard it was to get in here!"

I tried to smile slightly.

"Hey Rayne." I felt very relaxed in her company.

"Are you okay?! They wouldn't tell me shit!"

The doctor and a nurse entered then. They looked at me. The doctor looked like a mad scientist, with a mane of grey hair and dark bags under his eyes. The nurse was very short with light brown hair in a bun. Her eyes trimmed red as if she was stoned or very very tired.

"We can take her out of here, if shes disturbing you Serena." the nurse said.

Rayne scoffed. "Absolutely not!"

The nurse narrowed her eyes slightly.

"It's okay, she can stay." I put my hand over Rayne's on the bed.

Rayne turned back giving the nurse a look that read something like

"I told you so."

The doctor walked over.

"Just going to check your vitals."

Damon moved aside and walked to the back of the room where Darren was standing, as the doc came over on my right side. He checked my pulse, eyes and nose and mouth. The nurse left the room then.

"Wiggle your hands and feet please."

I tried and was successful.

Lift each arm then each leg.

Again I was successful.

"First name?"

"Serena"

"One plus one?"

"Two" I answered.

"The date?"

"April 19 2024"

"Birthday?"

"October 31 1994"

Rayne was stroking my hand and nodding.

"Well, no brain damage. Stitches need to come out in 4 weeks time if they don't on their own lots of rest. Light sensitivity, fatigue, mild discomfort around the stitches and brain fog are all very common with this type of injury. The worst of it will subside in a week."

He looked around the room at us.

"She can go home now."

"Thank Gods you are alright!" Rayne laid over top of me hugging me tightly.

"Shame that'll scar though." she pointed to my head.

I tried to laugh but it more just came out as a groan. I ran my hand along my head. Sure enough, I could feel the rough stitches from behind my right ear all the way to the middle of my head. I felt over it again and realized they had shaved my hair there. Rayne must've read the panic on my face.

"Oh right, I'm sure you haven't been out of bed to a mirror. Don't worry they just shaved underneath, you won't be able to tell your hair is still long."

A wave of relief washed over me, then I felt guilty for being so vain when there were things much worse than hair loss, we were all dealing with.

Rayne turned her attention finally to the brothers.

"Thanks guys for getting her here. I'm glad she was with you." Darren and Damon both nodded.

"Okay girl, come on. I got Matt to make your favourite homemade soup! The guest bed is ready for you too."

I glanced quickly to the guys. Darren shifted uncomfortably, Damon's smile momentarily faltered.

"Actually Rayne-" I started but Damon cut me off. As he walked closer to us.

"That sounds really great. I know she will be well looked after."

"But-" I started and Damon interrupted again.

"It would be for the best, you need to heal up. You can always come back and help once you are better."

Fear gripped me, I didn't like the idea of being away from them.

Rayne gave him a pointed look.

"Oh good for a second there I thought you were gonna deny her the time off."

'Of course not." Damon retorted, soundly slightly offended.

"Great."

I stole a glance at Darren, his fists were clenched but he remained silent.

"I'll gather your things!" Rayne almost skipped with each step.

"Can't wait to have you for a whole week! It feels like it's been forever!" She called over her shoulder as she packed my bag.

A week- no I couldn't. The guys needed me. We had no time to waste. We have a few of the 666 left to find and not to mention the demon, and the possibility of Henry being back from the dead.

Damon was watching my face and must have understood the internal fight I was having.

"It will be fine. We will handle it. We will grab you from Rayne's in one week." Darren reluctantly nodded in agreement.

"You'll be safe there." Darren said quietly.

"How do I reach you guys though?!" Damon wrote down their numbers, on the notepad by the bed and crumpled it into my hand.

"We will check in nightly"

I breathed slowly. "Alright."

We were talking too quietly for Rayne to pick up on what we were saying.

'What about-?" I cut myself off because Rayne walked up.

"All good here?" Rayne eyed Damon suspiciously.

"Yes, of course." He met my eyes then "Everything is fine."

I nodded in the deeper understanding of his comment.

"Well I got her from here guys. I'm sure you two have more important things to worry about. I'll have Serena back to you as soon as I can." She chirped.

Damon nodded once and walked toward the door, hovering near Darren silently beckoning him to follow. Darren stared at me for a minute. He looked concerned, but said goodbye quietly and they both left the room. Damon turned his head over his shoulder to wink at me before disappearing out of the hospital room door. I exhaled.

"Damn those men are so smoking. And, they did not want to leave you! God so hot. Makes me want to run home to Matt and take advantage, you know?"

I smiled halfheartedly. "Don't let me stop you."

"As if. You are so lucky Serena. Which do you favour?" Rayne giggled.

She was just looking for some girly gossip. It was more difficult then usual to meet her yearning for juicy details. All I could picture was the job at hand and keeping humanity alive. There were so many cursed objects left. What if the Demon followed me to Rayne's? What if I saw Henry?

Rayne interrupted my torrent of panicked thinking.

"That hard to pick huh?" She laughed. "I don't blame you!"

I laughed slightly. "I'm not- I don't see either of them like that."

Rayne rolled her eyes. "Yeah, sure you don't."

I looked back at her.

"Oh fine!" Rayne huffed. "I will get the answer from you at some point Serena. I'm oh so curious. Come on let's get you dressed and outta here."

Rayne grabbed my arm to help me from the bed and handed me my clothes.

I moved toward the bathroom on unsteady feet. There was a slight spin to my vision. Rayne let me lean against her to steady myself.

"You got this." She said encouraging me as I went into the bathroom to change.

I jumped at my dishevelled reflection in the mirror. Her voice tilled over to me.

"Did you get to spend some time at your new place?"

"Yeah a little, not enough though. I gotta slowly collect household items so it doesn't look so barren in there." It was sort of a lie, I hadn't gone into the house yet, but I imagined it did look barren.

"That's fair. The guys must be keeping you pretty busy I wager?"

'Yeah. I'm really enjoying my job though. I am still so grateful to you and Matt Rayne. Really thank you."

Rayne sighed in slight playfulness.

"You're honestly starting to sound like a broken record. But I am grateful you are happy with it."

"More than." I attempted to brush my matted hair with my fingers.

Rayne was right you couldn't tell where they had to shave my hair. I slowly undressed and pulled my black dress back on.

"And uh, your mom? Did you call her yet?"

My heart sped up momentarily forgetting we had plane ticket Wednesday next week. It was currently Thursday of the week prior.

"Not again yet, no." A small wave of guilt and newfound fear washed over me.

"We can do it together, if you want."

I appreciated what Rayne was trying to do, but it felt like something I should do alone. However, she probably wouldn't give me much choice in the matter. I stopped fiddling with my hair and walked out of the bathroom.

"Sure, I would appreciate the company when I call her."

It was a half truth. Rayne nodded and handed me my bag. We walked out to her car in silence. The lot was pretty full. Must be a busy night. The cool nighttime air felt amazing in my lungs. I glanced around but saw no sign of the guys. I sighed slightly and strapped into the passenger side of Rayne's car. After a moment I figured small talk was the way to go. Rayne would be suspicious, but she did love talking about herself.

"So how is moving up to fiancé level treating you?"

Rayne glanced over to me and raised her eyebrows. She pursed her lips.

"Small talk, really?"

"It's the best I can manage right now."

"I can hold space for that. Our life is charming so far actually. Although it does feel very repetitive in day to day. However in spite that Matt always manages to surprise me."

"Surprise you how?"

Rayne smiled thoughtfully.

"Well yesterday as an example. You know I just wasn't feeling too good, I had a long day it felt, you know just off my game a little. Matt made a snack platter for us and watched trashy chick flicks with me all night while cuddling me." She giggled then.

"I mean he fell asleep halfway through the second Twlight movie. But he made it through the first one! AND didn't make fun of it once this time!"

I tried to picture Matt whom loved sports and hated romance movies. I tried to picture him sitting through any chick flick and laughed.

"That's beautiful Rayne, but I don't know if I believe he didn't make ONE joke the whole movie!"

She held her right palm up over her steering wheel and said:

"I swear. But he will deny it if you ask him, I'm sure."

She burst out laughing as she turned the corner to her place. It was only a minute before she pulled into the garage and switched her car off.

"It's the little things you know? Little actions of love and care make the biggest impact."

I thought on her words.

"That's beautifully put Rayne."

"I know, I'm a poet and I know it"

We both laughed loudly, as she grabbed my bag without asking if I needed her too, knowing I would've said no even though I was in no state to carry anything. I loved Rayne for just helping. I didn't know how to ask for help. I had always tried to be everything for everyone. I hated feeling like a burden or a bother. I didn't like to have anyone help when I'm sick or behind on things. It was a toxic behaviour of mine, never taking care of myself before anyone or anything else. Rayne always knew that, so she would just take control when she picked up on it. I was eternally grateful for the relief of pressure over having to try and ask for anything; or having to delegate and break down all I needed in that moment.

"Thank you for the jailbreak and for grabbing my bag."

She laughed. "Anytime girl."

As we walked up the giant brick steps to her double door front entry, the smell of Matt's soup wafted down from the open kitchen window and my stomach growled. "Oh my god that smells incredible." I inhaled loud and deep.

Rayne smiled.

"Oh yeah, Matt is a fantastic chef as you know. I'm pretty good but he for sure is better. One day I aim to surpass his abilities."

"You can try!" Matt yelled from the window, laughing.

He waved to me.

Rayne stuck her tongue out at him.

"Come on in, soups ready."

I returned the smile and wave. Rayne opened the heavy oak doors and led me inside, locking them behind us.

"We will get you settled after you eat!"

Rayne said happily as she dropped my bag gently on the bench in the foyer.

I removed my shoes and made my way to sit at the 12 seat grand dining table under the massive chandelier. The space seemed so much bigger without all their usual lively guests.

Matt dropped a steaming bowl of soup on the white lace place mat in front of me then wrapped Rayne in a hug spinning her slightly and littering her face with kisses.

"Welcome home gorgeous." Rayne giggled uncontrollably then Matt slapped her butt and handed her a bowl of soup too.

"Thank you babe."

Rayne sat across from me and I couldn't help but smile it warmed my heart to see her so loved.

A few minutes later Matt joined us at the table. "Well bon appetite!"

"God its Wicked Thai yeah?" I asked Matt eagerly.

It was my absolute favourite. I loved how filling it was, and the variety of warm spices.

"You got it. Best you'll ever have I'd bet."

I laughed. "I wouldn't doubt it."

I brought a spoonful to my lips gently blowing the steam and took a bite. The explosion of savoury flavours was intense.

"Oh my GOD!"

Matt smiled confidently. "Told you."

"It's got the perfect amount of chicken, veggies and spice. Unreal. Thank you!"

"Of course! Glad you like it. What do you think baby?"

He turned to Rayne who just took her first bite.

"I second Serena! Delicious!"

He threw both his arms up. "And the crowd goes wild!"

Rayne and I burst out laughing. We all finished the meal greedily.

I peeked at the time on my phone: 7:08pm it would be too late tonight to call my mom. I would have to wait until it reopened in the morning.

I sent a quick text to Damon, saying I was safe.

A message popped up on my screen then.

"Hey Serena, hope you settled in good. We are just going to be in researching tonight. No need to worry. Call if you need. I exhaled a breath I didn't realize I was holding. I was glad they weren't tracking or killing anything tonight.

'Everything okay?" Rayne asked.

"Yeah, yeah everything is good. I will have to call mom in the morning it's too late today I think."

Rayne nodded. "First thing tomorrow then."

I stood up and gathered everyone's bowls.

"Oh hey I got that Serena." Rayne said. "Go get unpacked."

I lingered for a second with all the bowls stacked in my hand.

"Please let me help. It's the least I can do. Matt cooked this lovely meal and you guys are letting me crash here for a while."

Rayne shrugged. "Okay suit yourself. Feel up to a board game?"

Matt clasped his hands together in excitement. "Great plan!"

"For sure, only if you guys pick though, my head is not great for decisions right now." I snicked to myself slightly. I mean it wasn't a lie.

I walked into the kitchen and started to wash all the dishes Matt used for cooking plus our bowls. I couldn't hear them and took a moment to gather my thoughts. My head was hurting pretty profusely. I tried to shove the anxiety over what was going on with my mom out of my mind without success. I dried the dishes and put them away. My phone buzzed, I pulled it out of my cardigan pocket. Damon again.

"Serena sorry to bother you, but Henry, when you saw him did he look..like himself? Or..? We are trying to look at all avenues of possibility. Any cold spots?"

My head started swimming, so I was right, it might have actually been Henry. The thought froze me to my core. The pain in my head became overwhelming as I tried to picture Henry. His dark hair was the same, same outfit I last saw him in. Smile was the same but unfriendly. Eyes..I couldn't picture his eyes. Did he have eyes?.. I thought hard back to that night. Remembering him leaning against the wall laughing, black. Black eyes.

I quickly typed back. "Black eyes."

Damon immediately replied. "Okay, good thank you. It's okay, he can only really scare you. Wear the crystal we gave you, sneak sea salt in a dish under your bed and Rayne's. It'll protect you all overnight. Text me the address I can run by and salt the windows and doors for you too as an added protection if you want."

I thought back to the book I was reading back at the hotel. Black eyes were the lowest level of Demon. Salt would keep him from being able to come near us. A demon- Henry was a demon.

I walked to the kitchen cabinets and started hunting for sea salt. The second cabinet I opened was the spices. I found it quickly and grabbed the bottle. I walked back into the dining room.

"Guys- I'm sorry, rain check on the game? My head is killing me, I need some sleep if that's okay."

"No problemo! We couldn't agree on one yet anyways. Matt said as he winked at Rayne.

"Of course girlie, whatever you need let us know okay?"

"Okay, thanks again guys. Goodnight!" I rounded the corner as they both said goodnight back. They were wrapped in each others arms and gaze, they didn't notice that I was holding the sea salt; or if they did they didn't question me. I grabbed my brown messenger bag and threw it over my shoulder as I ascended the steps to the guest room. Their laughter trailing behind me. I checked the first guest bathroom for decorative bowls. The colour scheme was white and blue. There was an assortment of bowls in that bathroom. They all held different soaps. I had to admire Rayne for her maximalist personality that spilled into every room of the house. I grabbed two bowls combining the fancy soaps with one another hoping Rayne wouldn't notice right away. I filled both bowls almost to the rim with the sea salt. I walked down the massive corridor to Rayne and Matt's room. I hovered by the closed door feeling incredibly invasive.

"It's for their protection" I reminded myself quietly out loud as I pushed their door open.

The room was huge. Dark blue and white. Over the top tidy. I walked slowly to the 4 poster canopy king bed and slid the bowl underneath. I closed the door on my way out and retired to the guest bedroom. My phone buzzed again as I closed the door to the green and white room. The room reminded me of a 4 star hotel. I dropped my bag on the soft queen bed. My phone buzzed again.

"Serena, Darren insists we come give the extra protection detail. If that's cool."

I sighed out of relief. It would bring peace of mind if I knew Henry couldn't visit me or Rayne here. I typed back:

"Please. I would deeply appreciate that. 28 Royal Cres."

"Of course. Text me when Rayne and Matt are in their bedroom. Don't want to alarm them."

"Got it, thanks." I typed quickly.

I dropped my phone beside my bag and decided to draw a bath.

Of course each guest bedroom in this place had an en-suite. When I got into the bathroom there were vanilla candles laid out and a gift bag. I recognized Rayne's gift wrapping skills and smiled. On the bag there was a note.

"I know you don't drink but I figured you could wind down with this instead! It's more "You" Vanilla is still your favourite scent right? Enjoy!" With love: Your bestie.

I smiled and opened the package. Rayne always went the extra mile for everyone.

I pulled out a bottle of pomegranate-raspberry sparkling water. A small box of creme chocolates, a face mask, rose scented bubble bath and dark red nail polish. I started the bath and poured the bubbles in, loving the floral scent. I half skipped back to my phone so I could message her a thank you.

"I'll get up early and make breakfast as a thank you as well." I said out loud to myself.

I typed a message to Rayne: "Just got your gift! That is so very thoughtful! You didn't have to do that. Sparkling water was a great choice. Love you girl, night!"

She texted back hearts. "I'm SO thrilled. Knew you would love it. Matt and I are turning in, you shouldn't be able to hear us but just in case, there are ear plugs in the bed side table for you! LOL" I did indeed laugh out loud at that. Good for her.

I texted Damon. "All clear"

"On our way!" He immediately texted back.

I sighed with relief and went to check my bath.

It was full and steaming. I stripped down and lit the vanilla scented candles. The hot water felt amazing. I closed my eyes. Immediately my mind went to me freezing in the bath and I jolted them open. My breath was quick and my heart was drumming loudly. I looked around, but everything was fine. The water still hot on my body and the candles still flickering softly. I got out, draining the tub and pulled purple silk pyjamas on. I blew the candles out with a shuddering breath and walked quickly to the bed. The room was dark and warm and silent. I supposed it will take some time before I could enjoy bathing again, guess I would have to stick to showers. I wondered if the guys had come by yet. I walked over to the window, hoping to catch sight of them, but my window faced the back of the house and they weren't likely to show up there. They would do the back door. I sighed again drawing the heavy curtains closed and returned to the bed. I felt overwhelmingly lonely and slightly afraid. I texted Damon:

"You guys finish up?"

He messaged back quickly: "Just now! We just left. You all will be safe tonight. We will reapply nightly to ensure safety until you come back and we can work out the details. Goodnight."

My mind was rampant.

Another text: "Remember to try to have fun."

"Yeah." I whispered to the empty room. "If only it were that easy."

I closed my eyes and desperately hoped my dreams would be kind to me tonight.

Chapter 10

HOPE

"The prospect of creation, the new breath of spring, tiny buds spiral towards the sun, a birth, a rebirth, I bring forth this hope that new days will dawn."

Sunlight filtered through the heavy curtains, it felt warm on my face. No dreams. I'd never been so relieved. I sat up and checked my phone 9:01am

Wow, I slept in hard. I stretched and pulled the covers back. The smell of pancakes sifted through the air. I hadn't had pancakes since I was a little girl and I was warmed by the memory of the scent.

I had one message from Damon from 8am. "Good morning. Any complications?"

I smiled and typed back. "Peaceful. Thanks for checking in"

"Of course. Talk later. Oh yeah.. HAVE FUN"

I rolled my eyes. His concern for my entertainment was comical to me. Like "Hey remember to forget your responsibility to save the entire human race and have mundane fun."

I sighed and undressed. I stared for a second at the tub then opted to run the shower instead. My phone rang. Rayne. I picked up on the first ring.

"Yes?"

"Sorry to wake you but it's 9! I got a whole day planned so get your lazy ass outta bed!"

I laughed. "My ass is out of the bed thank you. Gonna shower."

Rayne groaned. "Ugh, hurry up!" click.

I wondered what she planned for the day. I'm sure it would be very fun, but part of me just wanted to get back to work. My head felt okay. I felt along the stitch line again. Thinking back to Henry. I was still having a hard time with the fact he was a Demon.

I tossed my phone on the counter and stepped into the hot shower. I washed quickly, pulling a pink dress out of my bag and I aggressively ran a brush through my hair. I didn't bother with makeup and headed downstairs my hair still dripping. I turned and walked toward the kitchen.

"Good morning!" Rayne scooped me into a hug. I hugged her back and smiled. Matt looked over his shoulder from the stove.

"Pancakes are done."

"Hey morning. Mm yeah they smell great."

"Matt likes to cook for me when he's not working. I cherish these moments."

"You mean cause I'm a better cook then you?" Matt said in a teasing tone.

"I'm not THAT bad."

I tried to remember Rayne's cooking growing up but she usually made a lot of frozen easy meals, outside of her amazing baking. However I hadn't tried her cooking in years so maybe her skill level had increased now.

"You get better all the time hun! I'm playing. Now desserts however, I could never hold a candle to yours." He kissed Rayne on the cheek. And she giggled playfully hitting him in the rib.

"You are such an ass, but you are right. I am the better baker."

Matt laughed. "An ass maybe, but yet I landed you."

"Yeah you are one lucky, lucky man. Never forget it."

"Nah." He kissed her quickly then dished pancakes out.

I loved watching them banter. Always so playful. Being around them made me miss Henry though. I thought about how we used to banter like that too, but ours was more aggressive. Henry was so unbelievably quick to anger. It felt like every time we were around one another it was walking on eggshells to not disrupt his mood. We laughed a lot too. He was romantic some days. I was naturally a people pleaser so I really waited on him. I would mould myself into anything he needed at that time. I would allow myself to be an outlet for him no matter what angered him. But I took everything that ailed him and healed it, whilst slowly decaying myself. It would be taken out on me and I embraced it. I trusted it. I was non existent, I existed only for him. I just wanted to heal him. Most of all he was openly unfaithful. It didn't bother me, he wanted every other women but in my mind it was fine because only I was his. All the other girls didn't matter. Whereas, I was his most prized possession and I feared to even dare look another's way. It didn't help that I had never really been with anyone else. So I truly was his. We didn't have the same rules. Now replaying that in my mind it sounded really messed up. That can't be love, not really, can it? I sighed to myself, and now, he was a demon. I feared him now, when I never had before.

Rayne spoke then: "Serena, what are you lost in thought about?"

I swallowed a bite of pancakes and shook my head slightly. "Not much"

Rayne gave me a pointed look not believing a word.

"Just wondering what you planned for us today?" That momentarily distracted her.

"Oh my gosh well, you've been working hard so I thought we could have a shopping and spa day!" She clasped her hands together excitedly.

"With a coffee first obviously."

I smiled. "Phew, I was worried you forgot."

"Your coffee addiction? Me? Never." We both burst out laughing. Rayne always made me feel so happy. I was lucky to have her in my life.

Matt stood up from the table suddenly. Staring at his phone.

"What's wrong babe?" Rayne asked stroking his shoulder.

"Mm well I just got called into work."

"What? You just got off a 12 day rotation."

"Yeah, I guess a few are out with a really awful illness. Time for the owner to step in and manage."

"I'll be home in 4 days. This branch is in Ontario, Short flight."

I felt bit ill suddenly. I didn't like the idea of Rayne being here without Matt if I needed to go, with everything going on. Rayne looked quite disappointed.

"I will make it up to you babe. They want me to head out this afternoon. But hey, you get girl time!" He over enthusiastically waved his hands with his voice raising an octave. When he said "girl time"

Rayne chuckled. "Okay. Love you."

"Love you too babe, I'm going to pack." He gave her a long kiss.

"Hurry up or you'll be late" He said between kisses.

Rayne's eyes widened and she chugged an orange juice. "Girl grab your bag!"

I obliged and went to grab my bag.

"Where are we going?" I asked as Rayne rushed past me throwing a beige coat over her and one of her black faux fur coats over me.

"No time! Get to the car!"

I smiled to myself. Gotta love Rayne and her dramatics.

I buckled into her Jag and realized that meant probably no coffee.

"Mani pedi?" I asked with forced enthusiasm.

I didn't do much to my nails. I used to when I was a teen but not in my 20s so much.

Rayne smiled. "Not this time. Another type of spa. I swear we will get your favourite coffee after okay? I have stuff planned the entire week!"

We pulled up to a spa that had lavender scents wafting through it.

Rayne practically jumped out of the car. "Come on!"

I followed, curious about what it could be.

"Hi Rayne!" The receptionist had dark ringlet curls and gorgeous mocha skin. She welcomed us with a smile.

'I'm so sorry we are late!" Rayne said.

"Oh, it's no trouble, only because you are a VIP customer of course." She smiled.

"This is Serena?"

I smiled. "Yes, nice to meet you."

"You too. Okay right this way!"

I grabbed Rayne's arm and kept my voice low. "What did you book?"

"Full body massage!"

"I've never-"

Rayne cut me off holding her hand up. "I know that's why I booked it but I promise it'll revitalize you."

I had never gotten a professional massage, I was actually quite excited.

"Rayne I can't afford this." I said quietly looking at the extravagant interior, thinking it was an inclusive spa for famous people.

"As if I would make you pay for an outing I planned. Just relax and enjoy!"

Again I felt like a charity case. I knew she was just doing what she felt was right for me. She always meant well.

We went into separate rooms. I didn't see who was assigned to Rayne. But the receptionist was the one to do mine.

"I know what you must be wondering. Why is the receptionist massaging too?" Its cause the actual receptionist called in sick today." There was a hint of annoyance in her tone.

"I guess there's some crazy illness going around."

That wasn't the first time I had heard this today. I wondered if any cursed object could have such a wide ranged affect.

"Okay undress to your comfort level, but please take your top off so I can get to your shoulders and neck. When you are comfortable slip under the heated blanket on the table. Your treatment will be an hour. I'll give you a moment of privacy." She stepped out of the room. I took a breath and admired the room. It was a deep purple and smelled strongly of lavender. There were a lot of nick knacks on the glass shelves at the back of the room. I wanted a closer look but the lady knocked again.

"Ready?"

I stripped my dress and my bra and darted under the blankets.

"Come in."

"Oh perfect I'm Marie. I will start at your shoulders if that's okay with you."

"Sounds lovely Marie, thank you."

She started pushing lightly in between my shoulder blades. It felt really nice. Slight tinges of pain, then release. I had no idea how much tension I was carrying.

She didn't say much. I closed my eyes and focused on the release of pressure as she moved her hands over me. I thought about the guys and wondered what they might be up too and if they had any luck finding any more objects. I also wondered what else Rayne had up her sleeve for the day. I felt two giant knots unravel in my upper back and sighed contently.

Then I heard..bells? High pitched tinkling bells. I tried to ignore the sound and recenter my focus to where Marie's hands were working a knot from my lower back. But they were so loud.

"Please, Marie I'm sorry to be a bother but, can you shut off the bell alarm sound?"

Marie paused where her hands were.

"What bell sweetheart?"

My heart stared to race as I bit back a cry of pain and abruptly sat up covering my ears.

"I-I'm sorry I have to go!" Marie looked afraid when I looked at her face. She stepped back slightly. I jumped from the bed and pulled my dress over my body forgetting my bra. I grabbed my bra and bag with my hand.

"Thank you so much, I have to go."

I said through gritted teeth as my eyes watered from the pain in my ears. I half ran to the front door glancing back to see if Rayne was out of her massage. It didn't look like it. God, how could she not hear it? How could no one hear the ear splitting ting of the bells? The other clients in the waiting room gazed strangely at me as I stumbled over my feet rushing to the door. Once the door closed the bells stopped, I fell to my knees, taking a shuddering breath. My fingers automatically moved to my ears to check for blood. They came back clean. I fumbled for my phone, dropping it on the cement. I cursed under my breath realizing the top half of my phone spidered. Not me breaking my phone screen twice in a week. I immediately dialed Damon, but it went straight to his voicemail. His voice wasn't even there it was just a beep indicating to leave a message. Now I was worried. I hung up, and dialed Darren instead. Same thing.

"Oh God." My mind started racing with all the awful possibilities. I tried to rationalize my thoughts. Rayne came out of the door then.

"Are you okay? Marie told me you ran out mid massage!"

I paused trying to piece together what I could to muster up some sort of rational explanation. But I failed.

"I-um. I heard bells."

Rayne narrowed her eyes. "What, like a fire alarm?"

I swallowed. Close enough. "Yeah." I lied, feeling immensely guilty for it.

"Well, I didn't those are pretty loud. Can you hear it still?"

I shook my head and looked down a little embarrassed.

Rayne's expression softened. "Now I understand why that would scare you so much. I'm sorry I had to think about it. I mean of course the idea of a fire would be terrifying after what happened with Henry and your apartment."

She gave me a tight hug.

"I'll explain to Marie next week when I go in again. You don't have to. Let's go get you some coffee."

I was baffled. She wasn't wrong, why didn't I think of that though? Henry and his black eyes popped into my head now. I exhaled and put on my best face.

"Yeah, that's right Rayne. I'm so sorry."

"Oh don't be." she smiled sympathetically.

We started to walk back to her car. I was looking forward to coffee and thanking the Gods she rationalized my outburst so perfectly. I tried not to worry too much about the guys. If they were at the hotel my call wouldn't reach them. I exhaled again. Right how could I forget? If they were at the hotel they wouldn't hear from me until they left. I decided I would not stress and wait to make sure they made their regular check in time and update them then. I believed there had to be another cursed object in there. Now how would I go back?

"How was your massage?" I asked her.

"Oh it was absolutely incredible! I do a deep cleansing treatment to my hair and skin here weekly as well. I will book you with me next time. Titania is truly an artist."

"Titania?"

"Yeah I only ever see her. Shes impeccably beautiful and swears by these treatments to stay looking youthful. I hope Marie was great too though. Titania highly recommended her."

"You are already very beautiful Rayne. I don't think you need anything like that. Marie was great, thank you. I feel so much less sore."

Rayne smiled. "Thank you. I suppose it's just nice anyways. It relaxes me like nothing else."

I nodded. "Fair enough."

We pulled up to "La Creme Cafe" again on Parron street. A huge smile spread across my face.

"My favourite. Thanks girl!"

Rayne laughed. "Whenever!"

"Do you want anything?"

Rayne shook her head. "I'll pass actually. Thanks. Don't be long! Still so much to do today." She smiled eagerly.

I walked in and ordered my regular raspberry vanilla latte.

When I walked back outside Rayne was staring off into the distance in the drivers seat.

I slowed my pace and looked the direction she was staring but saw nothing. I opened the door to her car and she didn't react.

"Rayne?"

She just kept staring.

My heart dropped.

"Rayne!" I grabbed and shook her arm slightly.

She turned to me. "Yeah, Serena?"

She looked perfectly normal.

"What are you looking at?"

I looked again trying to find what held her attention.

"Huh? Nothing. Sorry I think I'm just a bit tired. Maybe I will get a coffee too." She unbuckled and got out of the car. I hesitated wanting to follow her to make sure she was okay. But a few minutes later she came back to the vehicle, looking totally fine.

"There that should do it!" She took a sip. "Mm it is good coffee. Ready?"

I looked again trying to see what she was staring at earlier and couldn't.

"Yeah. Where too next?" I said kindly.

She smiled at me. "Thrifting! Thought we could find some stuff for your house together."

I felt overjoyed. "That sounds amazing."

"I figured you would rather thrift most of your house. HOWEVER I have a condition!"

"Ah, what's the catch?"

"Let Matt and I get you a bedroom set. I can't fathom the idea of you using a secondhand bed."

I started to laugh. Yep, she was herself alright.

"Okay. Deal. But only a new bed. I want to thrift all the dressers and such."

Rayne set her jaw. "Ugh, fine." She droned out the word "fine".

"You know I don't like modern furniture much. Vintage is so much prettier."

She rolled her eyes. "I know, I know. Although I disagree, I respect your love for it."

We pulled up to the "Old strathcona antique mall." In Edmonton.

"I love this place!" I was honestly ecstatic.

"Yeah, I know. Figured you would like this. I hope we can find you some things.

Oh! And if you happen upon furniture at all, Matt has a guy on call for moving big things."

"I am so excited, this was such a lovely idea Rayne. Thank you!"

She smiled and we walked inside. I loved how they had it set up almost like little rooms in a house. The floors and walls were all original for the most part. All wood. It had a large wooden staircase in the centre. There was also a small cafe inside. It was decorated with old signs of all sorts. They had everything from War relics, to toys/collectibles, jewellery, fine art and furniture.

"Well Serena where too? It is quite lovely in here actually. The set up is warm and welcoming. Unlike the secondhand places that are just in bare warehouses basically."

"I'm so thrilled that you came with me here for once!" I laughed.

"Let's head upstairs to the furniture first. I can't imagine getting anything prior to furniture."

Rayne nodded. "Okay well, lead the way girl!"

"Happily!" I bounded up the steps and Rayne followed close behind.

The main centre of the upper floor was all vintage furniture. To the right it was isles of collectibles and vintage toys/books. I scanned over the furniture with my eyes first.

"Jackpot." I said as I noticed several pieces of interest.

"Oh really? What do you like?"

I first saw a pink set of french inspired upholstered couch and arm chair. It looked it relatively decent shape. Maybe needed some cleaning. Easy enough. I checked the price. $100 for both.

"These for sure."

Raynes eyes widened. "Pink couches?!"

I laughed. "Well look at how intricate the wood frame is? The seats look already reupholstered."

"What on earth is your colour theme going to be?" Rayne side eyed me as she said this.

"Alright I mean it's your place go hard. I do know that you have a way of making a space look entirely chic and unique no matter what you use in it. It's your gift."

"Well thanks Rayne. I do enjoy interior decorating quite a bit."

As we moved through the store I settled on several furniture items.

"Let's wait until these are placed before I get anything else." I said decidedly.

"Okay!" Rayne half laughed.

We came up to the till.

"$719.21 for everything.

Rayne's jaw dropped. I laughed a bit.

"Credit."

Rayne told the store clerk a vehicle would be sent to load everything and take it to my place.

The store clerk nodded.

"Thank you so much, Transporting all that would have been a lot for us to do without help."

Rayne stared at me still baffled.

"How, HOW did you find all your house furniture in one go, for less then a grand?!" She almost shouted.

"That's just how I shop I guess." I laughed sheepishly.

"Also not all, cause you wouldn't let me pick a bed."

She laughed. "I'll get that right away. I can't wait to see the final result of your vision Serena."

There was quite a bit of pain in my head suddenly.

"Rayne?"

"Yeah?"

"Can we please call it a day?" I asked pressing my fingers to my temples.

Rayne looked at me about to protest then her face changed when she looked at me. I must've been doing a poor job of hiding my pain at that moment.

"Oh, of course, are you okay?"

"I don't-" My vision swam a bit.

I looked to the right and saw a mental institution. It looked outdated, and I didn't remember it here before. An ivy drenched brick of a building. With a sign reading "Black Rose ridge Home for the mentally ill." There was a black wrought iron fence surrounding it. A purple wisteria tree in front. You never saw trees like that here.

"Serena!"

I heard Rayne say my name but it was like my soul was floating from my body.

There was a young girl with long brown hair in a white dress spinning around the tree. I just stared.

I felt the cement hit the side of my face as I watched her play. She seemed so familiar. The whole building seemed familiar as if I had been there. But it must be like the hotel and the cafe, it must not exist today. She had a large heart locket around her neck. I watched it sway in the wind as she dancing around the tree. It looked so similar to mine, but yet- Then her eyes burned bright white and there was an inhuman earth shattering scream.

I must've screamed too.

"Serena Fuck- I need help!" She yelled.

"Shit- yes hi I need an ambulance right now my friend just collapsed! I don't know! She's screaming that somethings burning her!"

I didn't feel as though I was screaming. I felt quiet and still. My head hurt. Why was Rayne saying that?

"No, I don't know why, we were just in the store. Oh God I don't know what to do!"

Was the last thing I heard from Rayne before my vision went black.

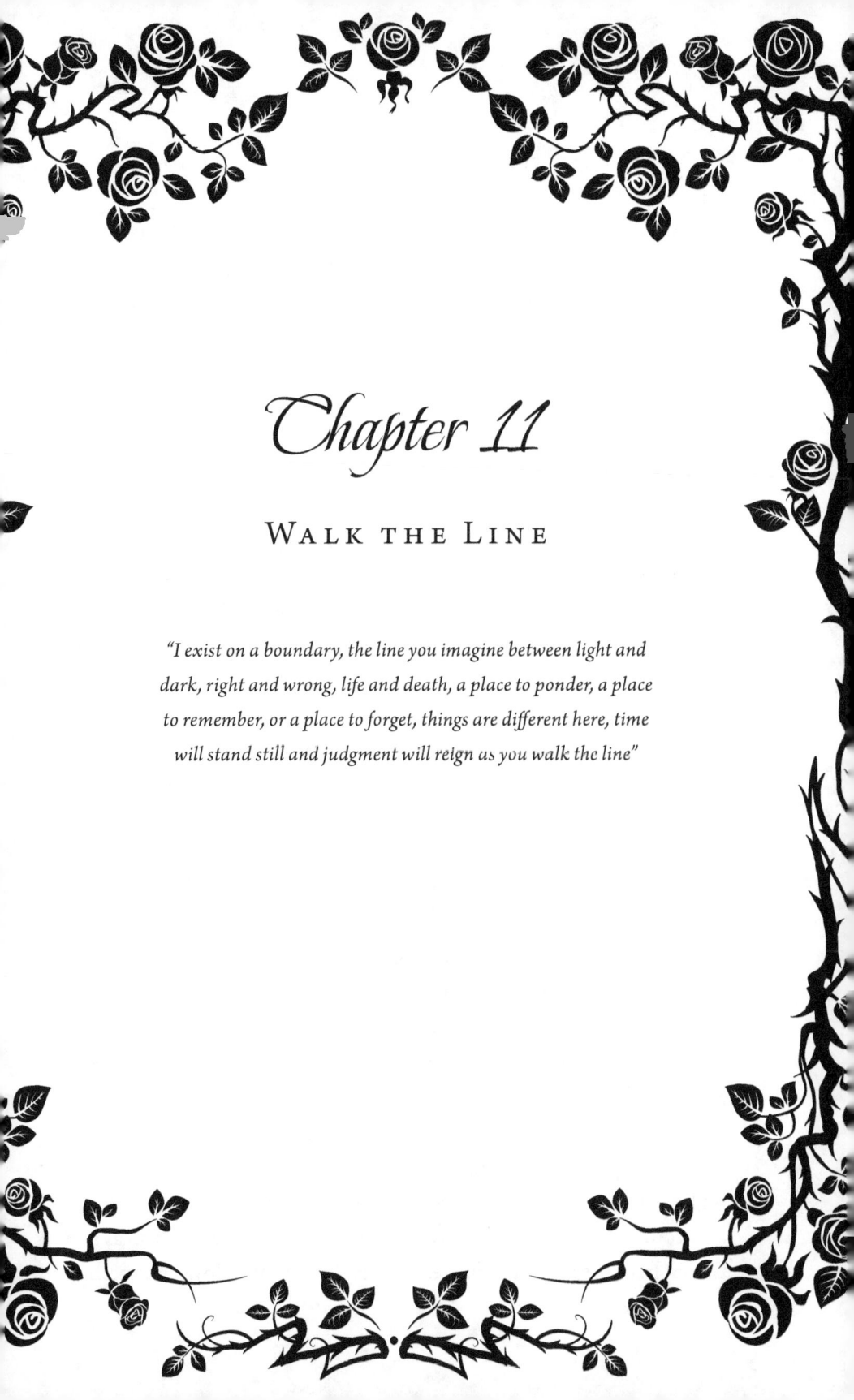

Chapter 11

WALK THE LINE

"I exist on a boundary, the line you imagine between light and dark, right and wrong, life and death, a place to ponder, a place to remember, or a place to forget, things are different here, time will stand still and judgment will reign as you walk the line"

"How are her vitals?" I heard Rayne's anxious tone.

"Working on it. You need to give me space ma'am." A women's tone, harsh and commanding.

"Is she going to be alright?" I could hear Rayne's voice breaking.

I could hear sirens very, very loud in my ears and I struggled to open my eyes. When I did red liquid poured into my left eye. I quickly closed it.

"Ahh" I groaned.

Rayne spoke up. "Serena! Oh my God, did you just speak?"

I could feel hands quick over my body, two maybe three sets of hands. I could feel a needle. I could feel where they were tying for my blood pressure. I could feel a cool damp rag pressing against my head repeatedly. All hand movements stopped momentarily. I opened my eyes again and tried to move my hands but they were tied down by something that was biting sharp into my wrists.

"What-?" I shook my hands viciously, feeling incredibly panicked.

"Serena, thank God! Oh my God, I've never been so scared."

Rayne started rattling off how happy she was but I hardly heard her as I again tried to free my hands and couldn't understand why I was tied down.

"Please- get these off, I need these off." I looked around only then realizing I was in an ambulance.

The paramedics looked stunned.

"She's conscious." The lady with the harsh voice stated.

"Serena, they had to tie your wrists, you were thrashing and screaming, you were in a full manic episode. You hurt your head again- I"

The paramedic held her hand up.

"Ma'am please, we don't know her mental state it's best to just try and keep her calm until we can get into the hospital."

I couldn't wrap my head around what she had said. I saw Rayne nod but her eyes never left mine. I was trying to calm down but being

tied down was making me feel absolutely petrified. I tried to frantically piece my memory back together but I still couldn't remember
screaming. I remembered the girl, the mental hospital the locket?
Another object maybe? I needed to talk to Damon and Darren.

I couldn't be in the hospital, it wouldn't be safe, Rayne wouldn't
be safe. It left both of us vulnerable to an attack from the demon. I
could not put Rayne at risk like that. We had to go.

"I- guys I feel fine. This is unnecessary, I'll be just fine."

The women looked at me considering her words carefully.

"Of course. We just want to make sure. Glad you feel better."

Her demeanour showed she was lying and it made me feel unrea-
sonably enraged.

Rayne and the other two paramedics gave her a look that read
"Are you crazy?"

"No really I-"

My heartbeat sped up. Too fast. It hurt. I tried to breathe but I
was hyperventilating.

"Shes slipping into cardiac arrest! I'm gonna need the paddles
stat. She's going to crash! How far to the hospital?!" The lady yelled
to the driver.

I looked at his eyes in the rear view mirror, so dark. Too dark.
They were black. The driver was a demon. They had to know. We had
to get the hell out of here now.

"Serena!" Rayne yelled tears streaming down her face. "Don't do
this!"

I tried again unsuccessfully to catch my breath. I had to get
everyone away from this demon.

"Ready the paddles and clear!" The paddles came down to my
chest and I screamed right before they touched my skin.

"NOO!" The scream ripped through my throat.

As I screamed the ambulance flipped and everyone was flung
away from me. The crunch of metal felt like it shattered the floor.
The scream of the windows as they exploded on impact was that of

a thousand gunshots. I watched Rayne fly to the other side of the ambulance, with a sickening crunch to the side of the vehicle and she fell unconscious. I watched the two paramedics that hadn't spoken fly against one another. The table I was strapped too rolled against the lady with the harsh voice, pinning her to the wall opposite of Rayne. I watched the driver crash against the windshield which split on impact. I felt the vehicle flip twice before landing. Then a familiar scene flashing in my mind, of the car crash, with the women expecting a baby and her man, that now looked remarkably similar to Damon except me in her space.

It happened within seconds. The moment the vehicle stopped moving I was the only one not unconscious. I tried desperately to unwrap my hands. I tried until I could feel blood trickling from my wrists and ankles, then I kept trying.

I kept looking at Rayne a heap on the floor. I couldn't find my words. I just stared at her as I aggressively tried to break free from the holds.

"Don't be dead, please don't be dead. You can't be dead, you are getting married in 14 days." I muttered out loud.

I needed my phone, I needed Matt to come to her. He had to know what was happening. I yanked as hard as I could until I felt a bone shift in my wrist. I would've cried out had I been able. I pulled my right hand free and quickly undid my left hand then my feet. I ripped the iv from my arm. I tried to crawl out of the bed, and fell beside the two paramedics that had collided into one another. There was blood pooling beneath both their heads. I forced myself to crawl, feeling every prick of shattered glass slid into my skin as I half dragged myself across the ambulance. Once I reached Rayne, I grabbed her into my arms and started to drag her out. I wasn't sure if she was alive. All my mind was thinking was I had to get us out, we needed to get out. The back hatch was crunched outward. I booted it several times until it came loose with a loud whine and clattered to the ground with a sound similar to if a dozen metal pots fell onto a hard floor at the same time. I carried Rayne out in my arms. Pleading she was alive. I dragged her about 5 feet from the ambulance. I could hear more sirens in the distance. I put her in the fetal position and tried to find her pulse. My breath shuddering with fear. My hands shaking violently.

After about 30 agonizing seconds, I stumbled onto the right part of her wrist and could feel her pulse. It was slow but it was there.

"Thank Gods.. oh thank Gods. You are alive, hang in there." I mumbled.

I left her and went back to the ambulance. I still mostly crawled, I couldn't quite stand. I pushed the bed away from the first women and dragged her out laying her near Rayne. Her pulse was strong but she was unconscious. Next I dragged each of the other two out. Both of them were still alive with weaker pulses but none as slow as Rayne's. I cringed remembering how her body crumpled into the side. The amount of broken bones it could be. I went back for the driver. The sirens sounded closer now. My eye kept filling with blood, I wiped it on my sleeve constantly blinking so I could see. I felt no pain. I pried the crunched door with my hands while kneeling, I didn't know where the strength was coming from and tossed it aside as if it were a bag of flour. I first checked his eyes, but they were a normal hazel brown.

"God had I imagined the black eyes?" I checked his neck for a pulse.

I waited 1 minute, nothing. I tried his wrist, one minute, nothing. I tried to drag him out anyways but the drive shaft was lodged into his ribcage. If I were to move him if he wasn't already dead, I would kill him. I had to leave him there. I fell to the ground then back into an army crawl. I stared at all the bodies strewn about and my nightmare resurfaced, the man after the plane crash- whom looked almost like Darren, I was in her space, the shallow grave of snow. I shuddered as if feeling the cold seeping to my bone as she did. I ignored it. Stress, Trauma there were so many explanations. I pulled myself slowly back to Rayne. As the sirens pulled up beside us. I closed my eyes in relief with Rayne's wrist back in my hand, feeling the throb of her weak pulse as I too fell unconscious.

When I came too I was in a hospital room. It was pale yellow and had some randomly placed art on the walls. The sun was struggling through some white blinds in the small window on my right. I tried to sit up and gasped in pain.

I looked down in horror as my upper body was wrapped tightly. I couldn't move my arms and I couldn't sit up. The realization hit only after a few minutes of staring. I was in a straight jacket.

I looked around the room but I couldn't see anyone.

"Hello?" I called out, helplessly trying to break out of the jacket with zero success.

A nurse came in then. She had grey hair in a bun and looked startled, no terrified as she entered, like she didn't expect to see me up.

She turned and ran out of the room without speaking to me.

"Wait! Please!" I fumbled again with the jacket.

Damon came in that minute and rushed to me. I was so relieved to see him that I almost cried.

"Serena! You are awake."

"Oh Damon thank God, I- is Rayne okay? Why am I in this? Please tell me what's going on. Please Damon." I bit back tears as my voice cracked.

He wrapped me in a very tight hug.

"Damon-please..Answer me." I whispered against his head.

I looked over his shoulder as Darren entered. He dropped two cups of steaming coffee to the floor and ran to my side. I watched it splash up the wall and pool onto the floor. What a waste of coffee, was my main thought.

"Get that damn thing off of her." He ordered Damon.

Damon without taking me out of his arms undid the jacket behind me and my arms fell free and immediately wrapped around him too.

"Thank you. Thank you." I locked eyes with Darren over Damon's shoulder.

Relief was plain on his face. His eyes were dark underneath indicating he hadn't been sleeping much. He was just standing at the end of the bed. For someone who was always so stoic that scared me.

"Rayne is going to be alright." Damon said against my hair.

I pulled out of his arms and he let me go, meeting my eyes instead.

"But wait- she's not alright right now? What happened to her! What about the others?" I shouted.

"Serena- keep your voice down." Darren warned, shooting a glance to the door.

I dropped my voice to a whisper.

"What is going on, please. I'm so happy to see you guys, but please tell me. Please"

They shared a look. Obviously communicating silently as they sometimes did.

I took a deep breath trying to calm down.

"Okay-" Damon started.

"Rayne is in surgery. The accident broke her whole left side of her body. They are repairing damage and pinning to ensure her bones heal correctly. She did not get any fatal injuries."

I interrupted. "Oh thank Gods, oh my god." I put my hands up to cradle my head.

"The others- I pulled them out- I don't know how."

"Everyone but the driver will pull through. You saved them Serena." Damon assured me.

"The driver- I thought I saw black eyes."

Damon seemed unfazed by this, my body flooded with unease.

"Guy's what's going on?"

Darren's eyes kept flicking to the door. He nodded to Damon.

"Look- this is going to seem crazy. But you have to trust us. Can you do that Serena?" Damon said softly.

"Yes." I meant the answer.

We had been through too much together for me not to trust them.

Damon slid the jacket off of my arms. I realized I was only in my white bra and some shorts that looked like they came from the hospital. I immediately covered my chest. Heat rushing to my cheeks. Darren chucked me a pink hoodie that I didn't recognize.

"Put that on quickly." He hissed.

"Okay, what's happening?"

But before I got an answer Darren was unhooking me from the machines and Damon was picking me up. I yelped in pain.

"Oh fu-" I began to yell in pain. Darren slammed his left hand over my mouth as he muffled my scream.

"Dammit, gentle Damon." He whispered roughly.

Doesn't matter how gentle I am Darren. It's going to hurt."

Darren kept his hand over my mouth as Damon adjusted me in his arms and I bit back another scream.

"Serena, I know it hurts. You need to be as quiet as possible." Darren spoke softly by my left ear.

I was unfamiliar with him having such a soft tone to his voice. This also didn't do anything to lessen the unease I was feeling. What was happening?

"Why are you carrying me- ahh!" Darren's hand clamped harder on my mouth.

Tears flooded my eyes, as they did blood flooded my vision again. Why does it hurt so much? I stared down in terror and realized my entire lower body from my waist down was in a cast.

My eyes must've beheld my panic because Darren looked away from my eyes now.

"Go Damon now. Serena, do your best. Our lives depend on it."

Darren said so coldly, so commanding you would think he was directing an army. Any hint of the softness he had a few minutes ago, completely vanished.

Damon broke into a sprint carrying me. Darren ran ahead scouting to ensure we weren't seen. We barrelled out the back door and I cried out again unable to keep quiet. The pain was siring. An alarm went off in the hospital then and we collapsed into a blue van. Darren ran to the drivers side and Damon quickly got us into the back hatch almost dropping me to the floor as Darren peeled out of the parking lot.

"What is going on?!" I yelled.

"I'm so sorry! Are you okay?" Damon threw a blanket over me.

"I- What's going on?"

Damon shook his head. We will explain everything but right now we need to get back to the hotel. It's the safest place.

"No! What about Rayne?! We can't just leave her there!"

"Rayne will be okay. Darren and I will take turns watching over her. Matt is on the way here on a plane right now. He will be here by tomorrow. Rayne will be in surgeries the next 3 days. They are keeping her under anaesthesia."

That did absolutely nothing to ease my fears. It just deepened them.

The van jerked aggressively right and left, I heard a faint sound of police sirens.

Damon held me firmly in place on the floor of the obviously stolen van while we careened at a suicidal rate through the city streets.

"But if we aren't safe, how is she going to be safe?!"

"They aren't after her."

"What does that mean?! The demon, Henry who is behind this?"

Damon searched my face a moment.

"Neither. They aren't after her because-well because she didn't rise from the dead."

Darren jerked around another corner.

"Dammit Damon! When are you going to learn to keep your friggin' mouth shut!" Darren yelled toward us as we sped through a red light.

"I-what?..."

We screeched to a stop and Darren tumbled out of the drivers side and yanked the back door open so fast it made my head spin.

"Go now!" Darren hollered.

Damon struggled to lift me. Darren groaned in frustration, and jumped up sweeping me into his arms in one fluid movement.

"Damon grab everything else and haul ass! We gotta beat the cops."

I realized they had parked into the dodgy hotel parking lot instead of the parking lot with the condemned building that was the hotel. Smart. Although it helped that regular people couldn't enter the hotel like we could.

"Darren! Back entrance. Below the terrace, so reception doesn't see her. There will be too many questions with her cast and all they won't understand. We can't be seen." Damon said as he filled his arms with stuff and jumped out of the back of the van after us.

Darren nodded and bee lined it to the back alley. There was so much pain I was holding back tears and I was biting my lip down hard enough to draw blood to keep from screaming.

"I know it hurts Serena just hang in there, we are almost at our room." Darren's voice was low and harsh.

We were racing up the stairs.

Damon looked ahead before we got to our suite, he motioned it was clear and we poured into the room. Damon locked the door quickly. Enchanting something under his breath and drawing a line of sea salt. Darren immediately laid me on the bed.

"How is she-?" Damon said to Darren.

Darren ripped his fingers through his hair which was soaked in sweat.

"I don't know- I'm checking!" He yelled back frantically.

He grabbed a medical bag that was obviously once on an ambulance out from under the bed. He had a stethoscope and was checking my breathing, my pulse. Counting my heartbeats. Then he was searching my face and head, the injuries there.

Damon was standing a few paces away in the kitchen staring at me.

"She seems fine Damon, all her levels are normal."

"Where is the pain Serena? Anything outside of your hips and legs?" Damon asked.

"Guys STOP. What is going on. Tell me right now."

I was even shocked by the edge in my tone. They both stared at me. After a few agonizing minutes of silence Damon spoke:

"We don't know how you are alive."

I gulped. I ran my hands anxiously through my hair and took a shuddering breath.

"You thought I was dead?"

Darren and Damon switched spots.

"We weren't certain. They only told us minutes before we came into the room that they said you wouldn't wake up that you had a heart attack from all the sedatives they had to give you, someone gave you the wrong dose. We don't know who or why."

He continued as he walked toward me. Darren started moving dishes around in the kitchen.

I exhaled slowly.

"Reiterate to me what happened. The last thing I remember was pulling everyone out of the ambulance. I crawled back to Rayne. That's it."

"That's the other thing, They didn't know how you could have possibly pulled anyone out let alone yourself. "

"Adrenaline?"

"That's what they rationalized. But that would be physically impossible. Even with adrenaline there are limits."

"Well I mean, my power or whatever you want to call it, I flung Darren across the room. I used it in battle. I know regular people wouldn't grasp that, but that must be it right?"

Damon looked sadly at me. "Serena the ambulance was crushed, you shattered your bones from your pelvis down."

Darren slammed a cup down so hard it broke, the glass pieces littered the floor.

"But-no, I was strapped down they strapped me down to the bed. The bed rolled into one paramedic."

"The bed was sideways, it wasn't face up. The lower half of your body was crushed against the ambulance and into the paramedic."

I shook my head.

"No, I sat up- I- I'll never walk again? That's what you are trying to tell me, you are tip toeing but I- I'll never-"

The realization hit me like a brick to the face.

My heart was speeding up again it hurt badly. I was having a very hard time calming my panic.

"Damon would you just shut up. Let her breathe a minute. You are laying too much on her." Darren barked from the kitchen.

Damon re countered. "She deserves to know! She asked to know!"

"It doesn't matter!" He howled.

The room started to spin again. "Guys" I whispered but they kept arguing.

"Guys please..." Barely a whisper.

All I could feel was my heart hammering in my chest. It was hard to breathe.

I grabbed Damon's arm as hard as I could. His eyes turned to me and flooded with panic.

"Darren!"

Darren was at my side in seconds. I was almost gasping for each breath.

"No! No! Serena!" Darren yelled as I succumbed once again to the blackness.

Chapter 12

CLIMB

"It is easy to set a goal, to pinpoint a dream, the hard part is the climb to get there, it is challenge after challenge, it is exhausting, it is scary, it is daunting, it is overwhelming, it will bend and break you, it will make you want to give up time and time again, there is safety in suppressing, danger in expressing, but if you don't keep moving, you'll always be in the same place, keep with the climb it's not about how fast you go, or how well you do, all that matters is that you keep going, or you'll never get to what's waiting on the other side."

I awoke to their voices, I didn't open my eyes, I just listened. I didn't feel much pain.

"She will wake up Darren."

"You better friggin' hope so. What do you think you were doing she just had a heart attack. Why would you-" Darren sounded more pained then angry.

"She needs to know everything!" Damon rose his voice.

"And she will! Slowly. Do you not understand that we almost lost her?" Darren's voice faltered ever so slightly.

"Oh, what you think your the only one who cares about her Darren?! Last I checked you only care about us"

"I look out for you because it is my responsibility to protect my younger brother. You always come first no matter what." Darren snapped.

"You think not telling her everything is how we protect her? Who is that helping Darren, us or her?"

"She has had multiple manic episodes in the last 48 hours. We don't even know what her mental state is. She is paralyzed, she had a heart attack, whatever the hell knocked her out this time. Shes suffered two massive head injuries. Do you want her healthy again?" Darren rambled.

"What kind of question is that? Of course I do." Damon's turn to snap back.

"Then we take this slowly." Darren spoke firmly.

"She's going to ask questions Darren, and what you think we should just not answer them? I don't know about you but that would seem more stressful."

"That's not what I'm saying. Whatever she asks she can know- Just don't dump it all on her the second she opens her eyes." Darren's tone softened slightly.

"We also may not have all the answers for her." Damon added.

"And we will deal with that as it comes Damon."

The coffee machine chimed then. Indicating the pot was ready.

I was having trouble processing all they were saying- I hoped to hear more but they stopped talking. I tried to move in bed and couldn't. I wanted to cry. There was no feeling in my lower body. I couldn't imagine not being able to do anything alone again. I fought against myself to move but I could only move my arms. It was like trying to swim up a waterfall. Utterly useless. So I used my arms to uncover my upper body. I would pace my questions slowly- as much as they all wanted to tumble off of my lips in one breath. I needed to know everything. But first I had to understand if I was okay physically. I must've fainted. But what manic episodes? I wished so badly that I could remember the whole night but no matter how hard I tried all I remembered was black eyes and pulling everyone out.

Damon noticed first.

"Serena! I'm glad you are awake. You gotta stop passing out jeez." He laughed.

Darren looked over to me. "I agree with Damon. Stay awake for a while at least."

"I will do my best." I looked at them both for a long moment.

"I'm not going to be able to sit up, am I?"

"Not for a while..We can prop you mostly up though. Want that?" Damon offered me a reassuring smile.

I nodded and they both moved to gather pillows and such to prop me up.

"We will find you a Wheelchair too." Damon continued.

Tears pricked my eyes and I forced them back.

"Better be one of the best and speediest ones around." I joked halfheartedly.

Damon laughed and Darren half smiled. Making light of the situation was the only thing I could think to do.

"Absolutely." Damon said.

After they propped me up Damon put a steaming cup of coffee on the side table.

Darren handed me a plate of food.

"Eat. Even if you don't feel hungry. You need the strength."
Darren said delicately.

I was actually famished.

"Thank you. How long was I asleep?"

"Not long, a few hours." Damon answered.

Phew. Only a few hours. It must have been me fainting. I was
so worried about Rayne, but I was beyond grateful she was going to
be okay. I couldn't pick my first question, it was so hard not to ask
everything all at once.

"Why did I get proclaimed dead?"

Damon sighed.

"They tried the paddle's on you the first time, and then the
ambulance crashed. They figured the adrenaline was keeping your
heart beating. They were monitoring you, but then you started
thrashing about and speaking incoherently. They sedated you but it
didn't take the first couple times. That's why the straight jacket to
keep you from hurting yourself or one of us."

He paused to take a deep breath then continued.

"But they gave you too much sedative. After the heart issue, they
assumed you would pass. And you did. According to their machine
your heart stopped beating. That's what they came to tell me, that's
why I rushed in like I did. Darren had gone to get hot drinks, unaware
of the OD. They also said if you didn't pass away they were planning
on sending you away, they didn't understand how you got everyone
out while supposedly paralyzed. In short, they were afraid."

"That's what we are working on figuring out right now. Do you
remember your day with Rayne where you went? We were trying
to figure out if you came in contact with one of the cursed objects
possibly." Darren added.

All I could try to process was the fact I was apparently crazy, and
also died. Somehow.

"I died..?"

"And then you came back." Damon said.

"But there, there was no bright light, no feeling of peace, no seeing a loved one. There was nothing... But death isn't nothing..We know that, we know that as a fact. Don't we?" I said slowly.

"We are trying to figure it out Serena. Try not to think about that." Damon said.

It wasn't hard to put out of my mind, I didn't fear death. But I did fear there was no afterlife.

"Do you think- Maybe, I might walk again?" I looked down at my useless legs.

Darren ran his hand through his hair and busied himself in the kitchen, I heard him crack a beer.

Damon was the only one really talking to me. Darren must not be so good at this kind of thing. Maybe he figured better to let Damon handle it.

Damon gave me a small smile.

"You never know- if this is an object, maybe we can reverse the affect somehow."

I appreciated the hope he was giving me, even if it was false hope. How was I going to help them save humanity like this?

"My day with Rayne, I had a bath, got dressed. We went to a massage parlour. I thought there might be an object there and was going to update you guys on the next check in. But I thought I had heard the fire alarm, it was blaring and I freaked out the staff by running out. It wasn't the sound of a fire alarm though. It was bells, like loud piercing tinging bells."

"Bells- Darren grab the folklore book for me. That sounds familiar. Did you touch anything there?" Damon asked.

Darren moved to the shelf to retrieve the book, he found it quickly and handed it to Damon.

I shook my head.

"Nothing outside of the obvious. Floor, door, massage table."

"Anything that looked old?"

"No, there was a huge display cabinet in the room with all sorts of things on it, but the bells were so loud. I couldn't stay in there."

"Anything that stood out among them?" Damon asked.

"No."

"Did you get anything other then a massage?" Damon met my eyes.

"No, but Rayne said she gets a skin and hair treatment they swear by for beauty and youth. Weekly."

Darren scoffed a bit. "Says every beauty product for women ever."

I snickered slightly. "That's true."

Damon was flipping through the folklore book.

"What about after, you heard the bells, you ran out and you, is that when Rayne called the ambulance?"

"No, after that we grabbed coffee's, somewhere I usually go, nothing off. Then we went to the-" I trailed off suddenly realizing there could have been cursed objects easily there.

"And?" Darren pressed.

"We went to the antique mall, to get furniture for my house."

"Dammit." Darren said quietly.

Damon lifted his head from the folklore text he was deeply concentrating on.

"Darren's right. You could've touched anything, came across any kind of cursed object there. We will have to prioritize that." He closed the book.

"Pause on the bells. We have to go to that mall."

"Okay. I moved to get up momentarily forgetting that I couldn't very well move in general."

"Not you Serena, you have to rest." Damon said.

"But I-"

"We can't very well carry you in public, we can disguise ourselves but cant disguise that." Darren said.

"And I would slow you down." I said quietly, dismayed.

"One of us should stay behind to help you." Damon said.

"No don't worry I will be fine."

Damon looked at me skeptically. "Serena you can't walk, how are you-"

Darren interrupted him. "I will stay here"

I was surprised he offered and had expected Damon would.

"Really?" Damon said.

"Yeah, you have a better eye for cursed objects bookworm. I'm good for fighting, but you won't find anything to fight there in the middle of the day. You can always reach me if you need."

"Okay, you are right. Serena anything else? What happened before the ambulance?" Damon pressed.

I tried to think but the last thing I remembered was going out the door after picking everything for my house. I remembered falling, bad headache. That's it. There was time missing and I couldn't account for it and the only person I could ask was in surgery.

"I- I've lost some time. I remember leaving the store, a siring pain in my head and falling, then I remember pulling people out of the ambulance. Then waking up when you guys took me out."

"Okay, we have to figure out what happened in that time span. I will also check your house, the new furniture okay? Can I have your keys?" Damon asked gently.

"Of course, they are in my bag by the door."

Damon moved to the door grabbing my keys.

"Okay I will keep you guys updated I will be back tonight."

"Take care of yourself Damon," I said.

"Don't be stupid and call me if you need me Damon, got it?" Darren said with a level of worry mixed into his authority.

Damon laughed a little and saluted "Yes sir, brother sir, I swear."

Darren snickered.

"Damon?" I asked hesitantly.

"Yes?" He hovered by the door. Flashing his brilliant smile to me.

"I know you have a lot on your plate and I know you are already doing me such kindness. But could you please.. please check on Rayne?"

"I would be happy to. I was already planning on it anyhow."

"Thank you so much."

He nodded. "Of course."

He closed the door behind him as he left.

Darren didn't look to me. He locked the door.

I stretched to reach my coffee. I was able too without having to ask for help thankfully. I hated this forced dependency.

I watched Darren busy himself in the kitchen cleaning up from the meal he made us.

I was having a hard time picking a topic to talk about. I settled for a compliment.

"You sing really well, you know."

Darren turned to me and raised his eyebrows. "Oh, really?"

"Your voice was what drew me into the club in the first place."

"Well I am no Elvis, but I try. I had no idea you were even there."

"I was having an internal conflict as to whether or not you wanted to be left alone."

"Yeah. You should've just talked to me. Then maybe I could have prevented your fall." He said a little coldly.

"Maybe. Maybe not. Don't put that on yourself. It happened. It was my fault. You looked really happy up there. Have you always enjoyed singing?"

"I've enjoyed it for as long as I can remember. We drove around a lot when we were younger. Used to karaoke the whole time."

"With your family?"

He thought for a moment. "No, we don't really, remember much of our parents. That's probably all lost with our other memories. Damon and I used to drive around, bullshit and talk for hours on end, then we ended up here." He was leaning against the kitchen counter as he was talking.

"Does Damon sing too?"

Darren chuckled. It warmed me to see his face light up ever so slightly.

"Sound's awful, doesn't stop him from doing it though."

"That's funny, I like when people live doing what they enjoy whether they excel at it or not. You don't have to be good at something in order to enjoy it."

"I like that point of view. It's also, just preforming live music in a bar, just relives some of the weight. Like wearing a mask briefly. It's just me and my voice and the guitar in my hands. Everything else just fades away for a while."

"That's lovely, I could see that when you were on stage. It was beautiful to see you happy. It must be exhausting though."

Darren met my eyes with a different look, like I'd stripped some of the wall he kept around himself.

"Exhausting?"

"To be stone. All the time. Rarely allowing yourself to feel anything but what fuels the fire to fight, to protect."

He looked away then and when he looked back his eyes were cold again.

"I don't have the luxury-"

I noticed his fist clench and I realized with dread that I was hurting him. I backed off the topic.

"So, when did you guys become like this? How did you learn about everything?"

Darren paused for a moment deep in thought. His fist fell open. I could sense him relax slightly, by the topic change.

"Honestly, again we don't really recall much of that. It's a missing piece that we hope to someday figure out."

"What about you?" He turned the question on me and I was unprepared.

"In a nutshell? My father was killed when I was 5, I barely remember him, but I miss him dearly. My mother-" I trailed off remembering the voicemail.

"We had a difficult relationship. We were close but when my father died she changed. Then she met Nick, and he was amazing- when he was sober. Mom one day left him. Then I left her when she went back to him. I haven't spoken much to her in the last handful of years."

Darren looked at me taking in the information.

"How old were you when you left your mom?"

"16. Same year I met Henry and well you pretty much know the rest."

I contemplated showing him my mom's voicemail, maybe he could make sense of it. Then I figured that would be best done when Damon was here too. I decided to revert to small talk. I didn't give him much time to reply.

"How was your day? The one I was with Rayne."

"Decent. We found 1 more item. It will require travel."

"Where?"

"Egypt. But we think the tomb might be headed to the States for display. It should by legend hold 1 of the remaining items we need. It was buried with a supposed ancient God."

"Ah, well Gods are fun to deal with."

"Yeah."

"Nothing we can't handle hey, we got this Darren."

I almost reached my hand to rest against his face. It felt like such a natural response, but I held off, because my judgment must be compromised. As I most certainly had never done so before.

He looked over to me. I couldn't read his expression.

"Ever the positive thinker."

I looked down and fiddled with a fray in the blanket to busy my hands instead.

"I don't see a point of thinking anything but positively." I said a little quieter.

"And this, what happened to you, what happened to Rayne, the Demon, Henry. All that and you still have hope for better?"

His words bit a little but that was no new thing. I stood my ground.

I looked down at my legs.

"I'm alive Darren, Rayne is Alive. How can that not be a positive thing?"

"That's not- never mind."

He busied himself again looking away from me. I paused, considering my words carefully.

"What's the alternative? What good would any other emotion do in this circumstance. Being sad, angry, feeling cheated, none of that would be productive. And it wouldn't change anything. Henry is out there it's a fact, we deal with it. The demon exists, all these horrible things exist and we can protect so many people. We can save the world. All of those are facts. You said yourself we do not have the option to fail so, we will not fail."

He paused in the kitchen then turned and walked slowly towards the bed. He sat in the chair beside me on my left.

"You make it sound so simple." He rested his face in his hands for a split second.

"It's for sure not simple or easy, but it's not impossible. We have to tackle one thing at a time. You guys maybe located another object. I for sure encountered one at the spa or the mall. We have found cursed objects almost everyday. We are well into the last few of all of the ones we need. Small wins. Even in a wheelchair I can still help locate items, I can still help with the spells. I can study books and spells I won't be much use in a physical fight anymore but that's not the only form of fighting."

Darren smiled a bit. "Thank you for being an ever shining light Serena."

He leaned toward me and ever so slightly brushed his lips against my forehead. For less then a second, and so gently that it felt lighter then a soft breeze. My heart thrummed in response. Again it felt like something we had done a thousand times before, but it had never happened.

"Sleep Serena." He didn't meet my eyes and went to the bathroom, closing the door. I heard the shower start a minute later.

I put my cup down. I ate a few bites of the soup Darren left for me. Then I realized I was extremely exhausted, and fell quickly into a peaceful sleep.

When I woke up it was dark in the room. I could hear both Damon and Darren breathing deep in sleep. Good Damon was home safe. I wondered why they hadn't woken me. I winced slightly feeling a strong burn in my bladder. Oh God. The catheter was burning. Then I realized I could feel it. I could feel it. I whipped the blanket off my legs and..moved my legs. Moved them. Tears welled at my eyes. I could feel my legs.

I didn't want to wake the guys. I suddenly was worried I was dreaming. I tried to pry the cast off with my fingers, moving my legs.

It made a very loud sound as it started to tear and Damon woke up.

"Serena? Is that you, what's wrong?" He whispered in the dark.

"Help me." I said urgently.

I heard him rustle blankets and his feet hit the floor so quickly that before I knew it he was at my side. He turned the small lamp on.

"Wait- what are you doing?" He asked in a hurried whisper.

Darren was still passed out on the couch the light hadn't stirred him.

"I need this off!" I whispered more urgently as I tried pulling at it again.

Damon grabbed my hands stopping me from grabbing the cast.

"Serena your legs are broken you can't take that off."

"Damon you don't understand, I can feel my legs. I can feel the catheter its burning like crazy."

His eyes widened as he loosened the grip on my hands.

"That's not possible Serena, you must be imagining-"

I cut him off. "I'm not! I am perfectly sane and telling you I can feel my legs!"

"Serena, it's a fever dream. You've been having them non stop for 3 days."

My heart dropped. "What?"

Damon sighed heavily. "I'm sorry Serena, your legs are broken, you gotta try to remember that." He put his face in his hands briefly.

"What do you mean three days?!" I raised my voice.

Darren stirred.

"huh Damon, she awake?"

"Yeah, she's trying to take her cast off."

Darren rolled off the couch. He looked at me and sighed.

"Guys, I am telling you I FEEL my legs! I FEEL the catheter. I- I'm not imagining this! What do you mean three days?! Where's Rayne?"

Damon pulled me into his arms.

"It's okay Serena. Rayne is alive, Matt rarely leaves her side."

"I promise you I can feel them! My legs."

I started to sob.

"You have to believe me." I whispered between sobs.

Darren sat beside me then and ran his fingers through my hair while Damon held me against him. I could smell liquor on Darren's breath.

"I-I'm so tired." I said quietly as darkness crept over my vision again. "Why am I so tired."

I felt myself collapse limply into Damon. It felt like my body was fluid, without form. I felt lost, floating and blind. But I could hear still.

"What the Hell are we going to do Damon? She needs a doctor."

"We can't, this isn't something a normal doctor can fix, they would dump her in a mental institute or worse considering how we left with her."

"She's losing her mind Damon. She's got such a high temp, the ice baths aren't helping. They make her hallucinate. Relive the nightmare of that night with the white eyed Demon. We are torturing her. I refuse to sit and watch her die. Make the call. It's time to contact Kallisa"

There was a long pause.

"Alright." Damon agreed solemnly. I felt myself being laid down but I couldn't move or speak.

"About damn time you listened to me Damon."

"I don't trust Kallisa." He stated.

"You think I do? I don't see another option, do you?"

"No."

I couldn't hear anymore. The darkness cradled me now.

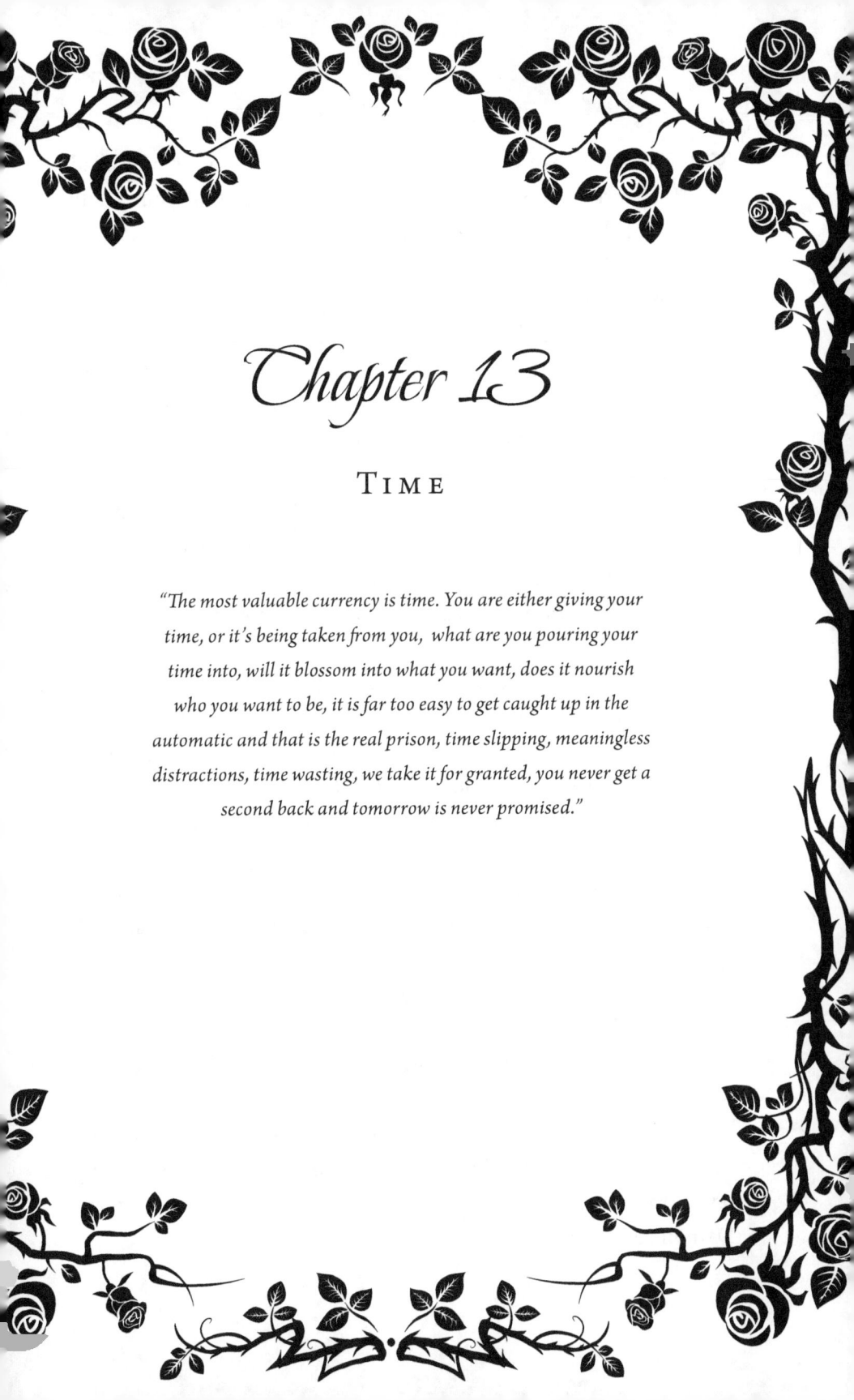

Chapter 13

TIME

"The most valuable currency is time. You are either giving your time, or it's being taken from you, what are you pouring your time into, will it blossom into what you want, does it nourish who you want to be, it is far too easy to get caught up in the automatic and that is the real prison, time slipping, meaningless distractions, time wasting, we take it for granted, you never get a second back and tomorrow is never promised."

When I awoke again. I could hear some sort of mumbled chanting. I opened my eyes, to a pretty and short young lady with blonde hair and- purple eyes.

"No..No!" I thrashed and screamed.

"No!" I screamed so hard it burned my throat.

"Don't touch me!" I cried out, but it went ignored.

I tried to push the girl, but my wrists were restrained. My mind flashed to what I had read previously about purple eyed demons.

"Heat and electricity, bounty hunter, lethal, can make blood boil with single touch."

"Serena, it's okay, this is Kallisa okay, we know her she can help."

Damon's voice said loudly and quickly. I took a few short breaths.

"But- but- but she- she's a Demon." I said breathlessly.

The words tumbled pathetically out of my mouth each word drenched in fear.

"What a displeasure to meet you, Serena."

Her voice sounded strange, like static but legible still.

"I can do no harm. Your boys here have me bound. Cleverly I might add. Never been trapped like this before."

"What are you doing to me?" my voice sounded so small and incredibly weak.

"Attempting to reconnect the nerve endings in your brain. Although with how ungrateful you are I don't think I even want to."

She smiled with pointed black teeth.

My heart raced and I started to shake.

"Guys please what is happening?!"

I could hear Darren chanting in the background, and see him reading from an ancient book.

"Serena it's okay, we thought she might be able to rewire the neural pathways in your brain to break you from this never ending fever dream/sleep cycle. You are perfectly safe, I promise you." Damon continued softly.

The thing laughed, and it sounded like TV static on full volume. I covered my ears.

"Ah but should you trust them? Here you are out of your mind, with a demon, as you so eloquently put it."

It gave me another jagged smile.

"Someone's in danger" It sing-songed as she rested her hands over my head. Darren's chanting grew louder.

"Pity." It seethed.

"What is?" I barely whispered unsure why I was talking to the thing.

"A pity they have me so bound. You are an interesting creature.. Serena. You have no ideaaaa what kind of price they would give me for you... ah. Done."

She put her hands to my head and I screeched like a banshee. It felt like my head was being dragged across gravel. I whimpered and put my hands over my head.

Darren didn't falter while chanting. But it sounded like he was doing it through clenched teeth now.

"Serena, it's okay, it's okay. Darren keep chanting!"

It let go of my head.

"She's all better." It singsonged again, bearing it's black teeth.

"Now let me go! We had a deal." it seethed.

When she let go of my head a ton of memories I didn't know I had came flooding through like a broken dam of knowledge that was inaccessible to me until that moment. There was no pain, no fog. But so much, I couldn't grasp, I couldn't piece it felt like I was drowning in my head.

"Serena? Are you okay?" Damon asked quickly, sounding rather alarmed.

"I- I- it did, I have so many memories, It must have done what you wanted."

The demon's voice sounded loud again like static.

"I have a name you ungrateful daughter of eve. I fixed your brain after all. Messy, messy messy, in there. I bet it will hurt- all those memories. I bet it's gonna hurt like Hell! Believe me, I've been there." Kallisa cackled viciously.

"Kallisa..Thank you." I said lacking conviction in my tone.

It was too saturated in fear and confusion.

"I can sense the falsity but I'll take it.. I wouldn't thank me yet... you might not want all your memories back."

It or she had an odd way of speaking, really drowning out words, almost hissing with each one.

"Okay Darren Banish her now!" Damon yelled.

They both began chanting.

"Always such a cold goodbye darling." It said to Damon whilst never looking away from my eyes.

There was a bright flash of Indigo and then it was gone. Leaving ash in it's midst.

Damon cupped my head in his hands. "Serena, are you okay?"

Darren rushed to my side and undid the straps.

"I'm sorry about the straps, we had to make sure you let Kallisa finish."

Damon said without looking away from me.

I couldn't even formulate a sentence, my brain had shattered memories, fragments all flying about like I was in the winds of a tornado.

"Serena, Serena."

I followed Damon's voice out of the chaos of my mind and focused on his green eyes. I put my hands over his on my cheeks.

"I will be okay. I- I think. She won't come back right? And Rayne she's okay? Is she home? Did you say three days?"

"Kallisa? No, she can't get to you. She owes us, she also knows that she is not a match for us. Rayne is still in the hospital, they needed an extra day for surgeries we are waiting for a check in from Matt. Last we checked all was well. We told them you were quite hurt and we were helping you. Today is day 4. April 23. We will tell you anything you want to know. What do you remember?"

"I don't know it's all loose pieces I can't really, I'm not sure how to put them together."

"It's alright Serena, are you feeling okay?" Darren chimed in finally.

"She doesn't feel feverish anymore Darren."

'I know my legs are broken. I don't feel ill, or tired." I said slowly.

"I'm relieved to hear that." Damon said and cradled my hands in his.

Darren exhaled loudly and put his hand on the top of my head touching his head briefly to mine. The smell of whisky was strong but I didn't mind it too much. I couldn't piece together anything that happened over the last few days, I hoped they would fill me in sooner rather then later. What had I done? What had I done to make them go to this length to bring me back to myself? It felt like 4 day's hadn't passed my last memory was Darren kissing my head and leaving to shower while Damon had left to check for the cursed object in my house and the antique store. I would ask if he figured it out, and for all the details but all I could feel was hunger right now and that was trampling everything else in my head.

"Honestly, I'm completely famished."

Damon laughed.

"I bet, we couldn't get you to eat anything the last few days. What do you want to eat? Anything your heart desires. I will order it and grab it."

"Can we go down to the cafe? I feel like I've been in this bed much too long."

"Of course." Damon and Darren both exchanged a look and stood there.

"We did get our hands on a wheelchair. It's not speedy by any means. But it'll work for in here."

Damon said as he rolled it from the opposite side of the bed. It was an old antique hand crank one. Similar to one you would see in an abandoned hospital.

I sucked in a breath. I never thought I'd ever need one. Yet here I was, but at least I was alive.

"It's got character that's for sure." I forced a small smile.

Damon bought it, Darren didn't. He looked away from me and scoffed quietly. Cracking and chugging a beer.

They both exchanged a look and I realized I needed help but neither moved to help me. In this circumstance, I appreciated them waiting for me to ask and not just helping.

"Damon would you?"

"Of course."

He moved quickly to help me and Darren cracked a second beer.

"Really dude you couldn't wait until we went downstairs?" Damon raised his eyebrows at Darren.

"I'm celebrating. Cheers to Serena, for being free of fever and nightmares."

He raised a second beer and chugged it. Damon shook his head and lifted me from the bed into the chair.

"You okay?"

"Yeah, I just want a moment to uh, freshen up first. I tried to wheel the chair and Damon put his hands over mine showing me how.

"Thank you. I can manage though."

"Of course."

It was hard to wheel at first but I got the hang of it. When I wheeled into the bathroom I almost cried. I looked like I just crawled out of a gutter. Everything was a mess. I worked to wash my hair over the sink, and my face, I laid a bit of makeup and brushed my hair. I sponge cleaned myself best I could. I pulled a loose dress over me. I stared for a minute trying and failing to recognize myself again, before the hunger was too overwhelming and I wheeled back out.

"Okay, ready."

Darren glanced at me and put the bottle down.

"Let's go then! Woo! Food!" he bounded ahead of us to the elevator.

Damon walked beside me.

"Is he alright?" I whispered towards Damon.

Damon gave me a long look.

"You look really beautiful Serena, a lot better then the last few days."

He said in a playful voice.

"Yeah I can imagine." I couldn't help but smile a bit too.

"You didn't answer my question though."

"Darren is- that's a hard question, you know how he is, he's just had a rough go."

I looked away for a minute. My arms were throbbing already from wheeling myself.

"Hey can you push me? I'm sorry my arms are just tired I guess."

"Of course! No trouble, I would be happy too."

He took over and I sighed rubbing my arms.

"Damon- I didn't..Did I hurt either of you?"

I didn't turn back to look at his face, I was too anxious about the answer.

"No, you didn't hurt us. You didn't hurt anyone, we kept you from hurting yourself though."

He said slow and sincerely.

"I'm so beyond relieved I didn't hurt you guys, what do you mean about hurting myself?"

"Let's just give you some time to enjoy being you again for right now. I promise you we will catch you up with everything. But let's take it slow please, you are just back on your feet. I know Darren would feel the same, alright?"

I pondered what he said. Remembering when I was half asleep earlier Darren was the one urging Damon not to say much too me. I guess he was listening. I figured humour was best right now.

"You mean back on my wheels."

Damon sputtered. "What?"

"Well you know, I can't walk so." I smiled as Damon laughed.

We rounded the corner to the cafe.

Darren excitedly waved us over. I chuckled cause he reminded me of a little kid for a moment, the way he had a cheesy grin on his face and was waving us over. However good it was to see him smile, and it really was. The amount he drank bothered me deeply. It reminded me of Nick a bit except for Darren was a friendly drunk and ice cold when sober. Damon pushed me to the end of the table and sat across from Darren.

Jane was serving us again.

"Oh my, why are you in a wheelchair Serena? Pardon my forwardness."

"I fell down some stairs broke my legs. I'm a real clutz hey?"

The lie came quick and smooth.

Jane made a mock face of pity. "I'm sorry to hear that."

She turned to Damon beaming and flipping her hair over her shoulder.

"Hey Sugar, what will be tonight?"

"Hey Jane, I'll get the special tonight please."

He half smiled at her and was watching me instead. Jane huffed.

"And you?" She turned to Darren.

"Oh just keep the drinks coming, Sugar" He smirked mocking how she addressed Damon. Damon narrowed his eyes at him.

"Serena?"

"I will get the special too, some soup and salad to start."

Jane raised her eyebrows. "That's a lot of food."

"Yeah." I laughed forcefully. "I haven't eaten much in the last few days."

She shrugged. "Suit yourself."

She headed away with our order.

"Darren how many drinks did you have at the hotel?"

Darren spoke slurring his words awfully.

"Oh two- three? I don't really remember you know. Just maybe five."

Jane came back with waters and another drink for Darren.

"Jane stop, I'm cutting him off." Damon said.

She nodded.

"Pffffft can anybody say BUZZKILL" Darren said obnoxiously.

He stared at Damon narrowed his blue eyes then whispered "Buzzzzzzzkilllllllll" Really dragging the word out, and pointed at Damon accusingly.

"You'll thank me in the morning." He said.

"Are you okay Darren?" I asked.

"Oh I-I'm perrrfect, I would be a hell of a lot better with another drink though Damon!"

He yelled too loudly for restaurant manner. A few heads turned.

"Try your water." Damon said.

Darren huffed, chugging his water.

Jane dropped our food off.

I had so many questions but all I could think of was how hungry I was, we all ate in silence. Jane cleared our plates doing nothing to try to mask the disgust on her face by the fact that I finished every bite of what I ordered and still ordered dessert. I spoke up then.

"Okay guys I need a run down of everything you guys know that I don't. Catch me up please. I can't do it little by little, the very thought agonizes me."

Damon glanced at Darren whom was busy eating still not really paying attention.

"Darren would tell me not too, but he's out of commission currently and I am choosing to tell you everything you want to know. Where should I start?"

"Did you speak to Rayne, does she remember what happened to me, or after, or anything?"

"No, She, God Serena I'm sorry she's still under anaesthesia from the last check in this morning. They had to do quite a few surgeries but shes healthy and expected to pull through."

I exhaled, "Okay, I- can you take me to her?"

"I can't Serena, I wish I could but the police, everyone is searching for you. You weren't supposed to leave that hospital. Matt knows everything, about you waking up and us looking after you. He will bring Rayne home when he can and you can go there unsuspected, by the time he brings her home, things should calm down enough where you aren't top news anymore."

I was horrified. "I'm wanted?"

"More or less, they are stating you are out of your mind and need to come back so you can be helped. Obviously you are safe in places hidden in the veil- like the Hotel here."

"Oh my God.." I put my face in my hands.

"Look Serena it's a lot to digest and maybe we should take it slowly."

I pressed my fingers hard into my temples.

"No." I pressed on.

"Did you find any cursed objects?"

Darren was staring at us he must've picked up on the conversation.

"Damon just what the Hell are you doing? Serena, he doesn't, you don't need to know this all right now. We just got her back man"

He was standing up and raising his voice now and people were starting to really look our way.

"Darren-" Damon stood up and clamped him on the shoulder.

"Take a walk, cool off."

Darren shrugged his arm off his shoulder aggressively and stormed out without speaking.

"I'm Sorry Serena, he's just really drunk."

I nodded. But I felt worried, I had an urge to run after him and ensure he was okay, But I stayed put, and pressed Damon for more answers.

"So.. Cursed objects?.."

"Yes. I found one actually."

"What? Damon that's amazing. What was it?"

"Well none of your house items are artifacts."

"Well, that's good, they seem really big to be part of a ritual." I said.

"Yeah it would look ridiculous trying to do a spell with a couch or table."

I laughed a bit picturing it.

"So no guardian that I saw or have seen. I simply bought the one we needed and moved on."

"Wow, how pleasantly uneventful."

"Stroke of luck. I will show you it if you are interested once we go back to the room."

"Yeah, I'm curious." I noticed Jane trying to nonchalantly watch us talk from the back. God she really liked Damon. I thought to myself. I wondered if Damon felt the same.

"Well, Damon you should celebrate I mean, you found one of the last items on your own. We have leads on more, and a whole month left yet. You should go have fun."

He laughed a bit, "What do you suggest? How do you want to celebrate. It's as much your win as ours."

"Damon, I mean-" I nodded my head toward Jane.

"Jane? What do you- oh. No, I don't think I should leave you to fend for yourself right now." He shook his head.

"Well not right this minute, I still have so much.. So much to ask. But after- I think you should."

"Alright noted. Next question."

"Were you guys able to get any more information about Henry, or- or the demon?"

Damon's face fell slightly, momentarily then he smiled again. "Not yet, but we will I promise you."

"I believe you, it's okay." I rested my hand on his for a second before pulling away forgetting Jane was watching and I didn't want to mislead my intentions in front of her. But he grasped it back into his.

"It's alright Serena, I know this is a lot but you aren't alone."

I hesitated then let his hand be. To my dismay Jane was watching and her face lit up red as she stalked off further into the kitchen out of view. Damn.

"I have some I'm afraid to ask. But, I need to know so here it goes. What happened during my fever dreams, what did I do, what did I try to do? And what did I do to land me in the predicament at the hospital?"

Damon was running his thumb over my hand and stopped meeting my eyes.

"Are you sure you want to know?"

"No, but I need to."

Damon exhaled.

"At the hospital you started to have these terrors that the doctors were demons trying to kill you. You were shouting and throwing the cords off of you, trying to hit the doctors and Rayne and you tried to take her and you out of the hospital twice before we got here and monitored you."

I swallowed.

"What- like I grabbed her and walked off with her to try and leave while she's broken and unconscious? On my broken legs and pelvis?"

"No- not exactly. More like, you tried to drag her from her bed whilst dragging yourself on the floor. That's another reason the doctors proclaimed you dead, because you were so amped up and doing thing's not humanly possible."

My mind flashed to every terrible zombie movie I could think of.

"God it's like something out of The Walking Dead. I must have scared everyone so much."

'A little." Damon gave me a soft smile. "We don't have to continue."

"There's more then that?"

"You were trying to exercise the supposed demon out of the doctor and wouldn't let anyone near you. That's why they gave you the sedation and jacket. They were afraid you would hurt yourself more or someone else."

"I can't believe that.. he wasn't a Demon? Rayne said I was in a manic episode before I fell. Do you know what that was?"

"I don't. You would have to see if Rayne remembers, when she's in a state to do so."

"Do you think the mania was derived from the affect of one of the cursed objects?"

He looked down again.

"No. Unless I didn't locate it, but of the one I gathered it does not have effects like that, that I could tell. But we will figure it out. However I could be wrong. You seem to react differently to the objects then we do."

"What about, the fever dreams?"

"I will gave you the basis. Mostly it was about Henry coming after you. The ice baths to keep your fever down you- well you thought we were the white eyed Demon, so you were difficult. We will find Henry okay? The white eyed Demon won't get you either."

He pulled me into a half hug. I was having a hard time grasping everything. Darren wasn't wrong this wasn't easy.

"Thank you Damon. For telling me."

"Of course, anything else you want to know?"

I took a long sip of water. "No."

Damon retracted back into the booth and took his hands off of mine.

"What can I do for you right now Serena?"

My mind was racing. I felt alien to myself, the memory lapses plus being unable to walk again were a lot to swallow. I thought again to my mom possibly in a mental hospital and worried that maybe I was crazy after all.

"I think- I'd like to go up to the room, would you take me?"

He jumped up. "Yeah, I got you."

He began to wheel me back toward the elevator.

"I will take you up then I will step outside to check in with Matt for you okay?"

I nodded. I glanced down the long bustling hall that led to the bar where I saw Henry and felt a bit cold.

"It will be fine Serena." Damon said softly obviously picking up on my unease.

"Will Darren be alright?"

Damon paused. "He always is."

That did little to help my anxiety. "Yeah he always is, until he isn't." I thought fearfully.

We started up the elevator and he wheeled me back into the room we shared.

He wheeled me to the table.

"Is there anything I can grab for you before I step out?"

I couldn't even think of something small that would help. Honestly I wanted to be alone. It was easier to take care of myself that way. I didn't know how to process stress unless I was alone.

"Honestly, I will be totally fine. Look Jane seemed upset maybe you should check in on her."

"Okay I will but are you sure you'll be okay here? I doubt Darren will return for a handful of hours yet."

"No problem. I might just sleep anyways."

"Okay, I will update you. Do you want me to wake you after I touch base with Matt?"

"Only if Rayne is awake."

"Okay deal. I won't be long. Lock the door, I got my keys."

"Okay, see you."

He closed the door behind him and I locked it immediately. I exhaled long and loud and slow. I stared down at my useless legs in dismay.

I felt the tears well in my eyes, and I gratefully let them shed. They flowed like water from a broken dam. It burned, it hurt and I let myself feel it. I only allowed myself to breakdown in private. Despite the tears I did believe fully that everything would be okay in the end. I believed it wholeheartedly, I had to believe it. I could not let my hope falter. I was afraid I would be irrevocably broken the day I let my hope die. I was grateful Rayne was alive, I was grateful we were progressing in this venture to save humanity. I accepted that my ability to walk was a sacrifice I had to make in order to save everyone in that ambulance that I could. To save Rayne. That price was more then fair. Although it didn't make it easier. I believed we could find Henry, I believed we could find the white demon, that we would figure out what and who I was; and I believed we would succeed at the impossible. We have too. It's the whole human race. It was such an unfathomable amount of weight resting on our shoulders. I was so grateful to have Damon and Darren too. I couldn't imagine my life without them now. I kept crying. The sobs ripped at my chest, my nose was impossible to breathe through. I held my hand against my mouth so tightly to muffle my sobs that the muscles in my hand were stinging and I was shaking harder then a tree in a hurricane.

"There, there."

I heard the voice then I felt an ice cold hand clamp down on my shoulder.

My body was drenched in absolute terror. I felt frozen in place. Everything in my mind screamed to run and I couldn't.

"Henry." I spoke barely a whisper, barely legible.

But I knew his voice as well as my own. I craned my neck to the right to look at him behind me. His black eyes shone in the moonlight of the room.

"Miss me?" He teased his mouth spreading into a smile of black pointed teeth.

A scream tore through my chest. Louder then I had ever screamed, louder then I thought anyone could. I wished I could take it back, I wished I could show him I was unafraid. I wished I could have pretended I wasn't horrified.

"No one can hear your pathetic shrieking Serena. It's just us baby." he seethed.

He grabbed my hair in a fist and used it to send me spiralling out of the wheelchair. I smacked into the kitchen cabinet, glass fell around me. I tried to scramble away but I couldn't move properly. As I tried he brought his hand to my throat and clamped down so hard that I could barely breathe.

"Henry, what do you want from me?" I choked out.

"What do I want?" He roared.

He whipped his opposite arm over the counter sending several dishes flying to the ground. "I just want you to walk alongside me again. It's better on this side. I can assure you."

Tears kept falling while I was trying to gulp air. I managed to shake my head.

"There's a rumour on this side that you have certain- abilities. See they are all watching you. Curious, curious they are." He sounded similar to Kallisa.

He got right up to my ear, whispering harshly while keeping his hand on my throat. I desperately needed air.

"And I thought to myself, Serena? My Serena? I couldn't believe it. So I rushed here to see for myself. However I am thoroughly disappointed, although not at all surprised, I got here, and I've never seen you so sad. You can't even walk. I bet you are wishing for those boys to come back for you. Hate to break it too you baby, they ain't going to make it in time."

He pushed my head hard into the cabinet 3 times. It was so loud. I could feel the blood hot pouring down my back. I tried to push myself up. Scrambling my hands against the glittering shards of glass surrounding me. It stung immensely as the small glass punctured my skin.

"You are weak Serena, you've always been so pathetically weak."

I strained against his grasp to no avail.

"However-"

He let go of my throat and I fell face down to the floor coughing, gagging and gasping for air.

"I don't want to kill you so quickly. They wouldn't like that. I'd rather it slow. They want to study you, I couldn't care less. I blame you, for me dying. Now I just have so much fury. I can't wait to kill you."

He said the words quietly by my ear.

I tried to grab his leg to pull him down he merely shook me off as you would a mosquito.

"Sad." He tsked.

"Sad that I can't just extinguish you here and now. Snuffed out like a birthday candle." He blew the air imitating doing so.

It was my worst fear come to life. The only man I had ever been with, been in love with was a monster. In all aspects.

"Who want's to study me?" I said rasping my words.

He whirled around. "Oh Serena, all of the under world. The over world. Everything. Apparently your abilities are disconcerted. That you are truly extraordinary. A key to a lock only you can open. I don't see the appeal. It is LIES!"

He yelled the word "lies" and sent another cupboard full of dishes flying.

I struggled hard trying to stand and kept failing.

"Oh please Serena. At least stand up."

I stopped struggling, at this point it was more demeaning to try then it was to be still.

"I will be seeing you, Serena."

Henry laughed an inhuman sound bubbling from his throat, he suddenly was no longer in front of me.

I attempted to drag myself across the glass and cried out. Damn it, I can't even get across the room. Damn it.. After a moment of struggling not to keep crying I gathered up all the strength I had and tried again. I screamed in frustration as I fell again. I got up again, ignoring the thousands of shards in my hands, my stomach and chest. I couldn't feel any of the shards below that, and for that I was grateful. I let the burn of the glass propel me to keep trying until eventually I was able to pull myself to the couch. I was astonished at how much upper body strength I had to pull myself that far up. The exhaustion hit me then and I starting to see black edges in my vision. I welcomed it and fell yet again into darkness.

Chapter 14

"Forgive me"

"Forgive me, I am usually too quiet or too loud no in between, I trust slowly, I won't make it easy to know me, forgive me, I don't know how to put myself before anyone else, I'm lost unless someone needs me, sometimes my thoughts are just too much, forgive me, I could spend a lifetime with you and it wouldn't be long enough, I will keep trying no matter how bad I'm hurting, I will lie to myself, forgive me, I get overwhelmed easily, I won't let you see me breakdown but please don't give me the same courtesy, I realize I'm a bit contradictory, Forgive me, my intensity, I know I love fiercely, I still believe my hope will never fail me."

"Serena!" I was awoken by Damon' voice, when light flooded the room.

"I'm here, Damon, I'm alright."

I half mumbled without opening my eyes.

"Serena, Serena, are you hurt?"

I felt his arms around me starting to lift me.

"I think I'm fine, just the glass-"

I opened my eyes then meeting Damon's green eyes that were filled with panic.

"What happened?" he asked cradling my neck and head in his arms.

"Henry was here. Just came to scare me mostly."

"What- but the enchantments, he shouldn't have been able to pass through he's the lowest tier of demon."

"I-I don't know. Maybe a border was missed. But it's- I'm fine. Okay, I'm fine."

"Let me get you back to the chair, I just want to make sure okay?" He said calmly.

I nodded as he lifted me sitting me back in the wheelchair which remarkably was still in one piece, Henry hadn't touched it.

As he sat me down I took a breath, and inspected my arms and hands, all were shallow cuts.

"See?.. I'm fine."

Damon was busy checking my back, then my legs he paused.

"Serena.." His voice was shaky.

"You, you can't feel anything from your waist down right?"

"No, why?"

He sucked in a breath and ran his hand over his jaw. Now I was nervous.

"Damon, please tell me."

He glanced up at me. "You need a doctor-"

"But I thought I was wanted?"

"I know, but in the Edmonton and surrounding area, they wanted to keep it quiet. Do me a favour Serena. Stay as still as you can. Try not to look at your leg. If you go into shock now we won't make it to Calgary"

I was stunned speechless.

"We leave in 5, I will pack you a bag. It's the closest big hospital that's outside the radar of their search for you which extends to Red deer. You will make it three hours."

He started throwing things into my brown bag. Of his, mine and Darren's."

I took a deep breath. "Damon you are scaring me."

"I'm sorry, it'll be fine. We gotta go grab Darren."

"Damon-can I help, pack or anything..?"

"Please just don't move. That's the most helpful thing for you to do right now." he snapped slightly.

My heart was pounding in my chest, and the internal battle of not looking at my leg scared me to death. How bad was it?

"I-what did Matt say?"

Damon paused for a split second. "Is that what you-?"

"I need something to distract me, good or bad, but please."

"Rayne woke up. Matt can take her home tomorrow."

I breathed a sigh of relief. At least one sliver of good news. I couldn't help thinking he was keeping parts from me.

"Damon- is that all?"

He hesitated so long that I almost asked again, then said:

"Rayne is awake, but she hasn't spoken. They say it could be a temporary affect, they are going to closely monitor her, but they are sending her home with Matt nonetheless. Nothing else is afflicted just her ability to talk."

I put my face in my hands. "Okay, but what does that mean?"

"It's possible, with the amount of surgeries and level of injury that it may be permanent side affect. However, she is alive still, and conscious of what's going on around her. I'm sure she will pull through."

"I hope so" I said quietly.

Within minutes I managed not to look at my leg and Damon was wheeling me away his arms full of bags.

"Are you still okay, can't feel anything?"

My mind was so crowded with fragments of memories that I was fighting to piece together. Kallisa wasn't wrong, It was messy in my head. Some of the fragments were so unfamiliar I couldn't begin to string them together. Perhaps I just needed time. So much was happening so fast. Then I thought to Henry, I wondered what he meant, and I wondered why my abilities failed me this time. I neglected to mention much to Damon as he seemed very worried about my leg. For the first time I was grateful I couldn't feel. We made it down toward the bar where Darren came to sing. I didn't hear him now. I was worried about him, I had never seen him quite so drunk. Damon draped his brown coat over my legs.

"Wait here, I will grab him."

I waited there for several minutes still afraid to look at my leg. I was tempted to try and wheel myself in. I got many strange looks as people passed by and I felt seriously exposed and under dressed. I was glad Damon had draped his coat over me it made it easier to not look at my leg. I felt at my throat noticing something felt a little cold and heavy and pulled on the locket I had around my neck. It was heavier then the silver heart necklace I had always worn from my great grandmother. This one lay over top of it. I traced my thumbs over it, forgetting when I got it and forgetting when I last had it on, or if it was always there. Damon emerged then. Without Darren.

"I left a note but we gotta move he will have to meet us there. Lets go."

"What? He isn't there? Are you sure?"

"Yeah the bartender claimed to see him leaving with some girl, I mean good for him for getting laid finally but just inconvenient. You can't wait. We have to move now."

"So you are what gonna smuggle me out of the city?"

"Pretty much, it won't be hard, we are not leaving the Province."

I started to laugh uncontrollably. Damon gave me a very concerned look.

"I- I laugh at inappropriate time's sometimes" I said gasping between each breath.

"Okay." He smiled and shook his head at me.

We got to the parking lot and Damon went straight for a jeep."

I kept laughing hysterically. "Why are we taking a jeep?"

"I'm hot wiring a car, the volvo is too bold and we can't use your vehicle."

"Ohh hot wiring a car? That's pretty hot Damon."

I joked still laughing. "Fast and furious."

He laughed too as the car rumbled to life. "Alright, lets get in."

He lifted me from the chair and fastened me in the passenger seat. "Still feel okay?"

"Aye, Aye, Captain" I sputtered between another bout of laughter. I felt like a maniac.

He collapsed the wheelchair and tossed it in the trunk. He got in and started to drive the direction of highway 2. I finally got a handle on my laughing. I watched the speedometer rev to 140 and hold steady.

"Damon, is this really necessary?"

"Yeah, absolutely. I-"

He stopped talking as he looked at my face. It must've shown how unsure I was, how scared I was.

"You'll be okay. Maybe try to sleep."

I was tired, perhaps that's what I needed.

"I will do my best." I closed my eyes. Sleep grasped me easily.

When I opened my eyes, we were still driving, Damon looked exhausted. I wished I could offer to take over driving. I would miss driving, it was always relaxing to me. I opted for light conversation.

"Damon you okay? We can pull over and grab a hotel? You look tired, I wish I could take over for you."

Damon smiled sleepily at me. "Nah, I'm good."

"How much further?"

"Another hour yet."

"I think that we should really pull in Damon."

"I need to get you there okay?"

"It can't really be that bad, right?" I tried to read his expression and failed. When he neglected to reply, I continued.

"Okay, then I will keep you talking to help you stay awake. Do you think we will find more items quickly? How many of the ones left do you think have guardians?"

Damon sighed sounded relieved for the topic change.

"I think the last of them will have guardians. I fear some of the smaller ones may have guardians that haven't shown because the items have no threat against them. However once we start using them to do the spells it might awaken one. That's just a worried guess though."

"Well, that would be quite a few guardians to deal with."

"It would but I think we have the resources to handle mostly anything that gets thrown our way."

He sounded sure of himself, which relaxed me slightly. Then he looked at me for a second.

"So, when Henry came, what did he do and say exactly?"

I felt goosebumps raise on my arms.

I breathed deeply, surprised at myself for not having already mentioned it to him. "He knows about my abilities but didn't believe that I have them, I couldn't prove it to him either. He also mentioned that he wasn't aloud to kill me, that they were curious of me, everyone of the over world and the under world."

"That- is concerning."

"That I couldn't use my abilities?"

"No, you were afraid that makes sense to me, just like with the white eyed Demon, your fear is a good blockade to your powers. I mean that you are sought after by many."

"What did he mean by that?"

Damon looked reluctant to reply.

"Well you know of demons, they reside in Hell. There are angels too of course."

I felt I would fall through my seat.

"Angels?! Like, radiant winged people?"

"Yes, but they aren't how you might imagine them, they don't really resemble humans at all. They don't meddle much in human affairs either."

"Wow.. that's incredible. I don't know why I didn't think of that, considering virtually every fairy tale/horror movie monsters are based off of the real thing. But does that mean there is Heaven?"

"We presume so. We don't know though."

I decided to switch the topic again.

"How do you think Darren will meet us here.. if he's drunk? Surely he shouldn't drive."

"I imagine he will be too plastered tonight to notice the note and that we were gone, he will probably meet us in the morning, and he will likely be really pissed about it."

"Has he always been angry?"

Damon pursed his lips in thought.

"Honestly, from what I remember, he was always a little more eccentric But there was so much weight on his shoulders at such a young age, I don't really blame him. I blame myself mostly he practically raised me. But we are both missing quite a bit of time in our memories yet."

I thought about that for a moment.

"You were only kids Damon, no one is to blame." I gave a reassuring smile.

"I know. It's hard not to though." He glanced at me then back to the road.

"We are almost there. How are you doing?"

"I'm more then okay Damon."

We pulled into the hospital parking lot now and he helped me into my chair without struggling even for a second and then he was quickly pushing me to the emergency entrance. When we went through the automated front doors a nurse came rushing in. Her hair was short and brown she had dull eyes and seemed to slightly limp when she walked. She was maybe 51.

"Serena?" her voice was scratchy.

Damon nodded and she took over wheeling me.

"Damon what?"

"I called ahead, I didn't want to drive all that way to waste time in a waiting room."

"It is bad then?"

Damon looked away from me.

"You'll be okay here. That is what's important."

We wheeled into a sterile bright white room. My heart was hammering as they hooked me up to a bunch of wires.

"She's been normal and lucid since the incident?" the nurse asked blandly.

"Yes." Damon answered.

"Good."

"Okay Serena. Look now. I need you to understand what we are going to have to do."

I swallowed as I dared to look down at my legs. Vomit rose in my throat as I stared at the dining plate size piece of glass jammed into my inner thigh. It must have pierced me while I dragged myself through all that glass.

"Can't-Can't we just pull it out?" I glanced to Damon who's eyes held fear that I hadn't seen before.

"If we pull it out, you could bleed out. That's why I needed to get you to a hospital Serena, but I needed you calm, and the glass is keeping the wound from bleeding but can also become very toxic very quickly."

The nurse agreed with him

"Yes, the doctor will be here shortly to decide a plan."

She left the room then. I couldn't help all the shaking in my body. How was it so perfectly placed? It was right in my femoral artery.

"Oh God." I took a shaky breath and Damon wrapped me in his arms.

I relaxed into them, grateful he just hugged me, without me asking. It was comforting to me.

"Damon, how likely do you think?" He held me a little tighter.

I felt his heart racing but he spoke calmly.

"Well you have supernatural abilities, I'm quite certain it'll take a little more then glass to bring you down."

I laughed a bit. "I suppose so."

The doctor came in now. A smile plastered to his young face like a ken doll. He didn't look real?

"Serena, okay I think best case would be to set you up in the OR and put you under to drag this out. The surgeons will have to work quickly to repair the damaged vein without you losing too much blood."

I was horrified at the idea of being put under.

"I don't-is that necessary? To be put under I mean?"

The doctors fake smile unnerved me as it never left his face.

"Quite, I'm afraid."

"I will be right there Serena okay, you'll be fine." Damon attempted to assure me.

"Okay."

The doctor kept smiling. I had an urge to run.

"Okay you have 20 minutes." He said, smile never leaving his plastic face

He turned and left the room, the nurse trailing behind him.

"Damon there's something off with that doctor." I kept my voice low and close to his ear.

"ah the joker?"

I sputtered. "Yeah you noticed too hey? Smile never left his face even briefly, like a mask."

"He isn't the surgeon Serena it'll be okay. We will look into him though, if that makes you feel better."

"It would. Have you heard from Darren yet?"

Damon shook his head.

"I doubt I will for a few hours yet. He is probably still out."

He unwrapped me from his arms as the fake doctor came again to wheel me to my room. Damon stood to follow and the doctor didn't protest. I was relieved.

As they wheeled into the OR Damon got told to stay back and panic flooded my body. But the fake looking doctor passed me to a doctor that seemed much more human in appearance and I felt relaxed again. Damon nodded to me and started to follow the fake doctor. I hoped he would have no trouble. He was pretty well versed with the hunt, I didn't think I needed to worry much. I smiled and closed my eyes silently praying I would survive.

As they wheeled me into the room I caught myself reminiscing about when I could walk. I felt guilty for thinking about it, barely a week in and I missed my legs. How selfish of me.

"Okay breathe this in." I felt straps against my wrists and started to writhe against them. When I looked up. I saw the doctors very human eyes.

"It's okay. It won't be long, it's just like going to sleep."

I loosened the tension in my body and tried to breathe. Standard procedures Serena, that's all. I reassured myself silently.

The gas burned my lungs and I fell quickly into sleep.

Chapter 15

"HERO"

*"It's a little too quiet, a little too dark, a little too lonely, I'm
wading through these memories like I'm knee deep in mud,
grasping for some semblance of sense like I'm underwater gasping
for a breath, all these things a temporary fix, then it's gone and it
all rushes back, then it's worse then before, just hold me steady, I
don't want to fall, I'm tired of being lost, I'm not done not nearly,
take my hand, bring me back home, I'm not sure I can keep
saving myself, please just take me home."*

There I could feel the plane drop much too fast. Oxygen masks fell from the compartments above. Screams of so many people. Ears popping, and then the impact. So cold, everything was so cold. I just wanted warmth. Dead everyone was dead... I'm so cold. My head is in agony, the air is too harsh in my lungs.. Arms wrapped around me. My legs are broken it's impossible to move. Legs are broken, just like now. No legs.. His arms are so strong so comforting. He's telling me he's gonna save us, he pulls us out of the wreckage, but I know I will die. The voice sounds achingly familiar. I long to see his face. I long for warmth. An image my husband? Two children, young 2 and 4 maybe, getting read to board a plane. Their grandparents maybe? "We will take the kids for the first week and then meet you there. "Enjoy your honeymoon!" I hug the two children tears spilling from my eyes. A bad feeling. Something's not right. "Maybe we should all go together?..."

"You two haven't gone on Vacation together since before the kids were born, enjoy some one on one time!" My husband nods his head. I lean down, I kiss their heads and tell them they are the best thing that ever happened to me and that I love them with all my heart. Their little hands it was like they were gracing my skin now. I wanted to cry harder then I already was. I miss them. I miss them so much. I held longer. I look to my children, and remember when I first gave birth, when I saw them for the first time. True love. The only form of true love I imagine. My first baby as he was laid on my chest. The feeling of overwhelm. The pain. I remembered not understanding why there was still so much pain when they put him on me. I cried as much as the baby did, I was so terrified I wouldn't do good enough and the need I had to give him the world was inexplicably intense. "Your an amazing mother. Never forget that." My husband kisses my forehead and wraps me in his arms. Time passed, Second baby comes along, I'm more prepared, I give birth not knowing the sex of the baby and without any pain medications. The pain is excruciating, I am slipping out of consciousness in between contractions. I remember not being able to speak there was too much pain. Then my daughter is brought out into the world and I stare in awe. Aurelia, she's beautiful. My husband speaks my name. I feel empowered. And beautiful. I cry happily.

Then I am in a car, Soft tunes, then the sudden whip of the vehicle, crunching metal, shattering windows, so loud in my ears, Blood, metallic and bitter it's all I can taste in my mouth my body crushed..I can't move, my face doesn't feel right, oh God help me. Please help me. I hear his voice pleading begging for me to be alive, but I cannot move my mouth to reply. I want to stroke his hair, I want to tell him I'm here but I can't move. His voice too is familiar, safe. I wanted to see his face, I wanted to speak.. what about the baby?...What will happen to our baby?..Then an image of us Younger then we are in the car. Blood in a bathroom, I'm crying arms wrapped around me, there so much blood. "We will keep trying trying for a baby. We will keep trying. We are at a hospital, long needles are being poked into my skin. They hurt. A nurse speaks "As far as fertility treatments go we have given every one under the sun. You may want to look at adoption if this doesn't take, especially after so many miscarries." My husband, the voice so light and loving, so familiar. "Don't worry. I have a good feeling about this one, don't lose hope my darling. We will do this. We can get through this. Emma, we will be parents I promise you. I am angry with his positivism. I feel helpless. Defeated. Cold. "I feel like my body is failing me. It's not doing what it's built to do. I don't understand. " I cry helplessly against his chest. "It's not your fault. Shh now" I held longer, It' later and im holding a positive test in my hands. My body aching from treatment. My heart swelling, nothing but pure joy. I can't believe it. *"You are one in a million." I whisper as I caress my belly. "I can't wait to tell your Daddy." I remember being scared to tell him, scared it would fail again. I plan a romantic evening at a diner late to tell him but I can't do it, until we are in the car. Right before it happens. It's all my fault.*

When I wake up I am looking down at my body. Wait down? Where? I tried to move and I felt lighter then air. My body was there, littered in so much blood. The giant piece of glass was on a table beside my body. There were surgical lights still on me but no surgeons in the room. I had all sorts of wires hooked up to me, but the machine they were attached too was unplugged. It looked like my leg was still slowly bleeding out. Only partly sewn.

"Oh my God, am I dead? Is that me? That can't be-"

I spoke out loud to no one. I tried to re enter my body but I went right through it to the floor.

"No..no no no no no. NO!"

I tried again to slam myself back into my body, I again slipped through. I searched for a clock my eyes fell on one on the wall above my head 10:07pm. I needed a date. I knew I got to the hospital that my surgery started at 330.

"Oh God what happened in those few hours. Why is my body like that? Why am I not in my body?"

I decided to leave the room. I had to find more answers. There had to be a way. I wasn't done here. I worried for Rayne, the guys. Oh God. The whole world was relying on us, I can't die before the fights even hardly started. I just can't. I leaned forward and as I leaned it propelled me forward. Or rather my spirit I supposed it was. I was still on that table. I found I could steer myself by leaning and I went out the door. I leaned right searching the halls for any sign of the guys. I headed towards where I figured the waiting room was and sure enough there Damon was. Head in his hands. I couldn't see

Darren I wondered if maybe he was still at the bar. 10 was pretty early when the bar was taken into account. The fake looking doctor approached Damon then. I watched Damon tense. Then he stood to face the doctor.

"Is she awake?" His voice was noticeably fearful.

His eyes were wide like a deer in headlights. I wanted nothing more then to hug him in that moment. But I caught a closer look at the doctor, he looked..slimy? Reptile like? He didn't look human by any means to me anymore, not even slightly.

"I'm sorry Damon she passed." he said.

His voice was garbled barely legible to me but must've been clear to Damon.

Damon moved his hands over his mouth.

"No, she can't be." Horror in his tone.

"I am afraid she lost too much blood sir, we couldn't stitch her fast enough."

"No, you're lying!" Damon roared and pushed past him.

I'd never seen Damon angry up until now. The unfamiliar emotion was unflattering to his features and his voice.

"God damn. How could I possibly comfort him?" I thought out loud. Not like anyone but myself could hear my voice.

I followed Damon as he rushed to the room where my body was.

He entered the room with his breath coming in shudders. Sure enough there my body was, still as stone and cold as ice.

"No! No, Serena!"

He ran his hands through his hair and started frantically trying to reconnect all the wires.

"There's gotta be something." He was muttering to himself.

He graced his hand slowly over my hair. Grabbed my wrist ever so gently feeling for a pulse. The machine's all crackled to life.

"Please, please." He was whispering so quietly.

Quietly begging for me. For my survival. But there's no way I could wake up, not when I'm not in my body, it's empty.

I wanted to scream that I was here but outside of my body. I tried to yell but he just continued muttering and trying different things. I tried to move an object to get his attention but my transparent arm went straight through it.

"Damn."

I heard Damon on the phone then.

"Darren, no just come here. I don't care how you get here but get here. Get a cab anything."

"I can't tell you right now, you need to come." He clicked the phone off.

Damon's voice sounded frantic and afraid.

"Damn it Serena! Come on." Damon slammed his phone to the ground.

"It's no use Damon."

The nurse entered then. No, I looked again, not a nurse. Kallisa poorly disguised as a nurse. If I was in my body my heart would race at the sight of her. I would squirm against the memories of her poking around in my head, unleashing things that were still even now unintelligible to me.

"Why are you conversing with her Damon?" I asked out loud to no one. Wishing I could be heard or seen.

"What do you mean? There's gotta be something."

"Damon-"

"Well how do you know?! Did you see her? Can you see her anywhere? Did she cross over! You would know if she crossed over!" Damon yelled now.

Fury in his usual kind eyes.

Kallisa looked directly at me. Or so I thought.

"Can you see me?" I whispered.

She gave me an unsettling smile of her pointed teeth.

"No I don't see her, I would only see her pass through to Hell Damon, if she's upstairs that's not exactly my area of expertise."

She had looked right at me I was certain. "Liar Liar." I hummed back to her.

Damon gave a frustrated sigh. "Is her soul still in her body?"

"Nooo.." She sing singsonged, dragging the word out.

"It's a bit entertaining to watch you scramble about though, pathetic attempts I might add."

"Shut up Kallisa, you can go straight to Hell."

"Oh baby, I've been there, you called me remember that Damon. I wouldn't be so keen on tossing insults, if I were you."

Damon hung his head low and breathed deep before he said anything else.

"Can you bring her back?" He whispered almost too quietly for me to hear.

"Hm, no not me."

"Who!?"

"I'm flattered really." She seethed.

"Flattered.?" Damon repeated through gritted teeth, his head still hung low.

"That you think I would be powerful enough to plunge a soul back into one's body."

"Who?!" He demanded again.

"I cannot get them myself." she said slowly.

"Then you are of no use to me. Leave." Venom dripping from his voice.

Kallisa tsked. "How very, very impolite of you."

"That was me asking nicely Kallisa if you make me ask again, I can assure you, you won't like the result."

"Don't call on me again Damon. I owe you nothing. I owe all of you nothing at all."

She left in a purple mist that crept along the floor.

When Damon picked his head up. I could see his eyes glisten slightly in the light.

If I could cry I would have. I wished I could communicate with him. All I could do was watch him struggle. I tried again more desperately to get back into my body, but something was blocking me, I just ended up going through my body as I would any other object.

"Damn it!" Damon screamed.

He swept his hand over the table sending surgical equipment flying.

He left the room then. Left my body hooked up to all the running machines. It was so strange to watch myself this way. I leaned toward the door to follow Damon. He was engrossed in a heated discussion with the reptile-like doctor. I believed that was the doctor with the plastic smile. So I was right, I guess.

"Do not tempt me, you have no idea what I'm capable of." The doctor whispered harshly to Damon.

"No." Damon said as he slid a small knife into the creature doctors neck.

"You have no idea what I'm capable of." he whispered back.

I never heard Damon sound so murderous.

The creature groaned slightly and Damon left hurriedly, pulling a pocket watch off of the creature's neck in one fell swoop. So fast I would've believed it never even happened in the first place if someone told me I saw wrong.

I watched the creature fall down and a few people crowded him. I stayed to wait and see if anyone saw what Damon did. But they chalked it up to the doc had a heart attack. I followed Damon outside. He was on the phone again.

"Darren how far are you?"

"A cab? Good how far?"

"I don't give a shit how expensive the cab ride is Darren. Try to sober up. I don't have the energy for your drunk ass. See you in 5."

He hung up the phone and hung his head in his hands, sitting on the front step of the hospital. I leaned toward him, until I was beside him and I wished I could comfort him somehow. Could he feel my presence?

"Damon?" I tried to speak. He didn't move to my voice at all.

I moved myself to touch his arm but my arm slid right through his.

I tried three times. The most he did was shudder as if he was suddenly cold. His eyes were watery, puffy and rimmed an angry red. He seemed to be deep in thought. A few minutes later a cab pulled up and Darren spilled out of it. Full smile and laughing to the cab driver. If I was in my body, I'm sure I would've laughed too. So happy to see a smile on his face.

"Thanks for the ride man, eh take an extra 20 dude! You are the best cab driver in Edmonton. Rock on whoo!"

He slammed the cab door as the Cab driver laughed. "Thank you man!"

He drove away.

Damon inhaled sharply and swiped his hand across his eyes.

"What's up lil bro?" Darren slurred laughing as he approached Damon.

"Big brother has arrived, whoop whoop."

He even motioned his hands up toward the sky.

Darren seemed to notice his face then. His smile dropped.

"Damon-? What?"

Damon soared up to him and cracked Darren steel in the jaw.

If I was in my body I would've winced.

Darren groaned and staggered back.

"Man what the Hell was that for!?" he groaned putting his hand to his jaw.

I saw Damon's eyes again watery and red with rage. He went towards him with his fist again.

"Damon stop!" Darren grabbed his hands still stronger then Damon even plastered.

"Damn it man! What the Hell has gotten into you? Stop."

His tone was back to stone.

Damon instead started to drag Darren by his hands, towards the hospital door.

"It's Serena." He said quietly.

Darren stopped walking all playfulness out of him. "What about Serena?"

Oh God, why couldn't I let them know I was right here? I was right here.

"Damon? Darren?" I tried again, except it was no use.

I went towards them and went straight through both of them.

Damon just shook his head in reply to Darren, a few tears managed their way down his face. Darren's face beheld a look of agony.

"Move." He pushed past Damon rushing through the doors to the hospital.

Damon sat back down cradling his head again, taking a few deep breaths. I leaned towards the doors and decided to follow Darren.

Darren walked right past the reptile doctor that was still surrounded by other doctors. They were covering his body in a black tarp. I followed him.

He got to the nurses station. "Serena Moonshale"

He demanded slamming his hand onto the nurses table. His eyes were furious. The nurse was blonde maybe 34 and thin. Her eyes showed a hint of real sadness.

"I'm so sorry." She said softly.

"No!" Darren slammed his fist again making the nurse jump slightly.

"Room 321." She said solemnly.

Darren stalked off so quick even in ethereal form it was hard to keep up with him. I still managed to beat him to the room though by a breadth.

He stopped in his tracks when his eyes fell onto my body. He just stood there for a moment. His eyes widened.

"No." He barely whispered.

I'd never heard his voice so hurt before.

He walked slowly towards my body. He checked all the wires and stared for a moment at the flat-lined monitor.

"Serena." He put his index finger to my throat, checking for a pulse. His eyes were hollow and faraway.

"I'm here, Darren." I spoke and wished I could comfort him too.

Is this what death was? You just endlessly float? Watch the ones you care about fall apart? Why was I a ghost and not a demon, or an angel or something in between? I thought I was special. Maybe I ignorantly thought I would live a long time. I wasn't ready to face death, there was so much undone, I was only 28. So much time left. I should have so much time.

"Serena! Damn it!" Now he was yelling, his voice full of anguish. He brought his mouth to mine and started compression's. I wondered what that might have felt like, his lips on mine.

"1-2" he counted out loud compression's. Another breath. Another.

A kiss of life, perhaps just a kiss of death. I thought to myself.

"Damn it Serena! Come back!"

"Don't you friggin' die on me. You are not dying on me today." His voice rough and full of pain, need and desperation.

Damon appeared in the doorway then, tears still pouring down his face.

"Darren- stop man. She's gone." He said slowly.

"Shut up Damon! We don't know that! 1-2-3" another breath.

"Darren! You think I haven't been through this already?!" Damon yelled.

Darren continued, ignoring Damon.

"Darren." He pulled Darren away from my body roughly.

"She's COLD. Feel her skin, you've felt her lips. She's gone. It's been too long. Man she-."

He said sadly and calming looking Darren straight on. Darren's eyes darted back and forth and his face was twisted with anger and sadness.

"Kallisa! Summon her." Darren said urgently.

"Darren I already- She can't do anything. I already tried that! You think I wouldn't try everything?! Everything to save her?!" Damon roared.

"What happened Damon. Why is she here! Huh!" He pushed Damon roughly.

"Why is she cut open like a-"

"How the Hell did she end up like this?!"

He ripped his hands through his hair and his eyes began to cloud.

"Answer me damnit!" He pushed Damon again.

"I- I left her to check in with Matt. As per her request! She was safe everything was warded-and then I"

Darren cut him off-

"Clearly not! This wouldn't have happened! You shouldn't have left her alone in the first place!"

"I know but-"

"Then what did you do Damon? You come right back inside? What else?!"

Damon grimaced. "I went to check in with Jane. But-"

"But what?! The girls in a damn wheelchair because of us! It was our duty. She was our responsibility to keep safe Damon! You put her in danger for what? Making amends with your little fuck buddy Damon?! The check in could've waited, it wouldn't have killed anyone if you waited until-"

"Until what Darren?! Until you stopped drinking yourself into oblivion? Until you decided to resume saving the world?!"

Darren punched his fist into the wall so hard it broke through the dry wall.

"It was too soon! I told you we needed to train her! We should've had her fully trained immediately way before her first accident! What did this to her?"

Darren rambled venomously, acid dripped from each word that he hurled at Damon.

"Henry got through somehow, she told me he was there, he gave her a message that those of the under and over world were after her, they were curious of her abilities, that he wasn't aloud to kill her. But he broke dishes, she must've fallen from her chair she dragged herself to the couch-"

Damon's voice was breaking as he relayed what happened. He took a shaky breath then continued:

"I got home and she had a piece of glass the size of a dinner plate deep into her femoral artery. She wasn't able to feel it, she had no idea it was there. I rushed her to the closest hospital I could, where the police weren't searching for her. They needed to do surgery, fix the artery before she bled out when they removed the glass- They failed." He choked on his words slightly as he finished.

Darren's eyes were enraged. He ran his hand over his jaw. He took a sharp breath.

"She's dead because of you Damon." He spat.

He glanced one last time to my body and left the room purposefully bumping into Damon's shoulder.

Damon leaned against the wall and slid himself toward the floor with his head in his hands.

"Serena, I'm so sorry." He whispered into his hands.

I went to him again trying to touch him to comfort him but I couldn't touch him. God damn what was I suppose to do? Am I really dead? I looked again to my body, afraid suddenly. Afraid I really was gone. That this was now my reality. I followed the direction Darren had went. I found him pacing the stairs outside of the hospital. He was talking quickly and quietly to himself. I had to move closer to hear him. It sounded like he was speaking another language. His eyes were focused. Determined. He stopped muttering and red mist appeared. I noticed then he had cut his arm. I rushed closer to see. It was a shallow cut made with the ceremonial knife. He had used his blood to draw a sigil on the ground. The red mist formed that into a beautiful women. Slender with long dark hair and bright red eyes. Darren looked directly into her eyes. Recognition flashing for only a millisecond then vanishing. Like he was remembering something that was suddenly lost to him again.

"Ahh what can I do for you Handsome?" her voice was sultry.

"No bullshit Demoness. I want to make a deal."

"Ahh well, let's get straight to the point shall we? What do you want?"

"I want Serena Moonshile's soul returned to her body." He said it like an army command.

"Hmm is that so? The rumours are true then, you really don't remember? Shame."

"Don't remember what?" he demanded.

It tsked. "I'm not at liberty to say."

"Whatever. Bring her back."

"I can't, Darren."

"What the hell do you mean you can't?! Isn't that your friggin' job?! How do you even know my name!"

"I make deals. You can't afford my price. We all know of you and your brother you are a hot topic in the other worlds."

"Try me." He challenged her

She laughed mockingly. "Trade Damon's soul for hers."

Darren staggered back. His face went slightly pale. His demeanour fell for only a second.

"No" I said out loud. Petrified he would say yes, praying he would say no.

"His soul isn't up for grabs." Darren continued his tone only faltering slightly.

I was relieved he didn't say yes.

"Then no deal. Good bye Darren. We shall see you soon."

With that she left in a swirl of red mist.

"You bitch! Get the Hell back here!" Darren howled into the night rage was not a blanket enough term for his tone.

A nurse came out then.

"Hey get outta here man, you are disturbing the other patients with all that yelling." He said.

Darren looked the nurse up and down as if sizing him up. The nurse took one step back.

"Just come on man, don't make me call the police." He said sounding small.

He was slender with long dark hair that he had tied back and dark eyes. He looked like a washed up rock star.

"I'm leaving." pure venom in Darren's tone.

He took a half step toward the man making him retreat half a step further. Then he whirled around and stalked off to the parking lot. I hesitated unsure what I just witnessed and undecided of whom to seek out first.

I was more concerned about Darren, but I moved to check Damon. I trusted Darren wouldn't leave without him. The body of the doctor was cleared up and the hospital was back in normal order. I went back to the room where my body lay and to my shock it wasn't there anymore. Damon was sitting on the made bed, wiped clean of any trace of evidence my body was ever there to begin with. Damon's head was in his hands, cellphone to his ear.

"Dammit Darren pick up."

He put the phone down and wiped his eyes. With one more look to the empty bed he left the room. I followed trying to accept the fact that I was really dead. The pain and fear I felt was unfathomable, if I could cry scream anything I would have. I went to follow Damon whom barrelled into Darren returning to the room.

"Damon where-" He ran to the bed touching the clean blankets.

"Where the Hell did they take her?!"

"Darren..she's gone. They took her body to the morgue. They need the beds. They can't just leave her there."

"The Hell they can't!" Darren stormed to the map of the hospital looking for the morgue.

"Dude, what are you doing? You gonna try to steal her body for what purpose Darren?"

"There has got to be a way to bring her back." He said under his breath.

Damon stared blankly at Darren for a second.

"Darren there is no way, the only way is a demon."

Darren looked up at Damon annoyed.

"Darren-" Damon's eyes fell on Darren's cut arm. "You didn't."

Darren tried to move to cover it. "Shut up."

"Darren don't be a dumbass! You know not to mess with that shit! I tried Kallisa and that was enough of a idiotic move."

"What deal did you make Darren huh?!" Damon shoved Darren then. Darren shoved him back.

"I didn't!" Okay?" He was frustrated and rushed in his tone.

"They let you off without a deal? Not a chance in Hell."

"They offered and I declined. They said they knew me okay? That it was a shame we didn't remember but apparently Damon we are pretty friggin' famous in the other worlds."

"Well what the Hell does that mean?"

"I don't know Damon but there has to be something."

"Serena told me Henry said the same thing about her." Damon said quietly.

Darren gave a pained expression. "Then why let her die?!"

"I don't know. Maybe, maybe there is something, but we aren't sneaking into the damn morgue right now Darren!"

"We can't just leave her there." He said dismayed.

"I know Darren, okay but we have to plan this carefully." He clamped Darren on the shoulder.

"Let it rest right now man. They will keep her body for 48 hours. That's how long the-" He trailed off.

"We come back tomorrow night. No exceptions." Darren commanded as he walked past Damon.

Damon sighed and followed close behind. I wanted to follow them, even in this form I still longed to be near them. I thought maybe I could still offer some sort of protection to them. Somehow, maybe with enough willpower. I followed closely behind them but as I existed the hospital doors once I got to the parking lot, I wound up right back inside.

"What the hell! No-" I said out loud.

I tried again, the same thing happened. I watched the guys as they slowly went out of my view to their vehicle.

I tried several times each time I grew more frustrated and desperate. But I had no luck.

"I'm-trapped here. Unfinished business.. I wager. Damn! Damnit!" I yelled to no one.

I floated to the map and started in the direction of the morgue. I had to try again, time was running out and I felt panicked that I might not be able to come back. Even more so that I was stuck here in this hospital of all places. I flitted my way down three narrow flights of stairs to the morgue. There were four bodies laying there covered. I was unsure how to figure out which one I was, as I couldn't touch anything. The one in the front the hand sticking out looked male. The one behind him, a feminine hand but not my own. The third one only had a few toes poking through. Female but not mine. The last one I couldn't see any limbs but my long blonde hair was trailing from under the blanket and resting against the gross cement. My white dress brushed to the floor, coated in black dirt.

"There I am."

I again floated toward the body. I was about to try to re enter it when I heard a voice.

"Ser-e-na"

Chills would've gone down my spine if I was in my body. I had heard the same voice before. In the bathroom at the hotel restaurant, when the glass shattered and Jenny patched me up.

"Damn what am I even afraid for? I'm literally a ghost myself. Nothing can hurt me." I reassured myself out loud.

"Where are you?"

I spun myself around, searching in the dark for the voice.

I backed up slightly when I saw a women standing in the corner of the morgue. Facing the wall. Saying my name over and over and over again. It was much easier to understand her in this form. Perhaps cause we were in the same veil. After a brief hesitation I moved towards her and paused maybe a foot behind her. She stopped saying my name and spun around. I could see her clearly now whereas before she was blurry.

"Mom." I barely whispered.

Chapter 16

(Written in Damon's perspective)

"I'm the one that's always laughing, joking, smiling, the life of every party, I am the one people know they can call anytime and I will come, the weight I bare is nothing, non existent I need no one and nothing if I can cheer someone up, I'm down for anything anytime and it'll be a great time, Always the bright side, people feed off that energy and I'm happy to give, but just once I wish someone would give me permission to fall apart too, is there no one I can dare trust to run too?"

We had taken a flight back to Edmonton. We were back at the hotel and we needed to look at all the options we could. We didn't have much time to lose.

"How many more items do we need Damon?" Darren asked me whilst downing another beer.

I thought to call him out on his drinking again but figured there was absolutely no point. What happened to Serena had wrecked me too but for once, it seemed I was holding myself together better. At least in my mind. Even just a tiny bit. Also, maybe it was part of me being optimistic, I thought maybe she would return some way, some form. I also knew the best way to honour her parting was to keep to the mission, and keep her best friend safe. My stomach twisted at the thought of having to tell Rayne and Matt the news. I shook my head slightly then cleared my throat.

"After inventory seems we are missing 3 only. Apart from the one we need to grab tonight while there is a blood moon. After counting all the items Serena located, plus those we have shipped in. I have absolutely no idea where the other 2 are located."

I wished I did. We only had 1 month left.

Darren nodded. "Okay. But we need to go back to Serena's body tomorrow night."

I looked again at Darren's arm. I was horrified that he had dared to take such a risk summoning one of the demonic patrons. Then I thought to how I immediately tried everything I could think of too. It was Serena, after all.

"I know Darren."

"Good."

Darren's eyes were pained. He was studying the Tome that was in the cabinet Serena had located. I wondered what he might find in there. I figured he felt responsible for her death somehow, even though outwardly he had blamed me. I thought he mostly blamed himself. I hated that he did. I was the one that left her here un-protected. I should have been more cautious. She was my responsibility. If anyone was responsible it was me. I was truly sick with guilt. There were so many things I wished I could take back at this moment. I failed her. Yet part of me blamed Darren too, as he was out just getting drunk, whereas I was doing our job. But that was just me compensating for my inability to keep Serena protected. I was just as careless. I ran a hand over my face and looked back to the black book that had called out to Serena the first night we met her. I was studying it religiously, it had lead me to one item that we needed to grab when the moon was at it's brightest. I supposed part of me hoped there was something in this book that would help us get Serena back. I was fiddling with the pocket watch I had snagged off of the doctor. I was pretty sure this was one of the 666, I don't know what stood out about it to me, I put it down beside the book as I read about seances. Of course why hadn't I thought of that? If Serena was in fact a spirit of sort we might be able to contact her.

"Darren, what about a seance?"

Darren hardly glanced up. "You know it's about a 98 percent chance we won't get her and just get some dark entity posing as her right?"

I sighed. He was right, and I knew that too. Wishful thinking. I changed the topic.

"Have you found anything useful in that tome?"

Darren ran his hand over his eyes and slammed it shut.

"Absolutely nothing, most of it is a language I can't read. It's not demonic either, because I can decode that. This? This is nonsense." He tossed the tome aside.

Demonic was one language I didn't understand but Darren did for some reason. We never really knew why, but it came in handy on occasion.

"Slide it here." I nodded to him.

He obliged and slid the black book over.

Darren sighed loudly, in anger. He walked to the fridge cracking yet another beer.

This time I didn't hold my tongue.

"Darren, seriously man can you stop with the drinking?"

Darren punched the counter roughly and I winced slightly.

"I'm not good at this Damon! I can't sit idly by and research like you. I need to fight something. Kill something. Do something. Anything!" He raised his voice at me.

"Well drinking is not going to help you on the battlefield man."

"You want me tolerable? Let me friggin' drink in peace or give me some creature to destroy. Now that I can do drunk or sober."

"We will likely have things to kill tonight when we secure this item. So put the damn beer down and conserve your energy."

Darren slammed it hard enough onto the counter for it to shatter. I rolled my eyes.

"Also if your watching my back, I don't want you drunk. We don't need to lose another one of us."

That made Darren pause. The look on his face made me feel guilty for what I said. But he simply sat back down and opened the black book quietly.

I opened the grey tome and to my surprise it was completely legible.

"I can read this. It's-it's Enochian."

Happiness flooded my chest like I was finding something long lost.

Darren looked up at me shock on his face.

"What friggin' ancient celestial language? Are you kidding me right now? How can you read angelic languages?"

I chuckled slightly in disbelief.

"I- I have no idea but if you can read Demonic and I can read Celestial, I mean- between the two of us we can understand every single language."

Darren half smiled.

"That mean's Serena might be-" he trailed off.

Shook his head and went back to the book.

I followed Darren's train of thought silently. He was referring to the possibility that Serena had become an angel. We believed angel did exist, as I remembered telling Serena once before. However, we had never seen evidence of angels in our time here, but if anyone reminded me of someone that worthy it would be Serena. I knew that true angels actually looked quite haunting. I pictured the common belief of what angels looked like instead. I pictured her beautiful long blonde hair as it blew gently in the wind. I thought to her ocean-like eyes that held such a depth you could drown in them. I thought about her voice, soft, light, kind. I pictured her milky skin, the natural floral smell she had when you were near her. Then I pictured her with Radiant wings, and smiled. Free of her wheelchair, free from this burden of saving the world. My thought process brought me a sliver of peace as well. It was a welcome thought that she might not be a ghost or a Demon.

"Man who the hell were our parents?" I half chuckled.

"I have no friggin' clue, but damn I wish I knew. Probably were a hell of a lot more interesting then most."

"You're damn right there."

We both laughed. A rare moment.

"The first place we need to grab from is that crypt, I saw on the news page it arrived today. It's sitting at the "Edmonton International Airport" right now. Said to be moved to a museum later this week."

Darren slammed the black book shut. "Let's go then. I'll drive"

He walked briskly to the door and I followed him.

I grabbed the keys from his hand. "No way. I'd rather us live."

The gentleman in the elevator greeted us. We rode down in silence. Then the receptionist greeted us happily. Darren ignored her and I smiled.

We exited the hotel and went into the volvo. Darren tried to go to the drivers side and I pointed to the passenger. He stood for a second then huffed and reluctantly entered the passenger side.

I chuckled a bit. I revved the engine which roared to life and tore out of the parking lot.

Darren leaned over fumbling with the stereo cranking "Save a horse ride a cowboy"

"Really?" I tsked as he started singing along.

"It's a Classic man."

I went to turn it off.

"No no, uh uh! My car my tunes."

"I'm driving!" I argued.

"Still my ride."

I shook my head and tuned out his singing. My thoughts floated to Serena. How I missed her, and what I thought she might say about the song. There had to be a way to bring her back. I glanced to Darren. I think he cared more for Serena then he led on. I honestly feared how he would handle it sober. He was so drunk, he was just keeping his buzz. I knew he would be better when he could kill something. But I had to watch his back, he would be careless if he was deeply hurt. This was our first real loss that we both could recall anyways. I wondered if maybe Kallisa could rewire our neural pathways too. Help us regain some of our lost memories, unlikely though we couldn't trap her again. That was the one shot we had to force her to help Serena. It was amazing my reckless summoning of her hadn't ended worse. I wondered why. Darren didn't say much just sang each song he put on. All classic rock. We pulled up to the airport then and we both headed into the building. There was a poster advertising the crypt.

"How are we going to do this Damon? What's the best course of action? Is it just in the open?" Darren asked.

Only slightly slurring his words.

The crypt wouldn't be warded, and it would likely be open for display.

"Maybe one guard, probably pretty easy to grab the three items with minor distraction."

"Three? Damon I thought it was only one."

"There are three of what could be the item, problem is I don't know which."

Darren nodded. "I'll distract."

I nodded jutting my chin forwards. He walked ahead we followed the signs towards baggage claim. There was one officer there. He was heavier and looked like he might fall asleep standing up.

"Bingo" Darren said as he slowly approached the officer.

"Hey officer." Darren did slur this time on purpose.

"Officerrrrrrrr.....laundry?" He laughed.

"Excuse me my last name it's pronounced Lone- drey" he barked.

"Yeeah that's what I said laundry." Darren pointed to his name tag again.

"Don't get your panties in a knot"

"What do you need, hurry up before I hang you out to dry!" He grumbled.

Darren chortled. "Hang me out to dry good pun Laundry!"

"Between you and me a dryer works really well."

"I'm going to escort you out of here if you don't tell me what you need now." The officer yelled furiously.

I moved toward the crypt after ensuring no one was watching. I leaned in to look taking care to ensure he was still engrossed with conversation. I rolled my eyes because Darren's distraction was honestly the worst I had ever heard, I couldn't believe it was even working. I reached into the crypt, grimacing at the mummified God as I grabbed the coins from it's eyes, and a jewel from it's crown.

The last thing I needed was the ring off of the mummified God's finger. However his finger snapped off. I gasped slightly dropping it back down. I picked it back up and Darren met my eyes for a split second a look of absolute disgust was there for barely a second, too long the officer was about to look behind him. Darren grabbed his arm.

"Hey hand's off! Don't make me call more security."

Darren removed his hands from the guards arm and I slipped from view.

"I need the restroom captain laundry sir." Darren saluted.

"Oh you little shit! Get back here!" The guard called after Darren. I laughed a bit. Kinda felt like we were just kids being delinquents. It was so lighthearted compared to the actual looming disasters. When we were outside all look of joy was wiped from Darren's face.

"Did you get the items?" he asked sternly.

"Yeah, I did."

"Good."

We got back into the car and I drove us back towards the hotel.

"Damon, can we stop at Serena's place?" Darren asked sadness edging his tone.

I swallowed remembering all the furniture she just picked out and how she never even stayed there for more then an hour, I wasn't sure she even went in it since she bought it. Now I would never know for sure.

"Sure, why not? I never, I never actually got the chance to return the key yet. So we don't have to break in or anything."

Darren grimaced slightly. "Good."

"First though, we need to go to Wabamun lake. It's only a few minutes from Serena's. There's something we need there."

"Whatever."

"So long as I get to fight something." Darren said as he slunk back in the passenger seat.

"You will, The lake is infested with Sirens."

Darren looked at me dumbfounded.

"Well that's just friggin' awesome." he said sarcastically. Shaking his hands dramatically.

"I have the music box on me, just incase."

"You think that might be too risky Damon? If we use it wrong it'll kill us too."

"I am quite certain I know how to Darren, I researched it enough."

"I trust you did the research bookworm. Just don't get us killed."

"I'll do my best."

We pulled up to the lake the blood moon was high and bright in the sky. There were no cars in the lot outside of us.

"I thought sirens lived in the oceans." Darren said.

"Yeah, most lakes connect to rivers which connect to oceans."

"Fan-friggin'-tastic." Darren replied sarcastically.

"Hey Damon maybe we will meet Ariel eh?" Darren joked.

I played along.

"Well you know actually, we might, she is based off a real siren. This music box is what is said to have cursed her in the first place. Serena mentioned it, when she picked up Grimm Fairy tales."

I trailed off again falling into guilt and realizing yet again that I hadn't accepted her death. That I simply couldn't.

Darren looked at me for a minute. "You okay man?"

"No, she should be here." I said, sadness clear in my voice, I didn't try too hard to hide it. Not from Darren.

Darren looked haunted for a minute. "I know."

We stopped talking as we approached the waters edge.

"So how do we draw these sons of bitches out?"

Darren asked clenching his fists together.

"We get in the water, it helps that we lost Serena, in the sense that we are easy prey, they can sense loss."

Darren pushed me roughly.

"Don't you ever fucking say it's convenient that she's gone. You don't get to say that Damon."

I stepped toward Darren and he held his ground. I would never actually go up against him, he's my blood, my brother and well he was way stronger then me.

"Look Darren that's not-"

"Whatever man-let's just kill some shit"

Darren waded out into the water.

"Darren! Wait, don't go right in the water, they drown you. Dumbass."

Darren came back out. "Well, what do you suggest Einstein?"

I motioned to two kayaks on the side of the bank.

Darren rolled his eyes.

"Ah capsize that's better then just getting dragged under I guess."

"It will give us more control. They are fast and dangerous Darren."

"Yeah, yeah, whatever."

He helped me heave the kayaks into the water and we each took one.

We paddled out about 15 feet. We were both scanning all the rocks and shallow areas. I kept listening for a sense of something but heard nothing. I looked over to Darren whom signalled to me that he heard nothing yet. Maybe we needed some time.

Suddenly Darren's kayak got bumped.

"Man you got something there?" I hollered.

"Yeah, yeah Damon I see three, three are right under me! Just friggin'g popped out from no where!"

I started to move towards Darren. "Hang on man, I'm coming!"

I saw two shimmering tails swish towards me as I got bumped too.

"Oh man. What's the plan here!?" Darren yelled.

"Gather them up and I will open the music box!"

"He tried to guide towards me, but one of them approached the surface of the water. No beautiful hair, just black and scaly, hairless, like someone in a skin suit with bright green eyes. Basically a giant water snake.

"Darren! Cover your ears!"

He did as the kayak flipped over.

"Damn it! Darren!"

I opened the music box then, out of panic for Darren. The melody tilled out and I felt light, peaceful. My kayak also capsized and all I could hear was the melody. The melody stopped as I entered the water. The creatures all began to shriek, an unholy sound, like nails on a chalkboard as they tried to swim away from us but couldn't move. I was pulled underwater too, Darren was floating a few paces ahead with three of the things circling him. I attempted to swim towards him when one grabbed my leg. I kicked viciously trying to get it off. When I succeeded Darren was much too still, They were all circling him.

"No- I will not let him die, he is not going to die."

I swam hard toward him as I neared the creatures with the music box. They all shrieked so loud that if I hadn't been under water my ears would have undoubtedly bled. I reached Darren grabbing him, as I did I accidentally dropped the music box. With a look to Darren's un-moving body I swam as hard and quickly as I could pulling him to shore. It was exhausting, it was a long swim and I was grateful that it was a still lake and not a rough ocean.

"Hang in there man-please"

I pulled us onto the sand gasping and gagging on each breath. My lungs were burning. But Darren still hadn't stirred.

"Darren!" I felt frantically for a pulse.

When I couldn't I began CPR.

1-2-3- breath-1-2-3 breath.

"Darren! Damn it, come back. Come back man!"

1-2-3 breath 1-2-3 breath.

A pulse, faint but there.

"Darren!" Tears and salt water poured down my cheeks.

"Please- not both of you- not the same day."

1-2-3 breath 1-2-3 breath 1-2-3 breath. I was choking on my own breathing. My arm's were limp from exhaustion and I knew I couldn't physically keep doing this much longer- but I would rather die then give up.

"Darren!"

I slammed my fist into his chest once hard. Darren's eye's flew open and he was immediately spewing and gagging on water as he coughed brutally turning onto his side.

I clamped my hand on his shoulder. I don't think I had ever been so relieved.

"Thank God. Man, I thought I lost you."

Darren kept coughing. Then looked to me. "Hey, hey, hey, okay Damon. Okay, okay man"

He pulled me into a hug. We never hugged. I leaned against him and quickly wiped my eyes taking a sharp breath and clamping him once on the back.

"I'm still here little brother."

"I'm relieved you are alright." I said forcing the shakiness out of my voice.

"Yeah, man..me too."

"Do tell me, you at least secured what we needed? That I didn't just almost friggin'g eat dust for nothing!"

"I dropped the music box, I have to go back in. As for the item, it's the sirens we need an abundance of their scales for the rituals, so it's not an item but we need it just as much. The music box will kill them, so long as no more come and drag them away from here."

"Frigging great. That's just- perfect really."

"There's a boat the next lot over, think you can commandeer that?"

Darren laughed. "Frigging just call me Jack Sparrow!"

I laughed too. "Alright."

We hurried to the lot over and with some effort got the boat into the water.

"Why the Hell didn't we do this first Damon?"

I shrugged. "Honestly I hadn't noticed it until now."

"Helpful."

We pulled the boat toward the water.

Darren got the engine purring without much effort. Just a quick hot wire job.

"Oh yeah baby!" Darren tapped the steering wheel excitedly.

"What did I tell you?!" He continued.

"Let's see em try to tip this thing." He concluded.

We made our way to the frenzy of splashing in the water.

"Here Darren." I handed him ear plugs.

"Will this work?"

I shrugged. "Theoretically."

"Great-that's just-Again why not the first time we went out?!" He shook his head.

"Honestly, forgot, I'm off my game Darren sorry."

"Just don't get us killed Damon."

We approached the frenzy of sirens and it was unbelievably loud.

"How do you wanna do this?" Darren hollered to me over the piercing shrieks of the creatures.

"The fishing pole! Stab them and pull them onboard. We need 6.

I have to go in. Tie this rope to me, don't let me drown." I called to Darren.

"I won't Damon." He gave me a steady look. "Be careful man"

I nodded. He secured the rope tightly to the base of the sail.

"Here goes nothing. Darren had already stabbed one of the things that screeched and writhed like a giant leech against the pole.

"Got you, you son of a bitch." Darren spat joyfully.

At least he was enjoying himself.

He then stabbed it to finish it off and it stopped moving. I looked to the water taking a deep breath, guessing where I dropped the music box and dove in.

The water was chilly. I knew I wouldn't be able to last long in here. I opened my eyes and the water burned slightly it was hard to see with all the sand flying around from the sirens thrashing about. I swam forward about 3 feet coming up for air.

I watched Darren successfully stab another one.

"HELL yeah, here fishy, fishy."

I heard him yell happily. I laughed a bit and dove back under. I spotted the music box a few feet from me and began to swim towards it. When Serena appeared. She smiled at me, holding the music box out towards me, beckoning me to her. I lost a bunch of my air in shock.

"How-How was she here?"

Relief flooded me. I wanted to rush to embrace her and never let her go again.

"I knew it. I knew she would return."

I began to swim toward her, engrossed by the sheer joy of seeing her smiling face again. As I reached her I went to embrace her, if I hadn't been underwater I would've cried. But as I grabbed her I felt scales and realized it was a Siren. Instead of Serena I was hugging a scaled black creature that shrieked in delight and started to pull me down. So quickly it was like a rush. It was much stronger then me and I was running low on air. My lungs burned in desperation for oxygen. I let my last breath out reluctantly. The water filling my lungs felt worse then anything I could ever describe. I had never been so afraid as the water rushed around me. I managed to grab the music box from it, confused why this one seemed unaffected. As soon as I got my hand on it I wound the dial. Black was creeping my vision now.

"Just a moment longer I have to hold on" I thought to myself.

As I wound it the melody restarted and the creature screeched and let go of me. I pulled desperately at the rope to pull myself back to surface. I was nearing the top, where I could see the boat when I lost consciousness.

When I came too Darren was leaning over me panicked as ever.

"Damon- Damon!" He hugged me again.

"Damn it man, you scared the hell outta me!"

I coughed and sputtered water as Darren patted my back hard.

"I was scared Darren. I'm not going to lie to you, I thought that was it for me."

"Well, you live to fight another day champ." Darren smiled.

"Anything else from this hellhole? I killed all but one."

"Ugh" I groaned and leaned against the side of the boat.

"No, thankfully."

I grasped the music box and closed it.

"Thank God." Darren steered toward shore.

I crawled to the dead sirens and started to tear the scales from them with Darren's ceremonial knife.

"Well those weren't friggin'g Ariels that's for sure." Darren half chuckled.

"Oh for sure not." I chuckled too.

"God man you really like fighting hey?" I asked.

"I'm just glad I got to kill something."

I nodded. "I get it."

"Hey man..what pulled you under?" Darren asked.

I paused briefly.

"Well?" Darren pressed.

"I-the siren tricked me, I thought I saw Serena."

Darren's face fell. "Oh."

We rode the rest of the way in silence. Darren dumped the siren's after I grabbed the scales and we headed back to our car. I had never been so grateful to be back on dry land until now.

We got in the car and I started it. Darren had a faraway look on his face.

"What man?"

Darren looked reluctant to reply.

"I guess, I just kinda wish I saw her too, even though it was an illusion."

He said solemnly.

I nodded in understanding and we didn't talk further.

We drove past the hotel and instead turned down her street, pulling up to cottage number 6. I parked in her drive. Staring at the overgrown ivy for a moment. Serena had seen magic in this place. Darren exhaled loudly and took a sharp breath in.

"Well, come on then." He was short in his tone.

He got out abruptly and started to walk up her driveway. It didn't feel right. Her not being here. I got out and followed Darren, unlocking the door. We entered and I looked around. All of the furniture had been delivered and was just sitting in a pile in the living area.

"What do you want to do here Darren?"

I felt as though we were trespassing. In my mind Serena would return somehow.

"Just seems to be a shame. A damn shame."

"What are you on about man?" I asked.

"She'll never get to live here. We took so much from her Damon."

Darren ran his hand over his jaw and his voice cracked.

I swallowed a lump in my throat I too felt trapped under this crushing guilt of failing her in every single way.

"She's gotta be someplace better Darren."

"And you really believe that huh?"

"What, you don't?"

He shook his head. "No. I can't. There is so much horror here on Earth but there is so much more horror, terror, anguish, in the other worlds."

"You are assuming. We don't know that for sure Darren."

"We know enough Damon, don't be so ignorant! You and I do not get to believe that fairytale." He howled.

As he spoke, smoke started coming from my pocket.

"What the Hell?" I fumbled through my pocket the second I touched the items I had grabbed from the coffer it felt like someone put a scalding pan to my hands. I threw the items onto the ground.

"These are burning hot!" I called out, shaking my hands off to ease the stinging.

Darren glanced over and the second he did. A sand like substance blew up from the items and spieled straight into Darren's mouth. He choked and gagged loudly. I rushed to him trying to get him to breathe. He suddenly stopped and looked at me. His eyes glowing gold. He spoke in a voice that was not his own. Horrified I staggered back.

"Darren, Darren no!"

I yelled as terror flooded me. I can't lose Darren, I can't, I just can't.

"Oh myyyy..What a strong vessel I have been gifted with this time. My subjects must honour me to their fullest potential. Ahh."

His voice was deep and beckoning, so deep it was almost hard to comprehend. The ring and the jewel and the coins flew to Darren's hands. It fixated on me now as if just noticing me. I was frantically running over everything I had read about Egyptian God's. There were several which one could this possibly be? Maybe it would tell me. I tried to think quickly. I had to shove the panic down and be rational. That thing had my brother and I would stop at nothing. Nothing to get him back to me.

"Yes, sir." I bowed down to Darren.

"Ahhhh you must be the one responsible. How clever of you to summon me into another God, surely no other vessel would be worthy of me, Osiris"

Osiris.. Great that was the Egyptian God of the underworld. That caught me off guard. I tried to remain stoic but that was Darren's specialty not mine. Did he just say a God?

"Ahh, you had no idea, did you? I can sense it. Oh the depths of this one. The demonic power, all that destruction, devastation, sadness, mmm, like honey to my tongue. Yes, this will do quite nicely"

I can't fight him. It's Darren, it's Darren's body. What was I gonna do?

"I will gather you later follower. Sleep. I command you to sleep and remember who you are."

Darren's hand flew up at me, gold eyes glowing brighter then flames. I felt a sudden force against me like I got hit by a car. I flew backwards and blacked out.

* * *

I am standing in the bathroom of my home, I have lived in this home for several years with her. There is blood coating the floor. My stomach is in knots. Her crying so hard, gasping with each breath and all I can do is hold her, and cry too. Another miscarriage. My heart aches for my wife, I mourn the loss of our 8th.

Child. I murmur softly in her ear that we will keep trying for a baby. That we wouldn't give up. I make a call that day after I tuck her into bed for fertility treatment options. When I tell my wife after she wakes she cries harder. I hold her tightly, reassuring her it wasn't her fault. The next day we head into the facility. I watch them poke long needles into her belly, wincing as much as she does. I stroke her hair. The first two don't take. I am low on funds. The nurse tells us that we may need to consider adoption if this one doesn't take. My wife looks defeated. All she wanted was a family, and I was struggling to give it to her. I reassure her, I believe that this one will take. I pray for the first time. Pray I can give her a child.

Then I am driving my car, my wife and I were heading out of town to meet family. I am exhausted, beyond exhausted. She asks me to to pull into a diner that's open late. I don't want to, I want to keep driving but one look at her and I oblige. She slams the door to my Volvo P1800 as she exits, I am angry until she pops her head back in laughing and apologizing. My lovely clutz. I order coffee, and pie..I love pie. She orders a cheeseburger and I tease her since it's 1am. I kiss her fervently against the hood of my car. Every time I kiss her it's like the first time. It's bliss to me and I know she felt the same. I playfully threaten her, that if she slams my door again that there will be consequences. We laugh. Soft tunes. She looks over to me with her Bambi eyes and I melt into the depth of them..dark blue. She tells me I am going to be a father. I am overjoyed, terrified, relieved. So many emotions that I forget for a moment that I'm driving. I lean over and kiss her. Soaking her in. Happy so happy that we finally did it. We would meet our child. My heart full, as I looked and saw the pure unrelated joy on her face. Then all too quick, The dream of a future shatters. Our unborn childs face only forged in memory. The sudden whip of the vehicle, crunching metal, shattering windows, so loud in my ears, Blood, metallic and bitter it's all I can taste in my mouth. When the car stops moving I look to her and she is too still..her jaw disconnected and her eyes are stuck open in terror. Emma.. my Emma. Why didn't I die? Why was it her? I want to scream..I hit the wheel hard with my hand, I try to move to her but I am trapped too. I beg..plead her to be alive..plead with whoever was listening.. Emma..looks identical to Serena. Red eyes and a voice that was not Emma's met mine. Using her broken mouth to speak, told me it was time, and laughed..as I ascend to Heaven.

Chapter 17

GHOST

"Your footsteps echo in these halls but your steps are long gone, your voice is lost in the silence that feels deafening, I've never felt such cold because you left me with no trace of warmth, I know I will see you again, I just know, but until then my friend, I will stand alone among the ruins of this disaster broken enough for us both."

"**M**om..." I said again.

I couldn't believe my eyes. I would've bawled had I been in my body. I didn't even know she died. The sadness that gripped me with that realization was overwhelming. She smiled to me. My mom looked completely like herself, just pale and ghostly.

"Momma?" She came to me and hugged me.

It was solid, real and I wished I could cry. All of our fights and differences suddenly didn't matter. I regretted not coming to her after that last voicemail she left. I felt like a monster. Every childhood memory with her came flooding back clear as day to me. I could remember when I was first born the first time I looked at my mom, all the way until the last time I looked at her. I waded though the memories comforted by the familiarity and safety of them. More laughter and love then pain. A beautiful childhood, an incredible mother. I saw through almost a birds eye how crushed my mom was when I left her when she went back to Nick. Guilt engulfed me again.

"Mom, I should have never left you." My voice is small and weak to my ears.

My mom stopped hugging me and looked at me.

"Oh my Sweetheart. You did the right thing leaving. You walked away and built your own life, your own happiness. In every mothers life there comes a time when their baby leaves them. It's painful. Beyond." She chuckled slightly.

"But knowing you were happy and safe is really all that matters. It is okay that you left my darling all the guilt you feel is okay, all is forgiven. I made mistakes. So many mistakes my darling, but I really did do my best to do right by you. I love you unconditionally. You'll understand the depth of a mothers love someday too my child. Just as you have in the past."

I shook my head.. "Mom..but we are dead."

She smiled again. "Death is merely a new beginning. Each day anew, like plants in the spring."

"You mean we live again?"

She smiled and nodded.

"Your story my darling, is not over. You weren't supposed to die yet my love. There is purpose and work left undone. You are so important. So much more then you could understand. Death is not ready to receive you. I've waited a long time to tell you this my love. There was a disruption in the natural order."

I was erratically trying to figure out what she was saying whilst my thoughts were overtaken wondering how my mom died and when.

"Disruption?"

"You must stop Cronos Serena."

I couldn't believe what I was hearing.

"You know?"

"I have knowledge beyond your comprehension, you will too, when it is your time. Damon and Darren, they need you as you need them. It is so much deeper then I can explain."

I could only stare at my mom in shock, there were too many emotions clouding my thoughts.

"Mom I don't-"

She cradled my face with her hands and kissed my forehead.

"You will."

"I love you mom."

"I love you too Serena. Do not fret, soon your fractured memories will come together clearly."

She leaned to kiss my cheek.

"And now I shall gift you life yet again my daughter. Aren't I lucky? To bring you to life twice. Then I will be free to move from this place. I will await you in Heaven my sweet child."

"Wait- mom!" I yelled.

But as she finished saying the words there was a warmth that enveloped me. Peace and comfort. Love, I felt it surround me, delving into every fibre of my being. Mystical, and suddenly I wasn't afraid anymore.

* * *

There was a bitter dry taste in my mouth. Like if you took a spoonful of cinnamon directly onto your tongue. My eyes flew open to a white sheet. I panicked batting it off of me. I fell to the cement it was hard and freezing. My body was gasping and gulping for air. I was keeled over coughing brutally and gagging on the cold dirty cement of the morgue. My eyes burned, the dim light's in here might as well have been direct sunlight for how bright everything felt. The smell was rancid, like meat that had gone bad and I continued to cough and dry heave for what seemed like an hour. After an agonizing 10 minutes, my laboured breathing started to normalize. I was relieved. I needed water, I was so thirsty.

"I'm alive." I said out loud my voice was raspy and unintelligible.

"I can't believe that I'm alive. Mom? Are you still here?" I asked barely audible.

There was no answer. I hoped she was in fact in Heaven as she mentioned.

I hadn't tried to sit up yet, I had been too wracked with coughing fits and dry heaving to move from where I fell.

"Oh God! Right I can't walk, God I need water." I whispered.

"Help! Please someone help me!" I tried to yell as loud as I could. It came out a wheezy whisper.

"I need water, it hurts so much I need water."

I attempted to drag myself towards the stairwell.

"I might scare some people, but I see no other option. I can't die again."

I began to pull myself and cried out. My arms felt weak.

"No. I have to be able to pull myself. I have too. I tried again and cried out again. How had I done this in the past? Dragged myself and Rayne and others with my broken body. Adrenaline I guessed and not being dead for 24 hours might have helped."

I tried to summon that strength. I tried a third time, I managed an inch. God my leg was sore. Wait- I could feel my leg. I focused hard.

"I need to get water. I need to move. I need to move!" I urged myself in my mind.

My body began to feel hot, like I suddenly had a fever. I felt similar to how I did when I tossed Darren across the room once upon a time.

"I can do this." I stared at the table I had fallen from.

"I will do this."

I grabbed the table I had fallen off of and stood. I could feel my legs and hips as they erupted in pain. The pain felt like needles dipped in acid on every speck of my skin. I heard the sickening crunching and shifting of my bones but I held with all my might onto the table.

"I will do this!" I yelled through clenched teeth.

I was biting back sobs. "I cannot give up."

"I will not give up."

The pain was unimaginable, indescribable. My willpower was untouchable.

Suddenly it all stopped. The pain, the crunching, the shifting. I found I could let go of the table. I stood there, too stunned to think about how dirty, how thirsty or how scared I was. I took a deep grounding breath. I moved my right leg. I bent it, lifted it. No pain. Then the same with my left, nothing- normal.

Tears streamed down my face in delight. I was standing. I could move my legs.

I dared to try and take a step, holding my breath in anxiety. Slowly I lifted my foot and placed it in front of me. I wobbled slightly, but shifted my weight. Then the next leg.

"Oh my God!" I was overjoyed.

"I'm walking! I'm really walking!" I laughed out loud and twirled in my dirty white dress.

I brought my hands to my face wiping the constant stream of tears.

Thirst gripped me again. "I gotta move"

I grabbed the white sheet I was laying under grimacing about the fact that my lifeless body laid there only minutes prior.

"Maybe I will just look like a patient that got cold and walked with a blanket over me."

"Surely will blend better then a women dragging herself across the floor." I thought to myself.

I walked to the steps. I couldn't wait to see Rayne, I couldn't wait to see the guys. I couldn't wait to keep living. I took one long look back at the other bodies that surely wouldn't get up again. I thought to my mom, and I felt light, and peace. I wrapped the blanket around me and gleefully bounded up the steps out of the dark dank morgue and into the brightly lit hospital hallway.

As I came up the lights were blinding. I whimpered slightly. A couple heads turned my way and I wanted to hide. I wished I was invisible. Thankfully no ones eyes lingered on me. I must pass for what I was trying to pass as. I shielded my eyes from the lights with the sheet. Looking for the nearest bathroom. There was one just across from the stairs.

"Lucky me."

I walked as calmly as I could attempting best I could to blend in. When I entered the bathroom I was even more relieved to find it completely empty. It also happened to have a small shower in it. It was like all the stars aligned for me today. I closed and locked the bathroom door. Hoping no one would need it until I was done. I rushed to the tap and kept filling my hands with icy water as I greedily drank from the tap, drinking directly from the running water and filling my hands with it and drinking that too. I didn't know one could consume so much water, that quickly. I stopped after a few minutes and swiped my hand over my mouth, the top of my dress was drenched, but my thirst was gone. I looked up and almost lost my balance. I did not look like myself. My skin was so pale and thin, you could see all my blue veins. My eyes looked slightly sunken with dark blue patches of skin around them. My fingers had purple on the tips. My hair was peppered and matted with dirt and dried blood. My thigh was still only half stitched but wasn't bleeding. The skin around it looked almost black.

"Necrosis?"

I watched myself breathe in the mirror for a couple minutes. Watched my chest rise and fall, I needed to be convinced I really was alive. My face was smeared with mud and blood. My white dress looked like ash in the bathroom fluorescent. After a few minutes of watching myself breathe, I stripped myself down, and walked to the shower. I scrubbed myself over and over with all the soap that was in there, I scrubbed until the smell of rotting meat was not obvious to my nose anymore. I scrubbed until my skin felt raw and painful to touch. I washed my hair so many times I lost count. I was shaking hard, the water wasn't that warm. I then proceeded to wash and wring my dress out. I wrapped myself in a towel and wrapped my dress in another.

I needed dry clothes and I somehow needed-

I stopped dead in my tracks as my train of thought screeched to a halt.

A young girl was standing in the bathroom. Long brown hair and a white dress.

I glanced to the door, which was still locked.

A memory came rushing back to my mind.

"I remembered coming out of the antique mall with Rayne right before I collapsed. Right before she called the ambulance. The one that crashed. I remembered that I had suddenly seen the mental hospital. "Black Rose Ridge" I remembered the little girl dancing behind the wrought iron fence, clearly another time. A heart locket swinging gently over around her neck. I remembered her dancing around the purple wisteria tree. Then her eyes. White eyes. Her scream. I remember how it felt like someone put a knife deep into my ear. I remember feeling like my entire body had suddenly gone up into raging flame. I remembered her. I knew her, I too had been at that same hospital. We both had."

I staggered half a step back. She looked to me then her eyes were white, but not like the white eyed demon, more like she was blind. She didn't move or speak when I staggered back. The heart locket was resting on her chest. It looked remarkably similar to mine from my great grandmother. I swallowed and wrapped the towel tighter around myself.

"Who are you?" I whispered.

The little girl met my eyes. Or so it seemed, it was hard to tell because she had no pupils.

"My name is Serenity."

She spoke, but not out loud, her voice came into my head.

I felt no fear towards her, I didn't sense any malice from her.

"Why can I see you? Am I not alive?"

"You have crossed the veil yourself, now all spirits you too will be able to see."

"Why can I hear you if you aren't speaking?"

"I cannot speak."

She opened her mouth revealing that she had no tongue.

I was mortified. Who would do that to a little girl?

"I've seen you before though?"

She nodded slowly.

"Yes, and it hurt remember? You were not ready to receive the memory. Your body rejected it, which caused you pain."

I swallowed loudly. "But I am ready now?"

"I cannot tell you that, only you can know that yourself Serena. Evidently so, you feel no pain right now."

"No, I don't."

"I have come to help you. If you'll let me."

"Help me? With what?"

"Saving the world."

I stared slack jawed at the ghostly girl.

"Okay." I breathed.

Life was so crazy already, it wasn't difficult to accept that a ghost was communicating with me and offering to help me. Perhaps that was her unfinished business.

She smiled slightly. It was eerie, but genuine and kind.

"You need clothes first, if you want to get outta here unseen, among your other stuff."

"Serenity?"

"Yes?"

"Who are you?"

She stood still for a moment.

"I told you my name already. I will be right back."

She dissipated into pinkish smoke and I sat there with my heart racing, wondering if I had gone insane.

I glanced over to the door again, still seeing that it was locked. I stood there awkwardly dripping wet and shivering from the cold. I hesitated unsure how long to wait. But then she reappeared. I jumped slightly.

"Here. Hopefully all this is yours."

She handed me a bag of my belongings I saw my phone, wallet and car keys. My matching heart locket. A change of clothes. I dressed quickly. So she was really here.

"Thank you."

"Hurry up. You can thank me after we get outta here."

I nodded and threw the wet towel into the hamper by the door.

"Lead the way I guess, can no one else see you?"

"No, only you. Try to look as casual as you can. If anyone recognizes you from the morgue we will have a hard time leaving."

"You can leave the hospital? But-I couldn't?"

"You were tethered here. My unfinished business does not tether me to a place."

"Serenity, I know your name but I could swear I know you-do I know you?"

She moved her head towards me.

"I can't tell you anything like that. Your memories have to come on their own. It's safer."

"Okay."

I trusted this little girl completely it was so strange to have such a deep connection to a stranger. I wished I could remember why I knew her, a friend maybe?"

We started to walk out of the bathroom and towards the doors. I shuddered slightly as I remembered when I first tried to follow the guys when I first was a spirit and how I failed. But we walked through the doors with ease. No one paid any mind to us. Or well me, I supposed most couldn't see Serenity. I exhaled loudly, relief flooding me.

She turned her head to me again.

"Your boys are at the hotel."

I felt my heart jump with delight, after seeing them in so much pain I was so anxious to return to them and make sure they were okay.

"Are they going to be able to see you Serenity?"

"No." she tilled

"Will you be staying with me?"

"I cannot enter there. I will meet you again when you leave. My job will be to help you on your missions until you all succeed in stopping Cronos.." Her voice echoed in my mind.

"Okay."

I got in my car and drove out of the parking lot, toward the hotel. Grateful that my car was still here and no one moved it just yet. I supposed it had barely been 24 hours. Serenity flitted into the passenger side. I exhaled. I couldn't believe a ghost was following me like this. I was also shocked how easily I was accepting it. I went as quickly as I could, without attracting too much attention. As I pulled up to the hotel my heart fell because I didn't see their car in the lot.

"Serenity are you sure?" I turned to look at her and she was gone.

"Great, that's just great" I muttered.

I drove past the hotel. I glanced back to my passenger and Serenity returned, it made me jump.

"Please don't do that, give me a heads up- at least."

"Apologies, Go to your house."

"My house? Why?"

"That's where your men are. I didn't get all the way there but I can sense it."

I nodded and turned left down the road that would lead to my little cottage. I thought about the house that I had such dreams for and bought furniture for. I wondered what might've happened to it after I died. If I had stayed dead. I wondered why they went there? Maybe an artifact.

I drove up toward my cottage and saw their car. Relief embraced me mixed with overwhelming excitement. I put my car in park on the roadside out front. Serenity nodded to me. I was almost out of the car, when Serenity grabbed my hand.

"What-let go." I shook my hand once and she obliged.

"Be careful Serena, something is off, there is a lot of power emanating from the house. I will be close by, but I cannot get past the warding on your house. I'm concerned as nothing should be able to enter, it's like a fortress against all the unnatural."

I paused for a moment and swallowed glancing once to my house.

"The white eyed demon?" My voice trembled slightly.

Serenity cocked her head to the side for a minute and looked quite- surprised?

"What do you know of them?" She asked kinda harshly.

I glanced anxiously again to the house. The guys might be in trouble, I didn't want to waste any time right now.

"Nothing much. One attacked me." I said quickly.

"Hm interesting. However it should not be able to enter either. The wardings on this place are intense and ancient. Plus, I would be able to sense the presence of a demon. It is not a demon. It's something else. However, powerful Serena, so please make haste, be cautious."

I nodded. "Okay."

I walked up towards my front door and felt petrified of what I might find. All I could do was hope and pray they were alright. I paused at the door with my hand lingering near the doorknob. I took a deep breath. Reminding myself that I needed to help them, in any way I could.

I twisted the knob and as I did my door opened silently into darkness and quiet. Too quiet. I walked slowly around, holding the knife I kept in my car near my chest. I walked to the living room, my furniture I had picked was laid out in a mess of a pile all over the space. I went toward the kitchen. Nothing, then the hall. As I rounded the corner near the back door there was a figure slumped in the middle of the floor. I rushed over. It was Damon. I quickly re-hooked the blade under my dress against my thigh and knelt beside him. He was bleeding and bruised but not enough to insinuate anything fatal.

"Please, please, please, please, no..no!"

I felt tears at my eyes and pushed them back.

"This is no time to cry Serena." I reminded myself.

I frantically felt against his throat for a pulse. It took only a moment to find and it was strong indicating he was just knocked out.

"Thank the gods."

I took my hand away from him and took my knife out again. I walked slowly around the rest of the main floor then headed upstairs. Worried whoever or whatever knocked him out was still lingering. I found no evidence of anyone else. Where was Darren? I silently prayed he was out or something. But why leave Damon alone? My heart was drumming so quickly I had a hard time not hyperventilating to keep up. I thought Serenity had mentioned they were both here. Maybe I was mistaken, or she was.

When I was positive nothing else was around the house, I returned to Damon's side.

I tried to gently rouse him. I was so unbelievably relieved, and grateful to see him again.

"Damon?" I spoke softly and gently shook him.

I was also worried he might wake up and be terrified, because here I was alive. I fully expected him to swing at me.

He didn't stir.

"Damn it. Don't make me drag you Damon."

I shook him harder this time. "Damon!"

I tried a few more times, being as loud as I dared too.

"I will drag you outta here. I gotta get you safe." I whispered.

I grabbed his arms and pulled. I strained but he began to move with me. I grunted and struggled with him. He was much taller and heavier then me.

I managed to get him to the front door with a great deal of effort. When I got there Serenity was standing on the porch.

"This is as close as I can get, bring him here, I will help you pull him. The powerful one is gone. I do not sense it any longer. It is faint enough to indicate it has been about an hour."

I was grateful for the insight. With a last yank and huff I got Damon's body onto the porch and Serenity grabbed his legs.

"It would be wise to return him to the hotel." Serenity whispered.

"How are you carrying him? When I was a spirit I just went though everything, like smoke." I asked.

"I have been a spirit for many years now, you learn over time. You were a new spirit."

We opened the door to my back seat and laid Damon there.

"Can you sense Darren, his brother?"

Serenity looked blankly at me for a moment before replying. "No."

I swallowed the lump in my throat again very afraid that something happened to him too.

"Okay." We heaved Damon onto the seat and I stroked his hair.

"You are safe now Damon." I said softly, closing the door to the back.

I got back into the drivers side glancing around once again to see if I could find Darren, or whatever knocked Damon out. I saw nothing, I rushed out of the driveway. We made it to the hotel in 10 minutes versus 20. I didn't get pulled over.

"Serenity, you can't enter here?"

She shook her head. "No. I will remain nearby however."

"Can you help me carry him?"

"As far as the door."

I nodded. I opened the doors to the car and grabbed Damon under his arms, Serenity grabbed his legs and pushed. Then she moved through my car to help me hold him on the other side. Her ability to glide through objects came in handy. We pulled him as gently as we could from the backseat of my car and, carried him to the front steps. Serenity stopped a couple paces from the entrance.

"I cannot go further."

I took a deep breath. "Okay." I heaved Damon best I could.

"Serenity?" I grunted between breaths.

"Yes?"

"Can you try to find Darren and whatever did this to Damon? I will tend to Damon, once he is awake again, I will return out here to meet you."

"Happy to."

"Thank you."

She nodded and dissipated. Leaving me alone in the cold weather. I hauled Damon best I could to the entrance.

I managed to get him to the door. The receptionist greeted us then immediately rushed when she saw what state Damon was in.

"Do you need assistance? What happened to him?"

I took a couple breaths unsure what to say.

"Too much to drink." I forced a laugh.

She gave me a strange look. "This one? Really? I mean his brother yeah but-"

I cut her off. "Please, just help me get him to his room."

She nodded and waved the bellhop over. He helped me heave Damon to the elevators. I looked over my shoulder.

"Did he leave with his brother?"

The receptionist nodded. "Yes they did leave together, he was alone?"

"Yeah, but that's okay, thank you."

"Oh and welcome back miss. We haven't seen you in a day or so!"

I forced a nod and a smiled to her as panic gripped me. That could mean a couple things, but it for sure meant Darren wasn't here as I had hoped. I took a steadying breath. Damon first. He was here, I was the only one that could help him. I was so grateful to be back to the hotel despite the circumstances. The elevator dinged it's familiar sound and I got us to their room. The bellhop helped me get Damon onto his bed, I thanked him and tossed him a couple dollars. He was overjoyed and left happily. I latched the door behind him. I looked back to Damon, and went to lay beside him. I studied his face, his tattooed arms, Handsome as ever and I found myself longing for his lighthearted jokes and voice. I had missed him, and Darren so very much. I felt for fever. He was boiling.

I went to the kitchen and ran a rag under cold water. I pressed it to his head and he still didn't stir. I sighed.

I got two more rags of cold water and pressed one the back of his head too.

I stripped his jacket and shoes. He was in a white t-shirt and dark blue jeans. I looked around for blood but only saw a little bit coming from the cut on his forehead. I felt behind him on his back for any spots of blood but he was clean. I put another cloth under his arm with that one he groaned.

"Damon?" I spoke anxiously.

I stroked his hair and cheek gently.

"Damon, please" I spoke louder.

"Damon!" I yelled.

His eyes flew open and he ripped the cold cloths off of him, sitting up quickly. Blinking rapidly.

"Emma?" he barely whispered.

I paused wondering who that might be, perhaps one of his lovers. But it had a familiar ring to it. It gave me butterflies when he spoke it. He must be so confused.

"Hey..hey take it easy, take it slow."I said quietly, putting my hand on his shoulder.

I watched him stare at me for a second while he kept blinking rapidly, he rubbed his eyes then refocused. I cupped my hands against his cheeks.

"Damon, it's okay, you are alright." I said softly.

He moved for a second and I flinched, expecting him to attack me out of fear, but instead he put his hand over mine.

"It's you." He rasped.

His eyes searched mine for a few minutes and filled with tears.

"Serena, I should know you would be the one to greet me."

My brows furrowed in confusion.

"No Damon- It's really me. You are alive, as am I." I whispered.

Tears fell from his eyes and he chuckled softly. He ran his hand over my hair.

"Serena." He pulled me roughly against him in a hug.

He sniffed once. "Is it really you?"

"Yes." I whispered against his chest. He pulled me tighter.

He pulled away only, slightly to look at my face again. 'I will have to make sure, I just promise I won't tie you up this time."

I nodded. "I know."

"I'm so sorry. I should never have left you alone. It's- it's all my fault."

I put my forehead against his.

"Please don't do that, don't blame yourself."

He cupped my cheeks again. Another soft chuckle as he swiped his right hand against his eyes and left his left hand against my cheek.

"How?"

I shook my head. "I'll try to explain, but where is Darren?"

His face fell. He got up abruptly.

"He wasn't with me?"

Damon started frantically searching the hotel room.

"No, I searched my whole house, before bringing you here. I saw no sign of him. I was hoping you would know."

"Damn it. We have to go." He said quietly.

He started towards the door then stopped.

"I will go look for him. Stay here Serena. Please. I-I can't lose you again."

"No, you are not leaving me here, I am coming. Didn't you say I shouldn't be alone?"

He looked towards me and nodded once. "Your right- Okay. I will have to carry you, I- your wheelchair-I'm sorry I don't-" I cut him off.

"No need."

I stood up from the bed and walked towards him, I couldn't help the small smile that came when I did.

Damon's eyes widened. "But-"

I nodded. "I know, it changed some things."

He gave me a small chuckle and quick smile. He grabbed my hand.

"We gotta go."

We rushed out of the room.

"We will need to take my car yours is still at my place. Or I can drive you to your car, we can split up. Where was he last?"

"We were both at your house and.." His eyes widened.

He stopped walking abruptly.

"Serena, I'm sorry, I'm so relieved you are here and I am still in a bit of shock but, Darren."

He trailed off and looked away.

My heart started racing. What was he going to tell me? Was Darren, he couldn't be dead right? I felt sick to my stomach and momentarily missed not having a body to feel such unpleasantness.

"What about Darren? Is he alright?"

"I hope so." His voice was distant.

"Damon just tell me what happened. I can be more useful if I know everything."

Damon sighed.

"I don't know exactly an item affected him. I- well I don't have an easier way to put this- he's possessed Serena."

I swallowed feeling much more nauseated. My heartbeat quickened.

"But I thought- the crystals, and you guys had measures to protect against possession?"

"Yeah. By ghosts and demons. Not God's."

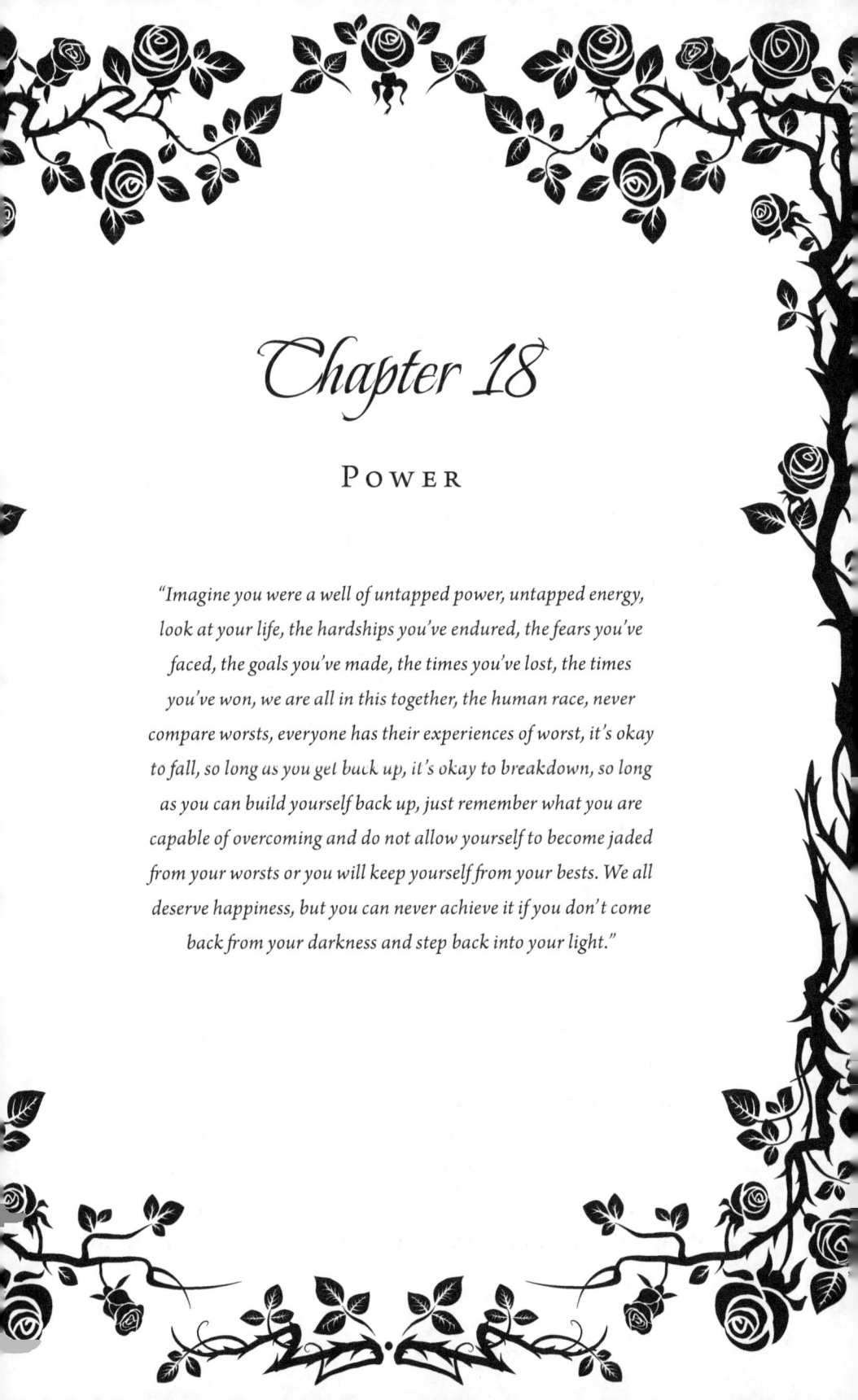

Chapter 18

POWER

"Imagine you were a well of untapped power, untapped energy, look at your life, the hardships you've endured, the fears you've faced, the goals you've made, the times you've lost, the times you've won, we are all in this together, the human race, never compare worsts, everyone has their experiences of worst, it's okay to fall, so long as you get back up, it's okay to breakdown, so long as you can build yourself back up, just remember what you are capable of overcoming and do not allow yourself to become jaded from your worsts or you will keep yourself from your bests. We all deserve happiness, but you can never achieve it if you don't come back from your darkness and step back into your light."

"**Y**ou mean to tell me, Darren is possessed by a God?"

Damon ran his hand anxiously over his hair and his eyes, depicting horror.

"Osiris. The Egyptian God of the Underworld."

I couldn't believe what I was hearing and I could only stare at Damon as we continued hurriedly to my car. I opened the door and we tumbled in. I took a shaky breath.

"How?"

Damon shook his head.

"We gathered items from a tomb, they just floated right over to Darren and took control of him when he touched them. He hit me with some sort of strong energy and I-"

"Ended up unconscious?"

He nodded. He looked at me again his eyes were trying to say a million things. Something was underlying in his facial expression and his energy like he was keeping something from me. I tried to shake it off. I clenched my jaw and focused on the task at hand. I had so many questions, and what if this God had killed Darren? I took a deep breath.

"Where do we start looking?"

"Honestly I don't know."

I glanced in my rear view mirror and jumped, steering the vehicle toward the ditch slightly. Serenity was sitting back there. She smiled slightly.

Damon followed my glance.

"Something wrong?"

Damn that means he couldn't see her.

"No. Except that I am worried about Darren." I half lied.

I was so worried, but it wasn't nothing that I was looking at. I glanced again to Serenity. Is this how spirits were normally, just existing with us, beside us but we couldn't see them or sense them?

His eyes lingered on me for a long moment. He was almost wistful?

"I am too."

"We will help him Damon."

He nodded. "With every fibre of our being."

I nodded. I pulled up to the house again.

"Are we splitting up?"

Damon was quietly looking out the window. I followed his line of sight and stared for a moment at the empty driveway. I could've sworn the volvo was there when I left with Damon.

"Damn it. He's got my car."

My mind raced momentarily.

"Make a call to the police station, report it stolen, they should be able to track it down for us."

Damon nodded. "That's a brilliant idea."

"Meanwhile we will try to track it on our own. He has two hours on us if he left right after I did with you. I didn't see him though Damon, I searched every square inch of my house inside and outside."

"I believe you. He is not- he's a God. A very powerful God at that, he was probably able to hide from you easily."

I sighed and looked to Serenity, whom was pointing to the right. I revved the engine and drove to turn right.

"Where are you going?" Damon asked quickly.

I paused unsure how to explain.

"A hunch."

Damon watched me for a couple minutes. I veered right at the stop sign past my house.

"I trust you. I will look up what I can on the God see how we could possibly, kill it. Or take it out of Darren without-" He trailed off.

"I understand." With my right hand I reached over and squeezed his hand slightly.

"Well we have taken down a God before." I continued.

My comment didn't seem to ease him even slightly. I didn't blame him. I was so afraid for Darren it was hard to keep focus to my driving. I needed something else to think about. I glanced to Serenity again. She motioned for me to continue down this road. It was gravel and treed in. We passed a few farmhouses that looked like they had long since been abandoned. Then I started to see people. They were glowing aspects of blue, green and red, wandering the empty farmers fields. I slammed my breaks and we screeched to a halt in the middle of the back road.

"What's wrong?" Damon said looking around us.

It was clear to me he couldn't see what I saw.

There had to be hundreds of ghosts surrounding these couple fields. I swallowed and looked frantically around. All had different styles of clothes. Some recent some ancient. Men, women, even children. My breathing was loud and erratic. If these were ghosts why weren't we cold? Then I noticed the corners of my windshield started to crystallize.

"Serena, answer me what's wrong?"

I looked over to him and glanced in the back, Serenity motioned for me to keep driving.

"Look." I nodded towards the frost creeping along my windshield.

Damon noticed that at least. He sighed.

"Ghost, can you see anywhere?"

I wasn't sure how to reply.

"Damon, Ghosts."

"There's two? Where?"

I shook my head. "Damon there are hundreds of them..wandering these two fields."

Serenity was motioning to keep moving more aggressively now.

"What do you mean? You can see them?"

"Yes."

He exhaled slowly and studied my expression.

"Let's keep moving. Have any taken notice of us? We must be headed the right way."

I glanced around but not a single one was looking our way.

"Not yet."

"Drive then."

I let my foot off the break and slowly accelerated. I slammed the breaks again as several wondered across the road.

"What-what is it?" Damon asked excitedly.

"Damon they are crossing right in front of us, What am I suppose to do?"

"Keep driving Serena. You can't hurt them."

I took a shaky breath and drove right through them. Wincing and closing my eyes momentarily as I did. Serenity motioned for me to turn right at the fork in the road up ahead. I did as she instructed. I was incredulous at just how many of them there were. We kept driving. The farmers fields seemed endless.

"There Serena!" Damon pointed to an abandoned mansion of a house, where the red volvo sat in the drive.

I glanced to Serenity whom nodded. I pulled up in front.

"Black Rose Ridge institute." the sign read.

My chest constricted with fear as I read the sign. Remembering having seen this before. Serenity and I were both very familiar with this place. Maybe I could discover what actually happened. The wisteria tree was even still around. I clicked my jeeps engine off and pulled behind the volvo.

Damon exited hurriedly. "Come on!"

Damon grabbed my arm as we raced through the yard to the entrance.

I wasn't sure if he had read the sign. But all of the ghosts seemed to be gathering and entering this building. Serenity spoke to me now, I knew I would be the only one to hear her.

"They are coming to Darren, or should I say Osiris. They are trapped here. Many are trapped here on Earth. They can sense the awakened God, they are gathering in hopes to be freed. Do not reply to me. I will be here to protect and assist as I am able, but you mustn't disrupt Damon's focus. Right now, he may be the only person that can bring Darren back from the claws of Osiris."

I wondered if Osiris could do such a thing. I silently prayed he could bring Darren back. A God of the underworld, how the Hell were we going to get through this?

We poured through the door huffing as we ran. Damon was frantically entering every room. The hospital was horribly familiar to me, and I tried to remember why. I knew at the very least I had been here, a patient. But how? When did this go out of operations?

"Damon, Let me lead. We should follow the ghosts, I think they are being directed to Osiris."

Damon stopped. "There are ghosts in here too?"

"Many, they all seem to be making their way through here."

"The sign, "Black Rose Ridge" does that mean anything to you?" I asked.

Damon shook his head.

"No. But I saw the sign. It is probably somewhere like the hotel. It must have some semblance of meaning, I would have to research it more. There has to be a reason Darren-"

He paused. "I mean Osiris is here."

"Damon, how do we get rid of Osiris?"

Damon looked at me for a moment.

"In the lore I found it is said Osiris brother Seth murdered him. Tore his body into 14 pieces and strewn the pieces all around Egypt."

I swallowed hard.

"Okay so we need to chop him up? But isn't he in Darren's body?!"

"The body Darren and I got the items from, was his, it was in pieces but I didn't pay much mind to it. It must've been that they gathered all the pieces, and something within that resurrected his spirit. I found no mention of Godly possession Serena, I have absolutely no idea how to expel him from Darren."

His voice broke slightly as he said this to me.

I thought about that as we rounded another corner and stopped in our tracks. Darren was standing in a room that looked like an old library. I was astoundingly relieved to see him. Possessed or not. The ghosts were surrounding him. There were so many overlapping voices. I covered my ears and crouched down. Damon didn't notice and started to approach Darren, without looking to me. Darren's back was too us.

Serenity crouched beside me. "Hold on."

She put her hands over mine and the voices silenced.

"How-?"

She put her hand over my mouth. "Shh. Approach with caution."

I nodded and followed after Damon.

"Darren!" Damon yelled.

Darren's body whipped around, his eyes were glowing amber. I swallowed the lump in my throat and pushed the tears that burned at my eyes back.

"Ahh I knew you would eventually catch up to me my worshipper. Tell me how fared your rest? You remember who you are yet? But how dare you address me by the vessels name. The blatant disrespect. Darren is not here anymore."

It's voice boomed and echoed like thunderclaps, it sounded nothing like Darren at all.

I lingered a few paces behind Damon breathing fast and heavy. What did it mean? What did it mean? Darren had to be here still!

"Perhaps I would worship you, if you weren't wearing my brother!"

"Hm disappointing. You do not yet remember. Perhaps another bout across the room then? As far as brothers go, well. They aren't all they are cracked up to be. My own murdered me you know. I've felt this one's power. He would kill you too false prophet."

What power was it talking about? What power did Darren have? I thought quickly to myself.

"Darren would never, ever hurt me." Damon said with venom dripping from his words.

Osiris laughed.

"How sad for you. However I do not blame you. I believed the same. Naive just like you. We have much in common you and I Damon."

"Give me Darren back. Or I will send you straight back to where you came from."

It laughed again.

"You dare threaten me?! When here I am doing your job. All these lost souls no where to go. I am helping you. If you two will not lead in your destined roles, then I will rule in your places."

I watched as each spirit approached him he touched them and they dissipated.

I glanced to Serenity.

"He is doing as he says..but he is dangerous, no limits and will annihilate many in attempt to free them."

"What designated role?! You seem to know so much, then shed some light on the situation for me. I will have Darren back. So either you will give him willingly or I will take him back." Damon's voice was acidic.

I had never heard him speak even remotely similar to this in the past.

"Mm. How unfortunate. You cannot have Darren back without me giving him up, and I will never let him go. Oh, how very frustrating for you."

"Darren! Fight back! Expel him. You can I know you can! Fight him!" Damon yelled.

"Enough!"

Osiris flicked his wrist and sent Damon flying into the wall of bookshelves which fell on top of him.

"No! Damon!" I screamed.

I rushed forward towards him. Darren's amber eyes focused on me as if just finally noticing me for the first time.

"You- how long have you been here? Who are you- the power emanating."

He paused and inhaled loudly, dragging his tongue slowly across his lips.

"It is absolutely tantalizing. Put's both these brothers to shame. What are you?"

I ignored Osiris and rushed to Damon. I started to frantically throw books off of him. I threw all the debris and books off of him, Osiris merely watched me. I cupped his face when I found it, it was horribly swollen and bloody. I frantically felt for a pulse. Praying he was alive still.

"Don't bother yourself. He is alive, I cannot kill him. I need him for now. He is just rendered useless, like a little broken toy."

I felt an overwhelming sense of absolute fury, I whirled around to face his glowing eyes.

"What are you going to do to me princess? I'm oh so curious. Despite your power, I can feel how much you care for these men. It's nauseating and will inevitably be your downfall. I can also sense you have absolutely zero control over your powers. Tsk tsk. Shame. Would make for such a delicious main event"

Serenity appeared beside me then. His amber eyes widened.

"The sister. It is as it was written. You are on the wrong side of this, misplaced. Lost. And you Serena, You have been through the veil, and returned."

He was staring at Serenity as he said this.

"Sister?"

Serenity nodded. "I am, Serena. But I could not tell you myself."

Tears welled for a moment. Looking to her blind eyes. Remembering how she had no tongue. This place- what happened to us?

"Why can't I remember?"

"Most of your memories are in fragments, for good reason." She replied.

"Away."

"No!" Serenity screamed.

I looked around and she was gone.

"Where did you send her?!"

I realized it didn't just send Serenity away but all of the spirits that were here presently. It was now just the three of us.

"Answer me!" I howled.

I felt a crushing weight of power as I lunged forward. Osiris was tossed back.

"Impossible. You are incomplete."

I felt a burning brim of power tingling throughout my body, my skin felt hot, and my mind was clear.

"Give me them back!" I screamed.

My back felt like someone stabbed a branding iron into it and I barely flinched as more power seemed to gather. There was so much energy it felt hard to contain within me.

I pinned him to the wall and as my hand made contact with his body he howled in pain. I could feel his skin sizzling beneath my touch. I pulled back horrified remembering this was Darren's body. This was Darren. I stopped. What was happening to me?

"Until later Serena. I told you, they will be your biggest downfall." He rasped.

As he did a glowing amber smoke began to detach from Darren's body. It lifted and shimmered out of him as Darren yelled in anguish. It folded in on itself above Darren for a moment before melting through the floor. Darren's body collapsed at my feet. The power and fury that was encased around me immediately stopped. I held Darren's body against mine.

"Darren..Darren..please please please! Darren! Darren.."

I begged holding his body tightly, I laid him gently on the ground and felt for a pulse. I picked one up, it wasn't weak but it was slow.

I let the tears out now. I grasped my hand gently over the burn I left on him. What kind of monster was I? So much so that a God flees from a fight with me.

"Please..come back to me.." I whispered.

I cradled Darren's head in my lap, stroking his hair gently and silently sobbing.

I glanced over to Damon whom was still unconscious as well. I grasped blindly in my bag for my phone and pulled it out immediately dialing 911.

"911 state your emergency."

"Hi- I'm-" I paused I didn't even know how to describe where I was.

"Please continue ma'am"

"I don't- look I don't know, I'm near the Alberta hospital."

I remembered the sign before Black Rose Ridge.

"Some abandoned farmhouse, I- I don't know the address."

"That's fine we can trace the call. What is the nature of your emergency?"

"My- friends they are both unconscious, both alive but unresponsive. One of the bookshelves fell onto him and the other, I'm not sure."

There was some clacking of computer keys. I held my breath in anticipation.

"Found you. Are you in intimidate danger? Is there anyone else with you? Are you injured?"

"No."

"Okay a unit will be there in 5 minutes."

"Thank you."

The phone clicked and I dropped mine.

"Darren..please." I gently tried to rouse him.

Oh God I hoped he was okay. I grabbed my cardigan and wrapped it under his head and moved toward Damon. I winced at his bruised swollen face. I was afraid to move him incase he was more injured then I thought.

"Damon-?"

He groaned. I gasped in relief. "Damon! Damon, hey, hey don't try to move."

He opened his eyes and the right eye only half opened because it was so swollen.

"Serena?"

He tried to move and groaned loudly.

"Okay, okay it's alright Damon, an ambulance is coming right now. Couple minutes stay with me."

"Where's Osiris?" He gasped.

"Gone." I studied his eyes.

"Where are you hurt outside of your face and head?"

"What do you mean gone?"

"Damon save your breath please. Please, okay I can't lose you."

"Darren, I need to get to him." He tried to get up and groaned loudly again.

"Damn it, Damon where does it hurt?"

"Leg. Right one. Darren!"

"Damon, Osiris left him, look he is over there but he's unconscious too, the ambulance will be here very soon stay with me."

I looked over and saw his right leg was buried beneath a mass of shelving. I swallowed hard. I hadn't noticed.

"Why did Osiris leave him? It doesn't make sense."

"Let's just let him come too and sort it out. Well if you can feel pain, that's a good sign."

"Yeah." He started to close his eyes.

"Damon, Damn it- come on. Stay with me."

I could hear sirens in the distance.

"Damon?"

He opened his eyes again.

"How many fingers?" I held up two.

"Four" He smiled slightly.

"I laughed with relief. "tsk two actually."

"Damn, maybe I'm dying."

I laughed slightly.

"Okay hang in there, let me check Darren."

I went back to Darren whom was still unconscious I felt again for his pulse. It was still present and I exhaled.

The paramedics rushed in then.

"Over there! By the shelves."

"Got it." A man replied and him and another guy rushed to help Damon as more men came this way to Darren.

"How long has he been out?"

"Half an hour maybe. His pulse is slow. But I couldn't see any injuries."

"You found them like this?"

I nodded. Unsure what to say exactly.

"Okay step aside we got him."

I did as they said and they heaved him onto the stretcher. I swallowed and pushed tears back again. Oh God I hoped he was alright. Once they were outta sight. I walked over to the man helping Damon.

"Can you distract him? You his girlfriend or something? We are gonna heave this off and it's going to hurt profusely, but he needs to stay still."

The man asked. I paused. "I- I can distract him yes."

I crouched by his head. "Hey love you hanging in there?"

"Yeah. Darren?"

"Darren was already loaded up, it's okay."

"Go- Serena go with him. Please. I cant obviously, but I don't want him to wake alone."

"I will but first I need to help here."

"Okay we are ready to move this."

"Damon hold my hand. Look at my eyes just focus on me for a minute okay, can you do that?"

"I could focus on you a lifetime Serena." He held my hand tightly.

"Oh even crushed underneath all that you are still flirting, ever the player eh?" I spoke lightheartedly, clearly kidding with him.

He usually would laugh when I said that in the past but this time he looked slightly wounded. I wasn't sure what to say and they heaved the shelving off of him and he cried out loudly. I held his hand with my right hand and his head with my left.

"It's okay, it's going to be okay now Damon."

He nodded his face twisted in such pain.

"Alright and up!" The paramedics lifted him.

He cried out and let go of my hand.

"Go to Darren, I'm fine." He urged me.

I kissed his hand and rushed toward the ambulance, without looking for his reaction.

"We can tow your car if you wanna ride in with one of the guys." The paramedic said.

I glanced back to Damon, hesitating. "Darren."

The paramedic pointed to the ambulance ahead. "Quickly."

I rushed to the side, he helped me in. They had Darren strapped to all sorts of wires. I sat out of the way, but I grasped his left hand in my hands and stroked it gently with my thumb. I played with the ouroboros ring on his thumb gently.

"Hang in there." I said quietly.

My heart raced being inside another ambulance, I was sure another accident wouldn't happen but the event had jostled me enough to have me very on edge in the vehicle as we raced towards the hospital.

"Do you guys know, will he be alright?."

The paramedics looked to me. "Are you intimidate family?"

I swallowed. "Close enough to, his brother is in the ambulance behind us. The paramedic nodded.

"He seems, completely unharmed. Just, dehydrated. Minor injuries except-" He lifted Darren's now cut shirt open to reveal the burnt hand print of mine scorched into the flesh of his chest.

I couldn't help the tears that came flooding over my face.

"Oh my God."

"I know we are unsure how this could even happen. He will need to be rushed to a burn unit as soon as possible. He should wake, we don't have a sign of any head trauma, but a burn that bad could put you into shock, we may be able to find a trace of DNA of the hand print but that could take weeks. Our best bet is to treat all we can and hope he wakes soon."

I nodded and sniffed. "Okay."

I was sick to my stomach, seeing what I did to him. It was revolting, wrong, unnatural. I wouldn't ever dare hurt him or Damon. I couldn't imagine anything ever happening to either of them.

I dialed Matt. I needed to know if Rayne was awake. All the most important people in my life were in such dire states. I worried they might have known I was dead already, but perhaps the guys hadn't told them yet. Matt answered on the third ring.

"Serena?"

Chapter 19

WALLS

"If walls could talk, the secrets they would spill would annihilate us, if mirrors could reflect our innermost thoughts and desires, we would shatter them all, if words could kill, we would have a massacre, if dreams and nightmares reigned true we would never dare sleep, if only to dream and never again wake."

"Yeah Matt, it's me." I said slowly afraid what he was going to say.

"It's so good to hear from you, The guys said you were quite sick and injured. You better now?"

I exhaled and relief encased me. He didn't know. They hadn't told him yet. Better now, yeah, more like, alive now.

"Yes, I am. How is Rayne?"

"She's awake. She's just not speaking much still. I was about to phone and update the guys but I hadn't heard from them today or yesterday. Everything okay?"

"No, they were in an accident, I'm headed to the hospital with them now."

"Oh God, serious?"

"Not life threatening thankfully, but yes."

"I would offer to come but my hands are pretty full with Rayne. I brought her home yesterday, shes up and about now."

"I am extremely relieved to hear that Matt."

Relived was an understatement.

"You and me both."

"Okay I gotta go, thanks for updating me. As soon as I can get over there I will. She's in great hands Matt, thank you. Tell her I love her. And I will see you guys as soon as I can."

"Of course."

Click.

I focused back to Darren. Staring at my hand print burned into him, fighting bile in my throat as I prayed he would be alright. At least I knew Rayne was okay. It was some semblance of weight and crushing fear off of my shoulders.

We pulled up to the hospital. It was not the same one I had died in, so we would not run into anyone who knew about it here.

There was a commotion of voices. I stayed by Darren's side, holding his hand. I walked with the paramedics with his body into the hospital and watched as Damon was also unloaded and rushed forward.

"Serena!" He called from the bed. He was trying to sit up. I looked over to him.

"Is he alright?" Panic drenched his tone.

"He's going to be fine Damon. I won't leave his side."

"Good. Good." his face relaxed ever so slightly.

"Damon enough chatting, let's get you inside. We need to operate on your leg right now so you don't lose it." The paramedic barked.

I swallowed. "You'll be alright Damon, I will be here when you come out."

He nodded and smiled. "Good."

"Prep OR 1 for immediate use!" A doctor that checked Damon hollered and he was wheeled away.

"This one for intensive care as soon as possible." The doctor that just checked Damon now looked Darren over.

"Can I stay with him, doctor?" I asked desperation in my voice that I couldn't hide.

"You will need to be sterilized first but yes."

I nodded.

I followed them to the burn unit. Never once letting go of Darren's hand. He deserved that at the very least.

"You need to let go of him for a bit." The paramedic said softly.

I reluctantly released his hand and was told to step back while they took Darren into his own room. God he had to be in a sterile room because of me, because of what I did. I took a couple shuddering breathes. I was lead to an area where I was to be sterilized and dressed in plastics. I was lost in my thoughts while they did all that, and let me back into the room. I knelt beside the bed as the doctors hooked Darren up and began to inspect the burn. They dressed the wound and all I could do was stare in horror at his unconscious face. I worried sick for Damon too. I reminded myself that he begged me to stay here for Darren. I wished I could somehow be with both of them.

"Doctor, is that burn, is he going to be alright?"

"My name's Leah" She said kindly.

She had black hair tight in a bun and a pinched look on her face. She looked to me:

"Yeah, so long as it doesn't get infected he will be, but he will need to be here for a week for it to even begin to be in a state of healing, if we don't need to do grafting. Which I am hopeful that we won't; but I won't know for sure for at the very least 24 hours."

"When do you think he will wake?"

"It's hard to say, could be any minute. Could be a couple days. His vitals do not say it's coma, so he will be able to awaken. Shock has varying responses. It's good that you are here, a familiar face will help graciously in his state. A burn like this on his chest will be incredibly painful even on morphine. If you come out of the room at any point for anything, you will need to redress in sterile gear each time you come in, we don't want bacteria on him."

"Okay. His brother Damon, can you keep me updated on him please?"

"Yes. I am his attending as well. Just ring the bell if Darren wakes or if you want to come out."

She left swiftly.

I exhaled. A few tears escaped my eyes. I grasped his hand tighter.

"God I did this- I did this to him. A familiar face, yes except, he thinks I'm dead. Now I worry it will put him further into shock to see me." I thought to myself.

I kept stoking his hand.

"Darren, can you hear me?" I spoke softly out loud. I didn't expect a reaction.

His hand twitched ever so slightly in mine.

"Darren?" I said slightly louder.

His hand grasped mine slightly.

"Darren, love please. Please." I raised my voice another couple octaves.

He groaned slightly and I was beyond hopeful for him to open his eyes.

I begged again. "Darren?"

His eyes fluttered open and he immediately tried to get up frantically looking around.

"Darren hey hey..it's okay.. you are in the hospital. There was a fight."

He stopped thrashing about at the sound of my voice. I found his hand and grasped it again. Holding it against my face. It felt as though I had done this before, even though I hadn't.

"Serena?" He rasped.

"Yes Darren, it's me you are safe, and I- I am so relieved- so happy to see you again." My words came out in a ramble of quiet desperation and relief.

"I'm dead. Either that or I am losing my damn mind." He whispered. His voice was small and shaky. It was unfamiliar to my ears.

"You are alive. You are just injured. You are safe." I said as soothingly as I could.

He didn't move his hand and I finally got the courage to look at his eyes.

I didn't know what exactly I expected to see in his eyes, but it wasn't anger.

His eyes were ablaze with such a depth of fury, that I instantly dropped his hand. Afraid suddenly, like I had been the first night I met him, when he held a blade to my throat.

"Darren wha-"

"Enough! How dare you wear her face, use her voice, play this act, are you amused you monster?" He yelled, yanking at the wires he was hooked up to, which sent alarms blaring.

"I swear I will send you straight back to Hell, regardless of the state I'm in, I can promise you that." He seethed. My heart was breaking by how he was looking at me and talking to me.

I inhaled deeply, he thought I was a demon. Had I expected different?

I took half a step back as he tried to get out of the bed, eyes blazing.

"Coward. Face me. You show up as her. I hope you writhe and burn in Hell."

My eyes teared up. I couldn't help it.

"Darren, please it's me. It's really truly me." my voice was soft and small.

I started to panic, worried my powers would take over again I tried to calm myself. I couldn't lose control again, I couldn't hurt him again. Either of them, ever again.

"Liar! You just shut the Hell up!" he roared.

"No- Darren." My voiced was breaking I tried to keep it steady and even and failed.

He started to chant in Latin as Dr Leah and several hospital personal came barrelling in.

"Sedate him, get him down! Serena you need to leave now, you can return when he is calm, We need the space."

I swallowed hard. Tears at my eyes.

"That is not Serena! That is a demon! It's a demon and you gotta let me stop it! You don't get it! That thing! It will kill all of you!" The rage in Darren's voice as he hollered was unlike anything I had ever heard.

"Okay he's in a manic episode, sedate him now. Before he hurts himself or someone else!"

"Serena out!" Dr Leah ordered. As a nurse began to lightly push me toward the door.

I glanced behind me on my way out as they slid a needle into his arm and he collapsed as all of them then lifted and strapped him back into the bed. I watched for a second longer then left the unit unable to stop the tears. I headed to the nearest bathroom outside of the burn unit. I fell to the floor gasping and sobbing hard beside the nearest sink. I hadn't even checked if the bathroom was empty. I didn't care how I looked. I just needed a release, it was so much. Everyone I cared about was in the hospital or in dire state or dead. I had a sister whom was dead that I didn't know about, whom clearly died as a child, and I had no idea where Osiris flung her. Why didn't mom tell me about her? How did mom die, when? The white eyed demon, Henry, I had no indication to how to control my powers, or what I was. I knew we only had 3 weeks left to save the world and on the other hand; I was overwhelmingly grateful and honoured to be alive again. My mom was right when she said I needed Damon and Darren. I just hadn't realized it until now.

"Chin up."

A familiar ghostly voice. I opened my eyes.

"Serenity?"

"Yes."

"Oh, I am so happy to see you!"

I stared at her now familiar white eyes and long dark hair.

"Where did Osiris-?"

"He merely forced all the spirits a distance away so he could focus on you guys. I'm fine. Not much can happen to spirits."

"I suppose, yeah. Darren he-"

"I saw."

"And Damon-"

"I'm fully caught up. But you should shake yourself off and go to Damon. He just got out of surgery. I may have located one of your missing items. I might be able to secure it but we need all of us in decent shape."

"Okay."

"I must go attend to other matters. Just get your boys healed up."

She dissipated without another word. I swiped my hand over my face, didn't bother to look in the mirror or around the bathroom. I made my way to the nurses station and asked for Damon she barely looked at me and handed me paper with the room written on it. I rushed there.

Damon was asleep but his leg was wrapped and propped. His arm and face were bandaged in gauze. He looked like a fallen angel.

I entered the room quietly and sat beside his bed, clasping his hand in mine.

"Damon?"

He opened his eyes and started to smile, then panic replaced the look.

"Serena. What's wrong? Is Darren okay? Why are you here with me instead? I asked you-" He said panicked, before I gently cut him off, holding my free hand up.

"Darren, had an episode, they told me to leave. He started freaking out, saying I was a demon. I mean, I- can we blame him for that? He has no idea I'm alive."

Damon nodded.

"I hadn't thought about that I was just so worried. But he's safe? He's him still? No Osiris?"

"He's sedated I can't go back in for a while, they need to keep him here for a week at least. He is himself, I promise you. How are you feeling? What's your time frame?"

"Thank god."

He studied my face, I'd imagined it was pretty evident I had been crying.

"Serena." he stoked my cheek gently, I leaned to his touch.

"I'm good, Damon. How are you?"

He paused for a while waiting to see if I would say more. When I didn't say more he dropped the topic.

"I'm good. They have me on a lot of medications though. They saved my leg. I guess I won't need to take your old wheels for a spin after all. The doctor told me at least a week."

I smiled. More grateful then usual for his humour and light-heartedness.

"Good, cause you wouldn't look as graceful as me in them."

Damon snickered. "Nah, probably not."

"I can run back to the hotel and gather a bunch of books so we can try to decipher some things, while we are here." I offered gently, I know our time frame is very tight.

"Good idea. But I don't want you to go far from us, alone. Not while we are here unable to protect you." He said concern in his voice.

"Damon.."

"Please." He met my eyes. "Just-please."

"Okay, I won't. Okay, I promise?"

"Good." he let go of my hand.

"I'm sorry Serena I'm a little foggy still-"

"It's okay, sleep hun, get better. I will be fine."

"Check on Darren too please."

"Of course, I will come back in a couple hours."

Damon had already drifted to sleep.

I exited his room. Heading back up to the unit Darren was on. I was stopped by Dr Leah in the hall.

"Serena I have been looking for you." she said as dread poured over me.

"Why, what happened to Darren?"

"Nothing, he just- he didn't- he didn't take well to the sedative he is still lucid but calm enough, I cannot push anymore into him without risking his heart and I won't do that. So maybe, it would be best to give him a couple hours to rationalize."

I paused for a moment considering.

"Call me immediately if anything changes with either of them please."

"What is their relation to you?"

I had no idea what to say to that. So I said the first rational thing that came to my mind. I figured I mean they were brothers so-

"They are my brothers."

The word felt extremely wrong on my tongue.

She nodded. "Good. If you weren't immediate family I would have to ask you to keep your distance."

I exhaled. "Of course. I will return later then."

"Visiting hours are finished by 8pm."

"Even for intimidate family?"

"Unless someone is dying, unfortunately yes."

I swallowed hard I didn't like that at all. That didn't feel right or safe in any way.

I glanced at the clock "7:49pm"

Damn.

"Okay, of course. Can I write a note to pass to them please? I don't want to go and disturb them just to leave again.

"Of course. Pen and paper at the desk. I will be back in a few minutes." she said kindly as she walked away.

I walked up to the desk and started writing.

"Damon, they wouldn't let me stay past visiting hours, even said I was your sister, no go. I am sorry to disappoint you, I will be heading back to the hotel. I would've told you but when I had left you were already asleep. I figured there was no point to wake you just to say bye. Darren is still okay, I couldn't go back in with him though, but they said they would keep me updated on the both of you. I will be careful and I will be back in the afternoon tomorrow. I will likely check on Rayne too.

Serena.

I paused about to write one for Darren, maybe it would be easier to read it for him. Easier to explain that I was back, easier to explain everything. I wondered about it too long and Dr Leah came back.

"Just for Damon please."

She nodded. "Absolutely. They are in good hands, otherwise see you tomorrow."

I nodded. I started to walk towards the doors.

"Serenity?" I said under my breath.

She flitted to my vision beside me and I did my best not to jump and remain nonchalant. I didn't want to look crazy, talking to no one.

"Yes? You want me to stay and watch over your "Brothers" She didn't laugh but her tone was slightly less monotone as she said it and I took it as her version of humour.

"Please."

"Of course sister, whatever you need. If you summon me I will come, just say my name like you did now, and I will come if you need. Be careful."

"I will, thank you."

She flitted out of my sight again and I existed the hospital.

My jeep was right out front the paramedic greeted me.

"We had it towed, here's the keys. They okay?"

"Mostly. Thank you so much again."

He smiled a bit. "Just doing my job."

I unlocked my car and got in exhaling loudly. I glanced in my rear view mirror. My makeup was smeared like a raccoon. My hair looked like I hadn't brushed it in days.

"At least at the hotel I can clean myself up, but Rayne first."

I thought to myself. I started to drive toward Rayne and Matt's so excited to see Rayne again. I rode in silence. My thoughts were too focused on everything to listen to anything other then them at the moment. When I pulled up most of the lights were on. I quickly parked and raced out of my car. I bounded eagerly up the steps.

Grateful I didn't need to explain how I was back to life, because no one knew in the first place. I knocked twice. Matt opened the door.

"Serena! Come in! I wasn't expecting you until tomorrow but Rayne is still up she's just in bed." He gave me a half hug.

"Glad to. Thanks Matt."

I walked in and there was an overwhelming, nauseating scent of lavender.

It reminded me of the massage parlour Rayne took me too a couple weeks ago.

"Can I just head to her room?"

"Of course."

"Are you okay Matt?"

"Yeah-yeah I'm good just tired you know."

"I understand. Well rest for a bit I can help for a couple hours if you need a break."

"That would be great honestly. Thank you. Are you okay though Serena? Looks like you've been crying."

I swallowed forgetting that I hadn't adjusted my appearance.

"Yeah, just a lot. I will be fine though Matt, thanks for asking."

He nodded and walked toward the kitchen.

I headed up the familiar staircase to hers and Matt's room, a huge smile over my face, being that I was so excited to see her again. I dashed into the bathroom and washed my face hurriedly borrowing a brush that was sitting on the counter. The bedroom door was open already so I just entered. I walked up to the bed and looked, but I didn't see Rayne. I looked around the room and didn't see her. I felt slightly panicked.

"Rayne?"

I left the room and walked back to Matt whom was just settling on the couch.

"What's wrong she okay?" He started to get up again.

"Well, she's not in her room?"

He jumped up. "What do you mean?"

He followed me upstairs then gave me a strange look when we re-entered their bedroom.

"What do you mean Serena, she's in bed right there?" He pointed.

I looked again to the bed, I walked a bit closer. My heart thrumming and my breath quickening. All that was on the bed was a very strange looking piece of wood.

Matt walked right up to the piece of wood and kissed it. I couldn't speak.

"Need anything my love? Serena stopped by to see you. It's nice to see you smile."

Had Matt lost his mind? What was I suppose to do, Rayne was not here. The piece of wood was the only thing in the bed.

"Well see here, she's okay, I will let you guys catch up. She doesn't talk yet, but maybe you can get her too."

I stared at him dumbfounded and kept looking at the piece of wood.

"I know she looks pretty sick hey? It is probably from all the medications she needed."

"Yeah-probably." Is all I managed to say in a shaky voice as he existed the room.

Chapter 20

MAGIC

"Imagine for a minute you are a child again, imagine finding joy in every tiny thing, curious, imagine laughing more then anything else, imagine being carefree, unafraid, imagine owning who you are with not a second glance to who might care what you do or say, being kind first, welcoming, loving fully and strongly, imagine that spark never being choked out by the world and never allowing that harshness to harden you, and holding that magic into adulthood, therein finding true happiness? What a kind of world that would be."

A million thoughts were flipping through my mind, I couldn't even think straight. The only thing I could gather was that Rayne wasn't here. I first dialed the hospital Rayne had stayed at being mindful not to say my name based on what happened to me there.

"Good evening, how may I direct your call?" A women's voice said quickly.

"Hi, actually I just wanted to know if my friend had been discharged yet?"

"Name?"

"Rayne Rivers"

I heard keys clacking.

"Yep! Says here she was discharged two days ago because she was healed enough, only issue was she wasn't talking yet."

"Her husband took her?"

"Matt yes. Is everything alright?"

"Thank you. Yes." Click.

I exhaled and looked over to the bed again. I walked up to the piece of wood.

I felt silly but I hugged it.

"I will find you Rayne." I whispered.

I rushed out of the room and down the stairs.

"Woah!" Matt jumped up. "Everything cool?"

"Yeah- I- I need to go check on Damon and Darren. Hospital called." I lied quickly.

"Oh, of course, I hope everything is okay."

"Yes I'm sorry Matt. Try to rest."

"See you Serena."

"Bye."

As soon as he closed the door behind me I broke into a sprint towards my car. I couldn't call Damon or Darren. I wanted Serenity to stay with them. I tried to run though what to do. I thought back to the scent, it was strong and overpowered like at the massage parlour. I googled the hours but they had closed at 8.

"Damn it." I whispered.

I unlocked my car and scrambled in. Slamming my door and ripping it into reverse. I tore out of the neighbourhood and towards the hotel. I was trying to remember what Damon had mentioned when I said bells and lavender.

"God, what did he mention?" I was still wracking my brain when I parked at the hotel. I got out and triple locked my car. I jogged to the front of the building taking care to ensure no one was watching me and went inside.

"Welcome Back! Oh you are all healed up! Walking on your own two legs that is wonderful." The regular receptionist greeted me happily.

"Thank you. I forced a smile.

"Happy to have my legs back for sure." I added hastily.

I started towards the elevators when Jane approached me. Her face was pure venom when she approached me. Crap, I really didn't have time right now.

"Hi Serena. See you are walking now. That's nice."

"Hi Jane, yes, I am grateful, just tired and ready to turn in for the night."

I moved to walk past her and she stepped in front of me.

"I'm just going to be straight up with you. Are you sleeping with Damon?"

"No." my voice was flat and stern.

"Don't lie to me, Serena I kill shapeshifters I can easily spot a liar."

"I'm really not, but I am very tired."

"Are your romantic interests elsewhere?"

I felt the urge to laugh at the mundane thought of courting someone, when I was just happy to be alive, and focused on finding

Rayne and stopping Cronos among much else. I sighed annoyed, out loud.

"Yes. I'm sorry if I gave you the wrong impression. I'm not going after your boyfriend. Just good friends."

"Well he's not really my boyfriend, but I like him so. Good then, thank you. You can go. He around anyway?" She gazed about.

I swallowed unsure if I should tell her he was injured.

"He's at the hospital."

Her face lit up in panic.

"What, why?!"

"Him and Darren were in a bit of an accident but they are both going to be fine, nothing fatal. Visiting hours start tomorrow morning."

"That's awful. I'm glad it isn't serious though. I will have to go see him. Thanks Serena, sorry for cornering you like that."

I nodded about to leave, then I saw Jenny hovering in the diner watching us.

"Wait-Jane?" she turned back to me and stopped walking.

"What?"

"I was wondering about Jenny."

Her eyes narrowed and she came closer to me dropping her voice to a whisper.

"What about her?"

I thought to Serenity.

"Does she know about-"

"Shapeshifters and all the other unnatural? Yeah."

"No- does she-"

Jane's eyes widened and she dipped her head slightly.

"Yes, she knows that she is dead. If that's what you mean. She didn't always. I told her recently."

"I'm sorry. Did you know she died? Have you known about her your whole life?"

"Why are you interested in my personal life? With all due respect I don't know you Serena and I don't appreciate the personal questions."

"You're right- I'm sorry Jenny just patched me up a while ago, she didn't seem to know then that she was dead."

"It's easier to pretend. I work here in between my hunts, to be near her."

"I just- I know it's personal, I guess, well I just found out I have a sister, one that died when she was a kid and I had no clue until a couple days ago. I suppose I was looking to relate to someone."

Her face softened slightly.

"I cannot imagine that. I'm so sorry. No, I've known about Jenny. I am actually her younger sister. I'm almost 20 years younger then her, that's why she's here. Mom had her when she was 15 and had me at 35. The hotel had already burned down by the time I was born. My dad told me about her when I was maybe 8 years old. So I stay close. But I can't imagine not knowing about her. That is tragic. I'm sorry as well. Older or younger?"

"I- honestly don't know much about her. She's a ghost, shes been helping me."

"She isn't tethered anywhere?"

"No, she appears when I call her."

Jane looked at me a moment. "Well she isn't an ordinary ghost then."

"Do you know much about ghosts?"

"My first serious man is part of the family that hunts them so yes by association, not by experience in field."

"I can look into her if you want help I mean." She smiled.

"Really? Okay. I have a lot on my plate, so I would deeply appreciate that."

"Sure. In return take good care of Damon. What's your sisters name?"

"Serenity Moonshile I would presume. She looks maybe 9 years old? Black Rose Ridge. It's kinda a place like this hotel, destroyed long ago."

"Okay that's enough to go off of. Meet me in the diner in 3 days at suppertime. I will share what I can gather about her. In the meantime. Be careful. I resent it, but I know that Damon and his brother care deeply for you, romantically or not. So stay alive yeah? Also, you know your makeup is running all over your face."

I must've not washed it all at Rayne's.

"Yeah, thanks Jane."

"Oh, and let's visit Damon tomorrow at separate times? I just don't think I could handle-" She began and I cut her off.

"I get it. I will go for 11 you go for 10."

She smiled and waved as she walked back toward Jenny whom also waved at me.

I walked quickly to the elevators. The same boy as usual tipped his hat. I smiled best I could.

"Glad to see you better ma'am if that is not too bold."

"It isn't and I appreciate that deeply. Thank you."

"Yes Ma'am."

The elevator dinged and I hurried out, racing to our room. I quickly unlocked the door. I locked it behind me looking around. The guys must've cleaned all the glass up. I shuddered remembering Henry. Wishing I could forget the memory. My eyes lapsed over the spare room that was brimming with the cursed items we needed. I walked over to the shelf.

"Fairy" Damon mentioned Fairies. The bells and lavender scent, signalled fae involvement. I was so relieved I remembered, then dread filled me. I searched frantically for a book that mentioned Fairy's.

"Changlings. A Whole Analytical list of Fae in each culture."

I didn't remember that book being there in the past. Not unlike the black book that found me. I grasped it quickly and settled into the nearest chair skimming the pages.

"Known for kidnapping babies and replacing them with fae offspring to grow in the human world- thought to need human milk in order to be strongest. The baby would look slightly different and be intelligent beyond its years, whilst the human child was taken to be raised as a fairy."

"In some cases human women were taken, especially newly married or new mothers to marry fairy kings instead and to nurse the fairy babies. Often when an adult is taken an object resembling a log was left in place of the stolen human, enchanted to look like the person, but appear sickly and would "Die" insinuating the human had died so no loved ones were left searching for it."

"An enchanted piece of wood- Rayne." I said out loud.

They took Rayne, Fairies took her. I turned that over in my mind several times and still had a hard time with it. I slammed the book shut.

"Oh God, it's my fault I exposed her to this world, by being part of it. Damon warned me in the beginning-"

I stopped myself. A pity party would not help Rayne. It was up to me to get her.

"Why could no one else see it wasn't Rayne, when I could? I wonder if it had something to do with why I didn't need spells to enter places like the hotel, or how I have unimaginable strength. The massage parlour. Titania. That place has to be run by fairies. The bells were so loud, the smell was so intense."

"But how the Hell do I find fairies?" I whispered.

I skimmed the book.

"Lots of the lore described deep in the forest, or fairy rings. But which Fairy ring? The massage parlour felt like my best option, but it wouldn't work right now. Then I remembered when Rayne and I were at "Le Crema Cafe" in St. Albert, she was staring like she was in a trance before I came up to the car, at seemingly nothing. But what if it wasn't nothing?"

"Lions park was where she was staring."

I have to go there.

I skimmed the book then again looking for fairy weakness in case I had to fight, in case my powers didn't work again.

"Iron. Burns them to dust. They are compelled to count grains of sugar or salt, if you pour it on the ground majority of them will have no choice but to start counting each grain."

I poured some of the sugar caddie into a plastic bag. The key to the room was actually iron.

"Seems too easy almost." I whispered to myself.

I rushed out locking the door behind me again.

I took the stairs, in hopes to sneak out without catching much attention. I half ran down the stairs, I reached the bottom and left from the back of the hotel. No one saw me. I rushed around to the front of my car. I pulled my phone out. "9:19pm"

It was still light out. Lions park was only about an hour from me. I started my car and headed in that direction. The drive was a blur, my thoughts rampant. I parked in the empty lot and rushed to the vantage point of the cafe. I couldn't see much but a big oak tree. I went to that, and again I smelled Lavender but couldn't see any. I looked around and there were hundreds of small mushroom rings. I was the only one in the park and I felt odd being here this late.

"Maybe she saw something, or someone, or maybe the fairies were already planning on taking her and that was her first glimpse. She never told me what she saw but shook it off and blamed being tired."

I felt around the tree, shocked when I hit the back end of it, it pushed inwards like a door.

"Woah!" I tumbled forward.

I pushed harder and a door opened in the trunk of the tree. It was tall and narrow, I had to turn sideways to fit, but I got in. As it did it enclosed behind me.

"Oh God, I'm in a tree, I'm literally in a tree."

I turned the other way and stairs appeared in front of me. It was so wide in here suddenly, like the little door in "Charlie and the Chocolate Factory."

I started to descend the stairs when they shifted into a slide and I fell flat on my ass and started barrelling downwards.

I screamed slightly. Within seconds I landed onto soft moss. All around me was floral of all different kinds. Much bigger then me. I had to have shrunk somehow.

"God I stumbled into Wonderland." I muttered.

I loved that story but didn't ever think for a second I would live it.

I was greeted by a pink haired lady. She was astoundingly beautiful. Her pastel hair was down to her knees and she was in a short white dress. Her wings were much like dragonfly wings. She stared at me a second.

"Who are you?" Her voice was very high pitched.

"I-I'm here to see Titania." I tried.

"Bold of you to not address our Queen as Queen." her eyes narrowed at me.

"My humblest apologies. I mean to say Queen Titania."

"Hm that's better, but you are not, well you are obviously not a fairy yourself, so how did you enter here? Are you one of our past human children?"

I shook my head. "I- don't think so."

"Hm. Curious. Quite Curious. You shouldn't have been able to enter our realms."

"The rules of entering magical places don't seem to apply to me, if I'm being honest." I said simply.

I stopped after I said that, unsure why I admitted that out loud.

"I see. Ah yes, well you won't be able to lie here. Try as you may however. Well I must take you to Jade. He is our prince. Queen Titania is not back yet."

"Follow me, human."

I started to follow her.

"My name is Serena."

"I don't need to address you as such. You are an unremarkable human."

I swallowed. "What about your name?"

"Silly. I won't tell you. Names are very powerful things. I don't trust you."

"I thought you said we couldn't lie?"

"I did not tell a falsity, I said I would not tell you my name and that is the truth. I said I do not trust you and that too is true."

She had me there.

"Right."

"Here is the Prince's quarters. Speak your piece. I will collect you later."

She flew away. Quite literally, I couldn't imagine having wings, it would be so beautiful to fly, I would wager.

"I can't believe, I'm in a Fairy kingdom." I whispered out loud.

"You are indeed. But why are you here?" A man's voice spoke.

I followed the voice and my eyes fell on a very very attractive man. He had dark brown hair, that laid at his bare sculpted shoulders, and a long beard. He looked similar to Jason Momoa from the Aquaman movie. But more, regal.

"Prince Jade. I am most displeased to meet your acquaintance. What brings you to the fairy realms human? Also how, how did you cross the barrier? Human's need a Fairy to let them in. Or they must know ancient magicks, ones we have never shared among the humans."

I was a little surprised by what he said, but no one could lie.

"Where is Rayne?"

I immediately clasped a hand over my mouth surprised at what I said. I hadn't wanted to, it just came out. God, this was going to be harder then I thought. Why hadn't the books mentioned this?

His eyes narrowed.

"You are here about my fiancé? I can assure you she is well. I will not be keeping her name of course. It is distasteful for the princess to bare such a barbaric human name."

I swallowed hard. "Let me see her, please."

"Your intentions?"

"Just to talk to her. I'm her best friend. I saw the wood and-" I bit my tongue before I could spiral into a speech about how she couldn't marry him that she already had a mate. I didn't know how I suddenly gained a moment of self control. I hoped it would stick.

"Saw? Hm. Curious. How did you find us then?"

"Yes, I will answer all your questions, after I speak to her please."

He stared at me a moment. I hadn't lied.

"Very well." He stepped aside to let me through.

I half ran forward. "Rayne!" I called.

Jade moved to close the door behind me.

"She's upstairs fitting a gown." he said plainly.

I stopped for a moment and looked around. The inside of the house was similar to a nice condo but it had no roof, simply was just plants, that the sunlight flitted through. Wooden furniture. It felt like I stepped into a life-sized antique dollhouse.

There was no stairs to get upstairs. Then I suppose why would a fairy need stairs.

"I can't get up there."

"I know."

He picked me up with one arm and flew me upwards and I yelped, not appreciating the unwanted touch.

He quite literally dropped me and then flitted back down.

Rayne glanced to me and her eyes lit up in recognition.

"I will return in some time, don't go down yourself, it is much higher then it appears and you are much smaller then you think you are. You would be quite dead, I'm afraid."

The prince called up and I heard the door shut. I found the bluntness that honesty brought humourous.

"Rayne! Oh my God."

I wrapped her tightly in a hug, and she seemingly had no injuries.

"How- how did you find me? Is Matt okay?"

Her voice was trembling.

It felt for a moment like we were kids again, where I used to comfort her when she fell, or someone said something mean to her. Not like being kidnapped to a magical world was anything remotely close to any of that.

"Matt is fine, I'm so relieved you can talk, and- you are healed? No injuries?"

She pulled back from me, staring at me with shock in her eyes.

"You mean he's not, looking for me? He's not worried sick?"

I shook my head.

"He doesn't know you are gone."

Her eyes filled with tears. "What-"

"The fairies when they take you, they enchant something to look like you, Rayne Matt thinks he is caring for you whilst you are bedridden ill, still injured from the accident and unable to speak."

She started to cry then and I held her closer.

"What is he actually caring for, if I'm here? I'm really here? Aren't I? I'm not- dead?"

"No hun, no. You aren't dead." I spoke softly, stroking her long brown hair as I had many times while comforting her when we were kids.

"How did you know it wasn't me at the house, if Matt is fully tricked? Oh God the thought of him taking care of someone thinking it's me is churning my stomach."

"It's a piece of wood."

Rayne sputtered. "Excuse me what?"

"They enchant wood to look like the person they kidnapped, they will appear sickly and eventually die, leaving loved ones to think they passed away when really they were in the fairy realm."

"Oh God the more you say Fairy realm the more I think I've lost my freaking mind."

"You didn't, look Rayne I know about this stuff."

"What do you mean? How could you possibly know about such an impossibility?"

"Because everything is real. Everything we see in movies and books it's all loosely based on real life things."

"Now you sound freaking crazy Serena. If all these unnatural beings and things and monsters exist why do we never see them?"

"You will find this hard to digest. But there are families, like a secret underground society, they are all in charge of different creatures. They keep them at bay and away from the public knowledge."

She was shaking her head and so I continued.

"Damon and Darren are part of it. They take care of demons, and right now they are trying to stop an apocalypse and that's what I've been helping them with."

"When you say everything?"

"Everything. Horror movie all the way to fantasy fairytales. Look, you are in a real live fairy world and you still don't believe me?" I said motioning to the room around us. She shook her head.

"No, I am way more comfortable with the fact that I've snapped and I am actually sitting in a mental hospital somewhere, being spoon fed while I'm trapped in my mind!"

I sighed. I understood, I was laying too much on her. I opted for a topic change.

I looked to the wedding dress she was holding in her hands.

"What do you remember?"

"I remember being in the ambulance with you after you freaked out, the ambulance crashed, I woke in the hospital with you trying to drag me from the bed, looking like a freaking broken rag doll, crawling on the ground. Flopping about, scaring the staff, and me. I remember Matt saying he loved me so much. I remember them telling me I could go home but I couldn't speak yet. I wanted to but I couldn't make my mouth talk. Then Matt put me to bed and then I found myself compelled to walk and leave the house, I walked to the cafe we went too barefoot and in my nightgown, in my casts and all, I felt no pain. I remembered when he were last at that cafe seeing a silhouette of a man standing by a big oak across the street, before you came back to the car. Then that night he- came through the oak tree I returned to. He sprinkled some weird powder on me and I ended up here. I was told I was marrying this Jade, otherwise they would kill Matt, so I obliged, now you are here, and I still don't understand how. I have been here 3 months. We can't lie so I don't speak much. I'm suppose to marry him tonight."

"3 months? You only got home 3 days ago, in the real world."

Her eyed widened. "Impossible."

"I promise you. Oh God Rayne, I'm so sorry. Come, I will get you home."

"I can't, I have to stay here, or Matt's life is in danger, this will be easier on him! If what you say is true, he will think he sees me pass away, and think he's done all he can."

"Rayne don't do this. Don't quit on me. Trust me, please. Have I ever steered you wrong before?"

"Queen Titania is here." Jade's voice echoed as the door opened. Rayne's eyes flooded with tears again.

"We are coming up." He said.

They both flew up then and Rayne and I stopped talking.

Titania was beautiful, she had sunshine golden hair down to her ankles and butterfly- like wings. Her eyes piercing pink.

"Why must you cry so much Ruby." Jade said as he moved to touch Rayne's cheek. She moved slightly away from his hand and he withdrew it. I cringed at hearing him call her by a new name.

"Your majesties." I bowed as low as I could.

"I've come to return Rayne to the human world."

Jade laughed out loud.

"You- human mean to come here and tell me, that you are taking my bride from me?"

"She is not your anything." I spat.

"She has been since I brought her here months ago."

"She has a mate."

"I do not care whom she thought her mate was before me."

Rayne just kept staring into the distance.

"If I may interject." The Queen started.

Jade stopped talking. "Of course your excellence."

She fixed her pink eyes on me.

"I remember you, from my massage parlour. You could hear our bells."

I nodded.

"Yes, Your majesty."

"I am curious Serena, I've heard much about you, a whisper through many realms."

That made Rayne look at me, slack jawed and horrified.

"Like what, your majesty?"

"That your powers worry even the strongest foes, although you do not express the ability to control them. I also hear you and the Elderwood brother Gods are working together, to stop Cronos"

That made Jade look at me, fear flashing in his features briefly.

"Yes, your majesty, all of that is correct."

She stared at me for a moment.

"And this-human? Ruby? How did you see past our enchantments, how did you find us? I compel you to answer these."

"I honestly don't know why, but I seem immune to the ancient magicks. I felt drawn to the tree, I placed my hand upon it and the door opened."

Her eyes widened.

"I've never seen a human, much less anything else express that kind of power. Only a Queen may enter through realms."

"As for Rayne-" I emphasized her real name which made Jade clench his jaw, which made me feel a slight satisfaction.

"She's my best friend. I went to see her as I heard she was released from the hospital and when I came to her bed, I saw the wood for what it was, a chunk of wood, in her bed."

"Curious. Our enchantments have never once faltered to the human eye. This proves to me that you are in fact not human at all."

Rayne's hands covered her mouth as she looked to me. The fear in her expression made me feel nothing but agony.

"I do not know, what I am if not human. My mother, my father, both human."

"Your body is human and was created as such. Your soul however is not a human soul."

"Queen Titania, do you know what I am?"

"All I can tell you is that your soul is very powerful, and that your body, your bloodline, you are a direct descendant from the first."

"The first?"

"The first soul in creation."

"You mean Adam and Eve?"

"No, I mean to say older then humans. It is the only possibility. I just do not know the specifics."

I swallowed. I was about to ask her to confirm that as true, but Fae cannot lie.

"So you may take your friend there home." She spoke kindly.

I gasped slightly in disbelief and Rayne's eyes widened.

"Queen Titania, mom, surely you don't mean that! She is my wife to be! You have readied her for me. I will not take no for an answer."

"Enough Jade. I shall find you another wife, I have many suitable clients that have received all treatments to prepare them for becoming one of us. Patience. I know you value your life as I mine. We will not be so daft as to make enemy of the first."

Jade backed down then.

"Of course not. My apologies-Serena."

He strained to say my name.

Rayne rushed to my side. I was dumbfounded and had a hard time finding my voice.

"Thank you, your majesty."

I moved to bow and she signalled me to stop and bowed instead.

"I do not favour Cronos's ideologies. His ending affects all of us, everything, every plant, every being, unnatural or otherwise, not just the humans. Now that I know you are of the first, you have my every faith Serena, your powers combined with the Elderwood brothers is our only hope, to secure a future at all. If I had seen you when you came in with Rayne, I would've known then and there. I wished I had, but I am however glad, we have had this talk, and for you to see our world firsthand. I believe it is quite exquisite."

"As am I. Thank you for your insight as to what and who I am. I do think your realm is one of great beauty."

She nodded.

"Serena, here, take this. You will need it. I have safeguarded this for many millennia. This is one of the 666 you need to stop Cronos. It is also the most potent antivenom to most harmful magicks. I know it will be of great use to you."

She ripped a bundle of small silver bells from her neck, and placed it in my palm.

I inhaled deeply, waiting for them to clang loudly but they didn't this time.

"They won't hurt your ears anymore, you have been to our world, you will also likely see many of us, in your day to day life now. You have our sight. I do ask you don't harm us, as we have done you a kindness."

I could not believe what I was hearing.

"Thank you, Queen Titania. I will not let you down. I will not fail. I would never intentionally hurt anyone."

"I trust that to be true in your mind, as I believe in mine, and really that's all that matters. I shall send you both to the surface now."

She blew some gold coloured dust toward us. I watched it shimmer in the air and I watched it blur as our surroundings became Lions park and we were both there in the field completely unharmed. The bells were still clasped tightly in my hands.

I exhaled loudly.

"Rayne, you okay?"

I turned to her but her eyes were watching me closely like a frightened animal.

"Take me home. Please. Please. Just- take me home."

I wanted to reassure her, soothe her anything, anything to make her not look at me so afraid. I couldn't fathom the idea of my best friend being scared of me. I merely nodded as we walked to my vehicle by the cafe. I knew it was a lot of information to digest, it was for me too, I wasn't really human. But I knew that didn't I? Was this my fate? Mine and Darren and Damon's fate, to stop this all from ending?

We buckled in and rode in silence.

Rayne spoke after about 10 minutes of driving.

"Only three days?"

"Yeah, only three days."

"I'm so afraid I will scare Matt, if he thinks I'm sick in bed. Can you stop here, I am so incredibly thirsty."

I nodded and pulled into the Circle K. I fuelled up while she ran inside for water.

My phone rang while she was in the store, it was Matt. I answered. "Hello?"

"Serena? Serena Oh thank God you are still up. Please come back to the house, Rayne, Serena I think- I fear she is dying! She is so thin, she's barely moving, she won't eat, can you please help me, God, Serena I can't lose her yet."

"Matt, don't worry, okay? I'm on my way."

"Thank you." Click.

Rayne emerged then with three bottles of water. She chugged two to herself and handed me one.

"Thank you."

We both got back into the car.

"They wouldn't give me water there. Apparently there, you don't need water as a fairy." She swallowed hard.

"It must have been really scary." I tried to emphasize.

"Beyond."

"I would be happy to listen when you are ready to speak of everything, if you want me to."

She nodded. "Perhaps, but not yet."

"I understand."

"Thank you."

"I have a plan to get you inside, do you have your keys?"

"Yeah. What is the plan?"

"You will sneak in the back door, Matt is expecting me to come, I will occupy him at the front door while you run to your bed. You will simply lay where the wood is and I will get rid of the wood. Matt will come to check on you as usual and see you are better. It won't look weird, it's better then just showing up, he won't be confused, just relieved that you are okay."

"Brilliant."

"Okay."

I drove a bit faster the rest of the way there. We pulled up to the drive.

"I can't wait to see him." She said wistfully.

I smiled. "I'm sure he will feel the same."

She got out of the car and ran towards the back door. The dark of the night kept her well shadowed. I walked briskly to the front door where Matt flung it open as I ascended the front steps.

"Hurry! I've called an ambulance, but they said 20 minutes."

"It's going to be okay Matt."

I rushed up the stairs with him, hoping Rayne had enough time to get into the bed.

We rounded the corner and sure enough there she was under the covers. She jumped up and ran toward us when Matt entered the room.

"Matt!"

Matt fell to his knees and he grabbed her tightly against him.

"You're alright?! But how- I was only in here minutes ago you looked so- It doesn't even matter!"

He hugged her tightly as Rayne sobbed.

I dialed emergency services to call off the ambulance and I joined them in the hug. It would have seemed suspicious not too.

"Rayne, I'm so happy you are alright! Matt had me so worried!"

It was by far my smoothest acting ever in my life. I broke off from the hug after a moment.

"I love you so much." Matt whispered.

They both kept pouring the words over one another as they held each other there on the floor. I watched happily. I was so glad and grateful Rayne was home safe. I checked the time it was 1:23am I could not believe everything had played out in a mere few hours. I moved to the bed to grab the wood as I did it turned to ash and burned away within seconds. I glanced to Rayne and Matt but they hadn't seen. They were too wrapped up in eachother's arms

"Good." I whispered to myself.

My phone rang then. It was the hospital.

I answered on the second ring, panic flooding my body.

"Hello?"

"Hi. Is this Serena?" It was Dr. Leah. I hesitated a moment before replying.

"Yes."

"I am so sorry to tell you this, Darren will not make it through the night, I am calling you to come say your goodbyes."

Chapter 21

(Written in Darren's perspective)

"Vulnerability I found at the bottom of the bottle, the only thing that breaks down the threshold of this armour, the only thing that crumbles this stone, the only time I can no longer hide behind steel plated walls, the only time I feel everything and I'm not just fucking numb, mask shattered, face to face with the monster, I cheers to the reflection of who I am and who I pretend to be, can't you see? I'll protect you with my life, you are everything I hope to be, everything, I want to keep, all I desire, I don't know how to tell you so instead I'll stay at arms length, and hope you'll stay."

I watched the demon posing as Serena, bile in my throat, how dare that thing disgrace her memory as such. Damn these injuries I fought against the staff. I had to kill it. I had to. The needles slid into my skin and I noticed something off about the nurse. It wasn't a needle at all, more so a single blade of a claw, a flash of glowing green eyes. A Djinn. No. Where was Damon? I have to remember. I have to remember everything that happens now is the poison. I have to get myself out of it's nightmare trap or I will die. Damon needs me alive. He can't lose me and Serena. I need to stay alive. The dream rushed and pulled me like a rapid current that held me underwater.

I was in a black room. Nothing around me but darkness. No shapes, no light, no sounds. Then I am shown an image, that moulds and folds and changes my surroundings.

It started after my set signing Elvis in the bar. I sit down and I see Serena. She greets me warmly. Her long hair curled slightly, in a beautiful dress. She emanated light all around her. Like a blinding aura.

"Darren." Her voice like silk.

She walks to me and plants a light kiss on my cheek and I am warmed by her light. Addicted to her presence, like an enchantment.

When she pulls back her eyes are red.

And I fall off my chair, instead of her. Henry grabs her. She is dragged away, eyes no longer red screaming, begging me to grab her and I can't. I can't fucking move.

Back to the black room of nothingness. I pace a few steps, looking for anything that resembled anything, but I cannot even tell which way is up.

Then the scene changes again and I am in our hotel room the night we met Serena.

It starts though with Serena dying, but it was me who took her life. The blade I had held to her throat I had cut into her, slicing her throat. I watched the life drain from her dark blue eyes. I shuddered. I grasped at her, her blood coating my hands.

"No- no- no- no- no! I didn't-I didn't!"

I never killed Serena. No.

Then I see Damon, humanity wiped from his eyes, as he stares at me horrified at what I've done. I stab him too. My own brother. His body falling limp beside Serena's. All I can do is scream. Something deep dark and evil lays beneath my skin. I turn the blade onto myself and the blade shatters unable to kill me.

"It's not real, it's not real-damn it! It's not real-"

I muttered over and over to myself.

The room swishes back to the blank darkness.

"I need to get out, but how?- How do I leave this place?"

"How do I escape my own mind?"

"It's just the poison."

My words echoing into the blankness does nothing to reassure me. I find myself questioning reality already, slipping, slipping into this trap.

A voice rings out in the still nothing.

"No, perhaps not, but the fact that you are capable of this, yes, that is very real. You are a killer." Osiris's voice.

"Get the Hell outta my head you bastard!" I holler to no one. My throat aches.

"We are one in the same you and I."

"No." I say through clenched teeth.

"I am not a killer."

"Oh but you are Darren. I've seen the depth of your soul. Barely human."

"Look around you, all those you love die. Are you still struggling to remember?"

"What the Hell are you talking about! Come out and face me you bitch!" I yell so loud it hurts my throat.

A laugh.

"You created me, to tell you everything you are too much of a coward to admit to yourself."

"Remember Darren, Remember what you are so desperately trying to forget."

"You were expelled from me! Get outta my head!"

"I am you."

I am back in the blackness staring at myself. My reflection? But it is not mirroring me. It's eyes are- my eyes are amber.

"How did Osiris leave, did he leave? No, I was possessed, I was trapped, in a mirror like world. He was taking souls, no I was taking souls, he was here. I was still possessed. I had to be.

"Let me go you bastard!"

"I am not Osiris Darren, I am how your brain is portraying your subconscious. There are things, things you need to remember."

"Darren!" I stopped. It was Serena's voice. Beckoning, a blissful echo over the vast nothingness.

"But she was dead- was I dead? Osiris came, I-I launched Damon. Was Damon okay?"

"Darren please. Please don't die on me." her voice held such sadness, it sounded so..real?"

"REMEMBER DARREN." Osiris's voice boomed, drowning Serena's voice out.

The nothingness shifted and pulled again.

"I am standing in a home that I have known a long time. It is charming, Victorian fixer upper. I look around at the vastness of the fields before me, my wife wraps her arms around me. Her vanilla scent enveloping me in it's familiar haze.

"We finally did it. It will be such an enchanting place to raise the children."

She runs her hand along her protruding stomach. I place my hands around hers. I agree with her. We spend hours together, planting wildflowers, and flax crop.

"I just want this place to welcome life of every kind. Over there we will have a great many gardens, weddings can be hosted." she says softly.

"It will darling." I say as I kiss her forehead gingerly, something I did many times a day.

"And the house well, My vision, it'll be beautiful. We can do it."She lifts our entwined hands and kisses mine.

I lack the ability to see the beauty and potential in such a broken down home. But Hell if I don't help her, I know she'll do it herself.

"Yes, I believe in you and your vision Aurelia I always do." I look to her face then, she looks so similar to Serena. Then we are in a hospital, Terrified our son is coming early. I have never felt such fear and such amazement as he is brought to her chest. She stares blankly, I tear up. I wish I could take all her pain away.

The days are hard, but we take turns, and she is radiant in motherhood as she shines in every aspect of her life.

"He is everything." She whispers as she kisses his head. Her eyes weary and puffy, from no sleep, same clothes as yesterday.

"Honey, go I drew you a bath. I will cradle him tonight, sleep my love. All is well."

She cries softly. "Thank you."

Out the window the wildflowers grow as her vision grows. Our house, she's made a home. She is everything.

The scene changes again, next child, she is more prepared this time, excited. I give her all she needs, we eat and down so much water, she births this one naturally and I am so proud. Her strength. A daughter. A second daughter. Twins. She cries as our little girls are laid on her with pure joy, proud too.

"I did it. All natural. I did it."

And this time she is graceful, she is handled, our little guy we have the best conversations.

"I am so blessed for you and our kids." I kiss her softly.

The scene switches. Our children are older, her parents encouraging us to go on our delayed honeymoon that they would follow the next day. I am excited but sad to leave them, but looking forward to being alone with her for a while. Aurelia, god she looked like Serena. She was reluctant.

"Maybe we should all go together?"

I encourage her to go, she parts them with a tearful loving goodbye. I didn't know then that this would be the last time I saw their faces. I would have never known.

The plane drops much too fast shortly after take off and the masks fall. My wife screams and I hold her, terrified too. We clasp the masks but the plane shudders and falls, all I hear is screaming, I can only hold her as we crash. I awaken she is alive but pinned.

"Thank God you are Alive."

"You too.. oh my God."

All around us is debris and twisted metal, fire and dead bodies.

I was able to drag her from her seat, she cries out in anguish. Her legs merely dangle. There was blood pouring from her ears, mouth and eyes.

"No..Aurelia."

She looks at me and cries tears of blood. "Darren-I-"

Her body let's limp and I scream as she perishes in my bloody, bruised arms.

"No!"

The pain I felt was like being carved with a hot iron. The winds and snow were so cold. Why didn't I die too?

I crawl and start digging as I sob. Digging in the snow until my fingers blackened. I dragged her body to the shallow grave and threw up everything in my system, I couldn't stop screaming, my throat was so raw that every breath felt like nails being dragged down my throat. Cold nothingness. Freezing, I start to burn the corpses the smell is acrid and I get sick over and over and over until I am merely puking blood. Days..Days go by. As I slip slowly to madness. I beg for death. Why will death not receive me? My children, my wife, never will I see them again. My humanity is gone, as I burn the bodies of those who once lived, for warmth then I feed off of them, like a feral animal. Survival instinct consumes me. Then I see her, Aurelia dancing, her skin blue from the cold, frost kissing her skin, her white dress and long hair billowing in the bitter winds. Vanilla strong enough to make my nose burn.

"Aurelia? I'm so sorry, I love you so much.. I love you.. I miss you..Aurelia."

Then her eyes turn to me, not my wife's eyes they were red and a voice that was not hers rang out. "It's time" I Went gratefully, willingly. She kisses my mouth a kiss with death, and a fiery pit opens beneath me as I descend into the fiery flames of Hell."

"Darren? Please, you can't do this."

Serena's voice again, softly, begging. Begging for me, why did she care so much about me?

I struggle to open my eyes the room begins to appear again, the black room with nothing.

"Darren?"

Her voice sounded as if she was crying. I wished it was her, God I wished it was her.

I struggle again to open my eyes and this time I am successful. My eyes are blurry and burn from the bright lights.

Wait- this is real now, it's the hospital, The djinn. I'm out, I'm free.

"Oh Darren! Thank God. Thank God!"

I met her eyes then, Serena's blue eyes, clearly not a demon. My body surged with joy, something I hadn't felt in what seemed like an eternity.

"Is-is that really you?" My voice was raspy.

I brought my hand up gently to stroke her long hair. She flinched as I moved my hand to her. The crushing devastation that she thought

I would ever hurt her was all consuming. I left my hand lingering. After a second she grasped it and brought it to her cheek and I stroked her hair gently. She was crying, and it felt like she would disappear. How was she here?

"Serena." I swallowed hard afraid I might lose control.

"It's me Darren, really, I'm not a Demon, It- it's a bit of a long story. I seem to have gotten a second chance."

I then remembered I had flung Damon across the room.

"Is Damon?"

She kissed my forehead gently, brief, like I had in the past. I surged with a feeling of peace.

"He is injured, but he will be okay Darren. He's at this hospital too."

I was beyond relieved.

"Thank you."

I was focused on her beauty and out of the corner of my eyes, I saw the djinn enter again. They looked annoyed that I was out of their poison induced illusion.

"Serena."

My tone was back harsh and she looked slightly stung and I hated myself for it, but she needed to know.

"The nurse-it's a djinn, stay back from it. Here. I should still be infected."

I cut the palm of my hand with the small pocket knife I kept on me and hurriedly pressed the bloody knife into her hands.

She understood immediately. She whirled around and stood up.

"He is awake, is he still going to die? Please, tell me he won't!"

Her voice was sincere and believable. What was she doing? I bit my tongue to keep from yelling at her to move.

The djinn paused, unsure how to respond.

"Perhaps he will after all, but this could be merely a side affect."

"Oh."

She started crying, hard and threw her arms around the nurse.

"Please- you have to help him!"

"That is my job." It was eyeing me viciously over Serena's shoulder.

Probably thought I was done for. Hell without Serena calling out to me, I probably would've been.

She pulled back slightly. "Thank you"

She whipped her hand around to it's front, while the djinn was focused on me.

A soft groan from the djinn.

"How the Hell was I bested by such a meek little?" He quite literally turned to dust.

I had to admit I was impressed. She rushed back to me.

"What can I do?" She was so afraid, like my wife in the past had been like she, had been in the past?

I tried to sit up and groaned in pain. Her eyes were full of worry.

"Hey, hey don't rush it, the djinn is dead, you are safe right now." she soothed me.

"I am safe, I woke up from the dreams. Thank you for calling out to me. Also nice job on that djinn, impressive performance.

She giggled a bit. "I could never hold a candle to yours, Darren."

"I'll bet you could. Can you get me outta here?"

"Jailbreak? Nothing we haven't done before." She smiled mischievously.

I couldn't help but smile too.

"Serenity" She whispered out loud.

I was confused for a minute then I jumped when a ghostly little girl appeared.

"Serena-"

"It's okay Darren, she's been helping me since I returned. This is Serenity."

She looked very similar to Serena, very similar to Aurelia from my distant memories, but I did not feel a pull of recognition as I did with Serena. I watched cautiously. She was only maybe 9 years old.

She had darker hair then Serena. It was a dark reddish brown. Her eyes were pale, like she was blind, and I could tell by the set of her jaw that she did not have her tongue. I was disturbed by my knowledge of such. Now I knew I had been to Hell before at some point. It existed, I must've seen so much horror.

Ghosts were not normally much of a threat but there was something off putting with Serenity. It didn't make sense that she didn't seem tethered.

"Hello Serenity." I said cautiously.

She did not speak but turned slowly to me, she gave me a slight nod.

"I'm sorry Darren she can't speak, I, she seems to be able to communicate with me telepathically. Wait can you see her?!"

Another thing that put my nerves on edge. "Yeah."

"Can you please lead us out of here? We can't be noticed." Serena asked the ghostly thing.

She nodded.

"Thank you." Serena said pleasantly.

Serenity dissipated into pink smoke. I had never heard of that or seen it before.

"Serena- I've never seen a ghost act like that. Are you sure she can be trusted?"

Serena looked slightly wounded and I recognized my tone may have been harsh.

She dropped her voice to a whisper.

"I know, I have questions too, but she has been extremely helpful this far, she's how Damon and I found you, when Osiris-" she trailed off and looked away.

I winced remembering the waking nightmare of being trapped in your own body while someone else controls it.

"We might not have been able to get to you in time without her. I'm surprised you could see her though, Damon couldn't. She's my sister Darren. I do not know when or how she died. I do not know why she is helping me but I've accepted it. I do not remember our life together yet. I do not know anything about her, my mom never told me anything."

Her eyes grew teary again as she came back to the bed but she quickly swiped her hand over them.

"Let's get you outta these wires."

She started to undo everything. I jumped when Serenity returned at the foot of my bed. She handed Serena a doctors outfit. She tossed a sheet over to me.

"She wants you to cover up and pretend you are dead, the staff all think you were dying outside of the djinn. it's the safest cover. Then to the tunnels under the hospital from the morgue."

Serena relayed the plan to me. I had to admit it was a good idea. A really good idea. I glanced to Serenity and shivered slightly. She did make it cold like most spirits. It was hard to see someone so young as a ghost, someone that clearly went through Hell when she was alive. The perfect concoction for a vengeful spirit. I would trust Serena on this, but keep a close eye on Serenity. Serena pulled the doctors outfit over her own pink dress. I placed the sheet over me. Grateful to not actually be dead, grateful Damon was going to be alright. I thought back to when we were kids. It was my duty to care for him. I was still fuzzy on our parents or when exactly we began on our own, fighting all these things. I remembered finding solace with Jane's family when we were boys. That's where Damon's care for Jane was fostered. I remembered we were starving, homeless and hitchhiking between towns. I struggled to get meals for us. Damon was younger then me. Jane's family took us in and cared for us. But we only stayed a few years then when we were teenagers we went off on our own again, learning about all the monsters in our world and studying alongside each family that was willing to teach us. Serena's voice pulled me from my reminiscing. Where had all these memories gone?

"Ready?"

"Yeah, let's go."

She began to wheel the bed as I covered myself being sure to breathe as shallowly as I could. Serenity was no longer in sight but I could still feel the cold. I shook slightly wrapping myself tighter. I tried to push away the memory of Aurelia, the plane crash. I could feel myself slipping from my emotional control and pulled out of it best I could. I felt the bed veer right and left. I thought back to when Damon and I broke Serena out of the hospital. We sure had been through alot. I wondered still how she was back, my relief was overpowering my concern presently, but I knew it would eventually waver.

I just couldn't shake how similar Serena looked and seemed to Aurelia. It was just the poison, those memories may not even be real. I told this to myself not believing a word of it. Did I want the memories to be real? I had to admit the idea of Serena being mine at some point, was intoxicating. There was no way she could feel the same? Right? Serena's voice again pulled me from my mind.

"Okay Darren, here I will help you up."

Serena lifted the sheet from me and helped to pull me up, I groaned. There was a deep radiating pain in my chest.

"Darren, what's wrong?"

"Nothing -I- my chest just hurts."

I was startled by how distraught she looked.

"I'm okay Serena, let's go." I stood from the bed.

I could tell she didn't believe me. Serenity began waving us toward the entrance to the tunnels, hidden in the wall.

Serena wrapped her arm around me. I started to move and was about to tell her I was fine when she said:

"Please just let me help you. For God's sake Darren must you always be so stubborn." She huffed slightly.

I leaned into her touch. Wishing I could feel more of it, be lost in it, in her.

I remembered when she said this before, when she tended to my wounds. She wasn't wrong, I was stubborn.

We rushed through the tunnels following Serenity. I could tell this was deeply uncomfortable for Serena to be in here and I bit back guilt for having asked her to get me out of the hospital in the first place. I wasn't a person that deserved her kindness. I had been to Hell. The thought was revolting to me, that I could've been something I killed for a living or worse. Even worse yet because I couldn't remember, but Osiris he said we were one in the same. We reached a man hole cover and we climbed the ladder up onto the sidewalk of downtown Edmonton.

"Thank you Serenity, please watch over Damon, we will be back to collect him tomorrow." Serena dismissed Serenity.

She nodded and left, taking the bitter cold with her. The night was warm again, the streets weren't bustling.

"God it's almost 5am." Serena said.

She ordered an uber and we clamoured in. I felt exposed and vulnerable in my hospital gown. Serena glanced to me.

"I'm sorry, we will be at the hotel soon, I thought you were dying- I mean- I would've brought clothes had I known, but I rushed out so fast. God Darren promise me you won't die on me, on Damon. We need you." She rambled.

"Serena."

I clasped her hands in mine.

"I will be fine. I promise you. Alright?"

She nodded and took a steadying breath.

"I in turn promise you Damon is alright, we will go to him in the morning."

I thought she would pull her hands from mine but instead she held them tighter and leaned against me. I took a quick breath, unsure how to respond to her closeness. I didn't move, I just let her lean against me.

I had so many questions, but I thought them best to leave until we got to the hotel.

I watched out the window, watching the streetlights and the rainfall. I decided to stroke her hair. After a couple minutes she sighed happily and her breath became slow and even. She had fallen asleep. I kept my arm around her, my fingers entwined in her blonde hair. I was too on edge to sleep. I groaned again at the pain in my chest. I reached to move the top of the hospital gown, there was charred handprint in my chest. I winced as I looked at it.

"What in the Hell?" I whispered out loud to myself.

I ran my free hand over the wound. It seemed to be healing alright, but where the hell did that come from? Osiris?

The hotel appeared on the right of the road and the driver pulled in.

"Uh, you guys sure this is the right place?"

"Yeah. Thanks." I mumbled.

I didn't want to wake her, so instead I carried her. I waited until the driver was out of sight then I headed into the back of the hotel, the hospital gown would draw many questions. I carried her effortlessly up the stairs to our room, reaching in her bag for our room key. I unlocked the door and put her gently down in my bed. She whimpered slightly and turned over. I pulled the covers over her. I turned to lock the doors and I went to the bathroom to shower. As I pulled off the hospital gown I got a very clear look at the burn. It was deeply embedded in my flesh. I inhaled sharply and moved to turn the shower on. I looked in the mirror a while longer. It was me, I was me, no Osiris, no other wounds really outside of minor scrapes and bruises. I wondered how bad Damon was hurt and the very thought that I injured him was enraging. I stepped into the shower. The hot water burned my chest relentlessly. I groaned loudly.

"Damnit."

I turned the facet off and stepped out my breath was shaky. I pulled a white t shirt and grey sweats on. I needed to hear how

Damon was. I checked Serena one more time. She was deeply asleep. I was extremely hesitant to leave her here, as I had chastised Damon for the same thing. God she died last time she was left. What the Hell was I thinking?

I stepped out of the room taking care to lock it behind me. I wouldn't be long. I got to the elevator. The same man greeted me.

"Going down sir?"

"No, Can you-"

I handed him a $5 bill.

He jumped back. "Sir what- I can't-"

"You can and you will. I need you to stand by my hotel door, the girl is asleep there, I just need to step outside briefly. I am paying you to stand guard I will return in 5 minutes, Guard her with your life if you must."

He stuttered. "Y-yes sir."

He moved to the door.

I rushed down the elevator. And half jogged outside. As soon as I got service, I phoned the hospital.

"Hello?" A women's voice.

"Hi, I was wondering how Damon Elderwood was? He's my-uh-cousin. I heard he was injured. I would be his next of kin."

"Oh well let me see, He had surgery on his leg, we have to keep him here for a few days, but he is doing well, just needs the time to heal. He won't walk on his own for a while. But he is expected to make a full recovery. We can phone you if anything changes? This number good?"

"Yeah thanks." I hung up before she could ask my name.

I rushed back inside and up the elevator.

I ran back to the room where the boy stood.

"Nothing, not a sound. Are you sure about the $5? That is so gracious. It really was no trouble. It wasn't even a full 5 minutes."

"Keep it, thank you, it was a big deal to me."

He tipped his hat. "Thank you very much sir."

I unlocked the door, relieved to see Serena still asleep and nothing wrong.

I breathed deeply.

I settled into Damon's bed instead, The couch didn't seem overly welcoming tonight. I didn't even grab a beer. I settled into bed and closed my eyes. I wanted. I needed to know what happened. How was she back? I was relieved Damon was okay. How did Osiris leave me? What was Hell like? The questions overtook my mind and I found it hard to fall asleep despite it all.

"Darren." Serena murmured.

I rushed to her bedside. "Yes? You okay?"

She opened her eyes slightly.

"Could you- would you please lay with me? She whispered.

I was taken aback from her request. My silence she mistook for no.

"Sorry-it's okay. I'm just a bit rattled from everything-"

I interrupted her in the softest tone I could.

"Of course I will lay with you Serena."

Her eyes watered slightly.

"God I'm such a mess, I'm sorry." She took a deep breath.

I settled beside her. I hadn't laid beside a women, in years. Not in the sense of innocently.

I took a deep breath too.

"I- probably need a shower.." She started to get up.

"Serena-it's okay, I don't care. Sleep."

She hesitated. "Will you wait?"

"Yes." I would wait years for her, but I wouldn't dare say that.

She awakened something in me I thought rotted away a long time ago, but I was wholly undeserving. I was always so cold, and distant and short with her. It killed me to do it, but I couldn't bring myself to stop. She was better off that way, disconnected to me, even though it was the exact opposite of what I wanted.

She gave me a soft smile in the moonlit room.

I watched her hurry to the shower. I laid there awake, the same thoughts rampant in my mind. But I remembered something, it was just a flash, but I was holding chains, sharp blades and laughing manically. Many people were wrapped among the chains, bleeding screaming. I jolted up, my heart racing.

"What the Hell was that- not me- It can't have been-"

Serena returned then, concern creased her face.

She climbed slowly into bed beside me.

"Darren, what is it? You look-"

She reached to stroke my face. I closed my eyes and clenched my jaw.

Her touch was light, loving and gentle.

"It has to be reminiscence of the Djinn's poison- it had to be- I could never-"

"Darren, did you have a bad dream?"

She asked so softly, barely a whisper.

I hadn't realized I said it out loud.

"The djinn, they trap you in a dreamworld right?" she asked me in the same soft tone, her eyes locked onto mine.

I inhaled sharply. "Yeah."

"You got out of that place, whatever it was Darren, it wasn't real."

She grasped my hand lightly and kissed it.

"This right now is real. I am real. You are, Damon. Our mission, is real."

I felt water burning in my eyes and I turned from her and she gently turned my face back to hers.

"Darren. It's okay."

I nodded, I was worried if I spoke my voice would break.

"Lay down, let's sleep, everything will seem better when we wake up."

She let go of my hand and laid down. I laid down beside her on her right. In the safety of the shadows, I let a couple of tears fall. Fair too embarrassed to show her how much that dream messed me up. I took a centring breath.

She turned over then and laid on my chest. I winced slightly when she laid on my burn. She smelled like Vanilla faintly.

"Is this alright?"

She whispered not opening her eyes. She wrapped her arm around me. The warmth it brought was beyond comforting.

I lifted one arm hesitatingly around her and she settled into my touch.

"Is this?"

"Yes." She barely whispered. "Goodnight Darren."

"Goodnight." My voice cracked slightly as I said this but she thankfully didn't seem to notice. Once her breathing was slow and even, I drifted to sleep too.

* * *

I awoke to the sunlight streaming in. I was still intertwined against Serena and she was still fast asleep in my arms. I didn't move. I focused on her long hair a mess on the pillow, her black nightgown clung tightly to her. With my free hand I laid the blankets over her. I couldn't lie to myself how comforting it was to be here beside her. After a few moments of studying her face. I slowly moved out of her grasp. I was reluctant too, but I thought she might appreciate a coffee. Having being back from the dead and all. I had no idea what she had been through in the last 48 hours either. I slowly got up careful not to wake her, I started a pot of coffee. I also began to cook breakfast. I was feeling-content. For the first time in what seemed like years. I started on eggs benny, and some hash browns. We usually had takeout or Damon would cook. I was terrible at it, but I hoped it wouldn't be too awful. She sat up slowly and stretched. She had a tired smile on her face. The coffee dinged at the same time.

"Morning." I smiled.

She beamed in return.

"Well, good morning to you too. Wow, aren't you chipper this morning."

I laughed a bit. "Oh man we can't have that." I said in mock annoyance.

She laughed too. "Well it is particularity out of character."

"Yeah, a little."

"It delights me to see you like this Darren."

I smiled a bit.

"Hungry?"

"Very."

"Good, I'm not the best cook but hopefully it's edible."

She laughed lightly.

"Well the cafe is right downstairs worst case." She teased.

I poured a cup of coffee for her and pressed the steaming mug into her hands, my hand lingered slightly on hers.

"mm thank you."

I let go of the mug and went back to the pan. She brought the mug to her lips.

"After we eat, I want to get Damon."

She nodded. "Me too. Serenity stayed with him, but she can't enter here. Jane asked me to let her go first this morning and I said I would go for 11, but I don't know the time."

I sighed slightly. "I've never left Damon's side, not since he was born, never more then a handful of hours. I would guess it to be around 10."

"Perfect. Let's eat, thank you for cooking."

"Now try it, and if you keel over I will know that cooking is just not for me." I joked.

She smiled and took a bite. I waited and watched curiously.

She started coughing and I watched her for a minute. She made an obnoxious choking sound and laid her head on the table. Laughter tumbling from her lips.

"Oh very frightening. That awful eh?" I teased.

She picked her head up and smiled. "I've had much worse."

She took another bite and I ate too. Shit it wasn't even that bad.

We ate in comfortable silence after that.

She stood up and took both our empty plates to the sink. I tried not to let my eyes linger on her, she was still in a nightgown.

"Thank you for breakfast." she spoke over her shoulder.

"Anytime."

"Here let me help, I stood up beside her."

"It's okay, I'm happy to clean up." She passed me a cup of coffee.

I took it looking at her for a minute.

"Oh, would you prefer a beer maybe?" she asked nonchalantly.

It bothered me slightly even though she had no bad intent behind the offer.

"I am happy with coffee."

She smiled. "Well, that's a first."

We stared at one another for a minute, perhaps both wanting to say so much but neither of us sure where to start. I sure wasn't sure. I knew that laying beside her felt natural and brought me comfort, she felt like home to me. I kept staring at her, I hoped she wouldn't pick up on it and misinterpret it. I was just still amazed she was alive. Then I realized with a sick twisted feeling in my stomach that she was walking. Why, why had that not been something I said, or even noticed. Or remembered, that when she died she couldn't walk.

I put my coffee on the counter, and gently brought my hand to her cheek she paused washing the dishes and gave me a confused look.

"What is it?"

"Serena, you're walking.."

She looked taken aback.

"What?! I can WALK?! Since when??" she lifted her legs up on at a time. Theatrically acting surprised like she didn't notice either.

"I was so caught up in you being alive, the sheer joy in that alone. I just- the thought- I didn't really think about it."

"I don't blame you honestly, You were in shock. It's been a hectic couple of days for both of us. It took me a while to accept that I was back. Yes, new legs came with my new life, and I am eternally grateful."

I didn't agree with her, it was completely unforgivable that such a vital thing escaped me.

I cupped her face with both my hands, and kissed her lightly on the head.

She smiled slightly. She leaned her forehead against mine, her lips lingered inches from mine. I inhaled sharply. It was very difficult for me not to kiss her. Her lips inches from mine were enticing. I was just so grateful she was alive, her closeness was agonizing for me. Especially, because despite the Djinn, I couldn't shake how much she reminded me of the past that I had forgotten. I wondered deep down if she was Aurelia somehow. I thought to our kids, if I did have kids in the past, where were they now? Did they live good lives? The climbing ache like a slow drip of acid that was my wife and children's memory lay heavily on my mind, and on my heart. I wasn't used to feeling anything apart from the ever burning rage. The crushing wave of melancholy was uncharted territory, as was this, peculiar contentment I'd felt since Serena returned to me.

"Let's go get Damon." She whispered, and pulled gently away from me.

I reluctantly let go of her. "Agreed."

We both downed our coffee and headed out the door. I was anxious to grab Damon, I didn't like him being far from me for long. My job is to protect him, protect her. I cannot let anything cloud that ever again.

"Ill drive us." I said.

"Perfect." She smiled to me as we walked out into the parking lot.

Chapter 22

LET ME

"Let me carry you when you can no longer bare the weight, let me
be the arms you fall into when you are too exhausted to move, let
me be the lips you taste, the skin you trace, let me know you so I
can show you, you are safe with me, your past is past, let me show
you I offer no judgment, only acceptance, let me see your darkest
side, so I can shower it in light, let me know your worst memories
so I can wrap them in love, let me be your mirror when you no
longer recognize yourself, let me pull you back when you feel you
are drowning, let me make you laugh when all you want to do is
cry, let me love you when you no longer love yourself, let me love
you when you do, Let me call you home."

I was almost relieved to leave the hotel, I was anxious to retrieve Damon. I hoped Darren wasn't too off put by my neediness last night. I was grateful to him for holding me. I felt so at a loss. So much had happened in the last couple days I could barely wrap my mind around it. I knew that talking about it would help, but I would rather talk to both the brothers at the same time as to not have to relive it again and again. I followed Darren to the volvo and got in the passenger side.

"Ready?" He turned to me smiling slightly.

I loved how much he had been smiling, I loved seeing him happier. Being close to him was unexpectedly surreal and comforting. I always felt safe with them, but this was slightly different. Maybe I had just been through so much that I was grasping for a semblance of comfort. Or perhaps that was wrong too.

I returned his smile and he drove towards the hospital. My phone came back on and I had a missed call from Rayne. I redialed her. She answered immediately.

"Serena?" Her voice timid.

"Hey, everything okay?"

Darren looked over to me curiously. He could very clearly hear her on the other line. I took a deep breath, worried something happened to her.

"Yes! Matt and I decided to move up the wedding, in light of what happened. I didn't tell him what truly happened Serena, I don't want to freak him out. The truth is the world that you and the brothers are a part of, I-I don't want to be any part of it. It's too bizarre and frankly terrifying. I'm sorry, I wish I could support you but, the idea that you could've been through worse then I have. I just- I think I would rather live in ignorance. That might make me a monster, but I just- I don't want the world to end, but by the sounds of it a lot of people have it covered and if it is the end, I just want to spend it with those I love. That includes you Serena, so please still come by as often as you can. I'm glad I understand more now, but I don't want to hear anymore. I can't."

Darren was watching for my reaction, he of course didn't know what happened yet, but I would tell them soon.

"Rayne, hey slow down. I think it's great you and Matt are moving the wedding up. I will be there. What day? As for the rest, I understand completely. I'm so sorry I couldn't shield you from it all. I wish I could have."

"Please don't apologize. You saved my life Serena. I owe you everything."

"I don't Rayne, you've done plenty for me too."

She laughed a bit. "I suppose, we call it even then?"

"Yes." I laughed too.

"Saturday, that's in three days. That's the new date. Meet us there please. The boys are welcome of course too."

"Thank you Rayne. We will all be there."

"Good. And hey Serena? Be careful for the love of God please don't die on me."

"You too Rayne."

We both laughed and ended the call.

"What happened with Rayne? If you don't mind my asking?" Darren asked instantly.

"I don't mind you asking, but I will catch you and Damon up together. It's easier that way."

"Okay. Well, are you alright?"

"Yes."

"Good."

"Yourself?"

"I will be better once we get my brother."

"Understandable."

We pulled up to the hospital and both clamoured out.

"I should scout first maybe hey? Try to semi disguise yourself, so no one recognizes you?"

He nodded. "Yeah right, I forgot."

He chanted something under his breath and to me looked the exact same.

"What did you change?"

He looked at me skeptically.

"I should look 70 years old, with a walker and no hair."

"You just look like you. I remember when we were all at my apartment and you guys were disguised, Rayne insisted you were both old men, but neither of you ever looked like anything other then yourselves to me."

"That's interesting. Something to do with your abilities maybe?"

"Maybe. But okay let's go."

We approached the nurses station.

"Hi, we are here to see Damon Elderwood?"

She barely looked to me. "I remember you from yesterday- go ahead, who's this?"

"Damon's father." I answered quickly.

"Okay go right in."

We both walked into Damon's room Jane was just leaving she pulled me to the side. Darren raised his eyebrows.

"I found out some vital information on Serenity. Meet me in the cafe tomorrow night."

I nodded. Darren watched her go.

"New friend?"

"Sort of, more so we related to one another. I thought she could help me find information on Serenity."

"Good call."

We entered Damon's room and Darren's eyes lit up. As did Damon's.

Darren moved and hugged him clasping him once on the back.

"Good to see you man."

Damon's eyes glazed with tears momentarily. He wiped them over Darren's shoulder.

"You too man. Especially Osiris free."

"Damn straight. Bum leg?"

"I'm done my surgeries, just can't walk for a while."

"I'm going to take you home."

He nodded. "Thank you Darren."

"I'm going to get you discharged. No need to break you out."

Darren stepped out of the room.

Damon turned to me beaming and opened his arms. I went into them as he wrapped me in a quick hug.

"Serena."

I pulled out of the hug smiling. "Hey, Damon."

"How was your night?"

I scoffed slightly.

"Oh, that bad?"

"Just, I can't believe it was only one night. I will explain, right now I am just grateful to have you both back."

"Ah well, you are the true miracle Serena."

I laughed a bit. Darren came in then with a wheelchair.

"Let's go, little brother."

"Oh, thank God." Damon breathed, relief clear in his tone.

Darren moved to heave Damon off of the bed and I held the chair still. Darren pushed it.

"Woo lets get outta here!" Darren jumped up happily.

Damon laughed. "What you drunk Darren?"

"Nah." He glanced to me and I held his gaze.

"Oh really, Darren not drinking?"

"What can I say? I've turned a new leaf. Let's get outta this place." Darren said lightly, without breaking eye contact with me.

Damon glanced skeptically to me.

"He really only had coffee today Damon."

"Good, I'm proud of you big brother."

Darren smiled. "Thanks."

We all left the doors and I whispered Serenity's name. Darren and Damon both jumped when she appeared.

"Thank you Serenity for watching over him. I deeply appreciate it."

"Of course. Summon me again when you need me. I am hunting one of the items down currently for you."

"Thank you." As I said that she left.

I looked to the brothers momentarily forgetting they couldn't hear Serenity.

"She said she thinks shes located an item. I don't know how she knows about everything, but she does."

"We will figure it out Serena, she could really just be helping." Damon assured me.

"She's my sister Damon."

His eyes widened.

"How?" He asked.

Darren gave me a sympathetic glance.

"I don't really know, Jane offered to look into it."

"Jane eh? We have a lot to catch up on hey guys?" Damon laughed.

"Yeah, but lets get home first." I smiled as Darren wheeled Damon and we left the hospital for hopefully the last time for a long time.

We all stumbled into the volvo.

It seemed we were all relieved to be back together heading home again.

* * *

We parked in our usual spot. We clamoured into the hotel.

"I'm starved." Damon said.

"We can order room service for you? Darren cooked us a really lovely breakfast, I'm still full myself." I offered smiling.

Stealing a quick glance at Darren, whom smiled slightly, not noticing my gaze on him.

Damon burst out laughing. "Darren cooked?"

"Shut up." Darren muttered.

"And you live to tell the tale eh Serena?"

"Honestly, it wasn't bad." I chuckled.

"Colour me impressed." Damon laughed.

We helped him up to the room. Jane wasn't here.

Once we were in the room it felt like a huge heavy cement block was removed from my shoulders. I felt as though the guys felt the same, I hoped they did. Here we were, together again in one piece. World still turning. Still breathing.

Darren helped Damon to the couch and propped his leg.

"Can I get you anything outside of room service Damon?" I offered.

He smiled to me. "Why not come sit with me?"

He opened his arms to hug me.

Darren eyed me for a second, he seemed curious what I would do.

I walked over and hugged him briefly. "Glad you are doing better Damon."

"Well, I didn't raise from the dead now did I? Not like you."

I scoffed a bit. "Seems as such."

Darren pressed a mug of coffee into my hands.

"Thank you."

Damon watched him curiously.

God why did everything seem so weird? I was sure it would be better when we started talking.

"So who wants to start?" I offered.

Damon started.

"Well Darren you were possessed by Osiris. We stopped by Serena's house after she-" he trailed off a second, before continuing.

"It was strange Darren, the items we stole from the crypt. Just sort of reacted and clung to you and voila suddenly you were possessed by Osiris. You knocked me out, telling me I had to remember what I had forgotten. When I came too Serena was here and I thought I was dead. I tested everything from Demon to shapeshifter but she is undoubtedly herself. I don't know how though. When I found out Serena was in fact alive. She had came by looking for us. She had Serenity with her. Serenity guided us to you Darren. You were sending lost and wondering souls back to the dead. Helping them cross over. Osiris said that if we couldn't do our jobs he would step in and do them for us."

"Our jobs?" Darren repeated and a haunted look came over him.

"Yeah, I don't really get it either." Damon shrugged.

"Then what?" Darren's tone was flat, stern.

"Then you, well Osiris got very interested in Serena and you- he pushed me to the wall and that's all I remember until Serena came to make sure I was okay, I heard you and her argue but- I don't know what exactly happened or when or why Osiris left you. Then the ambulance was here and you were unconscious and I made Serena stay with you. I got rushed into surgeries and Serena checked on me once before she had to leave cause of visiting hours. She told me you thought she was a demon. So clearly you didn't remember her being back prior to that."

I took a deep breath.

Darren held the counter in front of him so hard his knuckles were bright white.

I placed my hand over his, in an attempt to help him relax.

"You alright?" I said softly, meeting his eyes.

Damon watched me closely.

I could tell Darren's jaw was clenched.

"I don't remember a damn thing from when we got to Serena's house until waking up in the hospital, thinking she was a demon. I don't remember anything to do with Osiris or hurting you Damon. Damn it. I'm sorry."

He punched the counter with the hand I wasn't holding and I jumped slightly.

"It's okay Darren, it wasn't you." Damon said softly.

"How the Hell did that thing even possess me in the first place?! Damn it. If I could remember a thought, or anything it would help us find him and I am completely friggin' useless!" He rose his voice slightly.

I gripped his hand tighter. "It's okay, Darren."

He looked to me, anger swimming in his vision. I knew it wasn't directed at me, though it still made me weary.

"What do you remember from that night Serena?" He almost commanded.

"He left this on me."

Darren let go of my hand and unbuttoned his plaid shirt revealing the burned hand print.

Damon's eyes widened. "Holy shit."

I swallowed hard, tears burning in my eyes. It was time to tell him, and I wasn't ready.

"That hand print, Darren, it's not from Osiris." I swallowed.

Damon looked over to me.

"What do you mean of course it is, what else could do that? It looks like an exit wound, when he left Darren's body. Or marked it for returning."

Darren shot him a death glare. "That son of a bitch is not getting back into me."

"Guys-" A couple tears fell from my eyes.

"That hand print, is from me."

They both turned to look at me, disbelief painted on their faces.

"What do you mean?" Damon asked lightly, caution edging in his tone.

I turned to Darren. "I never meant to hurt you." My voice broke.

He stared at me for a minute. Studying my eyes. He swiped a thumb over my tears, then he wrapped me in his arms. I was so taken aback I felt faint, I swayed slightly and he gripped me tighter.

"You are why Osiris left my body, aren't you?" he said quietly.

"Yes."

"Then thank you, Serena."

"But- how?" Damon asked.

"I was, I just remember being so angry, and there was such energy, sizzling through me, I felt like I might explode. I was worried for you Damon, and especially you Darren and I just wanted so desperately to do something. When I pushed you Darren, well your body that's what happened, you were flung back. Serenity made herself visible and Osiris said something unsettling and quite literally vanished."

Darren was eyeing me.

What did he say? Can you try to remember?" Damon asked.

"The sister. It is as it was written. You are on the wrong side of this, misplaced. Lost. And you Serena, You have been through the veil, and returned. Your power is tantalizing, I have never felt anything like it." I repeated exactly as I remembered it.

"I will research the lore to look up any prophecies with a lost sister. Darren grab me a stack of books, I can't walk much may as well be useful."

"Prophesies? I chuckled slightly.

Darren nodded. "It's not impossible. Didn't Henry say something similar too?"

I shuddered slightly at the mention of his name. "Yeah, he did. So where was the crypt you guys robbed?"

"Edmonton airport." Damon answered.

"That's really public, if I remember correctly the legend of Osiris was his brother tore him apart and hid 14 pieces of him all over the world. So it was a completed skeleton?" I asked.

"Yes" Damon replied.

"Then we burn the bones?"

"That might work." Damon smiled. "We can try that."

"Okay. What else did I miss?"

"We got into a nasty bit with Sirens at Wabamun lake. We were pretty close to losing our lives that round." Darren said almost cheerfully.

"No Ariel?" I joked.

They both chuckled. "If only." Darren said.

"I wish I hadn't died, I hate the thought of either of you being in danger." I admitted.

"I'm sure I speak for Darren and I both that we wish you hadn't either. But I am grateful you returned, and can walk."

"Thank you Damon."

"Agreed." Darren chimed in.

"So how many items do we need and what is our time frame now?"

"We are missing 2 items. We haven't the slightest idea where they are, or what they are. But I have full confidence you'll lead us to them Serena. We only have 3 weeks.

"I can tell you where 1 of those are. Serenity said she found another but I'm not sure."

I pulled the bell out of my shirt that I got from Titania.

Darren's eyes widened. "How the Hell did you get that?"

"Fairies."

Damon looked horrified. "How? Queen Titania of the fae is immortal, one of the oldest immortals."

"Not to mention, you can't get to their world without one of them. They make it very difficult to enter their realms." Damon added.

"Like the massage parlour, what you heard there? Damon mentioned it, it was on our list to return. It looks like we need to ask you what happened while we were in the hospital." Darren said cautiously.

"And-" He paused briefly breathing deeply. "How did you come back to life?"

"I promise you I will explain it all to the best of my ability, I'm going to need more coffee."

"On it." Darren moved to make it.

"It is a long story but I will shorten it best I can."

"Go ahead." Damon urged gently.

"After I left visiting hours when Darren thought I was a Demon and they basically told me I couldn't see you until morning Damon, I decided to go see Rayne. When I got there, and Matt was just exhausted. He told me he was tending heavily to Rayne and could use some help. I went up to her room and he pointed to the bed telling me that's where she was but I couldn't see her. All I saw was weird piece of wood."

"Wood? You shouldn't have been able to see past the glamour, it should've appeared same to you as it did to Matt, that means-" Damon started.

"Yes- It means I am not human. Not fully."

"What about wood? We have never dealt with the Fae before." Darren asked, obviously not familiar with the lore.

Damon filled him in, I tuned it out.

"That's- wow." Darren sat back after Damon finished explaining.

"Tinkerbell is Bull too I guess." Darren half joked.

"Yes." Damon concluded laughter in his voice. "Go on Serena, sorry."

I smiled slightly.

"I didn't want to freak Matt out but I left in a rush. I figured out what was happening because of what you told me Damon, I remembered when you taught me the lore behind the faeries, and that we concluded we believed the bells I heard when I was in the massage parlour before my accident were that possibly of faeries. I was so relived to remember"

I sat beside Damon now on the couch, Darren was sipping coffee at the table.

"I'm glad I could help you." Damon said as he pulled me into a hug.

"Then what happened, how did you find the realm?" Darren asked concern evident in his tone.

"Well then I remembered a moment when I was with Rayne, I walked out of the cafe and she was staring oddly, blankly almost at a tree in Lion's park. She was super hazed and out of body almost for a few minutes, then she left to get a coffee too. So I took a long shot guess that's where it was and I was correct. When I approached the tree, I pressed on the trunk of the tree and a door opened, there were weird stairs, then I slid down, like "Alice in wonderland." I shrunk, I was greeted in this captivating floral world, by a beautiful pink haired fairy in a white dress. She lead me to Titaina's son Jade, because Titania was absent at the time. I didn't know you couldn't lie in their world. So I asked about Rayne. Turns out she was to wed Jade. He let me through to see her, she was so delighted, but she told me she had been there a few months, when really it was only a few days. Time passes much differently there too. When Titaina came, she recognized immediately I wasn't human, she knew about you two as well, she knew of Cronos and his plan, she knew everything, even she seemed surprised that I was able to enter without someone bringing me in, or being related to Fae myself."

"What do you mean, what did she say about us?" Darren asked firmly.

"She said that you and Damon were very powerful but that your memories were mixed up, just as mine are. She told me, soon we would see everything clearly, and knew you were trying to stop Cronos and that I was helping."

"So how did you get her to give up the bells?" Damon asked curiously.

"She handed them to me. Told me we must succeed and that Cronos ending, was an ending for all. She's on our side, she doesn't want Cronos to succeed in this undoing."

"Did you get Rayne back?" Damon asked urgently.

"I explained who Rayne was to me, Rayne was shocked by everything Titania let me take her back home. She said:

"In return, just don't fail."

"So then I took Rayne home, Matt thought she was dying, he was freaking out when I got there, She snuck through the back to her room and they were rejoined. She did not tell Matt anything, nor does she want to. She want's to remain in ignorance as much as she can."

"That's incredible that you got her home. I'm so sorry we weren't there to help." Damon half hugged me again.

"Then I got a call from the hospital saying Darren was dying so I came so afraid that it was to say my goodbyes."

Damon's face lit up in horror, he spun to Darren.

"How did you almost die??"

Darren took a long sip of coffee. "Djinn, the nurse was a Djinn."

"But how did you get out?"

"Serena drew me out of the nightmare with her pleading for my well being. Then Serena killed him." Darren smiled and said with pride edging his tone.

"Holy shit. What dreamworld of pleasures were you trapped in? The playboy mansion?"

"That sounds more like your dreamworld Damon" I teased.

Darren's gaze became hollow and distant. I walked up to Darren and softly rubbed his upper back for a second.

"What did you dream about? You never told me."

"It was a nightmare, a hellish nightmare, I really do not want to relive it. Not right now."

Damon's face fell. "I'm so sorry brother. Usually they trap you in fantasy."

"I wished it had." he said through clenched teeth.

"How did you come back Serena?" Darren asked, turning and facing my eyes.

"I awoke as if I was astral projecting over my body, I tried..I tried to re enter my body so many times but I just kept falling through it. It was strange to be as light as air, to move so fluidly. I couldn't grab any objects or make any sound that anyone could hear. I didn't understand what was happening and I watched my body die."

I trailed off for a second.

"I saw you both. I tried so hard, so damn hard to reach either of you and I couldn't."

"Oh my God, Serena I had no idea. That must've been terrifying." Damon said.

Darren looked to me almost like tears were welling. He turned away from my gaze.

"I saw you both, try everything to bring me back. Thank you for your efforts. I wish more then anything I didn't have to put you guys through that kind of Hell. I am glad and grateful to be alive again. Back to our mission. Back with the both of you." I half whispered the last sentence.

"We are just relieved you came back. All that matters is that we are all here in one piece and we can finish this battle." Damon smiled.

"That doesn't answer how you came back." Darren said slightly cooly.

"Darren does that really matter? Come on man" Damon said.

"Of course it matters! We need to know how and why, so it doesn't bite us in the ass."

"Darren-" Damon began but I cut him off.

"No Damon he's right. I went to the morgue where my body was and I saw a ghost that I had seen before in the bathroom of the cafe."

"You never told us, you mean Serenity?" Damon questioned.

"No, I didn't recognize it the first time but it shattered the glass, Jane's sister Jenny patched me up, it was one of the first nights we ate there together."

"And this time?" Darren pressed.

"It was my mom. She told me it was a mistake me dying, that there was work undone that I was destined for. That it wasn't my time. Then she told me how much she loved me, I reconciled with her. Then she hugged me and told me you guys needed me, and how lucky she was to give me life twice."

My voice broke slightly at the end and I swallowed to keep myself from crying.

"Did she say what she was, or where she was?" Darren continued to press.

"Darren, hey give her a minute, she didn't even know her mom died...remember?"

Darren dropped his gaze and finished his coffee as I finished mine. He got up taking both our cups to refill.

"It's alright Damon, he is rightfully concerned, and well honestly, I don't know. I was so in awe to see her, and horrified that she was dead. There was a great deal of emotions happening. She said she was waiting for me that I was her unfinished business so that to me means she was a ghost. But she made it seem as though she had been a ghost a long time."

"When's the last time you spoke to her?" Damon asked sincerely.

"Damon, honestly maybe 8 months. However she left me a voicemail 6 months back when we first started all this and it worried me. She was at the psychiatric hospital in Vancouver. She sounded rushed, like someone was after her, and asked me to help her. Not so much in words but still the implication was clear enough."

"What's her name, if you don't mind my asking? I will search her up." Damon asked.

"You have internet here?"

"Oh, right. Guess there's no books to help in that department hey?" He said dismayed and slunk back into the couch.

"We will look into in Serena, I am sorry for your loss."

Darren said as he pressed the refilled mug into my hand.

"Thank you."

"Damon can I look at the pocket watch you snagged off of that doctor?" I asked.

"Yeah of course, its in my coat pocket right hand side."

There was a knock at the door, I hesitated beside it while I was getting the pocket watch. I glanced to Darren and he came closer to me nodding for me to push forward. I opened the door, it was just room service.

"Order up." He said as he tipped his hat, it was the same guy from the elevator as usual

"Thank you very much" I pulled the cart into the room and closed the door behind it.

"Oh God yes. I'm starving." Damon said excitedly.

He was rubbing his hands together like a little kid. I laughed a bit as I wheeled it up to the couch.

"Here you go." I smiled a bit.

"Serena, will you come with me? I have a hunch on another item, but I can't be sure unless you are there."

Darren asked as he closed the black book he was holding. The one that called to me in the beginning.

"Without me?" Damon asked.

"Well, you are unable to walk currently, and you should eat. You'll be safe here nothing is after you." Darren said slightly sternly.

Damon eyed us back and forth.

"Where?"

"West Edmonton mall."

"Fine. Only because I know I will hinder you. Be careful please both of you."

"Always Damon, eh I'll even send Jane up for you." Darren said.

Damon chortled slightly. "Alright."

I smiled slyly. "Have fun, I'm sure there are still many ways to get laid even with a bum leg. Maybe, I don't know some pirate role play?" I joked.

Darren laughed gently and I smiled, his smile making my heart flutter. Damon laughed too.

"Oh, I'm sure I won't be hindered, but Serena, do you even want to go? You could stay here and keep me company."

He patted the couch beside him. Then paused.

"That wasn't-I mean an innuendo, or anything I just meant-" His face flushed.

"Oh- I- I didn't take it that way." I said as I felt heat rise to my cheeks. I didn't did I?

"No, Darren I would love to come with you. Sorry Damon."

Darren smiled slightly and grabbed my coat, draping it over my shoulders.

"Damon keep everything locked and warded, I will make sure we are back promptly."

"Yeah, yeah whatever, take your time."

"Oh and Damon?"

"What?"

"Get that booty ARRGH" Darren joked as he exited the door.

I laughed hard and we locked the door behind us with Damon's laughter trailing after us.

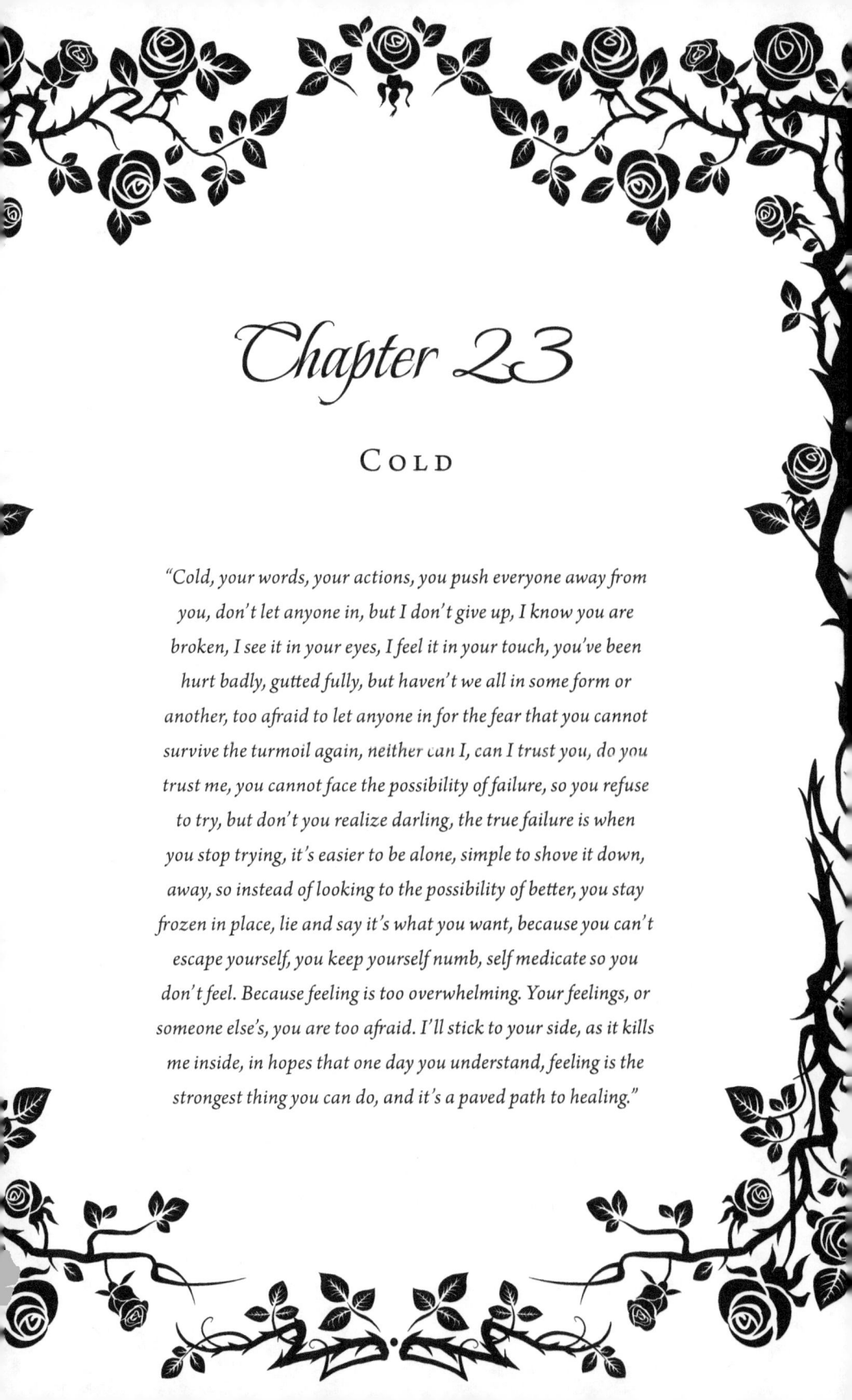

Chapter 23

COLD

"Cold, your words, your actions, you push everyone away from you, don't let anyone in, but I don't give up, I know you are broken, I see it in your eyes, I feel it in your touch, you've been hurt badly, gutted fully, but haven't we all in some form or another, too afraid to let anyone in for the fear that you cannot survive the turmoil again, neither can I, can I trust you, do you trust me, you cannot face the possibility of failure, so you refuse to try, but don't you realize darling, the true failure is when you stop trying, it's easier to be alone, simple to shove it down, away, so instead of looking to the possibility of better, you stay frozen in place, lie and say it's what you want, because you can't escape yourself, you keep yourself numb, self medicate so you don't feel. Because feeling is too overwhelming. Your feelings, or someone else's, you are too afraid. I'll stick to your side, as it kills me inside, in hopes that one day you understand, feeling is the strongest thing you can do, and it's a paved path to healing."

"Thanks for accompanying me." Darren said lightly.

He held his arm out for me to take. I did after a moments hesitation.

"Of course, I'm happy to if I'm being honest. What's your hunch?"

Darren studied my eyes a moment. "Well first we need to fetch Jane."

"Ah yes." Then I remembered I was suppose to meet with her today to learn about Serenity.

"Actually- she was looking into Serenity for me, I was suppose to meet her, is it alright if we talk with her briefly before sending her up to Damon?"

"Yes, I wonder what she learned. Hopefully it's helpful."

"I hope so too. It would be nice to not have to be unsure of if she's trustworthy or not."

"I would imagine so, but so far seems she has been only helpful right?"

"Yeah."

"Well that's a good start, I suppose."

We walked up to the elevators and rode them down.

We walked towards the cafe and Jane was working. She saw us and waved us in excitedly.

We headed that direction.

"Hey guys good evening, No Damon?" She looked very disappointed.

"Hi Jane! No, hes home though. He's just staying in for tonight."

"Oh! I should go stay with him for the night. I mean, if that's alright."

"That's fine Jane. We can come back in the morning." Darren said eyeing me almost seeing if I would agree or disagree.

"Only if Serena is okay with that though."

A night alone with Darren? Why not? I had plenty of one on one time with Damon in the past. Maybe I will get to know him a little better. Maybe he will let me this time.

"No I don't mind at all, he's been in an accident and just got home, I don't blame you for wanting to stay with him." I smiled and she clasped her hands together happily.

"Everything is warded up there so no need to worry." Darren added.

Jane nodded. "Thank you."

"Serena, so grab a seat guys I did find out a few things about Serenity, I am still looking though."

I nodded and Darren guided me to an open booth, I went to sit across from him. Jane slid in beside me.

"Okay I'm just going to lay this out quickly, because I want to see Damon."

"Of course, thank you for looking into her."

"She did exist, I found an old article online when I was outside the hotel, It was, well it mentioned Black Rose Ridge, so I dug deeper and I found the place."

She paused to sip water.

"So she's real?"

"Yes, I was able to find the obituary. The case states she died in the hospital, from an experimental trial. I cannot find anything on the trial yet. I do not know if you were also a part of the trial."

"Yes, she existed and all that shes said has been true this far. I will keep digging though."

"Thank you."

She nodded, got up and left quickly.

I took a deep breath.

"Are you okay?" Darren asked.

I wasn't really. I needed more details, but perhaps I could just ask her. Surely that would show me her intent.

"Yeah, it's nothing I didn't already know, apart from the twin thing."

Darren nodded. "Okay."

Jenny came over to us then.

"I will take over, what would you like Serena?"

"Actually Jenny, I think we are going to head out, just came to speak with Jane." I smiled at her.

"Oh great. Well have a nice day then."

She turned and left.

We got up and Darren led the way to the car.

It was very windy outside. I gasped slightly.

Darren walked around and opened the passenger door for me.

"Thank you."

"Don't mention it."

He closed the door behind me and half jogged to the drivers side, pulling his brown leather jacket over himself as he did.

"So you want me to stay the night with you?" I said in a playful tone.

"Well, we more or less live together anyways."

"Fair point." I chuckled lightly.

I was feeling slightly foolish. Was I nervous? I decided on a topic change.

"What, was your hunch at the mall?"

Darren pulled the volvo into reverse and left the parking lot before he answered me.

"Well." He eyed me for a second. He looked unsure of himself.

"What is it? Don't keep me in such suspense. It's impolite." I laughed lightly.

"Dragons."

I scoffed slightly.

"Dragons? I'm not 100 percent certain but even though a dragon could fit in west ed, I'm sure someone may have noticed by now." I teased.

He chortled slightly. "Yes, but there is a lot of dragon things, or there used to be not so much anymore."

I thought about it a minute, remembering the animatronic dragon that blew fire, at the movie theatre there. The multiple dragon themed rides in the amusement park and mini golf.

"You aren't wrong. What would a dragon look like now? Could they be human-like?"

"Yeah, I read about them a bit and the heart of a dragon is suppose to hold the power of the sun. I thought maybe we might need it for Osiris, or maybe even Cronos."

"You read?"

He scoffed slightly

"I do read sometimes you know. Also dragons are cool.. who the Hell doesn't like dragons? What- you don't like dragons?"

I laughed. "They are very cool indeed. What would they look like now do you think?"

"I'm fairly sure their eyes would glow. But in all honesty, I'm not sure. I'm sure you'll be able to tell if I'm right or not."

"You are probably right."

We drove in silence for a little while. He cranked the country station

"I'm surprised."

"Oh? What did you think I would play?"

"I've only heard you sing Elvis, so I didn't know what else you might be into."

We were about 15 minute from West Edmonton Mall.

"Well the hotel has limitations, but Elvis is king."

I laughed.

The song "Picture" By Kid Rock and Sheryl Crow came on.

Darren began to sing low and sweetly. "Living my life in a slow Hell-"

I listened intently to his singing. I loved his voice and I loved this song.

Sheryl crows part was about to start and I contemplated singing, but I was very shy to sing in front of anyone, and compared to Darren, God I would sound awful, I imagined. But as her part came up I couldn't help but sing, it bubbled out of me.

Darren looked over to me genuinely surprised and smiled so big it made my heart swell. I continued to sing as he patiently listened to me until Kid rock came back and he took over then we sang the chorus together.

"Well that was a first for me." Darren said a moment after we finished the song,

"What- hearing such a terrible singer?" I burst out laughing.

He smiled. "No, my first duet."

I glanced over to him.

"Well I'm honoured to be the first."

We parked at west ed now.

"You aren't a terrible singer Serena." He said to be as he closed the door behind him and walked to open mine.

"Well, thank you."

He extended his hand to help me up our of the car. I took it gently. He let go the second I stood up.

"Let's go hunt a damn dragon."

He laughed as he locked the car behind us and we bounded the iron steps up to the movie theatre.

"Bet you never thought you would say that out loud hey?" I teased.

"No, for sure not."

The mall was bustling with many people as per usual. We entered the movie theatre

Darren nodded. We walked around the theatre, looking at everything in the arcade and down the halls.

"Feel anything?" he asked.

"Not here."

"Well it's a big mall so lets keep looking." he said.

"Alright."

We left through the glass doors and descended to the main level of the mall. The smell of cinnamon bun filled the air.

"Oh yum, would you like one?" I glanced to Darren.

"Absolutely."

"Okay, I will grab some for us."

"Then I will find us some coffee?" He offered.

"Perfect."

He parted ways and I went to order cinnamon buns.

"Good morning how can I help you?"a young girl maybe 18 greeted me warmly.

"Good morning. Two cinnamon buns please."

"You got it."

I paid her and she handed me the buns. They were warm in my hands the sweet smell wafting to my nose.

I glanced around. I wondered where Darren might've hopped off too. I sat down staring at the giant life sized pirate ship surrounded by crystal blue waters. I lived around here that I sometimes forgot how crazy cool it was that this place had a life sized pirate ship, a full amusement park, A huge indoor waterpark, multiple mini golfing spots, an aquarium, a full sized ice rink, hundreds of stores, restaurants, bars, casino, dinner theatre, movie theatre you name it. I looked around at the people sitting in and around my vicinity. But I felt no pull, or calling. I wondered if Darren's hunch was correct. I hoped it was. I was also wondering where he headed off to for coffee. I was about to get up when he handed me a cup of steaming coffee from Starbucks.

"Here, wasn't sure what you liked there."

That made sense it was the closest coffee shop to where I was. It was attached to chapters.

"I'm not picky, mm Thank you." I handed him the bun.

"Arguably one of the best desserts don't you think?" He said taking a bite.

I followed suit. "Agreed."

We ate in silence.

"How about we just do a loop? Hopefully I can pick something up that way."

I said after taking the last bite.

He finished too.

"Sounds like a plan."

He grabbed our plates and dumped them in the trash bin."Shall we?"

"Let's."

We walked beside the fountains, heading to the opposite side of the mall. The demon he had summoned when I had died was on my mind. The extreme both brothers went to. I wanted to talk about it, but I didn't want to disrupt our goal, or Darren's focus. I thought of something else.

"So you still haven't told me your favourite show." I smiled.

Darren shook his head slightly and chuckled.

"You wanna know that badly?"

"Yes!"I laughed.

"I don't think I could pick just one."

"What about one from each genre that you do like?"

We began to round the corner of the ice rink.

He seemed he was about to reply when I felt very hot all of a sudden.

"Woah" I staggered back slightly.

His arm was immediately against my back.

"Serena! You okay?"

"I-yes, I just I can feel heat like fire."

The fire was overwhelming, like I was standing directly beside a campfire in the summer heat, even thought the ice rink was feet away from me.

"Which direction?"

"Around the bend." I said breathlessly.

"Hey, hang in there okay?"

We came up around the bend and walked the hall. Towards Galaxyland. The heat grew intensely. I only had enough energy to point. Darren's eyes followed where I pointed.

"Really, the amusement park?"

I nodded unable to speak and as we came up to it I start to feel pain and I yelped.

"What- what's wrong?"

I was shaking violently, I felt like I was writhing in flames.

"It burns, it burns so much please." I cried out.

"Come on, let's go." He started to usher me backwards.

"We can't!" I yelled between clenched teeth.

"What the Hell do you mean we can't?!" He yelled.

"We are here this is the dragon- it has to be there's not other explanation. We can't leave."

"Serena, I am not going to stand here while you burn alive. You are NOT dying on me again." He pulled my hand roughly backwards.

"Darren it's just pain." I said between gasps. "We need to do this, we have to."

"Serena-"

I ran forward before he could protest further. Trying my best not to scream as the pain became blinding.

"Serena! Damn it!" Darren ran after me.

"Serenity please. Help me."

I barely whispered, I didn't think it would work but I stopped short as she appeared in front of me.

Darren stopped a few paces behind me. Probably unsure where Serenity came from.

She held up a frozen pink peony. It looked encased in resign.

"Good on you for finding the dragon. Take this." she said.

I grabbed it and the ice immediately dissolved into steam. My skin was actually getting hot- it wasn't imaginary. Oh my God.

As I held the flower the burning stopped. I could've cried I was so relieved.

"But-how..?"

"I was looking for this very dragon for you, that was the lead I had. Apparently a frozen flower can douse the flames of a dragon. Remember Serena, there is more then one way to take a heart."

Darren caught up just as Serenity left again.

"What the hell. What did she give you? Did it make the pain stop?"

I held up the peony. "Ironically one of my favourite flowers. Yes."

He touched my arm briefly and yelped pulling his hand back. There were blisters forming as if he touched a hot skillet.

"Serena.." He said cautiously.

The peony erupted in blue flame briefly until it was only ash in my hand, I felt no pain at all.

"Put the ash into your locket..it will keep you from burning in the vicinity of the dragon. Now I must attend something else. Summon me if you need me again."

I heard Serenity in my head.

"A gift perhaps." I started.

"How did she get to you?"

"I asked her to come, I didn't think it would work. But the burning- it's gone."

"I'm glad for that-"

"But?"

"I never read anything about that in the book, and how the Hell did she find us so quickly and know of the dragon-?"

"I suppose we could ask Damon if it's been documented tomorrow when we go back home. I'm unsure of everything else myself, and if you think it doesn't worry me, you would be mistaken."

"So you dare still enter my lair even after I have doused you in eternal flame, ethereal one?"

Darren and I glanced towards the voice. A man stood with almond skin and glowing lime green eyes a few paces ahead of us.

"Ethereal one?" Darren re countered.

He adjusted his stance to defensive, like he was ready to jump into action at any given second.

"No, not you Elderwood brother. Your lady here."

I inhaled. "Ethreal like-angelic?"

"I did sense you Elderwood brother. I have been warned of your travels and your intent.

Darren challenged. "I'm glad you've been made aware."

The mans expression flashed annoyance.

"Hush. Her- however, never saw, or sensed her in any way, yet my fires burned her but not you. How odd. However I do suppose you-"

"Enough talking. You must know what we have come for then."

Darren said harshly and gestured for me to move behind him and I did as he asked.

It's eyes narrowed again. He had a black sleek cane, that he tapped twice and the amusement park around us froze momentarily then came back, there was a shimmer like we were in a soap bubble all around us.

"There- out of public eyes." it said.

"You have no hope as to defeat me Elderwood, God or no God. I will not go down easy."

"I will not allow Cronos to succeed." Darren seethed.

It laughed humorlessly.

"I've been alive many millennia, survived countless who have tried. I will not die at your hands. But you shall die at mine. Especially stripped of your power."

"Enough talking, let's dance." Darren challenged.

They began to fight. Lunging toward one another. Darren had the upper hand. But the dragon looked unamused. I watched intently and anxiously. I was trying to piece together what Serenity meant by there was more then one way to take the heart. Heart-heartbreak?

Love?..family..dragons-gold-collectors.. Darren took a hard knock to his jaw. I would step in without hesitation if he needed me too, but I also knew he loved fighting and that I was stronger then him. It was better I stayed out of it until he needed me, however I found it difficult to wait. I was looking over the man, trying to pin point what might be of importance, anything overly important I would assume he kept on his person at all times. He had many necklaces piled over his shirt. I scanned over them as him and Darren exchanged punches. A key. Darren's face was swelling and he had blood coming from his cheek.

"Ethereal one, are you not going to fight? Your mate is looking rough. Come on give me a show of that power." He challenged me.

"I'm bored, with this one- he doesn't remember who he is."

He flung Darren out of the way and he smacked into the side of the bubble.

"Darren!"

"I'm fine!" He spat blood onto the ground.

"In fact I am just getting warmed up."

He struggled up pulling the ceremonial dagger from his jeans.

"A holy weapon? Ah you are not so daft. Get on with it then."

I knew it was the key. I needed that key, I decided with distraction.

"Do you know who we are?"

He waved his cane and Darren was frozen in place.

"What the Hell!" He yelled trying to move.

Panic rippled my body.

"Quiet. I'm speaking to the ethereal one now, we can resume our play in a moment."

His glowing eyes pierced me making me feel the burn all over again. I stood firm and held eye contact.

"I said, do you know who we are?"

"I might." He countered.

I needed to play to his ego. I took a breath.

"Well for someone so strong and wise, that hardly surprises me."
He gave me an unfriendly smile.

"Well I have been alive a long time."

"Yes, longer then anything I can think of. And- this mall, this place, you created it didn't you?.."

Darren stopped struggling against the hold and listened to me.

"Of course. It is the perfect trap, I can drain energy from many sources, and the amount of treasures I collect here.. you couldn't fathom."

"I wouldn't dream of it. It is fair too vast for my small invalid human brain to grasp."

"Also true. I like you ethereal one. You say human brain, but you are not human. You can talk but can you fight?"

"You will not fight her! Your fight is with me!" Darren yelled.

The dragon rolled it's eyes looking briefly to Darren, I seized the opportunity to grasp the key from his neck, hoping he wouldn't notice. I reached and snapped it quickly shoving it into the pocket of my leather jacket, all before he turned back to me. I wasn't sure Darren had seen either.

"You are insignificant without your powers. Perhaps I will kill you Darren, perhaps that would incline the ethereal one to fight."

He fixed his cold eyes onto me.

I could feel the rage boil and the now familiar power tingling like electricity at my fingertips. I took a steadying breath. I had to stay calm. In control. I needed the information first.

"You will not take his life not here, not now not ever." I spoke low.

"What are you going to do about it ethereal one?"

"First tell me, who we are."

"Not a chance in Hell."

"If you want a fight with me, I want you to tell me."

"I'll just kill your little shell of a God here first then."

Darren's jaw clenched and he struggled again against the prison.

"I would advise you don't. Osiris himself fled a battle with me, after taking one hit."

Darren's eyes widened.

"Osiris.. you mean to say he is back at it again? All the pieces the humans must have located and returned. The sheer stupidity of the humankind never fails to amaze me. However he is nothing compared to me, he cowers in the very presence of dragon-kind. Darren, you are very powerful indeed. Your memories along with Damon's, locked away by yours truly."

He bowed sarcastically.

"Your missing powers however? What a wicked twist of fate. Not my doing unfortunately."

"How ironic you come to me in your time of need. Our one and only God of destruction and death. Osiris possessed you as a desire to do your job for you. A willing slave, an admirer of your works."

He laughed cruelly.

I glanced to Darren and his face was painted with a look of such crushing devastation, unlike any emotion I had ever witnessed anyone having before.

"The best part-" It spoke between heaving laughs. "Your brother is the God of creation."

Chapter 24

MAP

"Beauty in the eye of the beholder, A rose just as pretty wilted as it is alive, but in a different way, like echos of a past, whispers of a lost dream, something new, versus something coated in rust, the rust merely shows a detailed map of where it's been, as we all bare scars visible and not, after every battle we face as our story is written anew every morning, and our souls are the map of our being."

D arren's eyes were absolutely hollow and faraway. I couldn't believe what I just heard.

"You Ethereal one- I am curious myself as to what you are."

"You are lying." I spoke my voice losing it's edge as I tried to process everything.

"No. But I will put you out of your misery Darren, it's the least I can do! Your memories will return in waves each day now that I have revealed this concealment, it'll destroy you. And wherever that brother of yours is- he will remember now too. I have released your memories."

Anger overtook Darren's face then. He struggled fiercely against the hold the dragon put on him.

"You will not touch him." I seethed, the power sparking from my body.

"I dare you to challenge me little girl. I'm amused you would protect him with this new information."

I held up the key I stole from his neck.

"I accept your challenge."

"Serena NO!" Darren yelled.

"HOW DID YOU?! ARRRRGH!"

He howled and spun his cane around him. Darren's prison shook and fell freeing him from it's grasp as dark blue smoke encircled around the dragon. After a moment in it's wake, was a literal blue dragon.

Darren staggered back. "Now he's pissed."

"Yes, but as am I." I spoke calmly.

I exhaled as my power sprung from me.

I charged forward key in hand right at the dragon that began to spit flames in my direction. I ran through them, feeling no pain. I held the key above my head. I used the dragons right front leg to jump upwards and I stabbed the key into his stomach. I used every ounce of my strength the cut through it's scales and into it's flesh. The beast roared in anguish. Thrashing to get me off but as it thrashed down I dug deeper and dragged it across the frame of it's stomach. As I did Random jewels and items began to tumble out of him it was hard to dodge anything. Darren used the items to jump up towards the dragons head slashing it's tongue from it's mouth. The items fell harder and faster before long I was buried in miscellany treasures as the dragon fell limp beside me.

"Serena- Serena!" I could hear Darren yelling for me throwing items out of the way trying to get to me. I tried to speak but I was exhausted.

"Darren- I'm here." I whispered.

"Serena! I hear you. I'm coming hold on."

I could see light where he pulled things off of me and I struggled out. He immediately hugged me. I leaned against him panting hard, dropping the key into his hands.

"Thank God" he breathed.

The dragon returned to it's human form and made a choking sound.

"I will rise again, from ashes I rise. You cannot kill..a dragon." it said gutterly since one half of it's tongue was gone.

"Are you okay Darren?" I turned to face him.

He stared at me a second, then turned from my eyes releasing me from his arms.

"Are you?" He turned the question back to me.

"Unharmed."

"Let's go then."

He turned and started walking. Damn I can't imagine hearing what he heard, what thoughts must be rampant in his mind. I wanted to wrap my arm around him, but I refrained, worried it might make things worse.

"Do you still have that key?"

I held it up. "Yes. It's for sure one of the items."

He nodded and kept walking. Maybe humour was a good approach.

"Darren we just slayed a dragon! Your hunch was right!" I said excitedly and playfully bumped into him.

Darren chuckled slightly, but his tone was derived of joy.

"I never thought I would say that. I can't believe Dragon's actually exist. Will he though?" I continued.

"What? Rise again? Yeah they are reborn from their ashes. It will take a millennia before he matures again."

"Are they the same dragon that perished? Do they remember who they are?"

"I'm not sure."

"Wait-" I started back to galaxy land.

"Serena, where are you going?" Darren yelled after me.

He followed close behind. I wandered to the pile of ash that a maintenance man was sweeping up, probably mistaken it for dirt.

"Serena-what are you looking for?'

"Excuse me?" I said politely to the man.

He nodded to me. "Yeah, what?"

I was guessing the mountain of jewels and items was still invisible to public eye, due to the fact people were quite literally walking through it, unfazed.

"Serena-" Darren cautioned.

"Did you happen to find anything in that dirt pile?"

"This old rock yours?"

He eyed me oddly, picking up what looked like a gold speckled rock.

"Yes- I just-love rocks." I said with fake enthusiasm.

The guy shrugged. "Here."

"Thank you."

I took the rock from him and walked back to Darren.

He glanced at the rock then at me. "What?"

I shrugged. "Call it a hunch. Where are we going now?"

He gave me a slight smile.

"Wherever you like, we are barred from our hotel until the morning. It's early still."

His voice sounded solemn and heavy.

I glanced at my phone. It was only 5pm.

I winced looking at his face. "Darren, why don't we stop somewhere where I can patch you up."

"If you must." His tone was back harsh.

"Darren do you want to talk about-" he cut me off.

"No."

I inhaled loudly. "I'm here when you are ready."

"I can't promise I will be. I need to talk to Damon- can we just let that lie?" his tone was quite cold and angry.

I looked down feeling guilty for bringing it up. I selfishly wished he would speak kinder to me. The cold tones stung every time. Darren glanced to me.

"Please, Serena." His tone softened, as if reading my mind.

"Yes." I said quietly.

He nodded curtly. "Thank you."

"Are you hungry at all?" I offered.

He shook his head. "No, but if you are we can go."

"Honestly, I'm not right now. Where do you think we should stay for tonight? Maybe we could turn in for a bit at least, get you cleaned up, and put this someplace safe." I lifted the rock slightly, giving Darren a soft smile.

"I actually already booked us a place."

"Oh, wow thank you for thinking ahead." I laughed lightly. "Is it nearby?"

"Very." Darren pointed to "Fantasyland hotel."

I gasped slightly. It was difficult to hide my excitement. "Seriously?"

Darren chuckled lightly. "Yeah, I thought you might like this."

"Are you kidding me?! I love this place. Its expensive though- I'll pay half."

Darren shook his head. "No we are here on business." A playful smile at his lips. We approached the front desk.

"Follow my lead."

I laughed slightly. "Okay."

"Hey miss, he looked to her name tag. Eve?"

She had short black hair and dark eyes.

"Hi- how can I?- OH officer! Your room is ready. Complimentary dinner as well."

She glanced to me, then back to the Darren. I wondered what glamour he was using, I couldn't tell, he still looked normal to me.

"Here are your card keys. Boss has offered 2 nights at most complimentary."

"Thank you." Darren said and I followed him to the golden elevators.

"Free?"

"Yep. Total coverage."

I laughed and shook my head. "Not bad officer." I teased.

We went up to the second floor.

"Which room did you snag for us this evening?"

"You'll see."

We went up to the superior Romanian room. Darren keyed the door.

"After you."

"Well I'll be an officer and a gentleman." I laughed. When I entered the room it felt like we had just stepped into Greece. There were white pillars, the bed was circular. The jaccuzzi had a roman Greek god statue above it, the room was red and white with gold accent. There was two vintage style red couches by the huge windows. The walls were done in murals that looked hand painted. The crown moulding was gold. It took my breath away.

"Wow."

"It's pretty nice in here, hey?"

"Have you stayed here before?"

Darren shook his head. "But, I'm impressed."

I put the rock down on the counter and wrapped my black jacket over it.

"I'll get our bags from the car?" Darren offered.

"Sure, be careful."

"Always."

Darren handed me the key card and left.

I stared in awe around the room yet again. The jaccuzzi was in the centre of the room almost. It looked like it could fit 5 adults. My phone rang which made me jump.

"Oh right, back in 2024." I whispered.

I glanced to the caller ID it was Rayne. I picked up.

"Hello?"

"Hey stranger!"

I laughed a bit. "Hey Rayne how is it going?"

"Oh very well. I'm calling cause well the wedding is on Saturday."

I had forgotten she moved the day up, I immediately felt heavily guilty. It was Thursday today.

"Yes.."

"Look I know your suuuuper busy and all trying to save the world and such, but could you please ensure you take the night off of playing Hero and come to my wedding?!"

"What- of course I'll be there Rayne."

"I got you a dress! I know you have been occupied so."

"Yes, thank you love."

"Ohhh and bring a date! Or two.." She hinted.

"Rayne!"

"Oh what did you narrow it down too one?"

"None."

"I don't believe you guys all going through all this crazy shit and not catching feelings are you nuts?!"

"I care deeply for both of them. If I were to..choose one not to say I would, I mean it's just not a good time okay?! We have so much on our plates, romance seems irrelevant."

"Fine, I just want to see you happy."

"I am."

She sighed loudly. "And not lonely!"

"I'm not!"

She laughed. "Okay well I will see you Saturday then?"

"Yes."

"Wonderful! Just message when you are headed my way."

"Okay! Excited to see what you picked out."

"Ohh you'll love it. It's not boring at all, I swear. See you soon!" click.

I sighed. Was that true what I said to her? I wasn't even fully sure. I decided to run the jaccuzzi. I couldn't stay here and not go in it. Seemed like such a waste.

I walked over and turned the tap on, as the steamy water barrelled out. Floral, sage or vanilla were my options. I picked vanilla and poured it in. The room began to fill with the strong aroma of vanilla. I inhaled deeply.

The door clicked then, and every muscle in my body tensed.

"Just me." Darren said as he came in.

He inhaled deeply, his eyes faraway. He looked like he might drop our bags.

I rushed to his side grabbing the bags and putting them down gently.

"What's wrong? Darren, hey." I asked softly, steadying his shoulders with my hands.

He dropped to one knee, taking a couple deep breaths.

"Vanilla." He whispered.

"What? Are you allergic? Don't like the smell? I can drain it and put something else in."

I moved to leave and he grasped my wrist holding me in place.

"I'm fine." He nodded to me giving me a weak smile.

He let go of my wrist and got up. He glanced to the jaccuzzi.

"I can step out for a while, so you can enjoy that in peace."

"I-well, If your comfortable I'd really rather you stayed. I've got a bathing suit, no worries." I laughed nervously.

"Of course, I wouldn't leave you unless you asked me too." He gave me another gentle smile.

"Well, good. I'm relieved."

He loudly cleared his throat. "uh, I picked up some snacks just for in-case."

"I love snacks."

"They are just what I could find at the convenience store, didn't want to take too long."

"I'm not picky."

He started to unpack the bags, he pulled out chips and salsa, raspberry dark chocolate, cheese and crackers, caramel corn and a tin of coffee grinds with vanilla creamer.

I laughed a bit.

"That's fair you never get enough coffee in hotels."

Darren nodded.

Damn how the hell was I going to get him to open up? He can't shoulder everything that was said all on his own. He has to be overwhelmed. Maybe the key wasn't to try and fix anything maybe just a distraction of laughs and good conversation would suffice. I glanced to the water slowly trickling into the jaccuzzi.

"Darren?"

"Yeah?" He glanced up from the small table he was setting the food on.

"What's your favourite TV show?"

"We gonna do this again?" he said lightheartedly.

"Depends if you'll actually answer me this time."

"Depends on what you ask."

"Whats your favourite show?"

"Is it really that important?"

"No, but I would like to know anyways. I suppose I want to know you better, Damon he's an open book, you are closed off. I would like to learn anything you are willing to share."

He stared at me a moment and smiled slightly.

"Only if you'll do the same."

"Absolutely fair. But let me fix up your face, please." I chuckled and shrugged.

"What about the jaccuzzi?"

"It's slowly filling."

"I'm really okay, it's just some bruising and minor scrapes."

"Still."

"Fine."

I got up and went to the bathroom to get some soap and warm water.

I came back and he rolled his eyes. But allowed me to clean up his face.

"So what do you hope to get from that rock?" He asked casually.

I paused dabbing his left eye for a minute.

"Well-I think it will hatch. When you told me they are reborn from their ashes"

"What are you Kallesi from "Game of Thrones?"

I laughed dabbing at his right eye.

"Hardly. I just didn't like the idea of an infant of any kind being left to fend for itself."

"Well you do look like the mother of Dragons."

"Wow, thank you. Wait is that your favourite show?!"

Darren chuckled slightly. "No, but I did like it."

"It it something chick flicky? Is that why you don't want to tell me?"

"The x-files is my favourite show."

"A classic. I supposed you knew most of the things in that show were real hey?"

"I did."

"I'll have to re-watch it now knowing it's mostly non-fiction. Once we finish saving the world of course."

Darren chuckled. "Of course."

"What's your favourite colour?"

I raised my eyebrows. "Really?"

Darren shrugged. "I'm just warming up."

"Red. Okay done, face is cleaned up."

"Thanks, Serena."

I walked to the bathroom to dump the water and hang the cloth, I shut the jaccuzzi off on my way back to the room. Darren sat on the circle bed, flipping through channels.

I started sifting through my bag for my swim suit.

"Crap" I said under my breath.

"What's up?"

Apparently I didn't speak quietly enough.

"Seems I left my swim suit."

Darren glanced to me and put the remote down.

"I can go for a walk for a bit just message me when you are done."

I took a deep breath. "No it's fine."

I slipped my dress off.

"What are you doing?" Darren's hand flew up to cover his eyes.

"I have a bra and panties, it's basically the same thing."

He kept his eyes covered. "I suppose."

"It's fine Darren."

I wasn't wearing anything overly sexy, just a white lacy sports bra and white lace trimmed underwear.

"Honestly I think this covers more then the average swim suit."

I stepped up into the jaccuzzi. After hearing the water Darren uncovered his eyes.

The water was like a hot tub, the vanilla enveloped me in a heavenly scent and I relaxed to the back of the tub.

He glanced at me in the water. Then picked the remote back up and lounged backwards on the bed.

"I believe that."

"Water warm?"

"mm yeah, you should join me."

"No that's alright Serena, enjoy it."

'What's your favourite colour?"

Darren chuckled. "We continuing the small talk?"

"Absolutely. Need some way to pass the time."

"Fine, Green."

"How come green?"

"It's the colour of life, earth."

I nodded. "That's fair enough."

"Why do you like red?"

"Because it is associated with anger, hatred as well as romance, and love. It is also the colour our blood, which keeps us living and I think that's alot of responsibility for one colour."

"Hm. What a unique way to look at that."

"What's your favourite movie?'

I sucked in a breath. "God, that's a hard choice."

"Tell me your top 5 then." He shrugged.

"mmm "Number 23, Butterfly Effect, Pirates of the Caribbean, Grown ups, Legally Blonde. I also love anything Tim Burton."

"Solid choices. No particular genre, I noticed."

"I like a little bit of everything, same with music taste."

"What's your favourite animal and why? May as well get all the basic questions through first." I laughed.

"Dragons. Granted in human form they are quite rude."

I started laughing. "Well then if this one hatches, dream come true? Favourite animal as a pet?"

"I suppose as long as I am in his good books."

"Don't blame you for that at all."

I slightly swam to the tap to add more hot water.

Darren stopped flipping through channels and landed on the history channel.

"What are you passionate about, outside of singing Darren?"

"Well I'm quite passionate about fighting the unnatural and stopping the end of the world."

I laughed. "I mean more so hobbies?"

"Honestly not really. I enjoy movies occasionally. I like fighting."

"Remind me when this is over to find you some hobbies." I chucked lightly.

"You can try. I won't promise success."

"I can promise success."

He chuckled. "Okay what's your dream life?"

I paused to think for a moment.

"Well it's changed now."

Darren glanced over.

"Now my dream life is this. It's saving people without them knowing half the time. It's you and Damon and our mission. I do wish the world wasn't ending but, knowing we can make it, that we are so close. I suppose I am living in my dream life."

Darren gave me a soft smile. "What was it before?"

"I supposed, I wanted to be a mother quite badly. I guess your typical life. Be with someone whom I love and trust and connect with deeply. Have a small acreage, I would continue into the medical field given the opportunity."

Darren's gaze became faraway again.

"What's wrong?"

"Nothing. Are you sure you don't still want that, I mean once the world is saved and all?"

"I won't know that until then. What eager to berid of me?" I teased.

"Quite the opposite."

I was slightly taken off guard by his response. "Oh, well that's a relief."

"How's your water?"

"Warm. Did you want to try it out? The jets are really great."

"It's alright."

He seemed closed off again. Damn thought we were getting somewhere.

"Would you mind bringing me some water please?"

"Not at all."

He got up and grabbed a bottle from the mini fridge and went to pass it to me. After a moments hesitation I pulled him toward me and he half fell into the water. I burst into laughter.

"Serena!"

His upper body was toppled over the edge of the jaccuzzi.

He took his right arm and splashed a huge wave of water at me. As he burst out laughing too.

"Well your already halfway in. I mean." I playfully shrugged fighting another bout of laughter. It was the first time I had seen Darren laugh so much.

"Okay you asked for it." He said playfully.

He pulled himself up and took his white shirt and dark jeans off. He didn't have much for tattoos just one tribal snaking from his bicep that circled around an ouroboros, like the rings he and Damon always wore. He was muscular, built to fight.

Climbing in after me in his boxers. He jumped up suddenly.

"Goddamn Serena! It's so friggin' hot."

"Really? You'll get used to it."

I started laughing again and he joined me. He sat a ways away from me in the water.

"Why thank you for joining me sir."

Darren shook his head laughing slightly.

"My pleasure madame." He half bowed then splashed me again.

"Deserved." I laughed.

"Absolutely." he smiled.

"What do yours and Damon's rings represent? And I suppose same as your tattoo?"

"Ah. The ouroboros. Honestly we have always had them, both of us and matching tattoos as well. It must be lost somewhere in our memories. It represents the "Unity and the natural eternal cycle of destruction and re-creation." He gave me a half smile.

The dragon had said Darren was a God of destruction and Damon was a God of creation and he called me ethereal one, and I was reborn. My face must of portrayed my deep thoughts.

"What are you thinking about?"

I swallowed debating if I should share.

"About what the Dragon said. Your guys ring and Tattoo, and well me coming back."

Darren stared hard at me, as if the thought hadn't occurred to him.

"Holy shit."

His expression became hollow again, so I splashed him. And he shook his head breaking from his thoughts.

"What was that for?"

"To snap you back from your spiralling thoughts. We can wait and talk to Damon too, let's try not to worry about it. We can figure everything out together. We always seem too."

Darren stared at me a moment. "Your right."

I watched him for a moment and my eyes fell on my hand print, still charred and embedded into his chest. The guilt over having hurt him was so unbecoming, and overwhelming.

Darren followed my gaze. He swam over to me slightly. He picked up my hand.

"Darren what are you-"

He picked up my hand and placed it on his chest where my hand print was.

"Darren-I'm so sorry."

"This is nothing to apologize for. Remember that your hand print may have scarred my skin, but it is the reason I am no longer possessed. And for that- I cannot express my gratitude Serena."

He let go of my hand and I placed it back in the water.

"Okay."

Then he splashed me.

"Now enough with the heavy. Weren't we in the midst of some Bs small talk?"

He laughed slightly and I nodded. Feeling instantly more relaxed.

"Yes we were. Favourite food?"

"Burgers. Pie. Obviously. What about you?"

"I love burgers. I still need to take you to that place by my home. I quite like pasta too. If we are talking desserts I really like pudding and custard."

"Pudding and custard. You just aged like 20 years." He smiled.

"I am unashamed for being a granny at heart."

He chuckled lightly. "Good."

"Okay, let's get to some more introspective ones."

He nodded. "I accept your challenge."

"How would you spend a day, to make it perfect in your eyes? If opportunities and realism wasn't part of the question." I asked raising my eyebrows.

"Ooh good one. Give me a second." He said.

I nodded and moved to the tap again.

"More hot water? It's scalding!" he exclaimed.

"Hey if you can't handle the heat get outta the jaccuzzi." I teased.

"I was, you pulled me in."

"Touche."

"I'm teasing Serena, add more if you want."

I turned the tap on. I let it run while I waited for his reply.

"Big breakfast with those I am close too, then go out to a lake, do a nature hike and cool off in the lake, BBQ lunch. Tubing. Steak

Dinner, a professional massage without anything or anyone trying to kill me or Damon..he took a breath, or you and then go to bed without the weight of saving the world on my mind, next to someone I care for."

I smiled softly. "Well that sounds like an incredible day, and very possible too."

"Yeah. It doesn't feel possible right now. I'm also worried about Damon."

"He will pull through." I reassured.

"He's my little brother, its my duty to protect him and now with-" He cut himself off. "Small talk."

"Yes small talk-unless you want-?"

he harshly cut me off. "No. What about you? What's your perfect day?"

"Hmm. Breakfast in bed. Strong coffee and good conversation in the morning. Then a long car ride with all the best music, with all those I am close with. Karaoke in the car and all the road trip snacks, pull over wherever whenever to look at anything we feel like and just see where it takes us. I would want to finish off in the mountains, a nice hot tub soak. Then bed beside someone I care about. That's my favourite."

"That sounds like a good day, and doable too."

"When we aren't being hunted, and trying to save the world."

"True enough." he said.

"Best memory of late? I know you don't have all your memories from childhood but."

"All of our wins in battles recently, but most of all not losing Damon and you, coming back."

"I'm grateful to have not lost either of you either or Rayne."

"Oh speaking of Rayne her wedding is Saturday? Would you and Damon be willing to come do you think?"

"I would and I'm sure Damon would as well, providing he is not too sore."

"That would be amazing. Thank you. What a strange concept, a wedding when there's an apocalypse looming. Don't you think?"

He shrugged. "Ignorance is bliss."

"What's your best memory Serena?"

"Well my memories are still in fragments. I know I have many beautiful memories. But honestly? Finding you and Damon, learning about the unnatural and finding this unyielding strength within me. It's terrifying and beautiful all the same."

"That's lovely."

"Would you like to get out? I'm getting a little hungry." I smiled slightly.

"After you."

I got up and climbed out of the jaccuzzi. My skin was steaming-well he wasn't mistaken, I did have the water overly hot.

I grabbed a towel wrapping it hastily around myself and passed one too him as he stepped out.

"Thank you."

"I'm really glad you brought snacks! The water drained me, I do not wish to go anywhere else." I laughed.

"I'm more then happy to stay put as well."

"Movie?"

"Sure."

I headed to the bathroom to change into pjs.

I closed the door and exhaled. I was happy to be connecting with Darren and thoroughly enjoying my time with him. I was worried about Damon but I trusted Jane was taking care of him. I brushed my hair and pulled on black shorts and a black tank top. I attempted to scrub the raccoon-looking running makeup off of my eyes.

"Damn should have remembered this before the jaccuzzi."

I scrubbed until my skin was a bit red.

"God that looks worse, guess it doesn't matter."

I quit fussing with my appearance and went back out into the room. Darren was in white sweats and grey tank.

"What do you feel like watching?" He smiled to me.

"I'm not sure, I suppose we are limited too what we can find on cable."

"No, Netflix is on here."

"Pick your favourite Darren, since I don't know what it is yet."

He searched "Wedding Crashers."

I laughed excitedly. "Solid choice!"

He smiled at me. "I enjoy comedy any day."

"What genre did you think I would pick?"

"Honestly I guessed action, since you enjoy fighting."

"I like action as well."

He clicked play and we looked at each other, perhaps both thinking about the fact that it was just one bed. I glanced over the couch but it was a vintage chaise lounge, which would not be comfortable for anyone.

"I'll take the couch." Darren said politely.

The table he laid the food out was at the foot of the bed so we both settled comfortably at the foot of the bed.

The movie started playing and we both ate in comfortable silence.

We seemed to laugh at most of the same parts. I wasn't going to let him sleep on that couch, he wouldn't get any rest. I was playing around with the idea of just sleeping beside each other but I couldn't figure out how to ask. We had once before, I inhaled remembering how it felt the first time to be in his arms. I longed for it a bit, if I was going to be honest with myself. On the other hand, I hoped Damon was alright, but I trusted Jane was taking care of him. She seemed to love him quite a bit.

"Darren?"

"mm?"

"How long have Damon and Jane been together?"

"They aren't, not in Damon's eyes anyway, he has a friends with benefits arrangement with her in his mind."

"I don't think she shares the same mindset."

"No. Why do you ask?"

"Honestly, I was just curious. I saw how she looked at Damon and how worried she was when he was in the hospital. He just might be sleeping on a good one."

"Yeah, maybe. That's for him to figure out though."

"Perhaps. What about you?"

He scoffed. "Me?"

"Yeah when was your last relationship?"

"High school. 3 years. Outside of that, I've never really had a serious relationship, We were on the road all the time. It just didn't seem fair to make connections like that."

"What about yourself? How long were you with-" He cut himself off. "Nevermind."

"It's fine, I don't mind you asking. Henry was the only serious relationship ive had and that was 7 years."

"Only?"

"Yes."

"Well that's-uncommon."

"I know." I laughed

"I'm sorry he turned out the way he was."

"Me too."

The credits rolled then. I checked the time it was only 1030pm. I was exhausted.

"I might actually turn in."

"Honestly, I was thinking the same, I'm pretty tired too." Darren said.

"Well-we did fight a dragon." I shrugged. "No big deal or anything."

He smiled wide. "Nah just another day on the job."

We both laughed.

"Well Damon missed out on a Hell of a fight."

"Yeah he sure did, but we have a good story for him. Okay well, is it alright if we leave the TV on?" Darren asked.

"Of course. It doesn't bother me any."

He started to walk to the couch.

"Well Goodnight Serena. Thank you for coming with me today."

"Of course." I took a deep breath trying to calm my nerves. God why the Hell was I so nervous?

"Darren-?"

He sat on the couch.

"Yes?"

Now or never.

"Why don't you just-sleep beside me?" I asked sheepishly.

Darren's eyes widened slightly and his face was hard to read. I was so anxious my heart was pounding.

"You fought a Dragon today, you need a good night's rest, that couch won't do you any good." I half shrugged.

God shut up, don't ramble. I thought to myself.

"Are you sure?" He asked gently.

"Yes. If-if you want."

"I am honoured you asked, so long as you are sure?" Darren said. Eyeing me softly.

"Yes. Of course, I wouldn't offer if I wasn't."

I sounded confident which surprised me cause my head was whirling.

"Alright." He smiled.

"Well come on then."

I flipped the covers up on the right hand side and settled into the left.

He got into the bed slowly and covered up. The weight shift from his side was comforting to me. I spent a lot of years not sleeping alone, so this was soothing to me.

"Good night then." He said kindly. "Thank you."

"Of course. Sleep well."

"He turned away from me taking care to stay on the right-hand side of the bed and I shut the lamp off. The TV was on but almost muted. It was an action movie, but I couldn't pin point which one. I stared at it a moment then glanced to his side. He was already breathing deep and evenly, indicating he was already asleep.

I sighed slightly. I wished I could sleep that fast. I thought to myself as I closed my eyes and sure enough sleep met me in a few moments as well and I drifted into a calm dreamless sleep.

Chapter 25

CONTROL

*"We fit into boxes, perfectly cut, if you don't fit in this pretty box
you don't belong, sit down, shut up, bite your tongue, get in line,
forget your dreams, forget how to speak for yourself, words too
scared to offend, reckless sheep following a corrupt leader, they
don't like the ones that fight for the leader, pop another pill, it's
all a lie, here pull this wool to your eyes, take another drink,
smoke another toke, look what's on sale, it's not what you think,
it's your soul, your time, and you give up so easily."*

Iawoke to a start. Darren was thrashing about in his sleep, mumbling something I couldn't understand. I grabbed my phone and checked the time 2:31am. I put my phone back on the night stand and half sat up. He must be having one Hell of a nightmare. He was coated in sweat. I tried to rouse him.

"Darren? Darren, hey- hey." I gently grasped his arm and shook it a bit.

"No..no please..no." I heard him in his sleep it was clearer now.

"Darren, wake up!"

I shook his arm a bit more aggressively, his eyes flew open and he jolted to a sitting position. I put my hands on his hands and held them still.

"Hey, Darren, it's okay. It's alright. You were just having a dream."

His eyes were frantic, like a wild animal trapped in headlights.

"Darren. Shh, hey. It's alright. You're alright." I said softly never letting his hands go.

His eyes danced back and forth rapidly as he stared at me, like he was still delirious.

"It's okay. We are at fantasy land hotel."

He took a ragged breath. I could feel the sweat drip off of his face.

I moved my one hand off of his to rub his upper back for a second. His hand that was still holding mine squeezed it tightly, he rubbed his face with his now free hand.

He looked at me again. His eyes focused and-teary?

"Darren, what do you wanna talk about it? It wasn't real."

"I-"

His voice was hoarse.

"Come here."

He hesitated, so I put my arms around him and held him for a moment.

"Does the name Aurelia mean anything to you?"

He choked out, his voice still hoarse like he was holding back a wave of emotions.

I was shocked for a moment. My dream-the one that felt so real, that I kept having. In the plane crash he referred to me as Aurelia.

I let go of him suddenly.

His eyes widened. "It does?"

"I-what was the dream?"

He shook his head. "I don't think it was a dream, rather a memory."

I stared at him dumbfounded. But how would that be possible? How did we have the same dream?

"A memory?" I barely whispered.

He nodded and rubbed both hands across his face and stared at me again. Something forlorn and haunting in his expression.

"Was it-" I took a shuddering breath. "The memory, was it a plane crash?"

"How did you know that?-" the pure unrelenting shock was clear in his tone.

I shook my head taking a couple shaky breaths.

"I've had a reoccurring dream about a plane crash since I found the hotel. I die- I don't the whole dream is always in patches I seem to go further each time I have it."

"Impossible." He breathed.

"Serena I-" His voice was breaking.

I could feel myself seconds away from crumbling as well. It was impossible wasn't it?

"You think I was-?" I stopped to swallow hard.

His eyes were a storm of torment. "I don't-The -the dragon was right Serena. I remember what I am.

He inhaled sharply.

"Darren-" I whispered.

The familiarity I always felt, well I had felt with both Darren and Damon- the dreams. Is it at all possible that I was Aurelia at some point? What of the one with Damon?

I stared back into his eyes.

"Serena-I-"

He moved his face closer to mine. His eyes teared.

He brought his lips to mine. I was startled, but I didn't pull away. I put my hands on his neck intertwining them with his hair. It started off slowly, then it was crushing, fervent and needing. He inhaled and kissed me deeply. It was so familiar that even my dream felt more like a reality. My heart thrummed in my chest and I leaned back, laying down. He had his hands on the sides of my neck. His body moved in fluid motion to mine. I could feel the tears on his face. I kissed him back passionately, drinking him in. I never thought this would happen. Had I wanted it too? It felt blissful, I didn't want it to end. Then he abruptly pulled back and stopped kissing me.

"God, I'm so sorry." He said.

I put my fingers over where he kissed me.

"You don't have to apologize Darren."

"You don't understand. I do need to, you have no idea what I am, what I've done." He breathlessly mumbled.

"So enlighten me."

He shook his head. "No- I uh I need some air."

I think he meant for his tone to be harsh, but it only came across slightly cool.

He grasped quickly for his coat and stumbled putting his shoes on.

"Darren, where are you going?"

"I- just need a minute Serena."

That time he succeeded in sounding cold and I flinched slightly in spite myself.

"You'll return though?"

"I promise you, I will come back."

He walked out without waiting for my reply. I fell back onto the pillow. I tried to wrap my head over what just happened. He kissed me. It's just a kiss but, I felt like I had kissed him a thousand times before.

"Could that really be possible? Could I have been Aurelia, once upon a time? I had children before? If I had, what happened to them after I died? What year was that? But then again, my other dream- It was Damon. But I couldn't have been both Emma and Aurelia- I couldn't have been alive two places at once. That is assuming, Darren and Damon both had someone at the same time, the same years. Or was I neither, and it was just some strange connective dreams?" I whispered out loud to myself.

It was so complex to think about it was giving me a headache. I glanced at my phone again it was 330 now, I was shocked I had just spent 30 min in my own thoughts. I got out from bed and went to wet my face down with cold water. As I did the hotel room opened again. I jumped slightly. I glanced towards the door, I was relieved to see it was just Darren.

I stepped out of the bathroom. "I'm glad you are back."

Darren looked at me and nodded, he smelled strongly of booze. He half fell taking his shoes off. Damn. How had he gotten trashed so quickly?

"Darren how much did you drink?-"

He held up two empty mini mickeys from the fridge.

"Damn it, Darren."

I grabbed a bottle of water and handed it to him. "Drink this."

He reached to grab it and two other mini mickeys dropped from his arm. He laughed.

"Oops."

He laughed again and chugged the water, as he did it fell all down his chin and soaked his shirt.

I sighed. It broke my heart to see this, he was doing so well. I shouldn't have let him go alone. I took a breath and softened my tone.

"Come here, love." I guided him back to the bed, and covered him up.

He looked up to me and put his hand gently on my cheek,

"You take such care, of me. Everyone. Youuu are an angel." he slurred brutally.

"Sleep love. Just sleep, all will be well in the morning. You'll see."

I smiled and he dropped his hand from my face, burying his head into his pillow.

I sighed and settled into the bed beside him, I turned away from him. Once his breathing evened out, I fell asleep yet again, with a million things swimming in my mind.

Sunlight was pouring into the room when I opened my eyes again.

I glanced to Darren's side. He wasn't there. I panicked momentarily and flung myself outta bed.

"Darren?'

"Yeah..I'm here."

His voice was coming from the bathroom.

I was relieved.

"Not feeling too hot hey?"

"No." He groaned.

"Well you did have a lot to drink."

"Don't remind me."

He groaned again.

I walked over to the fridge and grabbed a bottle of water.

"Darren, would you let me in?"

He opened the door and fell back against the toilet.

"Here." I handed him the water.

"Thanks."

"You alright?"

"It's my own doing."

"Here I will help you back to bed."

"Don't, it makes it worse."

I nodded and stayed put as he got himself up and back to the bed.

"It's only 530am. You mind if I lay back down too?"

"No, I don't."

"Alright then." I laid back beside him.

I intertwined my hand in his and leaned against him.

"Is this okay?"

He breathed deeply. "Yes."

We laid there and both drifted back to sleep. I woke again and checked my phone it was 10. Darren was still passed out. I moved away from him slowly to not disturb him. I decided to run the jaccuzzi again. May as well use it one more time. I didn't pick a scent this time, just filled it with scalding water, and got in. Darren stirred shortly after. He sat up slowly rubbing his hand over his face.

"Better?"

He chuckled dryly. "Hardly."

"I put some Tylenol and more water on the table for you."

He stood up. "Thank you."

He took the Tylenol and a swing of water and groaned again.

He walked over to the tub, giving me a weak smile.

"That looks relaxing."

"Darren, would you please talk to me."

He knelt by the tub and I moved to the edge in front of him.

"About what?" he said softly.

"Do you really think..I'm well that it's true?"

His eyes clouded with agony for a moment.

"Yes."

I exhaled. "Wow."

"I don't expect it to be that way now, I just want you to know that. You are Serena now, not Aurelia."

His voice wavered slightly as he said the familiar name.

I felt unexpectedly sad at what he said. Then I cursed myself for being irrational. Much larger things at play. It was another life, if said life had ever really existed in the first place.

"I understand that, but can you tell me why you left so suddenly?"

He looked away from me.

"I really can't Serena, just give me some time with it, I want to speak with Damon too."

"I can do that." I gave him half a smile.

"Part of it was how I just-Lost control for a minute, with you..I had no right to you in that way, and for crossing that line I offer my most humble apologies Serena."

He studied my eyes for a minute, his blue eyes filled with sincerity.

I didn't really want his apology, a part of me felt betrayed by it. Part of me wanted to pull him in here and show him just how much I didn't want his apology. The other part wanted to, it wanted to put up walls and guard myself. I couldn't risk losing him or Damon in any way, they were too important. Focus on the big picture, do not be selfish. I do not have the luxury to give into this fantasy. We had a war to win.

He stopped crouching beside me then and got up. Making my decision for me.

"You don't have to forgive me now, I promise not to lose control like that again."

"I- do forgive you Darren, please don't worry about it."

I immediately regretted not telling him how I truly felt, but did I even know how I truly felt? Did I want him to never lose control with me again? Or was that all I wanted?

"Oh." He exhaled and smiled.

"Good. Are you ready to go back to Damon? I think we are going to get kicked out shortly."

I glanced to my phone it was 10:55. "Oh yes for sure. Let's pack up."

Darren nodded.

"I can pack both bags if you want to soak a while longer, just tell me which outfit to leave out for you."

"That's incredibly generous thank you."

"Don't mention it."

He moved about the room packing things quickly and I sunk deeper into the water. I closed my eyes under the water and when I opened them I screamed underwater. The white eyed demon- sure as day was standing above the water. It smiled and touched the water as I thrashed and felt it go colder and colder. I could hear Darren muffled through the water.

"How the Hell did you get in here!?" He screamed.

The demon started to laugh. An unholy sound.

I tried to get up and out of the water and he pressed down harder on me, the water was frigid and slushy, I couldn't stop shaking, oh God, not again.

"You son of a bitch! You'll let her go!" Darren's voice was acidic.

I saw Darren go forward with his knife in hand. It took the demons attention long enough for me to get above the water. I gasped, choking, gagging and coughing brutally so desperate for air.

Darren frantically tried to pull me out, he got halfway then dropped me back in as the demon knocked him away.

"Nonesense, it seethed. I can't hurt her. Even though I so desperately want to. Make her bleed, watch her struggle, scream and beg me to make it all go away."

It gave me an unfriendly smile as I tried again to get out as Darren was now on the other side of the room.

"Corvinus." Darren said in an unfamiliar booming voice.

The Demon looked-shocked? I was able to scramble from the water shaking, shivering and hyperventilating on the floor.

"Impossible. How is my name on thy tongue worthless human?" it seethed.

"What of Abraxas, Urxehl, Furcas, Morax, Abbadon, Sheol, are they in on this?"

"You cannot know. Unless- have you returned to us Master?"

"My memories have returned, I command you to let her go, state your business immediately, and promptly. Do not dare waste my time."

"Yes, Master."

"Fix Serena. Now."

The demon came closer to me and I tried to scramble back, when the demons clawed finger touched my shoulder I screamed as it felt the thing pressed a hot skillet into my flesh. After a moment of stinging I was warm again, dry and breathing normally. Darren looked relieved but he didn't let his guard down.

"State your business and get out of my sight."

"Master, wanted us to retrieve her and bring her to him. She is the only threat to Cronos that they can see."

"I am your master and I did not give such instruction."

The demon shifted uncomfortably. Urxehl and Osiris are leading presently, we were not informed you would return, your graciousness."

The demon half bowed and I sat there on the ground unsure what to say or do.

"Since when do you and your siblings leave Hell?"

"Since Osiris took over, sir."

"Run back to your boss and tell him he will face me personally for daring to crown himself in my absence. Tell Cronos, I will never follow him, and tell Urxehl for making himself take my crown, there will be hell to pay."

"You are the only master sir, I am grateful of your return. Yes, yes."

"Leave."

With that he did, he left only an icy wind for a second before dissipating entirely.

Darren rushed to my side.

"Serena?! Are you okay?"

"Y-yes." I stood up and Darren wrapped a blanket around me and then his one arm.

"So the Dragon didn't lie." I whispered.

"No, he didn't." Darren let go of my arm and looked to me.

"Are you sure you're okay?" I asked.

"Yes." He said plainly, I didn't buy it.

"Well he won't be around again, I can promise that much at least." He continued.

"I suppose we won't have to worry much about Demons no?" I offered lightly.

"No, but it's bothering me how lightly you are saying that." He said hurriedly.

"You are still you, and you are not Evil Darren."

He chuckled humorlessly.

"Don't lie to yourself Serena. My memories were gone, if I had known any of what I know now, I would have told you to run from me."

"Do you still want to do that?" I asked nervously.

"Would you listen if I did?" He said sharply.

"No."

I hugged him. He flinched slightly.

"Darren for all I know, I'm- my powers stem from evil too. I know you, You are not Evil, not truly."

I went to pull away and he pulled me back hugging me tighter.

"Good because I don't want you to run. And I am unbelievably selfish for that."

There was a knock then which made us pull away from one another.

"Maid service!"

I glanced at the clock 11:30

"We will be right out!" I called.

"You got it. I will be back shortly."

I looked to Darren whom half smiled at me. "Shall we get Damon?"

Darren nodded. "Absolutely."

We headed out quickly grabbing armfuls of our belongings. We headed out to the golden hall and down the painted gold elevator.

"I hope he had a good night with Jane."

"I'm sure he did Serena."

We walked to the car in silence. Darren opened the door for me and we headed back to the hotel.

Darren sang along too Jelly Rolls "Save me." And I sang with him.

We both laughed.

"For the record, you are not a lost cause."

He glanced to me and didn't say anything.

"You aren't."

"I believe, that you believe that Serena."

"You need to believe it too."

"I'm trying Serena."

I quite enjoyed these small moments with Darren, I was anxious to check on Damon just as Darren was.

We pulled up to the hotel shortly, nothing seemed changed. We walked in.

The receptionist greeted us, and we headed up to our room.

Darren went in first.

"God you are alive that's awesome." Damon hollered sarcastically from the couch.

"Hey Damon." I smiled.

"Glad you are as well." Darren said.

"Last I checked getting laid doesn't kill, normally."

"So did X mark the spot?" Darren joked.

Damon chortled. "Yes, she's gone now she has some stuff to do with her family."

"Oh Serena, she left you a book. Said it'll give you some information she found out."

"About what?" I grabbed the book off of the coffee table.

"She didn't specify, but I would guess possibly Serenity. So what did you guys get up too?" Damon asked us.

"Well we slayed a dragon." I said matter of factually.

He almost fell off the couch with how fast he sat up.

"You mean to say my brothers crazy ass theory was actually true? I'm glad you are both unscathed."

"Us too." Darren said dismissively.

"I cannot believe I missed a fight with a dragon! How did you take it down?"

Darren motioned to me. "I roughed it up, but she killed it."

"Powers again hey?" Damon asked.

"Yeah." Darren said blandly.

"I'm not going to lie I am a bit envious of your powers Serena." Damon laughed in amusement.

Before I could reply Darren spoke up.

"Damon, I need to talk to you."

Damon's expression became concerned. "About?"

'It's complicated." Darren's eyes flicked to me. Damn it was he really not going to tell me at all? I hoped he would still tell me, even if it was after he spoke to Damon. I couldn't deny I was slightly hurt he wanted me to leave, but I respected it.

"I-I can give you guys some privacy." I got up from the chair and grabbed the book Jane left.

"Seems I have some reading to do anyways." I smiled lifting the book.

"You don't have to go!" Damon said.

"She does. Stay in the hotel though Serena, please." Darren commanded coldly.

I suppose his guard was up.

"Of course Darren."

With that I picked up my bag and reluctantly left the room. I decided to go down to the cafe. The book looked like a journal and was leather bound and bright red.

When I got to the cafe I settled in the same booth I sat when I first met Damon and Darren, when I spilled the sugar caddy.

Jenny came up. "Jane's hunting, what would you like?"

"Just coffee, maybe some nachos?"

"You got it."

She dropped my coffee off and I opened the book. Swallowing the fear of learning more.

The first page was a newspaper article about Black Rose Ridge. I scanned over it best I could. It was fine print and weathered. "Printed in 1892" The front page had a picture of me and Serenity holding hands, among several other children.

I choked on my coffee briefly. I re-read it to ensure I had read correctly. Serenity was undoubtedly there. We were dressed in complementing outfits with big sunhats.

I read the article best I could.

"We mark this day as the tragedy of the children whom were part of the institute, Dr Kendolf Holster, experimental trails for gifted children went aery this afternoon When he claimed he had found the cure for these children to rid them of their demons which beheld their powers. Guaranteed to return the children to normal, unremarkable children, to return to society and their own homes. Dr Kendolf Holster is solely responsible for great loss of the lives of these children. His own daughters Serena and Serenity Moonshile suffered no different fate. Unable to live with what he had done, he took his life with the same cure two hours later. His wife has since been missing and unaccounted for."

I inhaled sharply shaking my head in disbelief.

"How could I have been alive over 200 years ago? My father was evil? My mother went missing 200 years or more ago yet I just had a phone call from her six and a half months ago??"

I shut the book, shaking and downing my coffee. Jenny came back for a refill. And I thanked her. I opened it again.

I flipped the page. On the next there was a photo pinned of the black book.

"The original occult text."

"This book belonged to the longest standing coven of supposed witchcraft in a millennia, with lineage being traced all the way to present day. The book is said to contain all of the most powerful spells in creation. The book is veiled and only one of the lineage may discover it and share it's contents with whom they choose. The last known sighting of such book was 10,00 B.C It is said it was transferred by the most powerful witch of each century as to keep with the times. It is mentioned in a handful of ancient texts from around the world."

"So I am part of a regal witchcraft bloodline of sort?" I whispered to myself.

The next page she had scribbled a phone number with a note:

"Serena I know this is so much to take in, but I was able to locate the phone number of where they kept your mother in Vancouver. Ask for Dell. He will be able to bring up your mothers file and share it with you. I couldn't because I am not a relative. Good luck Serena -Jane"

I flipped through the rest of the journal but it was blank. I knew Darren told me to stay inside, but surely the parking lot would be sufficient. He would have to understand. I dropped cash on the table and half ran out to the parking lot. I scanned around, when I was sure I was alone I dialed the number Jane left me. A man answered on the fourth ring. I took a deep breath to steady my voice.

"Hello, Dell speaking?"

"Hello Dell, I was told you might have some information on my mother?"

"Ah Serena, I've been expecting your call. Jane is a good friend of mine. Yes I have the file here."

"Your mother Ivory. Was a very ill women. She was brought to us 8 years ago. She was delirious and deranged. Assumed cult activity. She was convinced the world was coming to an end, she claimed she was 500 years old and believed it fully, told us she had powers beyond our imaginations. She claimed she had given birth to girls and a boy 200 years ago that had been reincarnated since the beginning of time. The last 8 years we worked with her she never changed her story or her mind. She took her life one night screaming it was the only way to bring her daughter back to life. We think she was referring to your sister Serenity whom died tragically at the hand of your birth father as a little girl, as did your younger brother. We were unable to talk her down and she was lost to us 6 and a half months ago."

I swallowed tears flooding my face. She did that the night she called me.

"That is everything on her, I'm very sorry for your loss. We would have contacted you sooner, but you are not easy to find Serena. She left her estate to you. Is it alright if I pass your number to a lawyer to read her will?"

"Thank you, yes. Thank you for telling me about her."

"A very solemn case indeed. At least you can rest knowing the truth now." He said.

God if only it were that easy.

"Thank you."

"Yeah you take care now." click.

I fell to my knees in the parking lot and cried. Serenity suddenly appeared.

I scrambled backwards.

"Sorry I didn't mean to frighten you, I left you alone yesterday and well, I can't enter here as you know. What's wrong? I see you fared well against the Dragon."

"I know about mom. But he mentioned a brother? We have a brother?"

"Ah, so you've learned that much at least. Good. Our brother is irrelevant. Forget about him."

"What am I missing? How did we perish 200 years ago, how did mom live 500 years?"

Her regular slightly monotone voice in my head turned acrid.

"She left me and our brother for dead and saved you that's what."

I shook my head. "What do you mean?"

"All those years ago, she put us in that institute, to save us. When she saw our abilities she was afraid, until she recognized and remembered who she was."

"And-who was she?"

"A witch clearly. The codex was hers. She was expertly cheating death for many years. She did the same for you when you died with me and our brother. But she never brought me back, or him!" Her voice was acidic and frightening.

"Why not all of us..if we are all her children?"

She laughed bitterly.

"Why? Because we both exhibited powers. She told me as a little girl I was pure evil. Our brother was unremarkable, he died outside of the trails. She couldn't bring me back with her. But you?" She paused.

"An angel in comparison."

"Serenity, I'm so sorry."

"I don't want your pity sister, nor your apologies. I've been in limbo for centuries. You cannot possibly fathom this prison."

I swallowed. "Then what do you want?"

"For you being the only standing regal bloodline, to bring me back as mom so graciously brought you back. Twice. I may add. I want to stop Cronos just like you. I know you have the book. Mom's spell is veiled in there. You would be able to find it Serena. You could use it on me and we can be together again. I can help you so much more if I am alive."

I hesitated for a moment "Of course Serenity."

"Good. I will be waiting. And just to ensure you keep your word, I know how to summon Crono's successfully trapping him to make the fight easier. I will share it with you the moment you revive me." She vanished.

I exhaled loudly and half ran back into the hotel. I scrambled to the elevator, ignoring the receptionist and a barely nodded to the bellhop in the elevator.

What was I supposed to do? Evil? What was true what wasn't? The elevator seemed to be going at snails pace. I rushed out the second the doors opened.

"Are you alright miss?" The bellhop called down the hall.

"Yes! Sorry!"

I waited until the elevator left and hurried to the guys door. I was about to barge in when I overheard them.

"Are you not understanding me?" Damon's voice.

"It isn't possible Damon!" Darren, heated loud.

"She was my wife in a past life Darren. I can feel her loss. My dream was a memory, I have been getting so many random memories since last night."

"Then you are damn confused!"

"If I can believe you are a God of the underworld, that Demons bow to you why is this unbelievable to you? Why don't you believe me?"

"Because I've had a similar dream Damon, Damn it."

I heard something clash.

"No." Hurt saturated Damon's voice.

"Not the exact same Damon but Serena was-" He paused for a moment. "In it too."

"As your wife?" The pain in Damon's voice was making me ache. I had to tell them. That somehow they might both be right.

"No." Darren said cooly.

I gasped slightly, why had he lied? Our kiss flashed in my mind. With the memory of it, I felt a longing like no other. Did he think he was protecting Damon? I cared for Damon too, just not in the same way and the dream had felt very real to me as well, devastating, just as the one with Darren.

"Then why?" Damon's voice was almost breaking.

"Forget it. I believe you. The Dragon also told me you were a God of Creation as I was one of Destruction. That Cronos held our powers but it held our memories so we should be getting floods of our memories over the next few days."

"With what I have already, I'm not certain I want all of them." Damon said solemnly.

"Yeah, same here. Honestly, it scares the Hell out of me man. God of Destruction..at least you are one of Creation. Figures, I would be the evil one."

"I don't know man the fact that we don't have to worry about Demons anymore is pretty damn amazing. You aren't evil."

Darren chuckled humorlessly. "Right. And you what? Create life?"

"According to you. Which is insane by the way. I have to at least partly believe it, after what happened with you. And the most important thing is you protected my wife."

Darren inhaled so loud I could hear it outside the door.

"Don't call her that. What about Jane?"

"Darren it's all so clear, I just can't wait to see her."

I put my hand on the door, hesitating.

"In a past life, Damon. Past. You can't expect her to be the same as your memory serves. She is Serena, not Emma, Damon." Darren said ice in his tone. "Or Aurelia" he added quieter.

I opened the door then, I couldn't bare to hear anymore. I had to sort this out with them and they needed to know about Serenity. When I opened the door they both turned to me. Damon smiled. Darren stared at me for a long moment then looked away, busying himself in the kitchen. I couldn't deny it stung slightly.

"Hey Serena." Damon greeted me warmly.

"Come here. I missed you guys." He opened his arms.

I walked and hugged him, grateful for the moment of reprieve.

"Wait Serena what's wrong? Why are you shaking?" Damon asked suddenly.

"I know about the dream Damon, I'm sorry I was listening."

Darren whirled around to face me.

"Serena-" He started.

"I have had a dream, reoccurring since I met you guys, I think its high time I shared it with you both."

Darren came to sit near Damon and I in the chair beside the couch.

"What dream?" Damon asked eagerly.

It starts off with me, I can feel the plane drop much too fast. I remember the oxygen masks falling from the compartments above me. There are countless screams. My ears popping painfully, and then the impact. Everything was so cold. I just wanted warmth. Everyone around me is dead... I'm freezing. My head is in agony, the air is too harsh in my lungs..Then strong arms wrap around me. My legs are broken it's impossible to move. Much like what happened a few months ago. My husband, he's telling me he's gonna save us, as he pulls us out of the wreckage, but I know I will die. The voice sounds achingly familiar. I long to see his face. I long for warmth. An image my husband, earlier before the crash, my husband is Darren. We have Two children, young 4 and 5 maybe, getting read to board a plane. Their grandparents maybe? "We will take the kids for the first week and then meet you there. "Enjoy your honeymoon!" I hug the two children tears spilling from my eyes. Then I get a bad feeling. Something's not right. "Maybe we should all go together?..."

"You two haven't gone on Vacation together since before the kids were born, enjoy some one on one time!" Darren nods his head. I lean down, I kiss their heads and tell them they are the best thing that ever happened to me and that I love them with all my heart. Their little hands, every time I have this dream it's as if they were gracing my skin now. I look to my children, and remember when I first gave birth, when I saw them for the first time. True love. The only form of true love I imagine. My first baby as she was laid on my chest. The feeling of overwhelm. The pain. I remembered not understanding why there was still so much pain when they put her on me. I cried as much as the baby did, I was so terrified I wouldn't do good enough and the need I had to give her the world was inexplicably intense. "Your an amazing mother. Never forget that." Darren says as he kisses my forehead and wraps me in his arms. Time passed, Second baby comes along, I'm more prepared, I give birth not knowing the sex of the baby and without any pain medications. The pain is excruciating, I am slipping out of consciousness in between contractions. I remember not being able to speak there was too much pain. Then my son is brought out into the world and I stare in awe. Aurelia, hes perfect. Darren speaks my name. I feel empowered. And beautiful. I cry happily. Then I am back in the wreckage, Darren is crying and holding me as I cry. The plane ablaze beside us. The smell is rancid. Then the indescribable pain of realizing we would never see our children again, or each other.

I stop talking for a minute. Because Darren's expression looked absolutely gutted. His eyes teary and Damon looked horrified.

"Darren was that your dream you mentioned?" Damon asked his voice breaking.

"A part of it, but mine-continues after Aurelia's death. I remember the five days of absolute Hell before I too died." His voice was shaking and he looked at me intensely.

"I can't even imagine. Mine was horrible too but not like that.." Damon said.

I went and wrapped my arms around Darren. He pulled away quickly trembling as he did.

"So you were Aurelia? But Darren-you said she wasn't your wife in your dream?" Damon asked hurt edging his tone.

"I lied." Darren said flatly.

"It-I'm not certain, but I believe so. There is a second part, about you Damon though, me and you."

Damon looked slightly hopeful and Darren looked sick to his stomach.

Then in the second part of the dream, I am in a car, There are soft tunes playing quietly, then there is a sudden whip of the vehicle, crunching metal, shattering windows, so loud in my ears, Blood, metallic and bitter it's all I can taste in my mouth my body crushed..I can't move, my face doesn't feel right. I'm pleading in my head to help me. I hear Damon's voice pleading begging for me to be alive, but I cannot move my mouth to reply. I want to stroke his hair, I want to tell him I'm here but I can't move. His voice too is familiar, safe. I wanted to see his face, I wanted to speak.. what about the baby?...What will happen to our baby?..Then there is a image of us Younger then the first scene. There is blood in a bathroom, I'm crying with Damon's arms wrapped around me, there so much blood. "We will keep trying trying for a baby. We will keep trying. Then we are at a hospital, long needles are being poked into my skin. They hurt. A nurse speaks " As far as fertility treatments go we have given every one under the sun. You may want to look at adoption if this doesn't take, especially after so many miscarries." My husband Damon, the voice so light and loving "Don't worry. I have a good feeling about this one, don't lose hope my darling. We will do this. We can get through this. Emma, we will be parents I promise you. I am angry with his positivism. I feel helpless. Defeated. Cold. "I feel like my body is failing me. It's not doing what it's built to do. I don't understand." I cry helplessly against Damon's chest. "It's not your fault. Shh now" It' later and I am holding a positive test in my hands. My body aching from treatment. My heart swelling, nothing but pure joy. I can't believe it. "You are one in a million." I whisper as I caress my belly. "I can't wait to tell your Daddy." I remember being scared to tell Damon, scared it would fail again. I planned a romantic evening at a diner late to tell him but I can't do it, until we are in the car. Right before it happens. It is all my fault.

I sit back on the chair, breathing shakily.

"Is that like your dream Damon?"

Now it was Damon's turn to be speechless. He nodded.

"It just continues after your death."

"So you were Emma..too?"

"I don't understand." Darren whispered into his hands.

Should I continue? Tell them about Serenity too? Just all at once, everything on the table so we can sort it together? I thought to myself.

"There's more."

Darren sighed loudly. "What else?"

I ran into Serenity in the parking lot.

Darren piped up. "I thought I told you to stay in the building."

"Damon shook his head at Darren. "What did she say?"

"Well I went out because I got a note from Jane with information on my mother and a phone number to call."

Damon nodded. "And?"

I reiterated everything to them. About my mom, her age my age, the book the spell and Serenity telling me to bring her to life that she could help with Cronos.

Darren ran a hand over his face. "Son of a Bitch."

Damon stroked his jaw deep in thought. "Wow."

"What should I do?" I asked them.

"I think you should bring her back." Damon said carefully.

"What are you friggin' insane?!" Darren yelled.

"Darren, we can trap her, we can make sure it's safe but we won't know she's a danger until we bring her back."

"She sounded too adamant. I don't like it." Darren said quickly.

"Yes, but don't you think you would be too? If you were a ghost that long? Because I was only a ghost 24 hours and that made me feel I'd lost my mind." I said.

"She makes a good point Darren. If you and I are indeed Gods, then she can't be much of a threat to us, regardless of if she is on our side of the living or not."

Darren sighed frustrated. "Then I will ensure Kallisa is here, she can kill Serenity, someone outside the three of us that has had no contact with her."

"Only if Serena is okay with that." Damon looked to me.

I remembered how she pawed around in my mind and shuddered slightly, but I also didn't fully trust Serenity, why didn't my mother take us both back? Perhaps Darren was right.

I nodded and breathed deeply. "Okay. Where's the book?"

Chapter 26

BLOOD

"We are blood, divine and infinite, spreading through the cascades of time, would you bleed for me, as I have bled for you, stardust in our veins, would you take my hand, follow me to the ends of time?"

"It's over on the shelf there" Damon pointed.

"How long do we have left Damon? How many items are we short?"

"We have a little less then two weeks only. But with what you guys gathered I mean. Hold on let me see."

He took the journal off of the coffee table and scanned through it. We have everything, except for one last thing."

"Then we need to do this. I have-I feel like it's something to do with her. I feel it has to be it's the missing piece of my past. It seems fitting."

"Serena-are you sure?" Darren asked hesitantly.

"No, but what choice do I have?" I said as I walked over to grab the book, when I got a strange thought suddenly.

"Damon?"

"Yeah, what's wrong?"

I walked over to the couch placing the book on the side table.

"Well, I have a strange theory."

"Go on."

"If you are a God of Creation, what if you can heal? I feel like that is involved in creation. Try to fix your leg."

"How?"

"I'm not sure- will it to be?"

"That's crazy, what makes you think that'll work?" Damon said.

"I don't really know, it's just a thought."

Darren was watching us curiously.

"I'll try."

He hovered his hands over his leg.

"Serena this is just-we don't have time for-" Darren started.

"Shut up Darren, let me focus." Damon said.

He tried for a couple minutes but it didn't work.

"I'm sorry Damon I thought maybe-" I put my hand on his shoulder.

"I know what's it's like to be unable to walk. At least it will heal." I said encouragingly.

"Thanks Serena." Damon leaned into my arms. Darren turned away.

I opened the book palming through it. Darren brought me coffee, as I sipped at it. A few hours went by while I flipped through to no avail finding a spell to bring Serenity back. Damon had fallen asleep and Darren was watching a movie.

"Any luck Serena?" Darren said quietly and walked up to me.

"No."

I was going through the last few pages, I stopped when red ink began to appear on the back of the last blank page.

"Wait-do you see that Darren?"

He looked and shook his head. "No, sorry what am I suppose to be looking at?"

I watched as the spell appeared seemingly from nowhere with ink that resembled blood.

"The spell."

"I don't see it." he said.

"Serenity mentioned it was blood locked."

He inhaled sharply. "Crafty, witches are always so damn crafty."

"At least I know she was telling the truth. We need a blood moon? Do you know when the next one is?"

"Ironically, yes I do, it's 1 week from today."

I sighed. "God that's cutting it close."

Darren reached around me and closed the book.

"You should try to sleep Serena." He spoke softly, and desire flooded me.

"So should you."

I looked up into his eyes, so much despair. I wished I could take it from him, unburden him. I wanted him to get lost in me, I wanted to be lost in him, his kiss, his touch. I needed to calm down.

He sighed deeply. "Honestly I don't think that is possible anymore."

"Do you want to-"

"What- talk about it? No." He inhaled deeply. "I really don't."

I sighed slightly dismayed. "If you change your mind."

"I will come to you, but don't count on me changing my mind."

Something else flashed in his expression. Desire? He looked almost like he might kiss me again. My body flooded with a glimmer of hope that he just might kiss me again. It took everything in me to not close the small space between our lips.

"Thank you Darren." I breathed when his mouth was inches from mine.

His brows furrowed. "For?"

"Saving my life- again."

"Those Demon's won't dare come within 10 feet of you. And if I see that bastard Henry, I will send him into oblivion. I can promise you that Serena." He pulled far away from me as he raised his voice while he spoke.

"Oblivion?"

"It's death for the dead, no hope of being reincarnated as anything more then an insect for eternity. No soul truly wants that. It is reserved for the worst of the worst." Darren stated.

I tried to picture Henry as an insect and it made me shift uncomfortably.

"I'm not sure he deserves that much."

"Really? Because he almost killed you twice and took your ability to walk."

"Well, he is not responsible for the surgery mess up. He is not a good person by any means, but unless he was secretly a serial killer or something."

"He wasn't."

"You know that?" The shock was evident in my tone.

He moved to the chair beside me.

"Yeah, anyone who has ever done anything wrong is catalogued in my mind. Like some sort of sick, twisted blacklist."

"Do you think that'll mean when Damon gets his memories back it might be similar?"

"Possibly."

"I think our next step should be to hunt Osiris. To get you guys back to full power before our showdown with Cronos."

"Yeah. I'm inclined to agree. In the morning though."

He reached his hand towards me hesitated for a moment then tucked my hair behind my ear gently. I took a shaky breath. Wishing I had told him the truth. Wishing I had told him I didn't want him to stay away from me. It's the opposite, I didn't want lines drawn. The situation was so complicated. I felt deeply connected to him. I shook off the thought.

"You need to sleep too Darren."

"I know."

I gave him a brief hug and I moved away from the table and to Damon's bed since he was fast asleep on the couch. Darren walked to his own and we said nothing the rest of the night. I lay awake for what felt like hours pawning over everything. I didn't know where to go from here. I feared bringing Serenity back. I feared our coming fight. I feared our potential failure. I was slowly drifting to sleep when I heard Darren and Damon talking hushed. I stayed completely still and tried to hear them.

"Sorry for waking you Darren."

"It's fine, I wasn't really asleep yet. Do you need something?"

"What do you think about Serena's dream?"

"What do you mean?"

"Do you think she was really Emma and Aurelia? From what you know of reincarnation?"

Darren sighed.

"Yes. She could have been both. Your relationship with Emma and mine with Aurelia were decades apart."

He sucked in a breath. "Well how do we go about this?"

"What the Hell are you talking about?" Darren said enraged suddenly.

"Well if she was at some point both of ours-" Damon trailed off.

"That wound is raw Darren, that memory pains me as much as it did then. Do you feel that way too?" Damon said.

"Why do we have to get into this right now?" Darren said.

"Would you just answer the question brother." Damon demanded.

"Yes it friggin' hurts Damon. It hurts like Hell. Is that what you want to hear? She is not Emma nor Aurelia not anymore she is Serena and neither of us have any sort of "Right" to her. If that is what you are implying." Darren said coldly.

Damon scoffed. "Of course not!"

"Then what exactly are you saying it for in the first place?!" Darren raised his voice.

"I just wanted to know if it still hurt you Darren."

"Damon if you don't need anything then I am going to bed."

"Do you want to keep talking about, you being the God of destruction?"

"I'm not sitting up with you to talk about my damn feelings okay Damon?"

"I can imagine that being very difficult and you can't shoulder that alone Darren! Don't be a dumb ass."

"You have absolutely no idea how this feels for me. What I've done? You are a God of creation. Sounds like a Goddamned dream! So screw you for trying to relate."

"Darren I wasn't comparing you to me. We aren't Good and Evil."

"That's almost exactly what we are brother and I'm done with this conversation tonight Damon."

Damon sighed loudly. "Goodnight then."

"Yeah." I heard Darren plop back into the bed.

They weren't alone in their pain. I grieved the same as I did in the memory even now. I felt both losses equally. But I am not Emma or Aurelia. I was once. But it felt like they were different people, but still parts of myself. As if I had split myself into three separate beings. So I saw the only way to go through this, was to finish what we started and save the world. Everything else had to wait. Everything.

I fell into a fitful sleep and awoke to the sound of breakfast sizzling in a pan and the smell of freshly brewed coffee. I sat up and stretched. Darren was still asleep in his bed. Damon was standing cooking. Wait-standing. I jumped from my bed.

"Damon! You're standing!"

He spun around and gave me the biggest smile I had ever seen and I raced to hug him. He picked me up and spun me once.

"It worked Serena. I healed my leg. It worked. You were right!"

"What of your memories?"

"Those came back in the night as well. It's a lot I want to wait until you and Darren are both up."

Darren groaned. "Well no ones sleeping through all that yelling. Whats the noise about?"

"Darren, Damon's leg- he healed it."

Darren got out of bed quickly then. "Well holy shit."

Damon laughed. "Yeah man."

Darren came and gave Damon a quick hug too, clamping him on the back.

"Glad you are on your feet again man. And you made breakfast. Awesome." Darren helped himself to a plate and I followed behind him.

We all sat at the table and started to eat.

"Serena said she thinks we should go after Osiris today."

Damon glanced to me. "Yeah?"

"Yes. I feel like that is the first step, to get both of your powers back, but the fact that you healed yourself, and Darren sent the white eyed demon away, it seems you both have a fraction of your powers?"

"He bailed from Darren after going one round with you Serena, I think we are safe. We have to ensure he doesn't get the chance to possess Darren again."

Darren shifted uncomfortably. "You mean that bastard could still possess me?"

"We should treat it as a possibility yes." Damon said

"Perfect. That's just friggin' swell." Darren said bitterly.

"It won't happen Darren, we won't let it." I added.

Darren sighed and took a bite of food.

"So how do we bring Osiris here?"

"There is a spell." Damon started.

"What do we need?"

"Nothing we don't already have."

"Well shall we?" I suggested.

He nodded.

Damon stood up and began collecting ingredients.

He pricked Darren's arm with the dagger.

"Ow. What the hell?" Darren said between a forkful of food.

"Need your blood to summon it." He shrugged.

"Would it kill you to give a warning?"

Damon shrugged. "It might. We will never know."

"Jackass."

Damon laughed. "All right."

I finished the rest of my coffee. "Do you think he will be upset or grateful we summon him?"

Darren chortled. "What do you mean? I don't know, I would be pissed if someone summoned me to kill me."

"Osiris worships you. He wants to be you. Admires your powers." I added

"Ah. Well that changes things then." Darren said. "Bastard should be grateful then. Honoured even." Darren added.

"Are we ready?" Damon asked.

"Yeah." Darren said and I nodded.

Damon began to chant something in Latin and the room got very warm. A few things clattered and fell to the floor.

"WHO DARES TO SUMMON ME!"

The voice boomed so loud Damon and I knelt to the ground covering our ears. Darren was unfazed.

A black shadow-like creature appeared, with glowing red eyes. It took up the entirety of the hotel room, blackening the walls.

"I do." Darren said in a voice unfamiliar.

"YOUR MAJESTY. Your memories have returned."

"Yes and I've been informed you are at fault for my powers lacking. For someone who worships me that surely could not be true? As it would be your life you would pay for that mistake."

Darren didn't sound normal, he sounded distorted and frankly terrifying, even Damon shifted uneasily.

"Safeguarding, your majesty."

"Return them to me unless you prefer to Enter oblivion"

"No, anything but that your majesty."

Darren out stretched his hand. "Now."

The shadow latched onto Darren's hand and Darren groaned loudly.

"Darren!"

"I'm fine." He said through a clenched jaw.

The was strange fire-like sparks that radiated from his hand. He groaned louder.

"Your powers are yours to do as you please sire. I do not value what Cronos wants."

Darren looked like he was in excruciating pain. He struggled to speak.

"My brothers too!"

"I would never sour myself with such light. I don't hold your brothers power." it spat.

"You can thank Cronos for that, he holds Damon's power. Stop him and Damon returned to power. And you- Serena you are incomplete, once you are no longer apart you will hone powers stronger then even I ever could."

"Leave us Osiris or I will send you to oblivion. Do not return unless you come to fight alongside us."

Darren said cooly, his strength seemed to come back but his face was twisted in pain.

"Happily, your majesty."

There was a wave of heat and Osiris was gone. Damon rushed to Darren's side.

"Are you alright?!"

Darren fell to his knees then and I rushed to his side as well.

"Darren?"

He groaned again. "I'm fine."

His voice was normal again. Damon helped him up and I backed out of the way.

"Well shit that wasn't even a fight. That was great Darren." Damon joked.

"Yeah." His voice was heavy with sadness.

Damon didn't seem to pick up on it but I did. He seemed to try and shake it off.

"Well what's next?" He tried to appear lighthearted, I wasn't convinced.

"You sure you're okay man? How does it feel to have your powers back?"

"No change really." A lie that I caught and Damon bought.

"Are you sure?" I asked.

He wouldn't meet my eyes. "Yeah."

I had a hard time knowing he was lying to me, and it scared me.

"Wait, what day is it?" I asked suddenly panic gripping me.

"Saturday why?" Damon answered.

"Oh God. Rayne's wedding is today."

I stumbled toward the closet searching for the bridesmaid dress.

"God she's probably just- flipping out."

"We will get you there Serena." Damon said.

"Would you both accompany me? Please?"

"Yeah-you-you want both of us to go with you to the wedding?" Damon said glancing to Darren whom seemed to be struggling to keep upright.

"Of course we will Serena." Darren said.

"Darren if you aren't-"I started but he cut me off.

"No- I'm coming. I want to make sure Henry doesn't make an appearance, if he does. I will deal with it."

"Okay. I will be ready as quickly as I can."

I rushed to the bathroom to start doing my hair. Updo- great. I did my best seated in front of the mirror looping and twirling my hair into an intricate design. When I was through I was actually impressed and I hoped it would be up to her standard. I brushed my makeup on lightly and quickly. I pulled the dress over my body. The white dress she had picked for me looked like a wedding dress on its own. It had a low cut neck, with a train and layered lace and sheer. Rayne had wanted to be unconventional and have us all in white like her. With one last glance to the mirror I rushed out. Damon and Darren were both dressed in the same tuxes as the day I first met them. They both looked absolutely stunning.

Damon offered his arm and I took it.

"You look beautiful as ever Serena."

"Thank you."

Darren opened the door. "Think we will be late?"

"Oh god I hope not. She'll have my head."

Damon laughed and we all walked quickly to the elevators.

Once in the lobby the receptionist wished us a good day and we headed out. Sure enough the second I stepped out of the hotel my phone chimed with 23 missed calls and over 30 text messages all from Rayne. I glanced at the clock on my phone, thankfully it was only noon.

I dialed her and she picked up immediately.

"Serena! Where the Hell are you?! Did you forget? Please tell me you didn't forget. Oh damn never mind. Get your ass here now. You are lucky we have 4 hours to spare. I can't get married without my best friend, so take a break from playing hero and get here."

"Rayne I'm on my way!"

"Better be." click.

"She sounds real pissed. Damon said.

"Rightfully. Weddings are really important to girls usually."

"We will get there in ample time." Darren said.

We loaded into the volvo. I took the back seat and we started towards Rayne's place.

When we pulled up there were at least 80 cars parked all around the road leading up to her property and loading the drive all the way to the main road and along the side of that as well.

"Wow." Damon sucked in a breath.

"Yeah it will be extravagant she would have spared no expense."

"Do you want me to drop you at the door and we will join you in a few minutes once I find a place to park?" Darren asked.

"That would be perfect thank you."

Darren drove up to the door. Damon stepped out to open the door for me.

"Thank you."

"Of course."

"Darren I can go with her, no point in us both parking the car."

He nodded. "Sure."

He drove off and I ascended the steps to their front door. Matt greeted us.

"Thank God Rayne is losing her mind. At least you look ready. Head right up, shes getting her hair and makeup done. Who's this?"

"Oh Damon- sorry this is Damon- his brother Darren will be joining shortly too."

"Aw and here I was thinking you brought a date. Get you a drink Damon?" Matt said.

"Sure."

I nodded to him and headed up the stairs. The set up was intense.

There were so many balloon arches of black and gold it was overwhelming. There were walls of white fairy lights on every open wall. There were white hydrangeas dangling from the roof, so many it gave the impression that the flowers were the ceiling. The entire drawing room and kitchen were covered with food of all different kinds. A massive 4 tier white ruffled looking wedding cake was in a giant glass container by the front door, where the guestbook was.

"I will see you in a bit Serena?" Damon called after me.

"Yes!" I stopped gawking at the decor and raced up to Rayne's room.

Rayne was already dressed and two of her friends that I hadn't met were fussing with her hair. Her dress fit her perfectly it was tightly fitted and had a medium length train. It was very classy and elegant her long hair was twisted up in curls.

She noticed me in the reflection of the mirror she was staring into.

"Oh my God there you are!"

"I'm sorry that I'm late. You look amazing!"

She smiled hugely. "I hope Matt loves it."

"He will probably tear up."

"Hell he better for how much this cost me." She laughed.

I didn't even want to know how much she spent. Me if I ever married that dress would be secondhand or on a very big sale. But Rayne and I were always opposite in money aspects.

"Well since I was late what do you need done?"

She handed me a coiled notebook.

"Check through everything and ensure it is all set up please."

"Sure thing." The notebook was heavy and the notes were on every line. I was shocked when I skimmed it that she had everything and I mean everything written the exact way she wanted it. Tables chairs, florals, decor, food. I exhaled.

"Okay."

"Thank you so much!"

The other two girls waved at me as I headed down the stairs. As I walked down I didn't see Darren standing in the entry and slammed right into him, the notebook clattered to the ground.

"Oh shit I'm sorry! Are you okay?" I said.

Darren laughed slightly.

"Just like the first time eh? Except me instead of Damon."

"Was that Damon, I ran into at her engagement party?"

"Yeah it was. We were both pretty drunk though."

"Ah well. Here we are again." I hesitated beside him then hugged him slightly.

"You look enchanting."

I smiled. "Why thank you."

"Where's my brother at anyhow?"

"Not sure, he went toward the kitchen for a drink and I went to see Rayne."

"And the notebook?" He nodded toward it.

"Ohh a very precise and detailed list of everything that Rayne wanted checked."

He cleared his throat. "Yikes."

"Yeah."

"Well the kitchen is the first part of the checklist."

"Let's go then."

We walked beside each other quite a few paces apart. Matt and Damon were in light conversation at the counter. There was so much food I was astonished.

"Oh my God. How many guests?"

Matt chuckled. "340"

"Holy shit!" Damon exclaimed.

"Well, where's the liquor?" Darren half joked.

"Around in the dining hall. Help yourself."

He clasped his hands together. "Don't mind if I do."

I went to sit with Damon as Darren went to grab a drink. I started scanning through the kitchen stuff.

"Oh wow she gave you her notebook." Matt said.

"Yeah, she sure did."

He laughed and shook his head.

"Well she always knew what she wanted and went for it."

"True enough."

"Can I look?" Damon asked curiously.

"Sure."

He took the notebook from me and read the first page.

"This girl measured the space between the place mats to the centimetre."

"Seems like it." I laughed.

Damon shook his head slightly.

"What about you Serena? You crazy like this? What's your dream wedding?"

Matt looked over and raised his eyebrows waiting on my reply.

Darren walked in holding a glass of I guessed whisky and coke.

"My dream wedding?"

Damon nodded and Darren glanced to Damon.

"Well to be perfectly honest I never thought much on it. I like the idea of a simple gathering, somewhere with natural floral and trees, outside, fall or summer, home cooked foods, unconventional in the aspect of guests attire. Basically just whatever you loved but never got to wear or only wore once. I wouldn't be worried about being out-shined. I think including the guests in the magic of dressing that fancy would be perfect. My dress I would buy secondhand or for very low, or buy a dress that's not a "Wedding" dress. It would have to be a ball gown I guess that's my only real want. The wedding doesn't matter so much, all I would want is to be 100 percent certain the person I was marrying was the one for me."

I glanced to Damon whom looked surprised and then to Darren whom looked enthralled. Matt let out a scoff.

"Well damn you're an easy please."

I laughed. "What? Was this not the wedding you dreamed of?"

"No, but it is the wedding she dreamed of and that's all that matters to me. Like you said, it's the person, and my person is Rayne." Matt said.

"I love how much you two love each other. I hope to one day find a love like that myself."

I kept my eyes downcast too nervous to glance to either of the guys.

"Well you'll find one you are still relatively young." Matt replied.

"Pfft. You're younger than me! You both are by a lot!"

Damon laughed slightly and Darren snickered. They knew how old I really was and "a lot" Didn't even begin to cover it. I still couldn't believe it myself. Mind you in comparison to the guys being ancient Gods I was young.

Matt shrugged. "We can't all be that lucky."

"Well I'd better get through this list for Rayne."

"Have fun." Matt teased.

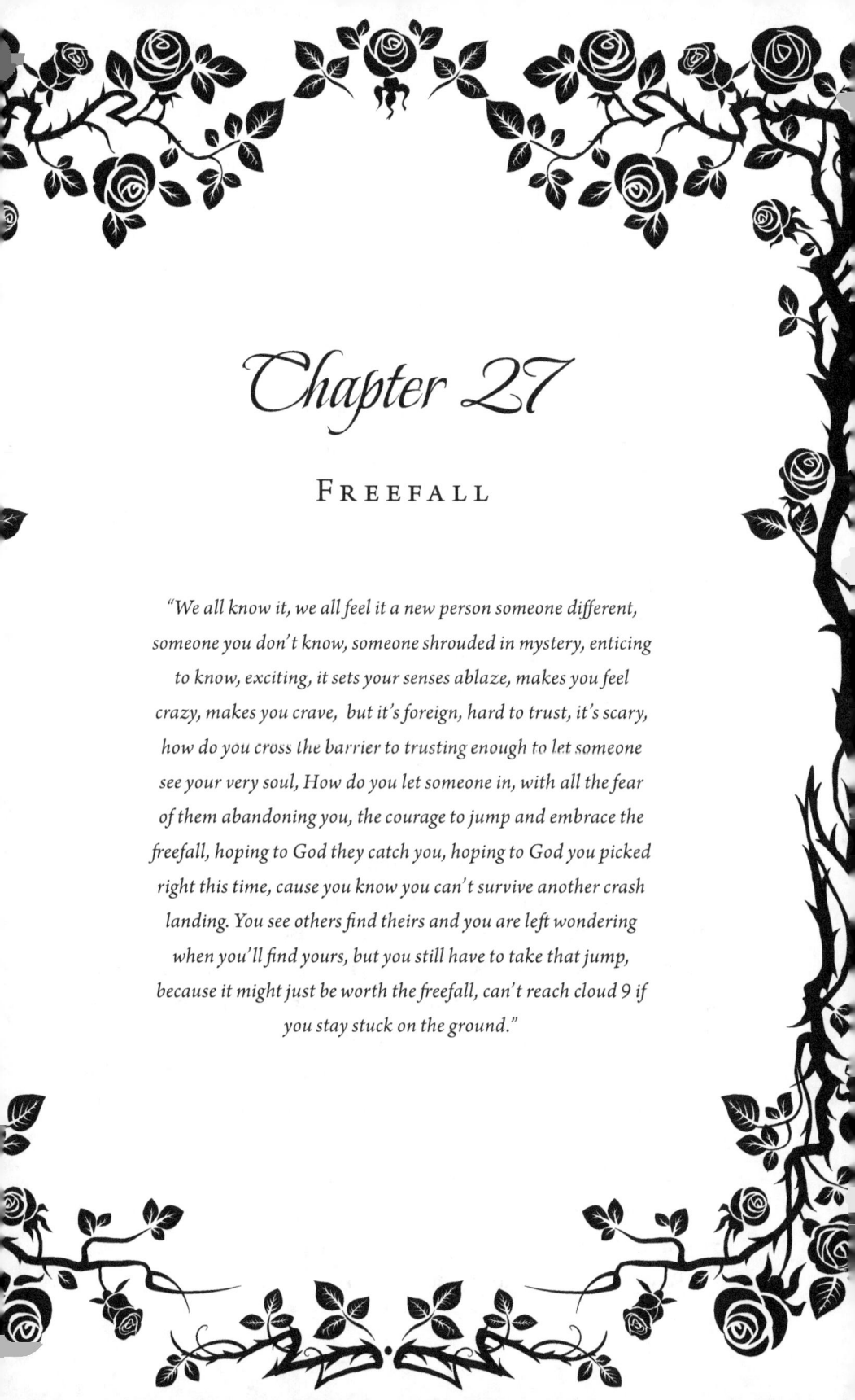

Chapter 27

FREEFALL

"We all know it, we all feel it a new person someone different, someone you don't know, someone shrouded in mystery, enticing to know, exciting, it sets your senses ablaze, makes you feel crazy, makes you crave, but it's foreign, hard to trust, it's scary, how do you cross the barrier to trusting enough to let someone see your very soul, How do you let someone in, with all the fear of them abandoning you, the courage to jump and embrace the freefall, hoping to God they catch you, hoping to God you picked right this time, cause you know you can't survive another crash landing. You see others find theirs and you are left wondering when you'll find yours, but you still have to take that jump, because it might just be worth the freefall, can't reach cloud 9 if you stay stuck on the ground."

It took me a couple solid hours to get though her mountain of notes. But I made it through and only had to fix one floral. Damon, Darren and Matt were conversing in the kitchen still and I could hear Rayne and the girls upstairs. I walked back up there to return the notebook. They were just finally finishing her hair. Which looked well- perfect.

"So?" She asked anxiously.

"All but one rogue flower, I got the best of him though."

She wrapped her arms around me "Thank you."

"Well you still have about 45 until the ceremony."

"More like 5. Limo is outside. Can you get the guys to go into the first and we will climb into the second?"

"Yes! On it."

I went downstairs and let them know to go into the limo. Damon walked past me and lifted my hand to kiss it.

"Until we meet again" He joked.

Darren was already quite drunk. He looked and me and kissed my head. Making an exaggerated "Mwuaah" Sound.

"See you."

I laughed. "Bye Darren."

Matt gave me a strange look and I just shrugged. It didn't feel weird to me, it felt playful and fun, but perhaps it looked quite strange. I'd better keep peoples attentions elsewhere.

I went upstairs after watching them depart and waving to join Rayne and her other bridesmaids. We all came down the stairs they held her train and I held her bouquet and veil. We all piled into the limousine and once we were seated we were off. The dark haired bridesmaid popped champagne carefully avoiding Rayne and her dress.

"Want?" She offered. I shook my head no.

"Serena. I know you don't drink but would you have a glass just to toast me tonight please? I promise you'll be fine!"

"Rayne I haven't had liqueur in years."

"Please?"

I hesitated. The girl put the bubbling glass of sin my hand. Would I be okay? I mean the world might end, we could fail.

Rayne shook her head and extended her hand for the glass.

"Never mind Serena sorry, it's not a big deal I'm getting carried away. I don't want to force you."

"No, it's fine. Cheers to you and Matt may you live happily ever after!" I drank the entire glass in a few sips the two maids cheered and drank theirs and Rayne drank hers.

"I glanced at the two girls that I hadn't paid much mind too. One had long dark hair and light skin and the other had ringlet auburn curls with very tanned skin. Both model like. I glanced and looked harder at their eyes. The girl with ringlets had dark brown eyes and the dark haired girl that poured the glasses had very dark brown. I could already feel the liquor kicking in. God I had forgotten how this felt.

"You good girl?" Rayne asked looking at me.

I took a steadying breath. "Yeah, no more for me."

"Of course not." She smiled.

They all chatted and my vision started to swim.

"Rayne I'm not, I'm not feeling too good. I gripped her arm suddenly.

"Serena, what's wrong?"

"I-I somethings not."

But the strange feeling was gone.

"Serena?"

"Sorry. I'm fine."

She looked concerned but then the maid that served me the drink distracted her.

I felt hazy but perhaps it was just because it had been so long. I was also upset with myself for giving in and having a drink.

We pulled up to a church on the outskirts of Edmonton. We all piled out helping Rayne out last.

We walked along the legitimate red carpet that was laid out. All of us entered before Rayne. I was first through and it was beautiful inside. She kept it simple in here. Just white flowers and petals strewn across the carpet. Matt was waiting happily at the alter. It wasn't super full in here just both of their immediate families.

I positioned myself on her side of the alter. The other two maids came up and I took the opportunity to try and spot the Damon and Darren. It only took a couple minutes of scanning and I spotted them near the back. Both of them smiled to me when I caught their eye. The bridal march came on and Rayne walked down. I glanced to Matt whom teared up slightly. Rayne was holding back tears and he immediately told her that she was the most beautiful girl in the world and how much he loved her. I started to feel really odd again. Just drunk I guess. I zoned out then when I came back they were kissing and the families were applauding. Strange, I couldn't remember them saying anything. I shook my head slightly. Then I spaced out again. This time when I came too we were already back at Raynes house at the reception. Rayne was hugging me.

"Thank you for such a beautiful speech Serena. I love you lots girl."

"Speech? Rayne, how long-when did we get back here?"

She looked puzzled. "Two hours?"

The horror must have been obvious on my face.

"Have I talked with anyone?"

"No you've been quiet outside of the speech you gave and toast you gave to me and Matt, which was lovely. Don't worry. You haven't done anything scary or embarrassing. I didn't even hear you say much to the guys. I think you might be blacking out."

"From one drink?"

She shrugged. "It's possible it has been a long time, but I will keep my eye on you. Let the guys know you are losing time patches. I'm sure they can help."

"God I'm sorry Rayne."

"It's okay, it's Marie's fault. She pressured you after you said no. I didn't help either, I'm sorry. I will talk to her Serena, just try to sober up. I'm here if you need anything."

"Alright. Well thank you."

"Stay outta trouble!"

I laughed slightly. I started palming through people trying to find Damon or Darren or both. People were starting to blur together. I bumped into Allan as my vision started swimming.

"Serena, you good?"

I half fell and he caught me.

"I- I don't, too much to drink I guess."

He smiled unfriendly. Unsettling. Something was wrong. He looked a little off, but maybe it was just because I was intoxicated.

"Allan- what's happening?"

"Come with me." It didn't sound much like Allan's voice either.

"Come with you where?" My words slurred slightly and it was hard to focus on his voice. Then he laughed slightly and pressed a cloth into my face I gasped and tried to struggle away but the drug worked quickly and effectively, within seconds I couldn't move my arms or legs and was dead weight in his arms. It burned to breathe and my breaths were panicked and shallow. I felt him drag me away, I frantically looked around but everyone was too engrossed in their mingling to notice Allan take me outside. I wished I could scream, move, anything. Tears were streaming down my face and I could merely whimper. I was absolutely petrified. Blackness crept my vision and the last thing I saw was a trunk opening as I was dropped roughly into it.

* * *

When I came too, my head was pounding and my mouth was as dry as it would be if you put cinnamon directly on it. My wrists were bound tightly as were my ankles. I was tied to a cold metal chair in a warehouse that smelled strongly of mildew. I tried unsuccessfully to free my hands. There was no light in here the only light was the midday sun coming through the small window about 9 feet above me. I seemed to be alone for the moment. I had no idea how long I was out or where I was. I was still in my bridesmaids dress which was now ripped and dirty. Then I remembered being drugged and Allan taking me away. I couldn't believe Allan would do this. I had known the guy as long as I knew Matt, which was going on 7 years. We had only ever had pleasant interactions. Rayne had tried to set me up with him about 6 years ago before Henry but then found out he had a preference for men. We only ever small talked we never have had a significant conversation. Friends by association because while I was around Rayne, Allan was around Matt. I had no idea he was capable of this though and I felt sick to my stomach that someone like this had been in and around Rayne and I for years. I attempted to summon my abilities to no avail. Why couldn't I summon them on a whim by now? I looked around the room there was a metal briefcase by a rusted metal table. There were a few knives and such laid out on said table. I swallowed hard.

"Serenity."

I tried to summon her hoping she would answer the call, to my dismay she didn't show.

I had no idea what to do. I rubbed my wrists back and forth but as I did they seemed to get tighter and I yelped. I tried to move the chair by rocking my body, after a few tries it screeched loudly forward an inch.

"Oh god, someones bound to have heard that." I whispered to myself.

I instead focused on my feet, I attempted to slid my shoes off using the ground and my other foot.

"Maybe if I wiggle them enough I will get the shoes off then the rope will be looser and I can maybe at least get my feet free.

I could hear footsteps in the distance and my heartbeat quickened.

I struggled more fiercely with my feet and I was able to slid my left foot out of my shoe. The rope rubbed and burned my bare skin but with that foot I was able to get my other shoe off. I kept my shoes over my feet enough so I hoped they would appear untouched. I rubbed my feet against one another, enough room I was certain to get them out of the bindings. Before I could do anything else Allan entered eyes as black as coal.

"Well mornin sunshine."

"What the hell are you Allan?" I spat.

"Mmm isn't it obvious sweetpea?" His eyes flashed red instead.

I ran back in my head, second tier, fire abilities.

"How long?"

"Oh as long as I can remember really."

"This whole time? What's this got to do with Rayne and Matt?"

He tsked. "A lot of questions you seem to have tonight Serena. Since tonight will be the last night you are breathing I would say it is simply a waste to tell you."

He inched towards my face so close, I could smell his breath which smelled of tar.

"But I do so love when they squirm don't you Henry?"

I choked in a sob momentarily, I was very close to crying and begging for my life.

I watched trembling as Henry entered then. His eyes still black.

"Make her beg first Allan."

"Oh this bitch will not only beg she will squeal. She's already crying."

I turned my face away ashamed that I was in fact crying. I tried desperately to swallow it back.

Allan came up and punched my jaw.

"You'll look at me when I'm talking to you." He spat.

My jaw was burning and aching from the impact.

"What do you want from me?" I turned and faced his eyes. My voice sounded small and pathetic.

"I want you to stop your pursuit to stop Cronos. He will make the world a better place. You and those Damn Elderwood brothers alike." Allan continued.

"I will never stop fighting for humanity. I will never support or allow the human race to be destroyed. Cronos perfect world is a world ripped of humans of life in general. Not just humans, plants animals, everything."

"Not us." Henry added. "Just all useless fragile life."

I took a breath and found my confidence.

"You really think he won't destroy you Henry? Or any other demons for that matter. Did Cronos tell you that directly? I'm curious."

Henry looked baffled. I continued.

"I'm going to take that as a no, in fact I'm willing to bet anything you've never even met him. Spoke to him. Yet you so blindingly follow the misguided belief that he will spare you because you are a demon. What about you Allan? Hmm? You speak to him. You best buds?"

"Shut her up Henry." Allan said

"Gladly. I killed you once bitch, it's easy enough to do again."

He started towards me with a knife. I immediately removed my shoes slipping my feet from the binding I stood up and whirled around at him using the chair to knock him back. He fell clattering into a metal shelf that fell on top of him. I caught him off guard and the knife clattered to the floor below me. I then swung at Allan whom went flying sideways. With this impact I felt my wrist snap. I screamed but it let my hands free from the chair. I knelt down with my unbroken wrist and grabbed the knife Henry had. Allan was closer and I started towards him.

He groaned getting up. "That won't do anything to me, stupid girl."

I sliced my arm open, spilling blood over the floor and then stabbed the knife into Allan's foot, holding in him place briefly. I used my blood and drew the same sigil that plagued my apartment walls. I don't know why or how I knew what it would do but it expelled both Allan and Henry in anguished screams. I was alone in the room now. I cradled my wrist, I grabbed the knife arming myself as I limped out of the room hoping to find a way out. The sigil was from the occult magic book I had found the first day I got tangled up in all this.

I tore the bottom off my dress off wrapping it tightly against my still bleeding arm and put my shoes back on.

There were two sets of muddied footprints.

"Must be the way out." I whispered.

Glancing around the warehouse was mostly empty it was just a lot of abandoned shelving. The footprints followed to the back of the building. I followed them staying alert for signs of anyone else. The Demons would be able to return in 3 hours. That gave me ample time to find a way out of here. The spells in that book were in my mind now, so many were flooding it was hard to keep up, It was like they were written on the inside of my skull. I came to a door that resembled a metal garage. It was jarred. I walked up and shimmied through the small space in the bottom. The sunlight hurt my eyes as I looked around. I was in an old grain shack, nothing but farmers fields and no vehicles or road that I could see. The sun was high in the sky, indicating it was in fact mid day. I had no belongings with me, so I began to trek through the field. Hoping I could find a road before nightfall. You never really think about how terrifying it actually is to be lost without a phone, until it happens to you. I never really thought I would be too bothered, I was wrong. I took a steadying breath and walked in the direction I hoped was north, I couldn't be certain. I also wasn't sure how long I had been knocked out. If I was drugged at Rayne's mixed with the booze, then the chloroform it might be easily 12 hours since I was taken. I could be anywhere. The thought made me shake with fear.

"Serenity" I tried again under my breath.

I waited a few minutes but she didn't show. I kept walking. I was so thirsty, my mouth had never felt so dry and it was making me dry heave. I was paused every few feet to attempt to vomit and couldn't. My feet ached. My wrist dangled useless at my side. My homemade bandage for my cut was stained deep scarlet. My head was throbbing. I reached my right hand to the top of my head and when I pulled it away there was blood on my fingers. Damn it. If I was struck with something I could be out even longer. I needed water, I could tell by how my body felt that I wouldn't last long without it. I would soon collapse, but as much as I willed it I couldn't force my feet to move any faster then they already were. I tried to remember. Rayne said her name was Marie. I was sure she put something in my drink. Being in the medical field I had seen girls affected by Rohiponal. Did Rayne drug me on purpose? No. She couldn't of. She did say to Marie not to pressure me that I didn't need to drink, but that could have been staged. I tried to remember if Marie's eyes were black, but in my mind they never were, maybe contacts? How long had Allan been a demon? Always? How long had him and Henry been coercing with one another? Could it have been going on all this time? Did they know who my mom was? What she was, what I am? Was this planned? I swallowed. Were Rayne and Matt in on it? Did they know all along? Was this some scheme to get to me? Is everything I think I know a lie? Why wasn't Serenity coming? If she did care about me, whats even more strange is even if she didn't she knows I will bring her back to life, so why not rescue the person that can do the one thing you want most? The questions swarmed my mind like a nest of angry wasps. I kept walking. My breath was heavy and my eyes were burning. The sun was setting now, I had seen nothing but field, no road, no signs, no buildings. Nothing. As the day began to fold into night I came to believe I may very well die here, yet again failing at stopping Cronos. I don't think I could be lucky enough to come back again. This was my last shot. I was struggling to the point where I felt I needed to sit down but I feared that if I did, I would not have enough strength to get back up. So I pushed until I wanted to cry because of the exhaustion. I pushed and pushed. After another 10 minutes of agonizing walking as dusk neared it's end. I saw a road but I couldn't move anymore my body refused. I collapsed in the grass maybe 30 feet from the road. Not close enough to flag a car. Perhaps after a little rest. My body yearned to sleep. I tried one last time.

"Serenity, please. Help." I croaked.

Before I closed my eyes Serenity appeared at the edge of the road. Relief wasn't the right word, but I rejoiced that maybe just maybe she could help me. She flitted in and out of my perception.

"Connection is weak, I see you. You are out of my range. I will get someone to you. Don't die. Don't you dare die, do you hear me sister?"

"Yes" I said weakly.

I struggled with all my might to keep my eyes open. But soon I succumbed to the peace of sleep.

* * *

An engine revved nearby. My eyes opened slightly. I was unsure how long I had been asleep. It was black out now. But I could see the volvo. I hoped I wasn't hallucinating. Thank God they found me. I still couldn't summon enough strength to move from the ground. Serenity Flitted to the roadside I could see her in the glow of the headlights. She pointed towards me and I saw two figures bee-lining it into the darkness toward me using their phones as flashlights.

"Serena!?" Damon's voice. I had never heard it so panicked.

"Serena!" Darren's voice. Commanding and worried.

I couldn't move my mouth to speak. My eyes were threatening to close. I counted my pulse. Slow, too slow.

"Serena! Damn it!" Darren, angry but closer.

"Serena Please!" Damon. Anguished. Sounded closer.

I still couldn't speak.

Then Damon came into view. And my eyes slipped shut again. I would live. I had to.

"Darren! Here! Help me!"

I opened slightly enough to see Darren's phone flashlight coming closer.

"Damon-" I barely whispered.

"Shh. Shh Serena just hold on. I got you. I got you love." He picked me up and again I was back into the quiet bliss of sleep.

My eyes fluttered open again and I looked up to Damon's terrified face. I seemed to be laying on his lap.

"Serena! Darren she's conscious." I realized after a second we were in the volvo still. Darren must be driving.

"Serena can you hear me?" Damon asked stroking my hair.

"Serena stay with us!" Darren hollered.

"Damon- don't let me die."

His eyes filled with tears. "I won't Serena, not again."

I began to try and close my eyes

"Damon! For God sake, keep her awake!"

"I'm trying!" He yelled back.

"Serena, keep your eyes open, just keep them open hon." Damon said calmly and quickly.

I tried to oblige but it was so hard, it was like weights were on my eyelids. It burned to try and keep them open.

"Darren she-how far are we?!"

"She what!?"

"HOW FAR!"

"5 minutes. Damon tell me what the Hell is happening!"

"Make it two."

I felt the car lurch forward.

"Serena you still awake?"

"Mmm" Was all I could say.

"Okay, good good keep with me." Damon said.

We pulled up to the hotel. I was confused, why not a hospital?

"Damon are you sure that this is the right thing to do! We don't have the time to fool around!"

"Yes. I'm sure Darren."

Darren hit the steering wheel in anger. "Get her out then."

"Come on, I'm gonna carry you okay?"

"Mhm"

Darren rushed ahead and Damon followed carrying me in his arms right tight behind Darren. I wished I had the energy to ask what was wrong, I was just grateful I was alive. It was hard to dwell on much else. We entered through the back unnoticed until the elevator where the bellhop did not ask questions. We got to the room in what felt like seconds and Damon laid me on his bed.

"Damon her head. Her head first please." Darren begged.

Darren started rushing about the kitchen gathering supplies.

Damon lay his hands over my head. He closed his eyes and started chanting something under his breath that I didn't understand. Darren came up dropping towels and a bowl of what looked like water. My eyes grazed slowly over him. I took many slow blinks to try and keep myself awake but to also ease the burning in them. Darren was pouring sweat and his eyes were rimmed dark red. He looked as though he hadn't slept in days.

"Damon. NOW."

"I'm concentrating!"

As Damon finished what he was saying in the unfamiliar language there was a warm pulsating feeling that began at the base of my skull and worked it's way upwards. Encasing my head in a pulsing light of warmth. I exhaled slowly.

"It's working Damon." Disbelief in Darren's tone.

He inhaled sharply. "Yeah."

The minute he pulled his hands away I felt relief. My mouth was still so dry.

"Water." I choked out.

Damon scrambled up and grabbed a bottled water from the fridge opening it for me and putting it to my mouth. I took the bottle with shaking hands. I drank the whole thing in a few chugs.

"More." I barely whispered. Darren got this one this time and Damon started hovering his hands over my wrist. The was the warm pulsing then, pain. I screamed as loud as I could manage through my exhaustion. The pain was bewildering. I felt my bones crack and shift back into place.

"God I'm sorry Serena hang on." Damon said as he kept healing me.

Darren half wrapped me in his arms.

"I know it hurts, it'll pass." Darren whispered soothingly.

He brought the second bottle of water to my mouth and I drank it greedily.

"Where else does it hurt Serena?" Damon asked as my bones shifted one last time and clicked into place. I was able to move my wrist again. Unbroken.

Darren pushed my sleeve up. "There her arm, deep cut."

Damon hovered his hands over me again and I grimaced against Darren's grip. I could feel the very fibres of my skin inching back together bit by bit.

"It's working Damon." Darren kept me tight in his arms.

He stopped chanting as the last of my broken skin pushed together. A warm tingling throughout.

"Serena can you talk?" Damon asked with concern drenched in his face.

"How-how did you do that? I thought your powers-?"

Darren wrapped me tightly one last time then let me go.

"We are just grateful it worked right Damon?"

"Beyond." Damon said and hugged me.

"Thank you- I need more water, my mouth is so dry please."

Damon got up to get it.

"I let Rayne and Matt know we found you. She'll probably want a phone call when you are up for it, but don't worry she knows you are alright." He said as he walked to the fridge.

Well that was good at least. I didn't have the energy to talk to her right now but I'm glad she had the peace of mind. God I did get taken on her wedding day too of all days. Darren's voice cut through my internal monologue.

"What happened Serena? You've been missing for three damn days!" Darren asked sounded more worried then angry.

Damon handed me the water then.

I drank it before I replied.

"Got taken by Allan at the party."

Rage flashed across Darren's features. Damon looked confused.

"Matt's bestie?" Damon asked.

"Yeah, hes a demon, he was paired with Henry and they had me in a warehouse, I don't know how long or how far I walked. But did you say 3 days?"

Darren nodded stiffly.

"Its good I walked long enough to get in touch with Serenity because I'm not sure you guys would have found me in time otherwise. I was monitoring my vitals best I could."

"Well you are safe now." Damon reassured sweetness in his voice.

"I'll kill that son of a bitch." Darren spat and stood up.

Damon raised his hand to settle Darren.

"Darren hold on. Guns blazing might not be the best approach."

"Well you let me know when you are done talking about what the Hell you want to do while I actually go out and do something about it." He shrugged Damon off and stormed out faster then I could formulate words.

"Damon go stop him please." I said urgently.

Damon took his arms off of me and followed out.

I heard frustrated chatter. Then Damon walked back in without Darren.

"He's determined." He said throwing his arms up.

I scrambled upwards. "And that determination is going to get him killed." I grabbed my bag and coat at the door.

"Serena you need rest." Damon protested. "I will go after him he just needs to cool off."

"I don't care right now. We need to fight together or not at all. I would do the same thing if you stormed out."

I moved to the door and Damon sighed but did not protest further.

"Serena-" He held up the keys to the volvo.

"He can't get far, snagged these off of him. Go sleep."

I dropped my bag. "Nice one." I laughed slightly.

He shrugged. "I tried, reasoning never works on him when hes like this."

"Do you think he will come back up when he realizes?"

Damon shook his head. "Too riled up he would probably go to the bar."

"Please for the love of everything just sleep Serena. We are all okay. We will figure it out tomorrow. You are safe."

He hugged me tightly and suddenly I felt quite emotional and pulled back from his arms. He studied my eyes for a moment. Could he tell? God I hoped not.

"Please don't realize I am crying, I will fall apart." I silently prayed in my head.

He looked like he was about to say something further.

"I will go sleep Damon." My voice was starting to betray my breakdown. Thankfully he didn't seem to pick up on it.

"About time." He laughed as he settled on the couch while I laid down on his bed. Tears flowed silently and I muffled them in the pillow. Three days. It felt like I was gone for a few hours. That meant the blood moon was tomorrow and I would need to release Serenity. I was grabbed by a sudden wave of nausea and I sat up not realizing I must've slept because Damon was asleep on the couch. It seemed

Darren wasn't home yet. I pulled myself to the side of the bed and got out. I wondered what time it was. I was worried about Darren not being back yet.

"You awake?"

I jumped slightly at Damon's sleepy voice.

"Yeah- I was going to maybe go check on Darren."

"He will be fine."

He sat up and walked to the end of the bed wrapping his arms around me, something felt off.

"Damon what's wrong?"

"Nothing Emma. I can't wait to meet our baby."

I swallowed hard. "Damon, it's Serena."

He hugged me tighter. "What a beautiful name."

"Damon stop!" I shoved him slightly and he let go of me shaking his head. His eyes looked glazed. I realized after watching his movements he wasn't actually awake.

He stood a breath away from me and brought his lips to mine. It was soft and brief. It did not feel full of longing and need like Darren's had. It felt like it was brimming with familiarity and genuine sweetness.

"I love you so much Emma." He mumbled as he laid back onto the couch.

I put my fingers to my lips for a second and raced out of the room, forgetting to lock the door behind me. I ran down the back stairs panting as I went. I hadn't changed, I was still in a black nightdress. I just kept going forward. Overcome by everything. I wound up at the entrance to the bar, hearing Darren's magnetic voice gloss delicately over lyrics that I didn't recognize. I rushed in and Darren glanced up as he was singing and met my eyes. A look of panic washed over his features. He stopped mid song and got of the stage. The was a clamour of confused voices but he didn't react to them.

"Serena what's wrong? Is Damon okay?" His voice was slightly off and he smelled lightly of whisky. His eyes searched over my face frantically.

"Damon's fine." I said unsteadily.

"Then what, Serena?" He put his hand to my cheek brushing my hair out of my face.

"What is it?" He said softer.

"Can we go somewhere?" I whispered the words tumbling out before I had the chance to think much on it.

He searched my face a moment and nodded. Ignoring everyone in the background telling him to complete his set.

I led him out of the bar.

"We can't go anywhere Damon jacked my keys."

"I'll drive then."

"What about Damon?"

"Your brother is okay hes safe and asleep upstairs. I won't take us far I promise."

Darren nodded and led the way. We walked out.

"Serena would you just tell me what's going on please."

"I will." I turned to him, once we were outside.

"Damon kissed me." I blurted.

Darren cleared his throat for a second. "And, you didn't want him too?"

I shook my head. "He thought I was Emma, he was sleepwalking and called me Emma, talked about our baby and I-"

Darren sighed. "That dream has really taken a toll on him it would seem."

I shook my head again. "Darren he kissed me."

"Yes, I heard you the first time, and? Do you not believe you were perhaps Emma once upon a time?" his tone was noticeably irritated by now.

"Why the Hell are you even telling me this anyway?" There was a hurt edge to his voice.

"Because you and I kissed too."

Darren's eyes clouded over. "I remember. But I told you it was a mistake. I thought I made it very damn clear Serena."

Snow started to fall around us, snow in May. My chest was burning and I felt sick to my stomach. He turned away from me angerly.

"Darren look at me. For Gods sake would you just listen for a second?"

I touched his shoulder lightly. He whirled back to look at me.

"What do you want me to say? You are your own person. What? Do you want my permission or something?"

"No, Darren." I swallowed cause I was worried I would cry.

"Then what?" he practically growled.

"Darren I don't know if I was or wasn't Emma if I was or wasn't Aurelia. I don't know."

He nodded. "I know look- I'm sorry I'm so drunk and this apocalypse everything is looming closer and closer and it feels like we are so Goddamn far from winning this. We can't fail."

"I know that it is heavy and it is unbearable but Darren we will succeed. I have nothing but faith in us. We will not fail."

"You don't know that for sure."

I grabbed his hands gently and firmly in my own.

"We will not fail, it is not all your own burden to bare Darren. We are all here to bare that cross with you. To walk through that fire with you."

"I know-" He said quietly.

"Right now, who I am is Serena. I'm not Emma, I'm not Aurelia. And Darren I brought you out here to tell you I fucking love you." My voice choked out as I said it.

The words hung in the air too long and I wished I could grab them back. The realization of what I had just come to terms with and spoken out loud. I had never understood silence to be so loud.

The strange mid spring snowfall whipped and twirled, melting as it touched the pavement around us. The silence was deafening.

"You what.." His eyes welled slightly.

He shook his head. "You don't."

"I do." I was still holding his hands in mine.

He kept shaking his head so I let go of his hands. They fell at his side then I put mine around his neck and hovered my lips near his.

"Serena-" He whispered in protest.

"I love you."

I was a breath away from his lips now, he leaned in slightly. I was about to close my eyes when from the corner of my eye I saw Serenity hovering behind Darren. I gasped slightly because she startled me. Before I could speak there was a glint off of a blade in the streetlight as she stabbed Darren's side.

"Ah!" Darren cried out pulling back from me grasping at his now bleeding side.

"Darren!" I yelled.

She grabbed Darren before I could.

"Revive me and I might let him live. I just had to see which brother you favoured to ensure I had the proper leverage."

"You friggin' bitch let me go!"

Darren struggled and swung at her but his punch went straight through her face. He struggled to get out of her grip as he couldn't grab onto her.

"Serenity let him go! I trusted you damnit!" I howled.

She laughed an unholy sound. "That was your first mistake."

I charged toward her to pull Darren back to me but she flitted from view and to my shock took Darren with her.

"No!" I screamed as I began to hyperventilate.

I turned from the parking lot and raced back to the hotel to get Damon. I couldn't lose him. What a fool I had been. I was bringing us out here unprotected, why had I trusted Serenity in the first place? I was spiralling in self pity knowing it would do nothing to help

Darren right now. I ran up the stairs ignoring everyone that said hi to me on the way there and I barrelled into the hotel room.

Damon scrambled off the couch.

"Serena, what are you doing? What's wrong?"

"It's Darren." My voice trembled as I was gasping for air.

"Serenity- she took him!"

Chapter 28

LEVEL

"What level would you go for someone you love, would you pick up their call at 3am, would you let them come in the middle of the night if they needed, would you be their peace, their safety, would you never go a day without telling them how much you love them, would you never stop going on dates and being excited about each other, would you be devoted, would you be an unwavering support, could you listen to them ramble about anything then just pull them close, make them feel safe with you no matter what emotion is plaguing them at that moment, would you stay for better and for worse, would you never stop being playful, laughing together, holding each other, could you love them at their best and even more at their worst, would you travel to Hell and back for them?"

As I finished explaining. Damon was running his hand anxiously over his jaw. I neglected to tell him much outside of what happened. I left out the part of me admitting my feelings for Darren.

"How bad was the wound?"

I thought back to it and grimaced.

"It was embedded in his side. Not fatal but I couldn't tell what she hit. They went so fast Damon."

"We need to get my brother back. When is the blood moon?"

"Tomorrow. Well it's probably past midnight so we have 24 hours before I can preform that spell. Do you think it's wise to bring her back?" I asked.

"She hasn't left us a choice, I won't leave Darren's life in her hands."

I nodded. His voice was frantic. I took a steadying breath.

"We will get him back Damon."

I put my hand on his shoulder and he put his hand over mine and nodded. Tears in his eyes. He swiped his opposite hand over them quickly. I pretended I hadn't noticed.

"What do you need for the spell?"

I let go of his shoulder and walked over to grab the book off of the shelf. Its familiar black cover and weight. I opened to the page I flagged with a pressed flower. I scanned over the ingredients. My heart was hammering so hard in my chest each beat it hurt. Darren could not die. I could not lose either of them.

"It's simple enough." I said.

Damon came up. "May I?"

I put the book in his outstretched hands as he scanned over it. His eyes widening.

"We need your blood. Serena, a lot of it. There has to be another way."

He slammed the book hard on the table.

"Damn it!" He yelled pressing his fingers to his eyes.

"Damon I'm so sorry, I had no idea-" My voice was breaking slightly and I swallowed it back.

"Serena, enough. It's not your fault. I trusted her too, she gave no inclination she had an ulterior motive. I'm angry at myself for not picking up on it sooner."

He half ran to the book shelf and was gazing over the titles.

"I'm not letting anyone die-there's gotta be another way." Damon said angerly.

I nodded. "I will help you look."

I grabbed another book off of the shelf and started looking through.

"She won't kill him so long as he proves a bargaining chip to ensure her freedom."

Damon started.

"I know."

He nodded. "At least that's in our favour, but we need to figure out how to bring her back without actually bringing her back." He suggested.

"Trick her?" I asked.

"More or less. We might be able to revive her for a time, long enough to grab Darren at the very least."

"Okay, what am I looking for?"

"Resurrection spells."

"Temporary?"

"All are temporary, except the one your mother used."

My stomach twisted in realization.

"But my mother was still alive a few months ago, so she couldn't have used her blood."

"I don't know how she did it. But there are ways to bring someone back for a short period of time. We just need to find one convincing enough, to fool Serenity."

We spent the next couple hours looking through books. A lot of the resurrection spells required a body, which we didn't have.

"Damon, what do you think she wants?"

He sighed loudly. "I'm not sure. We don't really know much about her. We can't even be sure she's actually your sister. You said yourself your mom never mentioned her, right? And you were close?"

"Yes, or she had a good reason not to." I said dismayed.

"It's possible, but we should entertain other avenues as well, to be sure." Damon said.

"Agreed."

We kept flipping through books for what felt like hours, continually coming up short.

"What if we did the same spell but with a lot less blood? Do you think that would be strong enough for a temporary spell?" I suggested.

"It might be worth a shot." he said nodding.

"It seems to be our only promising option at this point and we are running out of time."

I closed the book.

"Well let's hope for the best. It just needs to last long enough to get Darren back." I said.

"Exactly. We have to get him back no matter what." he said.

A panic rising in his tone. If only he know how terrified I was.

I noticed he was barely hanging on, so I kept my voice level and calm, even though I felt close to breaking down too.

"Damon it will be okay." I hugged him and he held me tightly.

"We can't lose Darren." He said against my hair.

"I know."

"Nothing to do now but wait."

I closed the book.

"Well I doubt either of us feel much up to sleeping hey?" I said gently.

"No, I suppose not." He pulled away from me now.

"How do you want to pass the time?" I shrugged.

He ran his hand over his jaw a minute.

"Did I kiss you last night?"

I as thrown off at his question. He remembered?

I swallowed unsure what to say.

"Yes, you did, I thought you were asleep though."

"I'm sorry, I was in a haze I thought you were Emma and I, I really am sorry Serena."

He let go of me then. Part of my reigned with guilt as I did care for Damon as well, I didn't like seeing him in such pain.

I wrapped him back in my arms. "It's no big deal. We can just pretend it didn't happen."

He looked to my eyes then and I was surprised to see him look hurt.

"What if- I don't want to pretend it didn't happen, what then?" He said quietly.

"Damon- I-I'm not Emma."

"I know that, but Serena-" he paused for a second eyeing me cautiously.

"I love you."

I broke eye contact and forced tears that welled past. I didn't want to hurt him. I did love him, but not in the way he wanted me to.

"What about Jane Damon?"

"She is not you, Serena."

"But she loves you."

"And you don't?" his voice broke slightly. I took a deep breath and turned to his eyes again.

"I do care about you Damon."

"Then kiss me Serena."

"Damon-"

Tears flooded his eyes and he pressed his lips hard against mine. I was reluctant to pull away, guilt pooling in my stomach. I knew he was unstable right now, and wrecked with worry for Darren just as I was. But as he kissed me and wrapped his hand in my hair it was familiar and safe. With the crushing uncertainty of Darren, and the world and having to bring Serenity back. I lost myself in his touch and his kiss. As I kissed him in my mind I pictured Darren and immediately pulled back. I couldn't do this.

"Damon." I said hesitantly.

He searched my eyes a moment.

"What's wrong?"

"I feel wrong with this."

He shook his head and pressed his lips to mine again and I put my hand gently on his lips.

"Please Damon."

He listened and sat back.

"I'm sorry for being so forward Serena."

I shook my head. "I didn't need an apology, I just don't want you to do something you regret."

I met his eyes and immediately regretted it as they were a storm of passion, need and fear. I changed the subject.

"Darren will be okay." I hugged him and he leaned against me.

He took a very deep breath.

"I don't know what I would do if I lost him Serena."

"You won't, I will get him back Damon. We will together. I don't want to lose him either."

He sniffed for a second and swiped his hand over his eyes

"I trust you."

"Good" I smiled and hugged him tighter.

"I couldn't ever regret it Serena." he whispered against my hair.

I turned slightly. "I can't imagine how you are feeling and I know how you need to relieve stress. I don't want you to risk it, you aren't in the right head space Damon."

He turned to face me. "Serena, I wouldn't regret it because I meant it when I told you I love you."

My eyes welled again and I kissed his cheek and held him close to me. I could feel his heart hammering in his chest. I felt tears fall from his eyes and land on my bare shoulder. I didn't pull away I merely tightened my grip on him.

"Damon it's okay." My voice cracked and I tried to swallow my own tears.

We laid like that intertwined with each other both pretending not to be crying and never once faced each other. Both our hearts were racing against each other. Both of us were too proud to face our emotions; so we laid there silently lying to ourselves and one another. We just held eachother until we fell asleep.

When the sun shone in, I opened my eyes. I was still laying against his chest and he was asleep. I brushed some of his hair off of his forehead and kissed him gently on it. I unwrapped myself from his arms. He took a deep breath in his sleep but did not stir. I got up and started to make coffee. Today was the day. Today I had to bring Serenity back, but today was also the day we would get Darren back. I worried and wondered what he could possibly be going through right now. Where was he? As I stated to pour water Damon stirred.

"Good morning." He half mumbled.

"Good morning. Did you sleep okay?"

"Yeah. I'm going to grab a shower."

"Okay, coffee should be ready when you are back."

"Sounds perfect."

I watched him walk to the bathroom in his white tank and red pj pants. I looked down at myself and realized I was still in the same dress as last night. I sighed slightly turning the coffee pot on. I walked to my bag and sifted through everything. It was hard to focus because I felt overwhelmingly terrified of what today would bring. But I knew it would bring Darren home. It had to. That's all I needed. I was embarrassed almost remembering how I had admitted I loved him, the way Damon had just admitted he loved me. It didn't matter if Darren loved me or not, it just mattered that I got him home, Damon needed his brother. If I did nothing else before the end of my life at least I could say I brought the brothers back to each other. I would never admit it out loud, but I was devastated that Serenity had in fact turned out evil. I settled on a red blouse and jeans. More practical then fighting in a dress. I sighed inwardly, I hoped it wouldn't come to that, and I was silently praying our feeble trick would work on her. Was she even my sister? I guess I won't know what she is until the blood moon tonight. Damon came out then.

He poured himself and me a cup of coffee.

"I think we should go on a quick road trip before tonight. I locked down another item. Honestly its our last item, if I'm right."

"Are you serious?! Damon that's amazing!"

'Yeah, I just wish Darren was here."

"Me too. We will get him back tonight."

"Yeah. I just wish I knew what was happening to him, you know?"

"We will know soon enough Damon." I said as I rested my hand on his shoulder.

"I know."

"Well where are we heading?"

He eyed me for a second.

"It might be difficult for you."

"Just tell me."

"You remember the hospital, your mom was at?"

Chills ran down my arms. "Yeah."

"It's there in Vancouver. I booked a flight. Leaves in an hour" Damon said.

"I'll pack. We should leave right away if we are going to make it." I said.

"Agreed." he said.

I left and threw a few things into my messenger bag and we headed out the door.

The drive to the airport felt longer then usual. We didn't even play any music. We were both probably too distracted with everything happening today to do much else. I was afraid actually to learn more about my mom, but perhaps we would get some answers concerning Serenity, my mom and everything. I was sick with worry about Darren.

We got to the airport. Damon took the lead and got our passes and led us through security, I appreciated that he just took over. My mind was too clouded to even think about speaking. We boarded the flight with no issues as we settled into our seats and the flight attendant began running through safety procedures.

"Are you alright Serena?"

I turned to face him. "No, are you?"

"Not a bit."

"Well we should be grateful I suppose, we are getting the last item right? And We will bring Darren home tonight. It's going to turn around."

He nodded. "I believe that too. Doesn't really make it much easier, I keep worrying we will fail."

"We won't."

He shook his head. "We can't that's the difference."

"Now you sound like Darren."

The plane roared up and I began to feel very panicked. Remembering the dream my past self, Aurelia and how I died then. I was so panicked that my breathing became ragged and I gripped Damon's hand. He looked confused for a moment before the realization dawned on him a few emotions moved through his features, shock then recognition and sadness.

"Are you thinking about when you were Aurelia?"

My heart was racing and I was taking raspy quick breaths. I managed to nod.

"So that settles it, you were Darren's too not just mine."

He inhaled deeply, and I felt hurt radiating from him.

"I think so." I merely whispered.

"Try to just focus on your breathing, I promise we won't crash. I'm right here."

I leaned into him and couldn't stop trembling, he wrapped his arms around me.

"You are completely safe Serena."

And for the moment, I did. I didn't remember the last time I was vulnerable enough to allow myself to feel safe. Not just physically but emotionally as well. If today was my last day on this earth, I was proud of myself for allowing those walls to began to crumble. I was glad I told Darren how I felt. I was glad that I had loved them both and maybe still now, but in different ways. I was happy to have known them. I wasn't going to go to this life or death fight with any regrets.

Feeling suddenly ill I realized I hadn't called Rayne and Matt to warn them about Allan just yet but I also believed he would keep his distance now, and be pursuing me further instead.

"I have to call Rayne when we land. Warn her to keep her distance from Allan."

His eyes widened. "Of course, but he's playing the long game he wouldn't harm them especially not right after your disappearance at her wedding."

"I know you guys just found me three days ago, it just feels like so much has happened since then."

"I know love."

I was shaking so hard that he kept fumbling his arms to keep me grasped in them.

"It's not a long flight. I promise you we will be alright."

I could only manage to nod.

The pilot came on then announcing that we were landing soon and to buckle up.

It did nothing to relieve my fear. Damon was holding me and stroking me arm gently. I kept trying to calm my breathing.

I felt the plane start to descend and I gripped Damon's hand so tightly that he grimaced.

"Serena it's almost over, can you loosen the vice grip? You're about to break my hand."

"I what?" I let go and was horrified when his hand was swollen, a nasty bluish bruise already forming.

He shook it gently, quietly cursing under his breath.

"Oh god I didn't mean to."

He laughed slightly. "Yeah well sometimes even I forget how strong you are."

I couldn't match his humour. I was too sickened looking at his hand, and thinking back to the burn I left on Darren. I didn't grab his hand again instead I busied my hands by folding them over and over and pulling at a fray on the seat ahead of me. He still kept his arm around me, and I still hadn't quite figured out how to stop trembling.

I felt the plane lurch slightly and bit my lip to keep from screaming. He tightened his grip on me best he could.

"This is normal we are touching down."

"Thank Gods." I breathed as the plane touched down.

"See, all is well Serena" Damon said quietly.

"Except for your hand." I said dismayed.

"Ah don't worry about it. He ran his opposite hand over it and when he pulled back it was healed.

"I'm kind of a God remember?"

I stared at him admirably. "Yeah. I forget that."

We grabbed our belongings and started down the aisle to get off of the plane. When we made it out of the hall and into the main airport seating I staggered back when I noticed Kallisa standing by some seats with a sinister grin on her face.

I grabbed Damon's arm.

He noticed and pulled me behind him with one arm in a fell swoop of a second.

"Kallisa what are you doing here?"Damon's tone was washed of anything remotely kind.

She walked up closer to us and Damon shoved me further behind him.

"I did not call you here." His tone ice.

She kept smiling. "I just thought you might want a word on your brother."

Damon's body flinched, he seemed to almost lose his composure. But he regained it within a moment.

"What about Darren?" He seethed.

"Come closer." She beckoned him with a hand of black claw like nails.

"I'll whisper it to you." She seethed again.

"Stay here Serena."

"What-are you kidding, Damon!" I whispered hurriedly.

He stopped about half a breadth from her.

"Speak Demon." He commanded.

"Your dear brother-" She hissed.

She moved her mouth right against his ear. Her pointed black teeth were glinting in the florescence of the airport.

"He's in Hell." She cackled.

I saw a shimmer of the blade for barely a millisecond as Damon plunged it into her side she groaned and turned to smouldering embers at Damon's feet. I quickly glanced around but no one noticed, she must be shielded.

I was shaking seeing her again and remembering her prying around in my memories. Damon stowed the blade and walked back toward me, his eyes full of anger that I'd never seen before.

"We have to make this trip quicker." He said through gritted teeth.

"What did she mean Damon? Is Darren trapped in Hell for real, is it possible she could be lying?"

"She wouldn't lie, it would not benefit her to do so."

I felt like I might vomit. It's like I could still feel her slithering and prodding my skull. I refocused, Damon was eyeing me curiously.

"Hell?"

"Yeah."

The panic gripped me and my heart was racing. "Then I guess we are going to Hell."

Damon met my eyes.

"You're damn right. Let's secure this item as quickly as possible."

"Do you know how to get into Hell?"

"I'm a God I must be able to do something."

"We have to get him, what if he's hurt Damon, can the item wait?"

""We might need it." He said quickly.

I nodded. Trying to fight bile in my throat as I worried endlessly. I couldn't bare the thought of him being trapped and tortured.

"How far do we need to go Damon? Please I can't- we can't wait that long."

"Serena I'm worried too but we can't go into hell unprepared, or we too will be trapped with Darren, and then the world ends. We lose ourselves and Darren too."

I swallowed. "Okay, lead the way."

We exited the airport and he hailed a cab. He got one within seconds of putting his hand up.

"Where to?" The balding heavy man said robotic.

"The asylum in the hills."

He stared at Damon for a second then his dull eyes flicked to me.

"Checking in?" He nodded to me.

Damon glanced to me, and I played the part.

"The walls, they are talking to me now."

Damon tried to hide a snicker.

The cab driver nodded in agreement. "Gotcha. Hop in"

We clamoured in. And I started humming "Ring around the rosy." And the cab driver glanced to me in the rear view and revving the engine.

I had to cover my face to hide my laugh. Damon playfully elbowed me in the side.

We pulled up to the institute. I tried imagining my mother here, when she was alive. Her medium honey coloured hair. Her green eyes. I thought back to how she looked in the morgue. I was petrified to find out the truth. I didn't feel ready. Not in the slightest, but the fact that Darren was in Hell and possibly being hurt or worse, I couldn't let fear get in the way. I had to face the mirror and reflect on my past, in order to look forward to my future.

Damon paid the Cab driver as he sped away. We rushed up the brick steps to the entrance as quickly as our feet would carry us. We walked through the automated doors. The fragrance of the pansies was overwhelming and only made my stomach churn more.

A brolly, grey haired, tattooed man greeted us.

"Checking in?"

Damon shook his head. "We are here about Ivory Moonshile."

A grim look crossed the mans features. "Next of kin?"

I stepped forward. "She was my mother."

The terror stricken in his features was unsettling.

"I-I have her papers here. I'm sorry for your loss. I will get anything else you need."

I swallowed summoning a brave voice. "All of her belongings and to see where she stayed and spent most of her time. Please."

"Right this way." His voice shook slightly and that sent goosebumps across my arms. Why was he afraid?

We rounded the corner passing a few different wards. I swallowed when I looked up, he was walking directly towards the maximum security section, that held two hulk-like men with batons and tasers strapped to their waists. They nodded us through with a swipe of the grey haired mans key-card. I stole a glance at Damon whom was looking to me sympathetically.

"It's okay" he mouthed.

I nodded. We walked through the doors and in room 333. My hand came up to my mouth in shock. The room was in absolute turmoil. My mind flashed back to how Henry's apartment has looked after the fire. Rummaged through. The furniture was upturned and there was scribbling all over the walls in red ink. Damon put his hands on my shoulders to steady me as I swayed in horror.

"I'll um- give you guys some time, take whatever you want. The room was left like this in tribute."

"Tribute to what?" I almost whispered, my hands still covering my mouth.

He seemed confused. "Don't you already know?"

I was unsure how to respond, but the man walked away so I didn't need too.

"Serena-" He started.

"Please Damon-just-leave it be." I whispered. Tears pricked my eyes as we walked around.

"Can you read the-" I cleared my throat. "The writing?" I choked out.

"Yeah- it's the same as the writing in Henry's apartment."

"Ancient witchcraft?" I brought myself to ask after a moment.

He nodded. I kept walking past the upturned furniture. I came to what resembled fragments of an alter of sort. There were many candles strewn about a few strange skulls and other bones. I fought bile again. God what was this what was she a part of? I kept searching and among the bits of glass and dirt was a photograph. I leaned down to pick it up. It was of my mom and me as a child. My breath was shaky as I studied the image of myself. Identical to the girl from the vision of this place, with the locket. But what of Serenity? I dropped the photo at the sound of Damon's voice.

"Serena, come here."

I glanced one last time at the photo and crossed my arms, trying to ward off an anxious chill and walked cautiously to where Damon was standing.

He handed me a birth certificate.

"Serena Ella Moonshile." born October 31 1921 3:00 am

"Serenity Belle Moonshile" born October 31 1921 3:13am

"Allan Kade Moonshile" born October 31 1921 3:23am

Triplets. Serenity was my sister, Allan was my brother. Born over a hundred years ago. All born here, in this room. Clearly they had died shortly after and became something different, so how and why was I still around?

I cried out slightly dropping the certificate. Damon moved to grab it from the ground, spun me to face him and pulled me against his chest.

"Let's keep looking. It's okay. Everything will be okay." He sounded so sure and I was so grateful because I was spiralling.

Chapter 29

ASYLUM

"Where do you run when it's yourself you need to escape from, your anxiety, your fear, the limits you put on yourself, when you can't calm the panic and your thoughts are spiralling out of control, you fall to the floor, tears pouring, screams ripping, who can you trust to witness you come undone, tied together with a smile, so no one see's you break, I seek asylum in your arms, will you grant it?"

W̲e rummaged through the rest of the room, finding occultist things everywhere.

Damon exhaled slowly. "There's a lot here. Dark magic, light magic."

I swallowed unable to look around anymore. "Damon-I can't. I'm sorry. I don't feel a pull to anything at all in here and I really just want to go. Please." I whispered the last word. Damon glanced over to me.

"Of course Serena, I'm sorry."

I shook my head. "We need the last item, I just don't think it's in here."

My stomach was churning at the idea that I was related to not just Serenity, but Allan too. Wincing as I remembered what him and Thomas did to me at the warehouse no less then 72 hours prior. I picked up my phone to dial Rayne, remembering silently that I needed to warn her still about Allan. She picked up on the fourth ring.

"Serena, hi I'm so glad you are okay! We only got one update but I'm glad to hear your voice, I'm sorry my wedding had such a brutal turn for you!"

I swallowed, she didn't even know the half of it.

"Hey." my voice came across shakier then I thought it would.

"What's wrong? Can you tell me what happened?"

"No I can't, but have you seen Allan since the wedding?" I asked trying to keep my voice low and even.

"Allan? Oh yeah, he's over right now, hanging with Matt, you want to talk to him?"

I clenched my phone hard and almost dropped it to the floor, I felt freezing cold, and my heart started racing.

"Rayne-" I started but she was already hollering to Allan to come talk to me.

I flicked my eyes to Damon and he obviously read the panic in them. He came close to the phone.

"Serenity? Allan's voice crept over the phone like venom.

"How nice to hear from you..' He continued. Now I was shaking so hard it was difficult to hold my phone.

"If you harm a hair." I seethed.

Allan passed the phone back to Rayne.

"Anyways yeah he's here, what was it you wanted to say?"

I heard a sickening sound like a knife being unsheathed.

"What the-" I heard Rayne say under her breath.

"Rayne listen to me, get the Hell away from Allan he's a demon, run get you and Matt and run." I said so fast but it was silent on the end of the phone.

"Rayne?! Rayne! I screamed.

The only thing that rang through the line was Rayne's blood curdling scream and there was a dial tone.

"Noo!"

I tried to redial but it went straight to voicemail.

"Damon we gotta move. We gotta move. You said-you said they were safe!!"

He held me then and ushered me from the hospital as we raced back to the cab. We would be too late. I phoned 911 and ordered an ambulance to Rayne and Matts. Praying Allan hadn't done what I thought he did. We sped to the airport and once we got to the front we were breathless.

"We need to get to Edmonton, now." I said hurriedly.

The lady nodded. Actually one leaves in an hour.

I nodded and was grateful something worked in our favour. Time dragged on and I wished that we could just teleport. I couldn't help thinking if Rayne was dead. What the hell could I do. I sat in a seat beside an elderly gentleman, he obviously rode motorcycles, he had a gang emblem I didn't recognize. He had a ring on that was gold with roses and thorns engraved into it. It looked as if the flowers were expanding along the length of his arm. Damon followed my gaze questionably.

"Ah Serena, not to judge but isn't he a little old for you?" Damon whispered by my ear jokingly. Obviously trying to calm me down by making me laugh.

"No I-"

"Excuse me, sir?" I started.

He looked at me "Eh? What're you on about?" His voice slurred.

"That ring." I pointed

His mouth opened into an eerie smile. "It's you." He said excitedly.

Damon shifted uncomfortable.

"I-It's you, it's you." He repeated over and over whilst almost twitching. He tore the ring off of his finger, however as he did his entire finger ripped with it. He dropped the disembodied finger into my hands and then vanished.

"Ugh!" I exclaimed almost dropping it to the ground. Damon wrapped it in the sleeve of the jacket that he took off.

"How much you wanna bet that was the last item Serena?" Damon said enthusiastically.

I was still horrified. "What was he?"

"A reverent." Damon said. "He just went to where he belonged."

I had no room in my mind to be excited that we found the last item I was far too concerned with Rayne and Darren to think on much else.

I shuddered. "Let's just go get Darren."

We walked down the aisle to grab our seats I prayed the flight would be safe again.

Damon wrapped his free arm around me and I leaned against him basking in his familiarity and safety. The flight attendant went through the regular safety procedures and I leaned closer to Damon closing my eyes just wishing things would slow down. I just craved peace above all else. I didn't want the world to end, I wanted Darren and Rayne safe. I wanted Demons to stop pursuing me. I wanted to understand what I was. I didn't want to feel like such a monster.

I could feel the plane descending and I took a deep breath. Relief flooded me when the plane came to a slow stop. Damon squeezed my arm once reassuring me. We hastily got off the plane safe and down back in Edmonton. Damon handed me a photo then, it was my mom just after she had the three of us. I stared at it before I took it shakily in my hands. I didn't really want it, god my mom looked like me.

"Just incase." Damon said and shrugged.

I nodded after staring at the photo for a second I tucked it into my bag. We rushed back to the car. It was 5pm. It was only 6 more hours until we has to try to bring Serenity back. Our sliver of opportunity to rescue Darren would come the second she became corporal so long as she wasn't faster then us. That was the catch, we had to be so specific and if we missed our window we would need to find another way to Darren. Damon seemed to sense my unease and he looked over to me in the passenger side.

"We will do this Serena. We can do this."

"I know. I'm just afraid."

"You aren't alone in feeling that." He said quietly.

"We can do it because we have one another." He said and perked up.

I nodded and looked out the window, watching all the other cars whiz past and wishing everything was already okay.

"We need to check on Rayne." I couldn't help saying it out loud even though I knew that's where we were headed already. Allan's voice ran in my head again and it sent chills through me. Especially now knowing he wasn't just a demon and my captor but also my brother. I could see Rayne's house in the distance and I sat forward anxiously in my seat, throwing the seat belt off of me before the car even came to a stop. I was trying to open the door even and Damon scolded me. The second he put it in park I raced up her familiar front steps and the door was ajar. A feeling of absolute dread crept over me. I stepped in and panic hit me like a wave when I saw blood all over the foyer.

"Damon!" I screamed.

He was right at my heels.

"Shit." He pulled a knife and went ahead of me motioning for me to get behind him.

I was shaking violently. My breaths coming in short bouts. As I looked to the walls they were just splattered with red against the white. We rounded to the kitchen and Damon rushed forward. Rayne was curled up in the kitchen motionless laying in a pool of blood on her white marbled tile floor.

I screamed, it was blood curdling, shrill and it tore through the silence like a hurricane. Tears rushed over my face and I ran to her body, shrieking into her bloodied hair and Damon held his arms around me. I tried to pick her head up and my hand came away coated in her blood. I vomited and cried my body wracking with each sob. Damon stood up with the knife to scout the rest of the house. I couldn't move from Rayne all our memories together poured through my mind. It's all my fault. It was all my fault.

Damon rushed ahead. It felt like forever that I laid there grasping her and crying. Damon pulled me up and I screamed for him to let me go, instead of listening he pulled me into his arms turning me to face him, he stroked my hair while my anguished screams were muffled against his chest.

"The house is clear, Matt and Allan are not here." He said quickly.

I couldn't catch my breath to reply.

"Serena, I know you are hurting but we need to move. We might be able to save Matt yet. We need to get Darren." He said quietly.

I took another shuddering breath, he was right.

"Can't you bring her back? Your Godly powers?" I barely whispered.

"Shes already crossed the veil, Serena. Slamming her back into her broken body.. she's better off where she is. We need to focus our energy to saving those we can. We can grieve later."

I knew he was right but it didn't make it any easier. He sounded like Darren then and my heart ached with how much I missed him. I couldn't stop the tears, my best friend was dead. There was no way for me to bring her back. Nothing made sense. The man I loved was trapped writhing in Hell and I never felt as powerless as I did now. I could feel the energy of my powers cackle and surge under my skin, but I still couldn't let them go. Damon kept his arm around me, I swallowed hard to keep from crying, my mind was rampant with memories of Rayne, and all I could think was today I still had to raise Serenity, and somehow get to Darren. The crushing overwhelm of everything was heavy, like walking with a hundred pound chain choking the life from you while trying to drag cement blocks with each step. All I wanted was peace. I wanted Darren back, I didn't want the world to end, I didn't want to have to raise Serenity, I didn't like that Allan was free. A sound in the trees broke my anxiety and my body erupted in a different state of panic. Damon quickly swooped me behind him while he held a light to the trees. Allan's black eyes glistened in the bush and a scream made it's way to my lips before I could stop it. He smiled with his mouth of pointed black teeth and lunged forward, locking eyes with me, dragging Matt's lifeless body behind him. His body flailing like a rag doll. Damon was quick to draw his blade and sunk it deep into Allan's chest, while Allan's eyes were focused on me. He turned to ash at our feet with an unholy howl of anguish.

"Matt!" I cried out and went to rush to him but Damon gripped my arm hard and shook his head.

I started to sob again, and Damon again threw his arms around me.

"Everything will be alright." He whispered against my hair.

"I'm so sorry Serena." He murmured and ran his hand over my hair stroking it in an attempt to calm me. It brought me a sliver of comfort, but even that was washed away with another wave of memories that rocked my brain.

"Serena, you have to focus now." He tilted my chin to his face him. He brushed my hair to the side in the same fluid movement.

I looked to the sky, shaking when I realized I only had 22 minutes before the blood moon was in optimal position for Serenity's rebirth.

"We are running low on time." Damon said and pulled me back towards the direction of the car. With a final forlorn glance to Matt's crumpled body, I allowed Damon to lead me to the car.

"We have to return to bury them." my voice broke when I said "bury".

"We will." We rounded the drive to the car and clamoured in.

"Where do we need to be?" I asked.

"The farmhouse where Osiris was."

I nodded. I typed it into maps, it was an 11 minute drive. Tight.

I turned my phone to Damon, whom nodded and revved the engine as we took off north. We pulled up to the farmhouse within 6 minutes and I felt so cold. I remembered all the spirits swirling and gathering here only a few months ago. I cringed remembering Darren's face when he was possessed. Damon put the car in park and we both stared for a moment at the farmhouse. Probably thinking about the same things, but here we were. The final battles.

I exhaled deeply. Damon put his hand against my shoulder gently. "You got this Serena. I'm right here."

I nodded feeling a little more confident. I reached into the back seat and grabbed my messenger bag, I could hear a few of the heavier items clang against each other as it's weight shifted to rest easy on my left shoulder. I took another deep breath and silently prayed, prayed to whoever was listening, that we could fool Serenity long enough to get Darren back. At a last glance to the sky I knew we only had 4 more minutes. We walked hand in hand up towards the abandoned farmhouse. I found my confidence, I knew I could do this, I would not fail. Damon gave me a nod of encouragement and we entered the building. The shelves were still a mess from when Damon was launched into them. He followed my gaze then squeezed my hand reassuringly. I laid the bag on the ground as Damon began with red spray paint drawing sigils copied from the black book, and I got set to laying out everything for the spell while Damon painted a pentagram around me, I took out the wooden bowl, and began to lay all the ingredients in it whilst reciting the spell my mother had written down. I lit a match and tossed it into the bowl, the ingredients smoked and a white flame came from them. I took a shuddering breath, reciting the second part and bringing the dagger against my wrist. Damon eyed me cautiously, probably just as worried if not more worried then I was. The last words fell from my lips and I pressed the blade into my wrist, cutting upwards and making sure the blood poured into the white flame. I gasped as the pain was sharp and blinding. I needed to let most of my blood drain and Damon needed to heal me before I died. Damon was beside me now with a finger against my throat counting my heartbeats. I began to feel faint and sick to my stomach but I held my bleeding arm over the bowl. I had my eyes only open slightly, when I saw Serenity materializing right in front of us. It was working. Serenity greeted us with a menacing smile as her face formed and her body formed. I was very dizzy now, I was focusing on Damon counting under his breath my heartbeats. I tried to count as well. Serenity began to laugh delightedly.

"I see you manged to hold our bargain." She seethed as she crouched beside me as I was starting to fade into sleep. Damon's voice was deep, threatening but calm.

"What about your end? Darren now."

Serenity threw her head back and laughed.

"Mm pretty daft for a God aren't you Damon?"

I could feel Damon's healing energy pouring into my wound, while he spoke to Serenity.

"We had a deal." His voice was ice.

"Yeah we did, and I will let you both into Hell. Daft, because you didn't even try to go yourself to fetch him.." She stopped talking to cackle.

"Worked in my favour of course. Now you get to go to Hell and I get to roam free. And you." She couched down and paused at my eye level. "Die instead of me."

I could feel my own powers sparking as Damon's energy stormed through my veins.

Serenity threw her head backward in laughter yet again as a pit opened in the cement behind her. A wicked wind ripped up and around, stronger then a hurricane and the pit fell inward, a relentless heat blasting from it's core.

I opened my eyes then, feeling nothing but strength and I grabbed Serenity by her throat. She yelped and struggled against my grip, choking and gagging as she thrashed.

"You are coming with us to Hell, or you are dying before you've even gotten the chance to live again." My tone was steel. My voice sounded almost unfamiliar in it's coldness. Damon put a warning hand on my shoulder.

"Let her breathe. Remember who you are Serena." He said calmly. I loosened my grip and let her fall to the cement amidst the wind and radiating heat.

"You bitch." She spat. I laughed slightly.

She tried to run but the sigils Damon had drawn created a semblance of a threshold that Serenity couldn't pass through. She let out a howl of frustration.

Damon tsked. "Sorry princess. Lead us to Hell hm?" He motioned towards the pit.

"Over my dead body." She seethed.

"That can be arranged." He met her tone.

She eyed him for a second and then flicked her gaze to me. She didn't say anything she walked up to the pit and simply dove in. As if it were nothing more then a swimming pool. Damon and I exchanged a glace.

"She values life too much, I say we follow her lead, she wouldn't choose death over life." Damon deducted. I nodded. Darren was down there and I would stop at nothing to return him to me.

I grabbed Damon's hand. "Together?"

"Always." He said as we jumped into the mouth of Hell.

The free fall was comparable to skydiving, the sudden rush of adrenaline and pure terror, as the wind whips around you, smothering the oxygen around you so that you can scarcely take a breath, almost like suffocating. The heat as we fell was severely intense, hotter then when you stand too close to an open flame. My skin felt as hot as it did when I was being burned by the dragon flame. If I had enough air in my lungs I would've cried out. Damon's arms enveloped my body and legs and arms were wrapped around his body my head tight against his chest as we spiralled down the seemingly never ending pit. When we neared the bottom, the air crashed back into my lungs. Damon and I both hit the ground sputtering and gasping. The landing did not hurt, not even slightly. At the bottom Serenity was standing leaning against a stone wall watching us with raised eyebrows.

"The gate will close in 24 hours."

Damon caught his breath before I did and cleared his throat.

"More then enough time." He said.

Serenity shrugged. "If you knew your way around down here then yes. Being that you don't have a clue, it's a labyrinth down here, and the longer a living soul remains the faster they slip into madness."

Damon narrowed his eyes. "You will guide us."

Serenity scoffed. "I haven't been to Hell Damon. I remained in limbo on earth."

Damon looked genuinely surprised. There was a pit in my stomach. It didn't matter. We had to get Darren.

"Damon." I touched his shoulder gently in a subtle attempt to reassure him all was okay. He lifted his hand to hold mine on his shoulder.

"We will find him. Let's go. You too Serenity." I said and started to lead Damon by his hand. He followed and Serenity walked behind Damon. I started down the nearest corridor. Each stone corridor was flooded with fire light. The air was hot and uncomfortable in my lungs. I was pouring sweat. The hollow screams of the tortured un-dead rang painfully in my ears. I winced, but I wouldn't let Damons hand go, I could feel his hand clenching and unclenching over mine, indicating his unease. I prayed again that we were going the right direction. I glanced back to Serenity, she met my eyes and smirked. I had a bad feeling that she knew exactly where Darren was. I was always very good at reading peoples emotions. Growing up I had to walk on eggshells, I memorized how to recognize footsteps, tone, facial expressions, how to tell if someone was angry, or unsettled or hiding something before they even spoke. Everyone was like an open book to me, and Serenity, she knew where Darren was. She just didn't want us to find him. The screams were agonizing to my ears. Damon was holding my hand tightly and he pulled me closer to him his demeanour shifted, protective. Perhaps he didn't want me to feel like I had to be the protective one when he was so natural the protector. Perhaps protecting me would allow him to combat the weakness he may be feeling mixed with the uncertainty and the fear. It would make him feel stronger right now, if I appeared weaker, I gathered. I leaned closer to him and tightened my grip on his hand, I slowly exhaled loudly.

"Don't be afraid, we will get Darren."

Damon pulled me close and half whispered with such certainty I realized I had been right and this helped him to focus. It felt good to be reassured but he didn't know that in reality, I wasn't afraid in the least and I had no doubt in my mind that we would succeed. I side glanced Serenity whom was eyeing me cruelly. We turned another corner the screams of the people chained in here were agonizing to my ears. It seemed the deeper we spiralled into the hall the louder they screeched. As we rounded yet another corner I was hit with a wave of emotion and real physical pain. I screamed myself and fell to my knees on the hard tears blinded my vision, my hands flew to cover my ears as if that could take the edge off. Damon rushed to catch me.

"Serena whats wrong?"

How could he not hear them? I cried out again as it felt knives were being stabbed into every pore in my body. The sadness and the blinding fury, all the emotions these people were feeling bombarded me. Serenity's laugh tilled out, and carried above the screams. If I could move, I would strike her. Damon moved to try and grab her and her eyes lit up white. She laughed louder.

"Not in here sweetheart. I'm in power here."

If I could speak my words would have been ripped from my chest. My memories flooded back to the first time I almost drowned, the white eyed demon. Damon hatred flared in his eyes for a moment. The true wrath of God. Serenity didn't even flinch as his power radiated from him. She laughed again.

"Angelic power doesn't work down here honey." She made a mock pout.

One of the screaming voices called out to me, I tried to focus and drown the others out. It hurt like peeling layers of skin slowly with a carrot peeler. Damon was focused on Serenity. I tried again crying out as the pain was unbearable. Then I locked onto it. Darren. It was him, he was hollering, his voice raw and gruff. I grabbed Damon's hand catching him off guard and rushed as quickly as I could ignoring the noise and the pain. Darren. Darren. I'm coming. Please hold on, please, please. I broke into a sprint dropping Damon's hand as he struggled to keep up and left him behind.

"Serena! Damnit! Come back!"

His voice was louder and louder. It was a labyrinth of cages and chains and fire. Tormented souls surrounded me, wailing, begging, pleading, screaming. I kept pushing past. Cold hands gripped every inch of my body as the souls tried to grab me. I struggled against them and I ran to the end of a hallway and there I saw Darren chained to a wall, his face pouring blood, wrists and ankles bound and bloody in metal chain. He was mumbling incoherently. I crashed into the front of his cage rattling it with all my strength.

"Darren! Darren! Can you hear me?" I cried out as I rattled the cage again. He didn't stir and my heart was racing so fast I feared it would explode.

I summoned all the strength I had as Darren thrashed against his holds.

I focused my energy and allowed my mind to clear, and focus on just the gate opening. I could hear Damon and Serenity gaining on me. And I exhaled deeply, as I did I pushed with all my might and the gate bubbled and lit up orange as it melted apart. I barrelled in. Darren did not stir from his feverish thrashing and mumbling. His eyes like an animal to slaughter darting back and forth. I was at his side in seconds. Channelling my power to break his bindings. They snapped easy like toothpicks. His body slumped forward and I caught him in my arms. He was still mumbling. I held him against me and stroked his hair. Pushing it hurriedly off of his face.

"Darren, please shh. It's alright. It's okay I got you. I got you. I'm getting you out of here. Its all going to be okay love."

I murmured against his cheek. He was shaking violently and still mumbling his eyes far away. I couldn't help but cry, I tried so hard to hold it back but it choked out easily. I couldn't bare him struggling. Why weren't his powers working down here? How could he be trapped down here, wasn't he the God for here? Then I looked in horror at his back and there was a sigil I didn't recognize carved into his back like a jack-o-lantern. It was still oozing blood. Oh God

he needed a hospital, or Damon's powers but we had to get him out
of Hell first. Damon caught up then his face beheld a look of horror.

"Damon" I cried out his name. "Please! We have to help him!"

"I will carry him. Serenity is behind but shes nearby, I don't
know how we are going to get past her."

I took a brief second to stop crying.

"I will deal with her. Get Darren out. I'm the one she wants
anyways."

Damon looked longingly at me like he didn't want to let me stay
alone. But then he glanced back to Darren and his condition and
inhaled sharply.

"Be careful Serena. Get out too. If not I will come back for you
somehow."

I nodded. "Just get Darren to safety please, please that's all I need
you to do. I will handle my sister and myself."

With one last look to me he scooped Darren up whom thrashed
and screamed against Damon's grasp as if Damon was hurting him,
in a total delirium. More tears fell from my eyes. I blinked them away
and tore my attention away from them. I tried again to drown the
voices and feelings to find Serenity. Before I could focus enough she
was in front of me.

"You got him out." Disbelief and a small flash of fear on her face.

I came right up to her so close that our noses almost touched.

"What are you?" I seethed

"Don't you understand Serena? Are you so blind that you haven't
figured it out? So wrapped up in your own goddamned mind that
you don't see."

I shook my head. "What do you mean?"

She tsked. "Pathetic."

I could feel the familiar flare of my powers sparking in my
fingertips. Anger cursed through me.

Serenity put her hand up to mine which confused me enough
to set the course of my powers astray. As her hand impacted me, I

was hit with painful energy like needles stabbing into the flesh of my hand. I cried out.

"I'm you." Serenity seethed. "See? Don't you feel it? Empty and hollow you are, we are incomplete and together we will be unstoppable."

Panic raced through my mind.

"Serenity." I almost whispered, shaking my head frantically.

She laughed as her hand began to dissolve and absorb into my own. My mind raced back to the photo, the photo of the special children that my father did experiments on. We were both in the picture, we had to be separate people, didn't we? Were we not? A thousand thoughts raced through my mind as the heat and pain intensified and she only laughed manically. I watched now as her forearm dissolved into mine. A word came to my mind a language I was unfamiliar. As the word dripped from my tongue I felt Serenity rip from my body and she screamed louder then all the tormented voices together.

"You bitch! What have you done?!" She howled in rage.

I spoke the next two words that came to my mind in sequence and her eyes went bright white like two light bulb's in the centre of her face. She tried to scramble away and as she did her skin began to crack open like porcelain. Fine fractured lines. A black ooze-like substance began to leak from every crack in her body as more cracks appeared her body shaking violently as she made a sound as if she was choking, I watched as it began to pour from her mouth, her eyes and nose as well as all the faint cracks in her skin. She continued to make raspy choking sounds. When I was sure she couldn't follow me, I began to step away. It stung me to watch her suffer, despite everything she had done, it hurt me to watch her struggle. I didn't know what those words did to her, or where I got them from, but it wasn't the first time something had come to me. I imagined it was from the codex.

"Serena, don't, you need me to beat Cronos." She choked out between agonized rasps. Ooze poured from her mouth as she spoke. She reached her hand to me. It was covered in cracks that leaked the same ooze.

"I don't need you. I will beat him myself." I said coolly as I began to walk away from her disregarding and attempting to swallow the stabbing guilt of leaving her there.

"Would you really doom humanity, for the sake of one man? One who doesn't love you? Or even want you? Doesn't that hurt baby sister? You give your being to anyone and everyone because you are so desperate for love yourself, it makes me sick."

I stopped walking against my better judgment and re-engaged in the conversation with her.

"That is what good people do Serenity. I love everyone unconditionally regardless of the pain it causes me. There is great strength in that, strength you have no access too because you are incapable of feeling love yourself. Every person needs to feel loved and cared for in some capacity, otherwise, are you even really alive? Without love Serenity, the world would crumble."

She laughed which threw her into a bitter gasping coughing fit as she spewed the black blood all over the floor.

"You think you yourself are capable of giving the world love? The world don't want it honey, they all want to die. If they knew what Cronos was planning, most would not only welcome it, they would beg for it."

I shook my head.

"No I don't believe that it is hopeless, there is so much beauty yet. I will love everyone I meet unconditionally and hope they spread that to those they love and so on."

She made a sound like a scoff. "Ask yourself this sister, What if you had to choose between Darren and the world? Could you let Darren and Damon die to save humanity?"

I opened my mouth to say that of course if I would save everyone else, but the thought made me sick. I pictured Darren and I would sooner die myself then lose him.

"If that doesn't get you, think to your past life, the children you had, what if in their sacrifice it would save humanity? Would you slay your own children?"

She paused to spew more black blood, then gasped before she spoke.

"You would never trade Darren or Damon or your children's lives for humanity. So now ask yourself who is the real villain here Serena? A hero goes for the greater good, and you sweetheart are no hero."

"I would find a way to save them all, no sacrifices. No questions asked."

My response made her laugh and choke again.

"Then you sister are a damned fool and humanity is doomed."

I hesitated unsure what to do, her words were twisting my mind, the voices around me didn't even bother me anymore. It was just what she said, and the realization that, if I couldn't save everyone, I would save those she mentioned. I shook it off.

"No you are wrong, I will save everyone. I have to."

I stood up from where I was crouching beside her. I noticed the words I had spoken were scorched into her flesh of her half exposed chest, where the porcelain cracks seemed to stem from. The scorched flesh seemed to be resealing. It wasn't permanent. She was stalling me. I stood up and raced back the way I came as thier voices crescendo.

"Save us!" They echoed in unison.

It was difficult to keep my vision straight. I remembered the way we came as if I had travelled it a hundred times. I remembered the words to speak when I reached the exit. I spoke them quickly and fluently. There was a blinding fire and vigorous heat that surrounded me and I screamed. When I opened my eyes, it was silent. I exhaled, so grateful for the quiet. I laid in the daybreak of a seemingly ordinary meadow. I made it, I was back on earth and Serenity for the moment was sealed in Hell. I prayed Damon and Darren had gotten out too. I was unsure how much time had passed. I stood up feeling dizzy and disoriented. Then my phone rang and it made me jump. I still had my phone with me? I picked it up.

Damon's voice poured over the line.

"Serena! Thank God you picked up. You got out! Are you okay? What happened with Serenity? Darren is stable right now. Where did you end up? I have been trying to reach you for hours! I will come get you. Drop a pin."

"I'm so relieved he is okay Damon and you too, thank you. We all got out. We did it. Yes I will drop my pin."

I did so and listened for the chime of my message through the phone.

"Goddamn, you are like a two hour drive. You hurt at all Serena?"

"No- no I am good."

"Good. I'm coming hang tight. If you walk share your location so I can find you."

"Thank you, Damon." Click

I looked up to the sky above, it appeared to be around noon. I looked around to see the hole I must've come out of but there was nothing but a seemingly ordinary meadow. I wondered if Serenity would find her way out, and if she did what would I do then? How was she a part of me? I thought back to the birth certificate, I rummaged in my bag hoping it would be there.

I pulled it out cringing at the mention of my brothers name. My mind flipped to him killing Rayne and I swallowed a sob. I looked over the names again. I flipped the page over and saw a note scribbled there.

"Serenity died aged nine after the energy transfer. Body to be studied. Serena survived. Operation a success otherwise. Serena is devoid of darkness, malice, hate. She is the purest soul in existence. The true embodiment of love."

I dropped the birth certificate. Energy transfer? Did that mean, they took everything out of my soul that could be anything other then good and gave it to Serenity, and took all that was good in her and gave to me? I felt nauseated suddenly. I swayed slightly in the field and dropped my bag to the ground. How could they tear part of someones essence and transfer it? Why? I felt nothing but sorry for Serenity, it wasn't her fault, she was stripped of anything other then darkness. I thought back to the image of her spewing blood and vomited myself. This also meant she was ruthless, no remorse or regard for anyone or anything. Just robotic. Devoid of her humanity, her soul. It was gut wrenching to me. If I could tear myself apart to give her back her soul I would. I stumbled forward trying to walk and was overcome with emotion. How could someone do that, to their child? I picked the photo back up. There was more writing on the bottom right.

"The other 5 of 6 children, survived with the energy transfer to Serena. All children died within the first year, all exhibiting extraordinary abilities and intellect.

Conscious transfer successful. My body was shaking so hard I put my hand to the grass to steady myself. We had 48 hours to complete the spells to face Cronos. Now I was afraid I would be unable to face him, without Serenity. I shook my head. I couldn't afford to think like that. I couldn't fail. Darren's words echoed in my head. "Failure is not an option." I exhaled slowly. I would win this fight for the sake of the people that died for my powers. I choked back tears, the guilt of having these abilities was overwhelming for me. I had to look through the journal when I got back to the hotel. There had to be more information. How did Serenity become white eyed demon? I swallowed another sob. Her hate and revenge was not her fault, I deserved it. I had part of her intertwined with my own soul and essence. The amount of hollow empty pain she must hold. I took a shuddering breath to steady myself, staring back to the invisible hole I had crawled out of. My mind flashed yet again to Serenity choking and spewing her black blood. I took another deep breath. Damon should be here soon, I recognized I had lost myself in my thoughts. As if reading my mind my phone rang. I fumbled to answer and struggled to find words.

"Serena?" Damon's kind voice poured over the line.

"Yeah."

"Road up ahead I can see you, can you walk?"

"Yeah." Was all I managed to say yet again.

I got up slowly and forced myself to walk to the car. Then I found more strength and broke into a sprint. Darren needed me.

Damon jumped out and opened the door for me wrapping me tightly in his arms. I fell against his chest, wanting to break down. But I held firm and pulled away.

"Take me home." I managed to whisper.

"Of course." He whispered against my cheek and helped me into the passenger seat. He half ran to the drivers side and throwing it in drive as we got back onto the road. After a few minutes of silence Damon spoke up.

"What happened with Serenity?"

I swallowed hard fighting tears again. Damon picked up on my unease.

"You don't have to say anything right now Serena, let's just get you safe."

A few tears escaped unnoticed by Damon and I merely nodded, feeling very weak now. I was grateful again as I always was for his consideration of my emotions. We had two hours drive and I couldn't formulate even a single sentence. The hours droned on. I needed Darren, I craved the peace his presence brought me, the reason I was so obsessed with him, The unconscious ability he had to calm the chaos in my mind and the storm in my heart. His ability to quiet the constant chatter in my mind that was always riddled with overthinking and anxiety, with a single touch. I couldn't imagine heaven even feeling better then the peace he brought me. How could someone make me feel so loved, when I was the embodiment of love myself? Did he not love me, like Serenity said? It wouldn't matter, I couldn't not love him. I supposed I was incapable of doing anything if not in love, a blessing and a curse, as I knew it hurt more then anything else a lot of the time. I wanted nothing more then to hold Darren, bring him back to himself, I couldn't bare the possibility of his mind being unreachable. I couldn't imagine, it would destroy me. It would kill Damon too. I prayed silently, I could somehow love him out of the dark depths of his mind. I couldn't begin to imagine the toll being in Hell had on him. He was completely delusional when I grabbed him, he wasn't even here. I swallowed more tears. Damn it I needed to get him back. I could feel Damon's eyes on me.

"Worried about Darren?" He asked hesitantly.

"Yes." My voice faltered as I said that and Damon sighed quietly.

"He is stable, as for his mind, well-"

He cut himself off and slammed his fist on the steering wheel. It made me jump and look at him. He looked like he hadn't slept in days. It hadn't occurred to me until that second that he might need to talk. I was being selfish by staying silent. I swallowed again.

"Are you okay Damon?" I reached my hand over to grasp his and squeeze it slightly, he grasped back in an instant and didn't let go. His eyes full of tears suddenly.

"No, I'm not okay. We got him back, but it's not him anymore Serena. He-his eyes are blank, he hasn't fucking said a goddamn word Serena!"

He slammed the steering wheel again and we swerved slightly. I put my hand on the wheel.

"Let me drive."

Damon stared at me for a second then put the flashers on and pulled over. I breathed a sigh of relief. He got out abruptly and yanked the passenger door open. I scrambled with my seat belt and moved to the drivers side by climbing over the glove box. I signalled left to get onto the highway again. I glanced to Damon as he tried to cover the fact he was crying. I turned my eyes to the road instead.

"Damon, it's okay to be upset." I tried hesitantly.

"It's not. I can't fall apart." He said his voice cracking.

I thought for a moment.

"You can for 5 minutes." I glanced to him.

He stared at me his eyes rimmed red, his face starting to turn crimson. When he didn't say anything I continued.

"Fall apart for 5 minutes. Let it out, feel it all and then close it all off in 5 minutes and focus on what you gotta do. I'm not going to judge you, and I will not lose any respect for you. Just allow yourself the freedom of feeling. If you can't give yourself permission to breakdown, then I give you permission to."

He stared at me a second and his eyes welled more and he buried them in his hands. His shoulders wracked with each sob. I swiped a hand over my own eyes. It was damn near impossible for me not to cry if someone else was. I felt everyone's feelings so strongly. I took a deep breath, GPS said we were 10 minutes away.

Maybe he could use the whole ten minutes. I took a few breaths myself trying not fall apart too. I would reserve that for when I was alone, after seeing Darren. I stepped on the gas a little, anxious to see Darren again. We were 3 minutes away now and Damon's crying and cursing had slowed enough that I thought he might be okay now. I glanced over and he was looking at me.

"Thank you. We will help Darren." He nodded and sniffed once.

"Yes, we will."

"When he comes back, you should tell him the same line. He's worse then me, he could use hearing it too."

"I will."

I smiled and touched his shoulder with one hand on the wheel. He put his hand over mine for a second. Then I put it back onto the wheel as I turned into the parking lot of the hotel. I barely had the car in park and Damon and I scrambled out. Taking care to press the lock button as we sprinted to the back of the hotel so that we could enter and avoid all of the greetings that would follow had we gone in the front door. We took the stairs because it felt faster. My heart was pounding so hard it my chest that my breath was coming in short bouts. Darren, Darren, Darren.

We got to the door and Damon threw it open. Darren was sitting on the couch cuddled in a ball mumbling to himself. I dropped my bag to the ground and tripped trying to throw my boots off. Damon gave me my space, he stepped aside, looking like he might cry again upon seeing Darren. I banged my hip hard against the end table as I tried to rush to his side.

"Darren, honey. Darren." I stroked his arm gently. He jerked it away. I jumped back deeply hurt by his rejection of my touch. How could I calm him?

"Darren, please it's Serena."

"She's dead, demon she died..she died- shes dead- she's dead."

"No, no- Darren, I came back, remember?- I came back and I could walk again."

He stopped mumbling for a second. "No, Serena you are dead."

"Darren please." I choked back tears. "I'm right here, my love."

He sat up abruptly his eyes were so cold and it scorched me. I cupped his face in my hands, feeling his stubble lightly press into my palms. Studying his beautiful blue eyes. This time he didn't pull away but his eyes were vacant. I glanced to Damon whilst still holding Darren's face. Damon looked absolutely destroyed. This would hurt him too but maybe. I loved Darren, I loved him more then words. I leaned closer to Darren, my heart racing and my breath became shaky. I slowly placed my lips against his. My heart soaring with the touch. I could kiss him for hours. I kept it slow and light. He didn't kiss me back. I pulled away, too nervous to look to Damon. I kissed Darren's forehead, then both cheeks then again on the mouth. This time parting my lips to coax him to do the same, it worked after a second. I entwined my fingers in his brown hair. Kissing him deeply I climbed onto him, until I was kissing him whilst sitting on his lap. After a minute his hands gripped my hips holding me in place and he kissed me back hard and needing. I opened my eyes to his crystal blue eyes that were now filled with familiarity. He pulled away for a second.

"Serena." he breathed.

"Yes, my love."

He moved his hands roughly up my back and kissed me deeper. Then he traced his hands to my neck and rested them against my neck and in my hair. I wanted all of him right now. I was flooded with ecstasy dripped desire. Darren stopped kissing me at the sound of Damon loudly clearing his throat. Oh, I forgot he was there for a moment, I was just lost in Darren.

"Darren?-" Damon said hesitantly.

"Yeah man it's me." He lifted me off of his lap and put me on the couch beside him.

Damon came over then and threw his arms around Darren clamping him once on the shoulder.

"It's good to have you back man." Damon smiled.

"It's good to be back. Thank you both for getting me back." He said but his eyes travelled to me and away from Damon. I had never seen such lust in his eyes and it only made me need him so much more.

Damon cleared his throat again.

"I'm just going to grab some air now that you are up and about." Damon stated after a second and exchanging a glace between Darren and I. I glanced slightly to Damon, his expression was very obviously hurt, but he nodded in thanks to me. I smiled and nodded too.

"I will see you guys later. Actually, I will be back in the morning. I will go visit Jane. Big fight tomorrow."

"Okay be careful man." Darren said without taking his eyes off of me.

"Agreed." I called to Damon whom closed the door behind him. Immediately Darren turned his eyes, like two blue pools of liquid sky, to me, hunger like I never seen.

"You told me you loved me, didn't you? Before." His voice hushed and urgent. I shifted slightly, feeling flush.

"I-yes yes I did. I do. I love you more then I've ever loved anyone before. I was terrified I was going to lose you Darren." My voice came out shaky and I looked down. He put my chin in his fingertips, guiding my face to look into his eyes. I exhaled slowly.

"You are never going to lose me. I will never go anywhere."

"I hope you mean that." I met his eyes.

"And-you love me?" His words like honey, dripping from his tongue.

I slowly moved closer to him and climbed back onto his lap my fingers tracing his back while I held him close to me.

"So much more then I could ever say." I whispered.

He relaxed against my touch. "I don't know what to say."

His words bit slightly, I wished he would just say he loved me too, of course it was possible he didn't the very thought of it made my chest clench painfully. How could I love someone so much, and not have it reciprocated? I took a deep breath to shoo my anxious thoughts for the moment.

"You don't have to say anything Darren, just-kiss me." I quietly pleaded, gazing into his eyes, as the need for him enveloped my body. His fingers still graceful against my chin.

His eyes locked to mine, then he closed them as he brought his lips against mine. He was running his hands through my hair while I ran my hand along his back. We parted lips our tongues touching slightly here and there. I moved my hands slowly from his neck down his chest, to the Hem of his t-shirt. I pulled it up over his tattooed chest. He left my mouth to let me pull his shirt over his head, as I slowly traced my fingers back down from his neck, his chest, his stomach and hovered there. He brought his lips back to mine and kept kissing me as he groaned slightly. His right hand travelled slowly under my shirt and unhooked my bra, while his left hand stayed tangled in my hair. He rested his hand there on my upper back, never stopping kissing me, tracing fingers slowly down my bare back. Was he waiting for my go ahead? I pulled away from his mouth for a split second.

"Darren, take me, all of me. I'm yours." I half moaned.

I placed my lips back against his as he tore my shirt over my head. He slid my bra over my arm gently moving his lips to kiss my neck and collarbone, then down my shoulder and my arm as he slowly slid my bra off. He dragged his lips back up to the hollow of my throat nipping slightly as I moaned quietly. Once his lips were back on mine he gently cupped my breast gently moving his hands back to my bare waist as he pulled me closer against him. He lifted me and carried me toward the bed but we stopped at the wall which he slammed me into, kissing me harder and groaning. I moved my hand from his stomach to his jeans and undid his belt, while his mouth moved back to my neck. His hands moved swiftly to my jeans unbuttoning them, he lifted me out of them and threw me onto the bed climbing on top of me, his bare tattooed chest resting against my breast, his muscular stomach against mine. He kept kissing me and I was melting like butter in his grasp and his kiss. I reached my hand down and unbuttoned his jeans which fell to his ankles he stepped out of them with ease half lifting me off the bed to keep kissing me. I reached my left hand down gently between his legs he inhaled sharply and groaned slightly as he brought his mouth back to mine. His fingers darted behind my lace thong and grasped me gently. I stopped kissing for a second to cry out in pleasure. Why did every touch with him feel so perfect and intense? Unlike anything I had ever experienced before. I slowly guided him into me and as we collided we both inhaled sharply, and kept kissing. We continued like that, for what felt like a couple of hours; before we stopped out of breath and dripping sweat. We laid beside one another wrapped in each others embrace. He kissed my forehead and I leaned against his chest.

"You alright?" He asked hesitantly stroking my arm.

"Oh better then." I laughed slightly. "Yourself?"

"I'm- I don't know what to say." He laughed slightly and moved my hair off of my face, planting a light peck to my lips.

"I think that was a perfect way to spent the night before the big fight." I joked.

"Yeah." Darren laughed again. "You could say it was the best way."

I laughed too. "Agreed"

I laid against his chest and listened to his heartbeat beyond grateful he was here.

"Darren when you are ready, please tell me what happened, but only when you feel comfortable enough too. I'm here for you. I always will be."

"I will always be here for you too Serena. But I-don't hold your breath on it, it's really not worth talking about." I felt all his muscles tense and listened to his heartbeat quicken. He was scared.

"Well, you are safe now." I kissed his forehead then his lips and laid back onto his chest.

"I know." He whispered. Then kissed me again.

Chapter 30

MEMORIZE ME

*"You want to know how to love me, memorize me, how my voice
sounds when I tell you I love you, learn to recognize the emotions
I hide behind these masks, learn me so deeply that my thoughts
and feelings are never secret to you, speak softly, listen closely,
learn me so you know me better then I know myself, then allow
me to be the same for you, understand me so I don't need to speak
so much, memorize my smile, the smile I give you every time I see
you, memorize how my fingers feel as they trace over your back,
your chest, how my hands feel when they hold yours, memorize
every curve of my body, every inch of my skin, as I will memorize
yours, memorize my kiss, how it tastes, how soft my lips are
against yours, how does it feel when I kiss you, can you whisper
it to me, it's pure ecstasy to me, observe how I react when you
touch me, how you touch me and where, memorize me so I linger
in your memory as you know you grace my every thought, and
love me, love me like you've loved no other, I will love you like I'll
never love again and don't dream let me go."*

D amon returned and Darren and I moved away from each other, now dressed in pjs. I had a pink silk nightgown on and Darren pulled boxers and blue pj pants on.

"Yeah like I don't know." He shook his head and laughed.

I chuckled slightly and Darren flushed which was weird to see.

"I will cook breakfast, why don't you kids stay in bed and snuggle." Damon smirked.

Darren gave him a look like "Shut up"

Damon laughed. "At least you finally got laid. Hopefully he was worth it Serena." He winked joking and I laughed.

"Wait- why are you laughing?" Darren asked.

I laughed harder. "It was perfect."

"Yeah Damon, you better cook, you are the chef. Good little house husband." Darren joked.

Damon burst out laughing. "Least I can cook a nice meal for a girl. But actually Darren is the better cook he just won't admit it."

Darren rushed over to me and scooped me into his arms twirling me around then kissed me hard on the mouth. I giggled against his mouth, kissing him deeply cupping my hands in his hair.

"Okay- okay, Get a damn room. Gross you guys." Damon teased but I could hear a level of hurt in his joke.

He fired up the stove and began making breakfast.

"Today's the day hey? We have all the items?" Darren asked Damon but kept his eyes glued to mine.

"Yes." Damon stated then followed with:

"I hate to interrupt your guys blossoming love, but Serena you need to talk about what happened with Serenity, we need the information for tonight to be successful."

Darren stopped kissing me and sat beside me. I took a deep breath all the jitters and bliss from my time with Darren escaped me like a rush of cold air.

I explained in detail everything. Darren and Damon both looked shocked but Darren seemed more angry then shocked.

"So you are essentially the first man made angel in creation. But somehow your father got a hold of the essence of the embodiment of true love. That or you were reincarnated as such with the original soul and he just added to your abilities." Damon said slowly. "I just don't understand why that was hidden to me until now."

Darren's eyes welled for a second and he wiped his hand over them quickly.

Damon continued pretending not to notice. "That also means that Serenity was the first man made demon."

"How is that even possible?" Darren demanded.

Damon shook his head. "How long have we been gone Darren? How long has the balance been disrupted? How many millennia have we been stuck as mortals without our memories?"

"That, Cronos might know. He holds the rest of our memories." Darren countered.

"So perhaps all will come to light once we complete the rituals to prep the trap." Damon said.

Darren sighed heavily and I wrapped my arms around his shoulders. I beckoned Damon to come the other side of me and as he did I wrapped my other arm around him too.

"We can do this. We have to. We have each other, and humanity is relying on us."

They both leaned against me then Damon got up to finish cooking breakfast. This might very well be our last meal together. Damon plated the pancakes, eggs, hashbrowns, sausage and bacon. We all sat together as Damon plated everything. Darren lay his hand on my thigh under the table squeezing once to reassure me. His coldness seemed absent for the moment, I finally broke through his walls, but would this be the only day I get with him like this? I pushed the thought away and tried to memorize his face, as he looked over to me. I studied his blue eyes, thinking I could get lost in them every day for the rest of my life. I studied his muscular tattooed arms, remembering how it felt to be wrapped in them, knowing he was everything to me, I would spend every night laying in his arms and that still wouldn't feel like enough. He saw me staring at his arms and wrapped me back into them, as if reading my mind. I relaxed against his touch in the familiar safety it brought me. I could kiss him for hours. I loved him so much. The only sound for the moment was the scraping of our forks on the plates as we ate in silence. Damon cleared the plates I moved from Darren to help him and Darren sipped at coffee.

"You feel ready Damon?" I asked as I dried the dishes he handed.

"Not even close. But I do believe that we will succeed."

"Me too."

We dried the rest of the dishes, I put the last one away and Darren wrapped his arms around my waist from behind me and planted a light kiss on my neck, which sent shivers through my body. Was it bad to want him again? I thought to myself and giggled. Focus Serena. I scolded myself in my head. Darren held my hand and led me to the spare room where we has all the items stashed. Damon followed us and opened the door. He let out a whistling sound as he exhaled.

"Oh yeah this is going to be a blast." Damon joked.

Darren laughed. "Best day ever!"

"It will be" I said as I pulled him against me by his hand and kissed him deeply.

Damon cleared his throat loudly and I pulled away from Darren giggling yet again.

"Sorry Damon." It wasn't a sincere apology, but he just smiled.

"Well little brother, where do we begin?" Darren asked planting a light kiss to the top of my head, which made my entire body flutter in response.

Damon was referring to the black book. He started to rummage through it.

I glanced to Darren whom was staring at me lovingly and I pulled his face to mine and kissed him again.

"Yeah guys don't mind me, I will do all the work" Damon said jokingly.

"What are you looking for Damon?" I laughed and let go of Darren to go and help. Was it selfish to be happy right now? This could very well be our last day on earth and though Darren hadn't said he loved me. I felt as though he did. I was too high on happiness, that the day hadn't dawned much on me just yet. I just had every faith that we would succeed. I hoped that after we did, we could all allow ourselves to be happy without the ever looming responsibility and duty to all of humanity.

Damon pulled out the first 6 items, he lay them on the makeshift alter and began to whispering something from his book. As he did the items flared to life a white flame over them all and as they burned I felt a surge of power in my veins. My hands were trembling and Darren looked at me and grasped them in his and kissed them.

"Are you alright?" He mouthed silently.

I couldn't really reply as my entire body was surging with energy. Damon finished the incantation and it was like a candle that blew out with the sudden shut off of power. I exhaled and Damon looked over to me curiously. He swept the ashes into a box that was black and littered with hand painted sigils.

"Serena are you okay?" Damon rushed to my side and Darren hadn't let go of my hands.

"I- I don't really know. I had a sudden surge of electric energy when you did the spell." Damon's eyes widened.

Darren's eyes clouded with something of crushing devastation.

"No." He whispered, gripping my hands tightly.

"She's the vessel Darren." Damon confirmed slowly.

"No." He said through gritted teeth. The anger radiating from Darren made me shiver slightly.

"We always knew it was a possibility." Damon continued.

"Then we stop." Darren said coldly.

"And let Cronos restart the planet?"

"We find another way." Darren was shaking with anger at this point. I swallowed afraid to ask what Damon meant.

"I already preformed the first of the seals, Darren. It's too late! We can't return the energy Serena absorbed." He looked over to me with tears in his eyes. Now I was petrified, but I kept my face as still as I could.

"No!" Darren yelled this time which made me jump.

He immediately turned to me and hugged me.

"I didn't mean to scare you." He inhaled sharply.

I could tell he was fighting tears. Darren whom never cried, always stone. My stomach turned. Damon was staring at me visibly crying. I exhaled. Vessel? For Cronos? I wondered. I couldn't quite bring myself to ask. My heart was shattering for Darren and Damon right now. It had to be bad, for them to react as such. I would die for them, if that's what had to be done. Die for them, for humanity. That had to be what it was, nothing else could be worse then that, that I could think of. I mulled over that possibility in my head for a moment while Darren still had me tightly in his arms.

"Damon you said she was reincarnated from the very essence of true love, so how can her whom is abundantly light and good, not a shadow of darkness how can she embody such evil?" Darren's voice was shaky but I could tell he was trying very hard to keep it level.

Damon shook his head. "Light cannot exist without darkness. In order for love to exist there must be hate. She needs Serenity too. I think that's the only way to protect Serena best we can. Just as you and I Darren. Destruction and Creation go hand in hand. Just as light and darkness. Love and hate."

I hated when they spoke as if I wasn't there.

"Guys what are you saying?" I managed in a shaky tone.

Damon swiped a hand over his eyes and Darren wouldn't let go of me, he kept his face against my neck.

"Serena, we believe you to be the vessel for all these seals."

Darren inhaled sharply again. "Elaborate, brother."

Damon looked away from me, he paused for a minute before speaking and cleared his throat.

"It means you are capable of embodying all of the magic from these seals. You are essentially-" He paused again to sniff and Darren was shaking now while he held me. Damon continued,

"Essentially- a walking bomb. You will absorb all the magic from these seals and trap it, contain it, until Cronos is here and then you release it- it's just-" He cleared his throat again tears flooding his eyes.

"It's suicide." Darren choked out mumbling against my neck which was now wet from his tears but he still didn't look at me.

I exhaled slowly and my body trembled slightly. Darren held me tighter and I leaned against him, breathing in his familiar cologne. Memorizing the love and peace in his touch. Remembering how his hands felt against my skin. How his lips felt against mine, how his hair felt in my hands. I inhaled letting a couple of tears fall.

"If we summon Serenity here- and she absorbs into you as she was trying to do we can-hope that her darkness can hold some of the power and between both of your souls one of you could survive."

I exhaled again. "Which one of us?" I barely whispered.

"I don't know." Damon looked defeated. "I don't know." He repeated with desperation.

"Is there no way to protect her Damon?" Darren's tone was steel. Damon shook his head.

"We are GODS for fuck sake! You are going to tell me that we can do NOTHING?!" Darren let go of me and whirled to face Damon.

"I know Darren but we don't have all our memories or all our powers and even still. Serena is more powerful then either of us. She is of the first, just like her sister. Allan was powerful too, but he is un-reachable and wasn't part of the Trial. I believe Serena can do this." He glanced to me.

"Damon, Darren." I stared a half a breadth longer at Darren's face, trying to hold back tears.

"I will do whatever needs to be done and if my life ends up being the price to pay for the sake of humanity. It's okay. I'm at peace with it."

Damon nodded curtly, and smiled.

Darren stared at me and his eyes filled with tears. "I will not under any circumstance let you go. I can't, Serena. I just can't."

I walked slowly to him resting both hands gently on the sides of his face. I spoke very softly, staring into his beautiful eyes.

"You can and you will. For the sake of humanity." I kissed his forehead and wiped his tears with my thumbs.

"I love you." I whispered so only he could hear. I didn't expect him to say it back.

He inhaled sharply. I went to pull away and he gripped me tighter, pulling me back against him. I was pleasantly startled.

"I love you." He whispered back.

Now I couldn't stop the tear flow. As if sensing it he just held me tighter. I got a hold of myself quickly, I knew if I let myself cry, I didn't think I would be able to stop.

Damon interrupted us by clearing his throat loudly.

"I have to do the next seal, the sequence has to be perfect. Or we have no hope of succeeding." His voice was cracking.

He didn't want to, but he had no choice. I pulled back from Darren and nodded. Damon returned my nod and took the next lineup of items out.

Nothing changed apart from the words he spoke. There was a blue flame then white ash which he swept into the box as well. I felt a small surge of power, it was not so overwhelming this time. Darren kept right at my side watching, waiting for any hint of a struggle from me.

"I'm okay, Darren." I reassured him softly.

Damon finished and all I felt was similar to a static shock. 2 down, only 64 left to go.

"We summon Serenity the second Serena seems even the slightest bit shaken" Darren said in a voice that sounded like an order more then a request. Damon nodded.

"Serena tell us the second it feels more intense. Don't wait. We don't want to risk anything by being tough right now." Darren continued.

"I understand." He knew me well, I would rather suffer in silence. I had to unlearn that immediately if I wanted a chance at living past today. I thought of Rayne. I missed her dearly. I wouldn't let anyone else suffer the same fate, it would be an insult to her memory. An insult to my mother gifting me my second chance. If I died today, but saved humanity and the brothers I would consider that a win. I wasn't afraid to die, I was more afraid of missing out on living. Never having children, never getting married, never growing old. It was just as tragic as it was beautiful. Damon took the next sequence of items and I had to stop glancing to Darren because he was unable to keep his composure and I needed to be strong for all of us. This continued sometimes I would get a rush of power other times just a spark. After about 3 hours Damon finished the 60th spell. We had 6 remaining before we were ready to summon Cronos.

"Are you sure you are okay Serena?" Damon asked cautiously.

"Yeah. I just feel very, energized-like I chugged a few 5 hour energies."

"Are you absolutely certain?" Darren said this time, the pain etched in his voice was overwhelming for me.

"Yes." I kissed him gently and slowly. "I'm okay." I whispered between kisses.

He kissed me back like he didn't want to ever stop. When he pulled away Damon wrapped me in his arms and I hugged him tightly.

He inhaled deeply then Darren joined on the hug. I stood there basking in the calming energy. I knew the final 6 spells were from the forbidden tome and from my moms personal list. They would be the most intense, the most powerful. I made it this far. I hoped we wouldn't need Serenity, I honestly wasn't even sure if she was alive. I pictured her spewing black blood and shuddered slightly. Both brothers immediately pulled off of me and were asking if I was okay. I nodded.

Damon moved to gather the items for the first of the final 6. I inhaled deeply. I would be lying to myself if I said I wasn't scared. I was scared out of my mind. But why do we let fear control our lives and our destinies? Nothing great ever comes from obeying fear, we would never progress, we miss out on some of the most incredible things. I swallowed the fear. I faced the demon of it. Greater good.

I looked at the items Damon had laid out. Darren placed the tiara and necklace on me as added protection.

"Darren do you have the summoning spell for Serenity at hand?" Damon checked.

"Yes." He said and looked back at me giving me a nod of encouragement.

Damon began the incantations. The surge of power began flowing the second the first word dripped from Damon's lips. I inhaled sharply. Darren was watching my every grimace with fear and determination on his face like a mask. As he continued the words I felt a bewildering amount of power surge and I cried out. Damon almost tripped up what he was saying but he held steady. If he screwed up any of the spells we would face more then just Cronos and risk failing it all. Darren was at my side in a second. I nodded to him telling him I was okay. I was wasn't I? Darren was watching my face intently. And he staggered back slightly.

"What-" I managed through my clenched jaw.

The last couple words Damon spoke put me on my knees. Darren was quick to grasp my arms.

"Serena!" Damon ran over.

"She's okay, Damon."

Darren met my eyes. "Woah, your eyes are white."

"Can you see Serena?" Darren asked me slowly.

I didn't know what the fuss was about I could see fine, the power cursing through my veins like liquid fire.

"Yeah, I can see fine. Why?"

"Your eyes are white." Damon said again.

"Like a demon?" I asked.

"No, like a blind person." Darren countered. "No pupils. Just white brilliant white."

"Like Serenity's?"

"Yeah, Serena." Damon said slowly.

I didn't like that, then Darren jumped back slightly. "Your skin Serena. Does it hurt? You are boiling hot."

"Like a fever?" I asked, feeling normal.

Darren showed me his hand which was bright red from his fingers grasping me.

"Oh God. Darren summon Serenity!" Damon said quickly. "She shouldn't be so hot."

"I feel fine guys. Damon continue the spells."

"I don't know Serena." Damon said.

"We have three minutes. Start the next spell, I will tell you if I feel off I swear to you."

"Darren-" Damon said hesitantly.

Darren watched me for a minute.

"Listen to her Damon only she knows how she's feeling we have to go off of what she says."

I was a bit surprised usually Darren would just make the call. He trusted me. Faith in myself soared with the confirmation.

"Okay." Damon grabbed the items for the second round of spells quickly.

Darren stayed nearby me but did not touch me again. I was worried about his hand, remembering in anguish the other burn I left on him. I didn't want to hurt anyone.

Flames. I wondered if the final seals was based on elemental. Damon began the second seal of six. I braced myself, a little nervous what this one would bring. He spoke the words that were lost to my ears in understanding. The items again the same thing they glowed brightly with the flames and crumbled to white ash. The surge of power like a tidal wave rushed over me, drenching me in strength. Water I thought to myself. I felt no pain just clarity, I was focused, I felt cleansed of my overthinking, my anxiety, the chatter in my mind. The voices I always heard since my trip to Hell. Everything was silenced. My subconscious like a clean slate. The purity was strange. When the incantations stopped both Darren and Damon came to me as quickly as their feet would carry them.

"Serena?" I no longer felt panicked by their reactions or emotions. Their feelings did not touch me it was like a barrier to feeling.

"I am perfectly okay." I said before either of them got the chance to speak.

Darren braved a brush of his fingers against my neck. "You aren't hot anymore."

"Good, I didn't want to burn you again. Do I look different?"

"No, not this time, do you feel different?" Damon said.

Darren shook his head. "You sound different, your voice is off."

"Really? I feel okay."

"Damon- continue then. Serena you are okay?" Darren's voice was sweet, tender.

"I'm okay"

Damon nodded. "Hang in there Serena, after this we are halfway."

He repeated the process with the third seal and I immediately felt grounded. I felt secure and safe and strong. Like the very essence of my being was reaching deep into the core of the Earth beneath me its like I could feel the mud on my skin, cool, knowing, grounding, then I'm falling, but I am not afraid cause my roots will hold me in place. I fall, down down, like a rabbit hole. Then trees envelop me and I open my eyes again, to Darren's deep sea eyes. "Serena." His voice as soft as velvet.

"I'm good Darren." I looked around the room.

Damon was watching me closely.

"Your hair." Darren said as he gently lifted it toward my eyes. It was well past my hips, close to my knees. When it was usually at my ribs.

"Anything else change?"

"Yeah your eyes. Ones green."

"Really?" I moved my hand towards my eye.

Darren nodded and Damon came to look. "Strange that it is affecting your appearance Serena, but if it's just doing that, not hurting you I would say that's a win." Damon smiled slightly and kissed my head. Darren squeezed my hand.

"Lets keep going. Three down, three to go." Darren said quietly to me.

I nodded. "Okay."

Damon began with the forth seal and I braced myself for another bout of power. This time it hit me like a train, fast. It whipped and howled like a mad wind. I felt cleansed. I felt my fear rip from me. I let the chaos storm around me and then I exhaled and it all stopped as I felt myself drift. I opened my eyes.

Darren and Damon were standing back and staring at me, seemingly in awe.

"What is it?" I asked hesitantly.

"You-you have wings, wings Serena." Damon said stumbling over his words.

Darren was watching me in awe.

"Do I?" As I asked, I felt my back ignite in a sensation comparable to peace.

As I moved my back muscles I felt the softest brush against my skin as I stretched and pulled the wings in front of me. My left wing was a brilliant white and my right wing was a shiny soft black.

"Oh my God." I whispered. The wings spanned triple the length of my body. Soft as rose petals against my skin.

"Serena, are you okay?" Darren asked hesitantly. It was killing me that I was making him nervous.

"I-yeah. I feel unchanged though it's obvious I have been changed."

Darren approached me slowly and I pulled my wings back behind me he paused briefly while I did. Then continued to walk towards me.

He got to me and immediately kissed me passionately with his hands cupping my neck.

"Two more to go. You look absolutely radiant." he whispered by my ear.

"I feel radiant." I whispered back.

"That is incredible Serena. It seems the rituals are returning you to your proper form." Damon added.

"I'm just grateful you are okay still, two more to go hon and then the fight, and we will win." Darren said encouraging me. He wrapped his fingers in mine and Damon started on the second last ritual. I was folded with this ever encompassing light that broke through me, filling all the broken pieces, all the spaces that were jagged or broken or lost came swirling back together. A rush of memories came through like broken dam and I knew who I was again. The light was blinding but I could see, it was cold but I didn't even shiver. I allowed myself to be consumed in it's alluring aura. When I opened my eyes Darren and Damon were tearing up.

"What changed now?"

"Nothing, but you are just absolutely gorgeous." Darren said as he came back towards me.

"What do you feel Serena?" Damon asked.

"Light." I said wistfully.

"Fire, Water, Earth, Wind, light, and-" He trailed off a second. "If it follows the same pattern, the next ritual will be for the power of darkness." Damon continued.

Darren tensed beside me.

"That is the real test, if such a pure soul as Serena's, can hold and wield the same level of darkness as it can light." Damon said.

"And what if she can't?" Darren asked.

"Then you need to summon Serenity."

Darren sighed in frustration. "I don't like that idea."

"Like it or not brother, you are talking about your girlfriends life."

"Girlfriend? She'll be my wife if we survive this."

My heart surged for a minute. "Wife? You didn't propose." I teased.

"You're right." He kissed me gently.

"Marry me Serena." he barely whispered in between each part of our lips.

"Ask me again if we survive." I said softly.

"When we survive, I will ask again."

"Ask?" I laughed playfully. "You more so commanded it."

"Then you'll oblige?" He smiled and laughed slightly. I giggled.

"I might." I teased while he pulled me against him into a hug.

"One last seal." He sighed.

"Guys, I hate to interrupt but I have to do the final seal." Damon's voice was pained, and he was obviously choked up. Darren stiffened at my side.

"I will be okay Darren, and if need be, it's okay to summon Serenity. Okay?"

He nodded and backed up towards his brother. There were tears in his eyes but he quickly swiped his hand over them and left me questioning whether they were even there to begin with. Damon gathered the last of the items. I took a deep breath. It helped that I had been wiped of my fear. When Damon began the incantation, the whole room around us shook violently. I heard screams similar to when we were in Hell. They were so loud in my ears that I cried out and collapsed to my knees. Damon kept speaking, Darren had the spell to summon my sister in his hands and was watching me with panic in his eyes. The items I watched they turned to black flames instead of blue and they eked thick billowing black smoke from them. Then I felt anger, such a blinding rage. It made me scream. Then I felt pain, it erupted through my entire body like barbed wire tightening around every inch of my flesh. Then a felt a great wave of absolute devastation, like every persons sadness at once and tears poured from my eyes. So much pain, sadness, despair, killing, so much sin, so much darkness so many people left hopeless, and finally a lack of love. When that wave hit me, the hollow empty void I felt within me was ever consuming like a black hole in the middle of my chest. I felt lost and so much fear. There was a mirror on the wall. I jumped up and screamed again in agony as the pain was overwhelming, I rushed to the mirror. Damon kept chanting.

"Serena! What are you doing?!" Darren screamed. I brought my fist to the mirror, over and over, ignoring the sting of the glass to my flesh and I was mesmerized by the glittering pieces all around me. I looked through and picked up the biggest one into my hand, I ignored the pain as it cut into my hand.

"Serena!" Darren yelled.

It seemed like the only answer, everything fell apart, nothing is okay, the world is hollow, we are empty, life is meaningless, pointless. Love doesn't exist. All these feelings were so prominent on my mind that I brought the dagger to my throat. The second I did I felt the glass turn to solid ice and I dropped it in pain.

I glanced up straight into my sisters broken face, that was still oozing black blood. Her eyes white with no pupils.

"Hello sister." She spoke into my mind.

I dropped the shard and she grabbed my arm and all I could do was scream as Damon's incantations continued. She exhaled and laughed wickedly as she began to drain into me. Unwelcome like a scarab digging its why through your flesh. Stinging like the fangs of a snake. The feeling of barbed wire intensified feeling like it was as hot as a branding iron. I screamed and screamed until my throat was raw. It felt like she was crushing my bones. Darren had to keep chanting but his eyes were full of terror. Finally she absorbed fully. Then her voice was echoing through my head. Taunting, tormenting, then the pain was gone. Damon continued chanting and the smoke from the last seal moved toward me forcing itself into my chest. I cried out again but Serenity silenced.

"You should be very grateful for me, you cannot hold all this darkness. I however-" she paused for affect then whispered "Can".

"You are in luck sister, we want the same thing despite what you think of me."

I prayed she was being honest. Damon stopped chanting and all the noise came to a stop. Darren was at my right side while Damon rushed to my left.

"Serena. Are you okay?" Darren pretty much demanded.

I could still feel Serenity moved inside of my body, like ants crawling, inching under my skin. I was deeply uncomfortable.

"I- yeah kind of. I can feel her though its so unwelcome. Like worms writhing in my blood, circulating my entire body."

"We will be able to separate you again Serena, I just- we have to trap Cronos first. But you won't be affected anymore, and that is the good news. You made it, we made it. Everything is set straight." Damon said.

I nodded. Darren wrapped me into his arms and as I hugged him back my wings also wrapped around him which made us both jump because it seemed we both forgot about them in the first place.

"I will summon Cronos. Is Serenity also ready?" Damon asked.

"Damon it's not enough time. I'm not.-" Darren cleared his throat.

"Darren if you want to save her we need to do this all as fast and as perfectly as possible. No risks."

Darren nodded and kissed me once gently on the lips.

"I did mean it when I said I loved you Serena."

"I love you Darren." He nodded and got up to leave but I grasped his hand.

"I need you to do something for me." I whispered and pulled him by his hand closer to me. Damon was preoccupied getting the trap ready.

"Anything Serena." Darren said kindly.

"When I die-" Darren's hands grasped mine very tightly.

"Don't say that to me Serena." His voice felt angry but I knew he was just hurt. I shook my head gently and squeezed his hands back.

"Darren-I know that you are shut down, I know you have a difficult time opening up, I know that deep down you feel unworthy and that's why you fight and you push and pull away. Why you are cold. I need you to remember that you are never unworthy. Everyone deserves to be loved, to be cherished, to be held, and supported. You are an incredible man. Being cared for or loved by someone or if for a change you needed someone else to be the strong one for once in your life- it would never make you less than. It does not make you weak. It would never cause you to lose your strength, resilience or independence. It just makes you real. I consider myself lucky to have known you. I wished it could be longer. You are so loved Darren. Damon loves you. I love you. You are a hero, you are my hero."

Darren was tearing up and not trying to hide it he moved his left hand to my cheek.

"Serena-" He barely whispered.

"Now go be the worlds hero my love. You and Damon."

He inhaled sharply. "You are not going to die on me today Serena. Promise me that."

I laughed humorlessly. "I will do my best."

He reluctantly pulled away from me to go help Damon. I waited in anxious silence for them to summon Cronos. Serenity lay still within me, waiting. I was already getting used to the discomfort of her essence in my body. As Damon and Darren both recited the spell work to summon Cronos. I inhaled deeply. I didn't know if I would die, but I knew Darren had to hear that regardless of if my life would be sacrificed to the greater good or I would be spared. As they worked through the spell every symbol, ward and outline that they had drawn on the walls and floor here began to glow gold, bright like staring into the sun. The lights flickered and light bulbs shattered. I felt an immense negative shift in the energy of the room. Damon and Darren kept reciting but as they kept speaking blood was running from their noses, eyes and ears. I tried to move to them but Serenity held me in place.

"Let me go!"

"They will live Serena, they need to finish you can't interfere with the natural order of what needs to be done."

"What natural order?"

She laughed loudly viciously in my mind. I wished I could block her out.

"There are two ways, either Cronos will kill you and we fail or we kill Cronos and win. I am aiming to win however, I don't fancy dying." She said.

"I second that."

"Here he comes" She sing-songed devilishly. I wasn't sure what I expected when I thought of Cronos. A man materialized then, with glowing blue eyes. He looked human esq, He was holding a glowing hourglass on a heavy golden chain that was wrapped around his huge muscled chest and shoulders. He had long white hair with a long white beard. Some sorta fucking Santa claus / God spin off. In the centre of his forehead there was a clock that was carved into his skull like some sort of nightmare jack-o-lantern. Over his legs and stomach lay thick Gold armour.

He seemed shaken at first, slightly delirious, and slightly confused. Then he locked eyes on me.

"She lives." His voice bounded loudly off of the walls it was deep and knowing.

He attempted to move towards me but was halted by the traps. All the sigils flared up in brightness again for a millisecond.

"Elderwood brothers!" He whirled around to face them.

"I should've forseen this trap. How did you outsmart me, when I hold all your memories?"

"We won't stand for you destroying time Cronos. We are here for the sake of humanity." Damon stated.

"Humanity!" he spat as he said it. "Humans are worthless, like fleas, little mindless cogs in a machine that are so unaware of their potential they destroy themselves everyday, with the emotions of infants and they cannot measure up. Vast majority would sooner die then live. Run on a schedule that they hate, slave to money, slave to other humans that think they can run countries. Too afraid to exist. Too selfish to be kind to others. Too greedy to coexist. Too enraged to be peaceful, Shaking and whining about every damn thing. It's pathetic! Lost fucking sheep."

"They need a leader, hope, a reason. They are capable of emotions far more vast then that of us Gods." Damon said viciously.

Cronos laughed heartily. "Disgusting plague, they destroyed everything their planet had to offer. We need a clean slate you both know that deep down. We need to restart, without humans to ruin everything."

"They need our protection, our teaching, our guidance." Damon continued.

"Spoken like our true God of creation. Always positive." His eyes flicked to Darren.

"My God of destruction, you should be in agreement, you deal with the filth of this planet firsthand. You are the judge and you execute the punishment. Are you not on my side?"

"I do not believe all humans are evil." Darren said low and cold.

"Being that I am trapped here. I will return your memories. Only because I believe you will understand me better. You will understand my way is the only way. We must return this planet to the God's it was intended for."

With a dip of the hourglass he had stuck to him, a flowing blue stream came from the hourglass and dissipated into Damon's head then Darren's head.

Both of them seemed stunned for a minute then both looked to me. What were they thinking? What was wrong? Serenity held my body in place and I hated that she could control my movements.

"You however are extraordinary. So he was successful, your father in merging your soul with that of the first. The prophecy of 6, Devils numbers. You all went to a great length of trouble to secure me. I truly, did not believe it was possible. No matter how hard you try you will be unable to kill me though. Nothing can kill me. I am time itself."

"You know what I think you son of a bitch? I think you underestimated us and will continue to. We aren't planning on killing you. Now!" Darren yelled and 6 people stepped out of the shadows. I recognized none of them except for Jane.

"Impossible."

"Seems you are the one lagging behind Cronos. Following behind Jane was about 100 shape shifters. There were 5 other leaders. Vampires, werewolves, sirens, ghosts, fae. There was a lead for each group, plus 100 or so soldiers of that group. I remembered back over the last few months. All the creatures we had faced. These must be the families? But the leaders? They were the children like me and Serenity and Allan that my father destroyed?

"How cute, you brought an army."

"Charge!" Jane yelled and all 500 or so creatures came flying at Cronos. There were hundreds of unholy sounds as every single being attempted to damage Cronos. Cronos waved the vast majority off as if they were simply flies. There were cries of battle and Damon and Darren both also charged ceremonial daggers in hand. Serenity still wouldn't allow me to move, she forced me to watch helplessly. Cronos kept his focus on me. I sensed he felt I was a danger. The bodies were piling quickly at Crono's feet. None of the leaders had fallen just yet. I tried to move against Serenity again but she held firm.

"Soon." She whispered in my head.

Jane fell then and Damon stopped fighting and rushed to her side. I assumed to try and heal her.

Cronos hit Darren so hard that he went flying against the wall. He was up right away. I fought hard against Serenity.

"Your man can handle himself. Hold steady or you'll screw the whole thing."

Soon enough there was a mess of blood, guts, chunks of bodies strewn all over the room. The leaders were the last ones fighting alongside Damon and Darren. Cronos barely looked phased.

"Now" Serenity said.

I lurched into action heading directly at Cronos. He was preoccupied with Damon. The ring from the reverent was on my finger and as I surged my powers the ring turned into a sword. I lunged the sword against his shoulder when I jumped up I used my wings to elevate me which felt natural to me even though I had never exactly flown before. The blade sunk into his shoulder and he groaned loudly, clearly this hurt him. It left a scorch mark on his flesh. That sparked determination I went for another swing whilst still flying and he swatted at me, but the impact of his fist didn't even cause me to stagger back.

"What in the Hell? Where did you find that blade?"

I thought back to it. The ring had been our final item that we grabbed in Vancouver.

"The original sword paired with the first." Fear flashed across his features slightly. I struck him again while Damon and Darren both hurled at his side. Jane and the other leaders were hurling weapons into his back, but he seemed completely unbothered. I struck the blade into his chest this time and literal tree roots spilled out of the wound wrapping him in a series of tree roots. He howled, an inhuman sounds from his throat. I stabbed him again this time his whole arm frosted over and then Darren brought a hammer-like weapon down on it and his arm shattered. I stabbed him again this time in the stomach and light poured from the wound. Like someone shone a flashlight through the wound in his body. He yelled again. I stabbed his neck next and he began coughing and choking as water bubbled out of his mouth. Fear was evident in his eyes now. Serenity took control of my body then and I lost my balance flying and began to fall, she caught us and swung at him again this time stabbing him through the timepiece on his forehead. It bubbled and hissed like acid as a tar-like substance leaked from it.

"Fire, earth, air, water, light and darkness." She breathed. "6 elements. 6 months, 6 seals, 66 rituals and 666 magical items. And now we, absorb. We will become the ultimate being Serena."

I felt a magnetic pull from my body and it was drawing a strange essence from Cronos that looked like rippling water dancing and glimmering in the air.

"No!" Damon screamed and pushed me out of the way. Darren came right beside his brother and grabbed him, as the essence was drawn into both of them instead.

"Damnit no!" Serenity screamed in my mind.

"I watched the essence pull from Cronos as he made a series of unintelligible sounds. Everyone around outside of the Elderwood brothers and me were unconscious.

The brothers turned to me both of them now had one glowing gold eye. Cronos body shuddered and turned to dust on the floor.

Serenity was losing her shit in my head, screaming and screaming. I got so fed up.

"Out!" I yelled at the top of my lungs, and as I yelled it I imagined myself in my head grabbing Serenity and plucking her out of me. As she detached from me, the feeling of worms squirming in my veins, beetles under my skin. Faded. The feeling of needles in my flesh, softened. I exhaled and imagined light, bright light filling all the space in my body thought about radiance. Luminescence. I pictured the light shying the dark away until my entire spirit was cleansed of any reminiscence of the darkness. I pictured Rayne, when she was alive, my mom and imagined their light surrounding me as she was cast out of me.

"Serena!" Darren cried out and rushed to me.

She materialized back into what resembled her body, broken and oozing.

"How could you do that to me sister? I helped you." She choked as she spoke unable to move her body that now resembled a broken doll. I was still shaking there was too much power still residing within me, it felt unobtainable yet. Darren had his arms around me in a second.

"Are you okay?" He half laughed, relief flooding his features. I looked into his different coloured eyes. I wasn't ready to tell him the power was still too much. My time was thin.

"What happened?" I asked. "Is Cronos?-"

Darren nodded eagerly. "We beat him baby."

"Damon and I now have split his power. It'll never fall into the wrong hands again. We can recreate the world in the sense of opening their eyes to the truth. We can elevate the humans to their highest potential.

"Jane please!" Damon was yelling pain in his voice.

Darren glanced over and ran towards Damon.

"Darren-Darren she-she's not breathing." Damon was crying.

I glanced to Serenity. She stared at me with black empty eye sockets.

"I don't want your pity sister."

I couldn't leave her like that. We were once a part of one soul, hers all darkness and mine all light, but we used to share that. I reached out to her.

"Take some light, Serenity." I whispered. The power within me was crashing through my body like waves.

"I don't need you." She coughed brutally and spat black blood.

"No one is all good or all evil. I'm just tipping the scale."

After brief hesitation she took my hand. I imagined my light as tendrils of a willow, billowing and softly creeping, I imagined pouring light into her wounds. She gasped slightly. I pulled away after a moment. Feeling a bit less chaotic, but still too much power. The darkness that had crept into me from her was nothing but an unwanted infection. I could heal it. I looked at her again and she stopped coughing and stood up. Relief flooded me. She glanced to me and nodded.

"I knew I could count on you sister."

I watched curious of what she might do. She walked slowly to where Damon was cradling Jane's head. I followed. Serenity crouched beside them.

"Let me." She said. Damon looked at her in confusion.

"Let you what?"

"I can fix her." Damon watched her for a minute and recognition sparked on his face. Serenity leaned over and kissed Jane as she did she absorbed into her. Jane's body convulsed a bit then stilled. Serenity was no longer in sight. Jane opened her eyes and coughed. She stood up and Damon watched her in awe for a moment.

"Emma?" He choked out.

Jane's appearance changed slightly when Serenity joined her.

"I was in another life, before I was Serenity. I just couldn't remember, my soul was too corrupted. You have Serena to thank for that." She whispered. Damon shook his head in disbelief and wrapped her in his arms. Then he hugged me.

"You did it Serena, you did more then just save everyone, you healed Serenity's soul."

Darren wrapped me in his arms. "I was so scared I was going to lose you Serena."

The power flicked and raged and coursed through me. Not much more time. How do I tell them?

Damon kissed Jane, then rushed to try and heal all the fallen troops. But as he tried he was unsuccessful. "Too far gone. We lost so many people today."

Jane looked around. "The leaders won't stay down, all of them are immortals. The rest though, their sacrifice will not be in vain."

Damon wrapped her back in his arms as Darren held me. Darren brought my mouth to his. I kissed him with all my being, like it was the last time, because it would be. It had to be, I knew I wouldn't survive much longer. It broke my heart, it scared me, it angered me. But if I am the embodiment of true love, perhaps in my death it'll return real love to humanity. I hoped my death would bring everyone of them their soulmates. I prayed someone would love Darren in my absence. Love him as hard and as much as they could, cause he deserved it. It was devastating, that I could not be that person for him. Every fibre of my being poured love for him. He was my home. He was my safety, he was my adventure. I would've given him everything, time and time again I would have always chosen him. How to tell him that, and then tell him I wouldn't survive past today?

I let his hands wrap in my hair as mine cupped his face, he ran his hands up and down my back gently, but needing. As my mind was rampant with thoughts. Damon and Jane were also kissing. Who would've known that Serenity was Damon's soulmate? I thought I was both of theirs but now it made sense as Serenity and I were two parts of the same, as we returned to ourselves our souls were rebuilt. I was so glad Damon had someone, it was Jane all along she was just missing some pieces. But now, Darren, when he finally let someone in, I had to leave him. I feared he would never seek love again. I swallowed as tears were pouring down my face, I hadn't realized. Darren stopped kissing me.

"Darling, what is the matter?" His voice sweet as honey.

I stared into his beautiful blue eyes and I couldn't stop my tears. I cried so hard that I fell to my knees shuddering and gasping as sobs wracked from my chest. The kind of crying you would do when you breakdown, when it's all too much and you collapse on your bed, or the bathroom floor and cry so hard and so loud until your chest aches and burns and your throat is so dry you end up gagging. Unable to get up, unable to stop. The kind of breakdown you only ever do alone, you never let anyone see. The kind you question if you'll ever be able to smile again.

Damon and Jane rushed over. One look at Jane and she understood.

Her eyes welled slightly. "No."

"Serena, why are you crying?" Damon asked putting his hand on my shoulder.

"Serena honey, we did it, we won, the world is saved. Are you in pain?" Darren's voice was killing me because it was drenched in concern and longing and confusion.

"Why did you say, no Jane?" Damon asked turning to her. Darren glanced to her too. I was gasping and crying too hard to speak.

"She's still dying." Jane barely whispered. Tears dripping slightly from her eyes.

"Jane what do you mean?" Damon rushed over to me, seemingly trying to heal me.

Darren one look at his face was gut wrenching. He was staring at me in disbelief.

When Damon brought his hand to my skin he was jolted back. "Woah! What the hell?!"

Jane shook her head. "You can't save her."

Darren glared at Jane for a moment." "What the Hell do you mean Jane?! Can't save her my ass!" He yelled walking up to her aggressively.

Damon stepped in front of her and put his hand up to stop Darren from coming closer. Darren obliged.

"She's still got too much power. Even with releasing me, there's too much, I wished I noticed it sooner it's coming off of her in waves."

"Then we need to get power out of her!" Darren screamed.

Damon watched me for a moment, I still couldn't get a grasp on my emotions.

"We can't Darren." Damon said through gritted teeth.

"Don't fucking tell me we can't! "We have to, we have to!" He yelled and punched the wall beside us, denting it and hurting his hand.

"We knew it was a risk." Damon continued.

"To Hell with that, and you!" He punched the wall again then groaned in pain exhaling sharply.

"We found loopholes for everything tonight! We have our powers our memories." Darren was so angry. I was so humiliated that I couldn't stop crying.

"I'm so sorry brother. But stop with your damn pity party and go comfort her. She needs you. She needs you Darren. She needs to be held. She needs protection. She needs love, she needs you to calm her fears."

"I don't know how to do that!" He ripped his hands through his hair.

"Don't be such a fucking coward Darren. You love her. Show her how much right now. Words, hold her, kiss her, calm her, don't let her die in fear and confusion. It's the least you can do. Put aside your Goddamn ego and emotions as she's done for you many times and be there for HER! It's not about you!" Damon yelled.

I heard them and was trying to get a handle on my hyperventilating. Damon was right with what I needed, but I also needed Darren to be okay, not fake okay, actually okay. Darren came to my side then. He wrapped me in his arms and I folded into him, muffling my cries in his chest.

"Serena, I'm so sorry. I would give anything I would do any-" His voice cracked and he held me tighter. I felt his own tears on my skin.

"How long?-"

"I don't know." I choked out. "Not long."

"Then I'm dying with you."

"No, you are not!" Damon yelled. Jane put her hand on his shoulder to calm him.

"Even if he wanted to Damon- you guys are immortal."

I took a deep breath. I was beginning to calm in his arms as his touch always did, when he held me all I felt was serene peace. He brought that peace now for me, just as he always had. Such a magical power over me. I took a deep shuddering breath and grasped onto him.

"Darren I want you to find love, happiness. I want you to learn to live without me. Think about humanity, we saved everyone, you guys and the abilities you can change the world, not just this plane but Heaven and Hell too. You guys have the power to reshape the future for the better. In my death I believe it will restore love to everyone, we have been without love for so long. My death will bring peace to so many.

"I don't want to let you go Serena. I can't." he gasped against me. MY turn to be strong. I ran my fingers over his back tickling him gently, soothing as I could.

"Hey, we knew this was a one way ticket right?" I tried very hard to be lighthearted. I wrapped him tightly in my arms.

"I love you Serena, I have loved you for a long time, I just didn't know how to accept love. You deserved it all along. I felt I could never fill those shoes. I wish, I just wish I told you sooner."

"You were always enough Darren. Even when you weren't all here you were enough. You literally just saved the world Darren. We all did, Take the win. Humanity lives. Time goes on. You hold the key to reshaping a future for everyone. That's amazing. And now my hope for you is to keep your heart open, and find love again. You deserve to be loved Darren."

The power bubbled and surged and I felt very hot. "I need to get away from here." I said quickly.

"No-" Damon said. "Not now."

Darren grasped me tightly and kissed me again. "Please, please Serena." I kissed him back. Too much, it was painful now. I had to move.

"Darren let me go, please I can't hurt you guys, we just saved everyone, but the jobs not done."

"No.." He said. I looked to Damon. His eyes filled with tears but he nodded.

"Come on brother. He pulled Darren away from me holding him back."

"Let me go!" Darren struggled but Damon was stronger right now.

"We are soulmates Darren. Find love. Find happiness and trust our souls will meet again." I wiped my eyes. He stared at me a minute.

"We are all immortal in the grand scheme of things. We are just Echos of the everlasting." I said and flew up high as fast as I could once I was high enough that I knew I couldn't hurt anyone I released the power. It was surreal. Painful, screams that tormented me raised then silenced, the pain of everyone else intensified then released. My fear tightened then let go. My sadness curled around me then flitted out. Until I was left with nothing but light. I screamed again as I felt myself tear into thousands of shards, like glass, glittering and falling around me. Then I felt peace. Back in ethereal form. The pieces fell and turned to rain, the entire planet now I could see as my essence left the stratosphere, the entire planet coated in rainfall. I knew it was returning love to here it belonged, and deep down. I knew the brothers would recreate a world more beautiful then imaginable.

Humans would revolutionize how they should. Third eyes open. True potential in every single being. I would see my mothers soul, Rayne's. I just knew. I also knew, my soul would rejoin Darren's when the time was right. Until then I would guide him and Damon and Jane on their journey. I knew eventually I would return, it was just a matter of time. There were never any endings, just new beginnings.

Thank you for completing *Echoes of the Everlasting*.

We would love if you could help by posting a review at your book retailer and on the PageMaster Publishing site. It only takes a minute and it would really help others by giving them an idea of your experience.

Thanks

Kyra Romanyshyn at the PageMaster store
https://pagemasterpublishing.ca/by/kyra-romanyshyn/

To order more copies of this book, find books by other Canadian authors, or make inquiries about publishing your own book, contact PageMaster at:

PageMaster Publication Services Inc.
11340-120 Street, Edmonton, AB T5G 0W5
books@pagemaster.ca
780-425-9303

catalogue and e-commerce store
PageMasterPublishing.ca/Shop

About the Author

Kyra is an author and artist based out of Edmonton, Alberta. She has always enjoyed creative writing, ever since she was a kid. She is actively pursuing her dream to write books with *Echos of the Everlasting* as her debut novel, with more books of similar genre to follow. Kyra uses her free time to write, paint, and read. She enjoys helping others to seek happiness and fulfillment in their lives. She has two kids that she loves more then anything. Kyra aims to use her writing as a way to teach her kids and those who read her stories that you can make your dreams a reality, no matter who doesn't believe in you. Believe in yourself, and it will become your reality.

www.ingramcontent.com/pod-product-compliance
Lightning Source LLC
Chambersburg PA
CBHW052340020726
47503CB00001B/41